DAMNATION'S DOOR

I tore my eyes away from the ceiling and pushed to my feet. My ankle fired up with pain the moment I put the slightest amount of pressure on it, but I concentrated on moving. Sitting on my ass and praying for a miracle would only end with me being torched.

I had just hobbled to the entryway when a huge *whoosh* fell behind me. Light flared at my back, like the fire had gasped in awe. I spun around too quickly, lost my balance and landed on my ass.

The column of white fire that circled my sister was in front of me.

For a moment, I didn't so much as breathe. Not that I could, given the lack of oxygen in the air, but what little I had was locked in my lungs next to a heart ready to break from my chest.

I knew Dro was in there, but I couldn't scream. I couldn't move. Couldn't do anything.

Come on, little sister. I know you're in there. Wake up.

Just as I finished the thought, the blaze began to dull. It receded inward, getting smaller and drawing back to its source.

Dro pitched forward, slapping her hands on the ashy floor and dipping her head. She was shaking. I started crawling toward her, trying to get her to snap out of it.

Dro lifted her head, and I stopped.

Her eyes glowed brighter than I could have ever imagined. Even in the drowning red, orange, and black world around us, there was no avoiding that electrified blue gaze.

Just like there was no missing the anger in it.

"Dro." My lips mouthed her name, though my voice couldn't speak it. Whether that was because it was too cracked, or I was too scared, I couldn't tell.

I had never seen Dro look like this before. For the first time in my life, I couldn't see her as human.

DAMNATION'S DOOR

A *Cursed* Novel

Amy Braun

For my loved ones and everyone who's supported the CURSED series.

More From Amy Braun

CURSED

DEMON'S DAUGHTER

DARK DIVINITY

DARK SKY

CRIMSON SKY

STANDALONE NOVELS AND NOVELLAS

PATH OF THE HORSEMAN

STORM BORN

NEEDFIRE

ANTHOLOGIES AND COLLECTIONS

THE MAKER OF MONSTERS in SPAWN OF THE RIPPER from April Moon Books.

HELL TO PAY in LEGENDS OF SLEEPY HOLLOW: ORIGINAL TALES OF TERROR FROM AMERICA'S SPOOKIEST VILLAGE.

SURVIVALISM in THE DEAD WALK: VOLUME 2 from FOF Publishing.

DISMANTLE in THE STEAM CHRONICLES from Zimbell House Publishing.

LOST SKY in AVAST, YE AIRSHIPS! from Mocha Memoirs Press.

SECRET SUICIDE in THAT HOODOO, VOODOO, THAT YOU DO from Lincoln Crisler and Ragnarok Publications.

BRING BACK THE HOUND in STOMPING GROUNDS from April Moon Books.

HOTEL HELL in DEATH'S CAFE from Mocha Memoirs Press.

CALL FROM THE GRAVE in TOIL, TROUBLE, AND TEMPTATION from Mocha Memoirs Press.

CHARLATAN CHARADE in LOST IN THE WITCHING HOUR from Breaking Fate Publishing.

DARK INTENTIONS AND BLOOD in AMOK! from April Moon Books.

Hell is paved with good Samaritans. – William M. Holden

What other dungeon is so dark as one's own heart? What jailer so inexorable as one's self?
Nathaniel Hawthorne

Chapter 1

It was supposed to be simple.

I actually thought we would be able to step outside our shelter, get the supplies, and be back before anyone realized we'd been there.

This is what happens when my sister's optimism rubs off on me.

But it wasn't Dro's fault that we walked into a damn trap. Hell just hated us.

That was fine. I hated Hell right back.

The cheap metal door was still clanging against the plaster wall of the store I'd just busted into. Max had looked into it when I asked, and told me there would be demons, but he couldn't tell what kind because his precog was still blurred. I was expecting a couple Reds or ghouls, maybe a Shredder.

I was not expecting Possessors.

The possessed humans weren't surprised to see us. Even in their human forms, the Possessors should have been able to sense my sister, because she was the most powerful half-demon known to exist. Since she was still on Hell's Most Wanted List, we had a serious problem on our hands.

The Possessors looked like regular humans, except their irises were solid black. I held back my shiver, knowing just how much pain their souls must be in. Being possessed was one of the worst things a human could experience. I had barely survived it.

These Possessors had taken over a group of tall, bulky men in black clothes. Their hair ranged from shoulder-length to bald, and their arms were covered in tattoos. Each had the tattoo of a rose thorn that appeared to be weaving in and out of their skin, blood dripping from the points. I had the same one inked behind my ear.

This just keeps getting better and better.

Finally, we snapped out of our shock. I went for the hatchet on my hip and grabbed a knife from my inside jacket. Beside me, Warrick took out a handgun. Next to him, Sephiel drew two short swords. Max wisely stepped back, knowing he couldn't fight half as well as the rest of us. Dro's shoulders were tense and ready, but I moved in front of her not just to protect her, but to keep her from doing anything that would get all of us killed.

I started reconsidering this when all of the Possessors drew enormous handguns.

But they didn't shoot. Why weren't they shooting?

Because someone else was in the room with us. Someone bigger than the Possessors, who stalked out from the shadows into the dim light. My hand tightened on the grip of my weapons, and I expected Warrick to pull the trigger.

Drake Talbot smiled when he saw our anger. He was a huge bear of a man, about six foot three and probably two hundred and fifty pounds of muscle. He had on his black duster and dark pants, his hands on his hips to display the guns and the thick, blunt hilts of his knives easily visible next to his clothes. The top of his head and his chin were covered in dark stubble. Two abysmal black eyes stared at me, filled with sadism and malice.

"Well, look who showed their faces after all," Drake sneered, standing confidently behind his bodyguards. "We didn't think you'd make it to Party Town."

Party Town. I supposed Drake would see it that way. I didn't think a city full of murderers, rapists, and generally wicked people was a place to party, but Drake was the definition of a masochist. He would see a city of death as home, sweet home.

Warrick didn't have a kill shot, and that was the only reason I could imagine for Drake to still be standing. All it would take was one missed shot to set off a chain reaction of bullets and blood.

I wanted to see Drake bleeding under my boot just as much as he did, but I wasn't throwing my knife, either. Something wasn't right.

"What are you doing here, Drake?" I growled.

He laughed. It was an awful, rasping noise. His black eyes met mine, the same way they had when he stabbed me twice and left me to die. I blocked out the memory, keeping away the phantom pain of a knife sliding into my stomach and ribs.

"Had to pick something up for the boss," he said mockingly. "You can imagine how fussy he is."

My blood went cold, and I barely heard Dro's sharp intake of breath. I could picture Sephiel's face tightening with anger. Drake looked at all of us, relishing the hatred, pain, and fear we radiated. I controlled it as best as I could, knowing answers were more important than revenge right now.

"What the fuck did you do?" I asked again.

His grin widened, and this time he only looked at me. "It isn't what I did. It's what I'm *going* to do." He dipped his chin, fixing me with his black gaze. "He's got plans for you, *chica.* Serious plans. So much detail has gone into them that even your ex isn't allowed to intervene. Matt's pretty pissed about that too."

Not as pissed as he would be if he heard you calling him 'Matt.'

"See, I found something really, really special." Drake continued. "It's the last thing we need. But don't worry, sweetheart. You'll get introduced to it very, very soon."

My stomach turned. I expected him to say something about wanting Dro. My sister was the real supernatural force in our group. I was human, born and raised. I'd never been anything but. I didn't want to be.

Whatever was being planned for me by Drake, my former lover, and the creature I feared above anything else could only involve pain. A substantial amount of it.

I'd been on the receiving end of their tortures before. I had no intention of going through them again.

Though if they wanted me for something, they wouldn't risk shooting me. They would take me alive.

No, they're not. They're going to try. And they're going to fail.

I took a risk myself, and threw my silver knife at Drake.

I didn't miss–I hardly ever miss–but I didn't hit my mark.

The thin silver blade slammed into the neck of the Possessor standing beside Drake. The huge bounty hunter had stepped to the side so the blade wouldn't get anywhere near him. He stepped so far I was a little embarrassed at how off my aim had been. Deep down, I knew better. Drake was fast for someone his size, but it looked like he'd gotten quite a bit from his deal with the Devil.

The man lurched, blood gushing from the wound in his neck. He opened his mouth as though to scream, but a spiral of thick black smoke shot out of his mouth. The Possessor's true form screeched and twisted away in the back room. Then room exploded into action.

At first I thought the Possessors were going to shoot us. At their cores, they were still gangsters. Yet as soon as I surged forward, I saw them hesitate.

They were here to stall us, not kill us. At least not me, and probably not Dro.

Everyone else though… they were fair game.

Two shots cracked in rapid succession. None of the bullets hit me, though two of the possessed Blood Thorns dropped from the bullets that crashed into their skulls, scaring the Possessors out of their vessel's dying mouths. Warrick had exceptional aim, and shooting demons with blessed silver bullets was good way to keep them from returning to rip us apart.

I went for Drake, who was backing away to escape through the storeroom exit. Fucking coward.

Two Possessors blocked my path. They tucked their guns away and threw out their fists. I skidded to a stop and stepped back, one of their clenched hands brushing along my temple.

Admittedly, I didn't think this whole plan through. Seeing the man who murdered my mentor, kidnapped my sister, tortured and tried to kill me sparked my already short temper. So it wasn't long before they got their shots in.

The man on my left jabbed his fist into my ribs. I winced, giving the man on the right the chance to loop his arm around my throat. I was pinned to his back, my neck straining painfully as he wrenched it up. I used one hand to claw at the meaty arm on my throat, leaving my front completely exposed to the second man. He grinned, thinking he was going to get some revenge on me for the sake of his employers.

Stupid bastard forgot I was still armed.

He pulled back his fist to hit me, and even as his fist was flying for my face, I was moving. I kicked him in the knee with one foot, making him stumble. His fist brushed over my shoulder and into the chest of the man choking me. I kicked his stomach with my other foot, making him double over. Then I sliced the blade of my hatchet into his exposed neck.

Blood squirted out of his severed carotid artery, painting the dirty floor before he collapsed onto it.

The man behind me growled and slammed his fist into my kidneys. I winced at the crushing pain. He was so much stronger now that he was possessed. His grip tightened on my neck, causing black spots to dance in front of my eyes. The Possessor's free hand shot out to catch my wrist and keep the hatchet away from him. He squeezed until I thought he was going to break my hand.

Then he stiffened and released his hold. A warm liquid peppered my neck, filling the air with the coppery smell of blood. I pitched forward, touching my throat and coughing to get back the oxygen I'd missed. Assured that my neck wasn't broken, I turned around to see what had saved me.

My little sister stood over the Possessor, the knife in her hand dripping fresh blood onto the floor. The man crab walked away, blood oozing from his fingers as he tried to put pressure on the wound in his throat. He looked terrified of my sister.

At first glance, Dro wasn't the kind of girl anyone would be afraid of. She was sixteen, and utterly beautiful with the face of a saint. Her skin was flawless and paper pale. Long white hair rested in a braid along her back, ending at the base of her spine. But over the last few weeks, there was a darkness lurking behind her ice blue eyes. A danger that needed to be avoided at all costs.

A malevolence that reminded me of her father.

"What did Drake steal?" she demanded in a cold voice that didn't belong to her.

"We– we never knew," the Possessor pleaded. Usually these were the kinds of demons that toyed with their prey. The demon that possessed me had felt Dro's power, which meant this one must have been sensing it too. I started to understand why he was so afraid.

"We were just told to wait here. They knew you'd be looking for him, and we were supposed to keep you from killing him."

I glanced at the back door. It was open, and Max was beside it, keeping Warrick from going through. He was likely trying to explain that the revenge-crazed demon slayer wasn't going to be able to find his nemesis tonight. Warrick was standing profile to me, though I could only imagine the anger burning in his neon green eyes.

"You're lying."

Dro's hollow tone made me look at her again. My eyes flicked down when I saw the light coming from her left hand. Blazing white flames were curling around her wrist, clawing their way up her arm. The Possessor's eyes widened as he stared at the hellfire she was controlling. He'd probably seen what it could do, and I didn't blame him for being scared.

"I'm not!" the Possessor cried, snapping me out of my thoughts. His voice was becoming hoarse from the blood loss. "I'm not, I swear!"

I'd been in this situation before. You accused

someone of lying, they said they weren't, and then you started beating the truth out of them. Eventually, you got the answer you wanted. I could tell when someone was putting on a façade, and when they were being honest.

This demon didn't know shit.

"Dro," I croaked. I muted my cough. She still didn't hear me. The fires continued to rise up her arms.

"Dro, that's enough," I warned her.

She didn't listen to me, clenching her fist and increasing the light from the flames until I could no longer see the outline of her hand.

"*Andromeda*," I half shouted.

My adopted sister turned her head slightly at the sound of my voice. Her eyes locked on mine, and I was amazed at all the anger she was holding back. It softened when she saw me, but not nearly as much as I wanted it to.

"He doesn't know anything," I told her. "We're done here."

Dro twisted her head back to the dying Possessor, white hair swishing against her back. The hellfire dulled and evaporated from her fist. She looked at the bloody knife in her hand, then went still.

This was the first time Dro had ever killed a human on purpose with her bare hands.

I walked to my sister. I gently placed my hand on her shoulder. She jumped under my touch, glancing back at me. I saw the terrified, ashamed little girl who would never forgive herself for this. I wasn't happy with that, but it was better than seeing the look of a cold-blooded murderer.

These days, I took what I could get with Dro.

"Go outside with the guys. Make sure Drake's not waiting to trap us, and that Warrick doesn't chase after him."

Dro's light eyes held my dark ones. "I don't need to go outside. I can do that from in here."

I clutched her shoulder just a little harder. "No. You don't need your powers for this."

"But–"

"No."

One look at her narrowed eyes and harsh frown told me that we were going to fight about this later. Probably the moment I saw her again outside.

Regardless, Dro put her knife on her belt, glanced at the dying Possessor one last time, and stormed to the front door. Her guardian and ex-angel Sephiel gave me a small nod. He would protect her from anything while I wasn't there. As he followed my aggravated sister, I watched Max hesitantly show Warrick the front door. He was smart not to touch him. Warrick looked ready to punch the lights out of the first person that crossed him.

Once they were gone, I picked up my silver throwing knife and sheathed it in my jacket. The other Possessors had vacated their human vessels, leaving behind their dead bodies. Usually Possessors put up more of fight than this. I couldn't help but remember that they were fodder for something much more sinister. I stood by the dying Possessor, who was now flat on his back and choking on his own blood. Possessors hated to leave their vessels, but I wasn't going to exorcise him. I didn't have the time, and even if I did, he was a dead man. The wound in his throat was too grievous. The Possessor was the only thing keeping him "alive."

I knelt beside his head, dangling the hatchet in front of my knee. When my eyes locked onto his, they weren't filled with the pain I'd expected them to be. If anything, he seemed proud. Whatever his goal had been, he appeared to have accomplished it.

"Tell me something useful, and I'll end it," I told him.

The Possessor made a noise between a rasp and a gurgle. It took me a moment to realize he was laughing.

"Not... long... now," he choked out. "She'll be... his... soon..."

He grinned, blood staining his teeth. I decided against the mercy killing. I slowly pushed myself up, ignoring the aches and pains in my body. I walked around the shop, looking through the cabinets and drawers to salvage anything I could. I found some packets of dried and canned food, as well as some bottles of lukewarm water. I never once looked back at the dying Possessor, knowing it couldn't take me over since I had an anti-possession sigil tattooed over my heart.

Yet I couldn't shake the foreboding words the Possessor had given me. As I walked out of the store and back into the dark, bloody streets, I recalled what Drake said.

See, I found something really, really special. It's the last thing we need. But don't worry, sweetheart. You'll get introduced to it very, very soon.

There was only one reason Drake, Mateo, and Lucifer himself would target me.

They wanted to capture my sister.

Chapter 2

Nobody was in a good mood when we got back to our current "safe house." It was a place where I'd once done a job during my time with the *Espanis de Sangre*– the Blood Thorns. I'd kicked in the door of the house, scaring the fuck out of the man and his family. I remembered the way his wife tried to defend him, raising a frying pan to hit me with. I'd stopped that by grabbing her hand in one fist and breaking her nose with the other. The children cried when I took their daddy away. That had been the worst part, because I knew their father was never going to come back.

I locked the door behind me and placed a chair under the doorknob. It was a pitiful form of defense against demons and psychotic drug lords, but now that Sephiel was human and unable to make protective wards, cheap solutions were all we had.

I turned around and looked at my friends. All of them were slumped in various positions across the living room. Sephiel stood vigilantly in the corner closest to me. He was dressed in his white leather trench coat, white shirt, white pants, and boots. His wavy auburn hair was flatter now, and I thought I saw hints of grey at his temples. His blue eyes were slowly losing their brightness. I noticed the bags underneath them.

Brooding in the left corner was a professional demon slayer, and my new lover, John Warrick. Broad shouldered and tall, Warrick was the definition of ruggedly handsome. His thick, dark oak hair was almost past his ears now. He was starting to grow some stubble around his mouth and cheeks. He wore dark blue jeans, a grey T-shirt, brown leather jacket, and black boots. Warrick's arms were folded over his chest, and I started to wish they were around me instead. Then I caught a glimpse of the angry twist of his lips, and figured this might not be the best time for some cuddling.

Sitting on the patchy olive green sofa directly across from me sat Max, who was working on honing his psychic abilities. He was able to sense things about people, like emotions and intent, though it was more powerful when he touched them. He was trying to use his gifts to discover what the demons were planning, but they were much stronger than he was. He'd be turning nineteen soon, though he looked more like an unpolished sixteen year old. Like Warrick, the young psychic was growing a small goatee. His skin was a dull gold like mine, and his eyes were a gentle, dark brown. Max didn't have much in the muscle department, but he focused on keeping us optimistic and looking out for Dro. He was the kind of person who didn't need physical strength to be strong.

Max was nestled beside my sister, holding her pale hand in his bronze one. I wondered if his ability was on, if he could feel the emotions rushing through my sister.

I hoped not, because she wasn't happy.

Dro stared at me with resentment, disappointment, and guilt. I wondered how much of it was directed at me, or if she was trapped with dark reflections of herself. In the nearly seventeen years since I had found her alone in the forest, crying in patch of scorched earth, Dro had rarely ever looked at me with disappointment this obvious. Sure, I had screwed things up for both of us, but she always found a way to forgive me.

This seemed like a last look, as if I was finally drying up all of the patience she once had for me. And if she directed all these dark emotions at herself...

I matched her stare. I'd told her over and over again that what was happening to us wasn't her fault. Dro and I wanted nothing more than to live normal lives. We hadn't asked to be tangled in a pissing contest between Heaven and Hell. Dro hadn't asked to be the Key to unleashing it all. She had just been born.

Being alive shouldn't have been a burden.

"So," Max finally said, attempting to break the awkward silence. "Are we going to talk about what just happened?"

I marched through the room, taking out the slim pickings for food and placing them on the scarred coffee table.

"What's there to say?" I muttered.

Max blinked at me. "Oh, gee, Constance, I don't know. Maybe we can talk about how we walked into a trap with Drake *fucking* Talbot, and none of us knew it."

I raised my eyes to Max's. For whatever reason, he had never been very afraid of me. I respected that. I also respected his desire to see Drake's head fall off his shoulders. Drake had killed Max's father, Manny, in front of us because he'd been looking for me. Manny's cruel murder was something I would never forgive myself for, even though Max held no blame over my head.

He did hang onto a lot of rage, however.

"If you'd known, you would have told us," I said.

"Well, *duh*," Max snarked, testing the limits of my patience. "But it was just a stupid convenience store. What the hell could he have been doing there?"

"I don't know," I replied, backing away. "I didn't find out."

"You should have let me chase him," Warrick said from the corner. His voice was deep and rumbling, which usually made him sound sexy, but right now was making him sound dangerous. "I'd have found out why he was there and what he was taking."

Of all of us, Warrick had the most cause to hate Drake. He'd raped and murdered Warrick's sister because of money, and had been eluding Warrick ever since. He'd been furious when he was forced to abandon his fight with Drake and run from a full-scale battle between Heaven and Hell. His temper wasn't getting any better now that I'd been openly threatened by his archenemy.

I looked at Warrick directly. "He would have expected that, and he would have killed you."

Warrick's head lifted, sharp green gaze locking

onto my dark one. I hated seeing the bags under his eyes, illuminating the scar under his left eye that Drake had given him years ago. Warrick wouldn't hurt me, but pushing his temper wasn't going to win me points with him.

Which was bad, since pretty much everyone in the room was pissed off at me right now.

"You're one to talk," he snapped bitterly. "You charged a room full of armed thugs."

"Who weren't going to shoot me," I pointed out.

"Really? I thought all the Blood Thorns hated you."

Now I was the one who was getting pissed off. "They do." My tone warned him to drop the subject.

"But you attacked them anyway."

"I thought I could get Drake before he got out of the door," I told Warrick. "I figured if everyone was focused on me, they wouldn't try to kill the rest of you. Besides, you heard what Drake said. They aren't going to kill me anymore than they will Dro."

"That is what perplexes me," Sephiel commented from behind me. I was grateful he intervened, because I liked arguing with Warrick about as much as I liked arguing with my sister.

"Why is it that they wish to draw you out, Constance? We have been moving through the city for weeks, staying in the shadows to keep safe and obtain information to close the Hell Gate, but what has prompted them to expose this new plan now?" Sephiel's eyes went dark. "Lucifer has not been seen since we entered the city, and he should be ecstatic at the return of his child."

Warrick hated Drake with every fiber of his being, and even that hate paled in comparison to the fury Sephiel held for Lucifer. Their feud began when Lucifer kidnapped Everiel, the love of Sephiel's life, and forced her to bear him a child in Hell.

That same child I had found in the forest sixteen years ago.

Sephiel might not hold any ill will toward Dro, but

it was impossible to miss the sadness in his eyes when he saw the similarities between my sister and the woman he loved, but wasn't able to save.

"He has a plan," Dro muttered. We all looked at her.

She stared at the food on the table without seeing it, holding Max's hand tightly in hers.

"I know he has a plan."

A warning flag went up in my head. "How?"

She paused. "I just do."

That flag started snapping in the wind. "Dro, did you...?"

My sister's frosty blue eyes rose to mine. "Did I break my promise and use my powers to find him?" She heard the sarcasm in her tone, and dialed it back. "No. But we've been running in circles since we got here, Constance. We're going to have to take the fight to Lucifer eventually."

"Then we'll find out what Drake stole for him and what they plan to do to me."

She narrowed her eyes. "We've tried doing that for the Hell Gate. It hasn't worked. No one is talking, because no one knows anything. Lucifer hasn't been seen since the Heaven Gate was shut, and the Blood Thorns are loyal to Mateo. We're running out of options."

Dro wasn't wrong. It wasn't just options we were running out of. It was places to hide. I knew this city like the back of my hand, but so did Mateo. He was born and raised in Ciudad Juárez, the son of the most powerful drug lord in all of Mexico. As leaders of the Blood Thorns, Mateo and his father Emilio were untouchable.

Then I came around. I entered the gang, stupidly fell in love with Mateo, learned of their plan to betray me and Dro, was tortured by them both, only to finally escape and kill Emilio right in front of his son's eyes. As a result, Mateo was hunting me to the ends of the earth, and he would find me eventually.

All of us were involved in some sort of revenge scheme that just wouldn't go away. But that was no excuse to walk into the hand of the Devil himself.

"Then we'll just have to wait until we've got absolutely nothing left," I stated. "That means Max is still the only one who uses his powers."

I sounded like a scolding parent, and Dro reacted like the accused child.

"They don't always work," she shot back, regardless of Max's hurt expression. "We've already figured out that Lucifer is blocking him on purpose, only letting Max see what he wants him to see. That's why we walked into that trap today. You think he won't set up another trap if he can?"

"Dro, you lost some of your powers when we shut the Heaven Gate. Whenever you push them, you damage yourself. You don't know how far you can go, and it's too risky to try."

She yanked her hand from Max's and got to her feet. Her fists were balled at her sides. I couldn't remember her being this angry with me before.

"Then I better go get some sleep so I can take a watch," she bit off. "It's the only useful thing you're going to let me do."

I blinked, unable to think of anything to say, or to stop the hurt digging into my heart. I tried to tell her that she was useful, that I just didn't want her to get herself killed, but Dro was already storming for the stairs. Nothing I could say now would bring her back. For the first time in my life, I didn't understand my sister. I didn't know what to say or do to make her believe in me again.

That hurt me worse than the punches I had taken tonight.

No one dared say anything to me. Max slowly got up from his seat on the couch. If my sister hadn't left in such a dark mood, maybe he would have cracked a joke. Something about having to clean up my mess again, that he had to literally play kiss-and-make-up, or that if I kept fighting with Dro, he would get more time alone with her.

Max wasn't afraid of me, but he knew when to stay back.

"I'll talk to her," was the only thing he whispered as he passed.

I didn't even nod. I imagined they would have their own making up to do. I wasn't worried about them. Max nearly always took Dro's side, so it was hard for her to stay mad at him for long.

I was less easy to forgive.

"I shall remain on watch," Sephiel said gently. "You are tired, Constance. You need to rest."

More words I didn't want to hear. Being scorned by Dro made me want to do something to prove that we weren't stuck in quicksand, with every little problem leading us to one giant suffocation.

Hearing Sephiel say I was tired actually made me feel the exhaustion in my body. I didn't sleep more than four or five hours, barely ate, and was constantly running or fighting. It had been weeks since I relaxed, but it felt like years.

I nodded to Sephiel, then stalked out of the room. I had lost my appetite. I didn't expect anyone to follow me, though I shouldn't have been surprised to hear footsteps at my back. I stopped at the staircase and turned around.

Warrick was standing behind me, sharp green eyes watching me with patience.

"What?" I breathed. I really wasn't in the mood for another tirade.

Instead of berating me, Warrick slipped onto the staircase with me and opened his arms. I stayed in place, but let him curl his arms around my back and pull me against his chest. The moment I felt the warmth of his body and inhaled his musky pine scent, I began to relax. I started to feel safe, comfortable, loved.

In the three weeks we had been together, Warrick had shown me more kindness and compassion than Mateo had done in two years. Clearly my choice in men had improved.

"Don't do that again," he whispered into my hair. "You scared the shit out of me."

I curved my arms around his back and hugged him

tighter. It was better if I didn't respond. That way I wouldn't have to lie to him.

"I'm sorry for lashing out at you," he went on, stroking the short, black strands of my hair. "I just saw him, heard him say those things to you, watched him get away again, and..."

He sighed instead of saying the rest. But he didn't have to.

"I know," I mumbled into his chest. "Guess I need to think before I act, huh?"

Warrick stifled a laugh, the rich sound sliding through my ears until it warmed my chest. He gently rubbed my back, and I melted even more.

"That would be a relief."

I wanted to smile, but my heart and mind weren't in it. Staying in Warrick's arms was easier than facing my problems. He loosened his hold for a second, until he realized that I wasn't letting go. He put his hands and my shoulders and slowly pushed me back so I could look at him. All his anger and impatience was now pushed down somewhere. It wasn't gone, but at least he was trying with me.

Not everyone was.

As if he was sensing my thoughts, Warrick cupped the bottom of my chin and lifted my head. There was so much tenderness on his face it broke my heart. I didn't deserve any of it.

"It's going to be okay," he promised. "You and Dro will get through it. You always do."

I didn't tell him that it was different this time. Something dark was growing inside my sister, and I had no idea how to stop it. If I even could.

Warrick stalled my thoughts by pressing his lips to mine. It took me half a second to respond. I was still reminding myself that Warrick could be trusted, that he'd saved my life and my sister's life without hesitation. He wasn't going to turn on me or torture me. He wanted to protect me, because he knew I wouldn't protect myself.

I stood there and absorbed him, enjoying his smell

and the sweet saltiness of his kiss. When Warrick pulled back, I nearly pouted. He smiled and stroked my face with the backs of his fingers.

I don't know what he saw in me. I wasn't that pretty, certainly not on the scale Dro was. I was slim with an athletic build and almost no curves. My dirty hair was black, razor straight, and chopped just below my chin. My dark gold skin was almost always covered in blood, and my dark brown eyes nearly always matched my mood. Yet Warrick looked at me like I was a queen.

"Come on," he whispered. "Let's get some sleep."

This time I did pout a bit. "But I'm not tired now."

He grinned, and gave me bedroom eyes that weakened my knees. I knew he'd spend the next hour stripping away my problems. After he stripped off my clothes.

"Good," he said, taking my hand. "Neither am I."

Chapter 3

An hour and a half later, Warrick was sleeping beside me. His arm was curled over my ribs, his strong heart beating against my back. We were sleeping on the floor of a spare bedroom deprived of all its furniture, using our clothes as blankets. It wasn't much, but Warrick's skin was warming me better than any fabric could.

Despite the comforting heat of him and the gentle breeze of his breath in my hair, I couldn't fall asleep. It wouldn't be long before my watch, and all I could think about was what my sister had said to me. No matter how badly I wanted to deny it and prove her wrong, I knew we couldn't run and hide for much longer. I hated that, because it used to be the simplest thing in the world, even when it seemed like the hardest...

I'd used the last of my money to take a huge risk. If it didn't pay off, I was going back to that little shack in Holanda to introduce that con man to my hatchet.

On the other hand, the first thing I showed him when I went to get our fake passports was the Blood Thorn tattoo behind my ear.

That got his ass moving pretty quickly.

"We're next," Dro whispered.

My sister tugged at the strings of her hoodie. She looked small for a fourteen year old girl. I wanted to tell her this would be easy, all we had to do was stay calm, except that would mean I had to be calm myself. Dro could sense my emotions if she pushed herself, so she knew I wasn't relaxed.

I was gripping the steering wheel of my stolen car with white knuckles and frequently glancing in the rearview mirror. *The passengers in the cars behind me were staring blankly ahead, impatiently waiting for their turn to drive into America. Any one of them could be working for my old boss. Or the new boss. It had been a week since Dro and I left the Blood Thorns. Seven days since I murdered my employer in front of his son, the man who betrayed me. The man I had been stupid enough to love.*

I rubbed my right shoulder out of habit. Dro had healed the bullet wound, leaving a small patchy scar on my skin. Less easy to heal was the giant hole in my heart.

I pushed the ache away and put my foot on the gas, easing the car forward. I stopped at the yellow line to wait for border security. The man who approached my car window was almost exploding out of his uniform. He was about two hundred pounds and six feet tall. His shirt strained under a combination of fat and muscle. He wore dark sunglasses with tinted shades that matched short brown hair. He tilted his sunglasses down and looked between my sister and me. His eyes stayed on Dro for longer than they needed to. It made me uneasy, but I wasn't surprised. Dro was becoming more gorgeous every day. It was impossible for her not to catch the eye of most males. Or the occasional female.

"Passports, please," he said with a bored Texan drawl.

We took our passports out and handed them to the guard. He read them carefully, confirming the details. My face was blank, but my mind was doing laps around the never-ending What If track.

If that con artist gave us faulty passports, I'm going to shove his head through a wall. Then I'll have to find someone else who isn't willing to talk, but who the fuck will that be? The entire city knows I ditched the Thorns by now. Mateo will have a manhunt on for me and who knew how far he'll reach–

The border guard handed us back our passports. "Please step out of the vehicle."

My first thought was to ask why. But then I

remembered this was standard. I unbuckled my seatbelt and got out of the car. Dro did the same. The sweltering Mexican sun beat down on my head. I showed my back to the other cars. Dro pulled up her hoodie and shoved her hands in her pockets.

"Where are you and Ms. Raymond coming from, Ms. Horatio?" asked the border guard as he circled the vehicle.

"We were coming from Ciudad Juárez," I answered.

The border guard raised his eyebrows at me. "Nasty place for two young girls to be. How long were you there?"

"Four years," I answered. "Visited family."

It was almost true.

"So where are you going now?" he asked, turning toward Dro. My sister shifted on her feet.

"El Paso. My friend's family lives there." Those were the lies.

The border guard turned and looked at Dro. She lowered her eyes.

"Aren't you hot in that, sweetheart?" he asked.

Dro shook her head. She was terrible at lying, and she was too memorable physically. I would get her something ice cold to drink if we ever got out of here.

"She's not feeling well," I said. "She has a fever."

The nosy guard looked at Dro again. She lifted her eyes just long enough for him to be satisfied, then flicked them back to the ground. The man went back to examining the car, peeking inside.

"Any fruits or vegetables?"

"No."

"Drugs, alcohol or weapons?"

That almost made me laugh. Drugs? No. I worked for a drug cartel, but I never sampled any of their products. Not after I saw how destructive it was.

Alcohol? No, but I could damn sure use some.

Weapons? Now those I did have. I was carrying my father's hatchet under my oversized shirt, four throwing blades in my jacket, and had two handguns under the front seat. The guard walked back around to the trunk and asked me to open it. I did so. There was nothing inside.

The border guard looked at my face one more time, then gave me a curt nod.

"Welcome to the United States, Ms. Horatio."

I nodded to him and got in the car. My sister was already inside, waiting for me. I buckled up and watched the yellow bar blocking us from the States. I felt someone watching me, and looked over my shoulder to the border guards in the booth.

The man I talked to started speaking with his partner, a tall Hispanic man. My windows were rolled up so I couldn't make out what they were saying, but they kept flicking their eyes back to me. I gripped the wheel tightly.

"Connie, the bar's up."

I turned my head forward and stepped on the gas. It took a lot of effort not to punch it to the floor and get away as fast as I could, but that would definitely get me caught. So I drove just a hair over the speed limit. About twenty minutes later, the border wall was a faded grey line behind us.

"Are you okay, big sister?" Dro asked me after a long time.

"Yeah," I replied. "Glad to leave that shithole behind."

Dro watched me with concerned blue eyes. Ever since she watched me collapse under the weight of Mateo's betrayal and Emilio's torture, she'd been waiting for my next breakdown. I didn't have many. I toughed out the hardest shit and came out stronger. I didn't complain, and I didn't hold many regrets, I just did what I had to. Even when my parents were brutally murdered in front of me, I put on a brave face and kept going for my sister. She needed me to be strong, so that's what I was.

I didn't understand why Mateo and Emilio had been the exception. They were monsters. Mateo enjoyed hurting people, and it was Emilio's greatest pleasure. I'd been no better than them. I had liked the power of it sometimes.

There was nothing more superior than facing someone who wanted to kill you, and killing them instead.

I knew it was wrong. I knew it would damn my soul. But I did it anyway.

"Constance, pull over."

"What?" Why was my voice hoarse?

"You're shaking."

Instead of arguing, I did as she said. The road we were on was empty so I wasn't going to hold up traffic. I pried my hands from the wheel. The leather had left a red impression in my palms, flushing my skin with blood. I stared at my hands, watching the blood turn darker and darker, thickening over my hands until it painted my fingers–

Dro unbuckled and threw her arms around me. I jumped a foot in the air, but wrapped my arms around her. Then I noticed that my breathing was raspy and my pulse was pounding. I closed my eyes and took a deep breath.

A little while later, I reached up and patted Dro's shoulder.

"I'm okay, little sister," I whispered. My voice wasn't trembling anymore. "I'm okay."

She pulled back and looked at me, doing her own assessment. I gave her a weak smile. I might not be entirely better yet, but I was at least trying. Dro smiled, and helped me immensely.

"Where are we going now?" she asked, buckling up her seatbelt.

"North somewhere. Any suggestions?"

Dro looked out the front windshield as I pulled back onto the main highway. "Hawaii would be nice. There would be a lot of hot guys there."

I laughed. Dro always knew what to say to make me feel better. The problem was that I was jaded. It was hard for me to see the good in anything unless I knew I was stronger than it.

"Maybe we'll get up there," I said. "Most important thing we can do now is lay low. Mateo will send Thorns

past the border."

And there I went, killing the joy Dro was trying to put in me. She nodded solemnly, and my heart sank. I was a bitch, but at least I knew how to play things safely...

Something was on my shoulder, gently rocking me awake. I jumped and whirled myself around, ready to come up swinging. Warrick– fully dressed, unfortunately– raised his hands and leaned back.

"Sorry, didn't mean to spook you," he said without any shock to my actions. "Thought you might want to get up and have some food."

I sat up and rubbed my eyes. "Sure. Is it my turn for watch?"

"No, I took your turn."

I lowered my hands and looked at him. He smiled sadly at me. "You haven't been sleeping much lately, Constance. You needed it."

I tried to protest, but he waved it me off. "It's too late for you to get pissed off because everyone else is awake. We're all waiting on you."

Goody, I thought. I pushed off the clothes and stood up to look for my underwear. As I moved around the room with every piece of skin available to the eyes, I felt Warrick watching me. I looked over my shoulder and found him smirking with his laser green eyes fixed on my ass.

"Do you mind?" I asked impatiently.

He kept staring. "Not at all. You have a beautiful body. I'm just appreciating it."

I snorted. Beautiful, sure. If you don't count the scrawniness and the dozens of scars from knives, bullets, claws, and fangs.

I finally found my clothes and yanked them on. I could have used a shower, but that would have given Warrick more naughty ideas. As much as I would have enjoyed those ideas, we had problems that needed to be dealt with.

"What's everyone doing awake?" I asked, pulling

on my boots and grabbing my weapons.

"Watching TV," Warrick replied.

I stared at him. "Are you serious?"

One look at his face told me he was.

"You need to see this, Constance."

That didn't sound good.

Chapter 4

Seeing it was worse.

I was barely listening to what the shaky voiced reporter was rushing to say. She was going on about the U.S. government telling everyone in the northern states to make their way south to avoid the massive forest fires stretching from Washington to Iowa. There was also something about Mexican officials willing to open the border for refugees if the American government began erasing some of its debts.

All I could focus on was the images on the screen, the aerial shots of a giant red blaze snaking over mountains and blackening the earth. The next image was of a bridge packed with cars, their owners carrying half closed suitcases and crying children toward wary eyed border guards.

What stuck with me the most was the strung together clips of blood stained streets, demons scampering after fleeing humans, wild monsters smashing through cars and windows to get their victims, thick black clouds that spiraled and drilled into the mouths of anyone unfortunate to be close to them...

I shivered, nearly glad about our split second decision to come to Ciudad Juárez. The States were being completely overrun by demons. The NSA was cautioning everyone to arm himself or herself and stay in their homes. Military units were swamped and doing their best to eradicate the monsters. Hospitals were overcrowded and shutting down because they were perfect targets for hungry demons that wanted easy prey.

"Have you heard from the other demon slayers?" I caught Max's whisper to Warrick at my back.

Warrick's sigh was heavy. "No. They're blocking

my calls. Even Jackson."

All of the other demon slayers Warrick used to work with were assholes, but Jackson was a genuinely good man. He was Warrick's friend, and if he wasn't answering his calls, then I had to assume it was because he was either swamped with the chaos we had brought to the States, or he was dead.

I hoped it was the former.

I wondered, not for the first time, if this would have happened if we hadn't closed the Heaven Gate. After Dro's blood was used in a ritual to open both Gates to the other worlds, Lucifer's plan had been to invade Heaven and bring sinners into it, corrupting every soul inside. Alternatively, Heaven's plan had been to descend to earth and restructure Hell to relieve it of the worst sinners, while simultaneously blocking out anyone else who made mistakes in their life and condemned themselves.

Dro and I destroyed the Heaven Gate by burning paradise on earth. We had locked the Gate and banished the angels on earth to live in their mortal vessels. Their wings and powers were stripped, only the most powerful beings like Dro and the archangels preserving some of their abilities. But those abilities were starting to wane, and it wouldn't be long before they were totally gone.

However, if we hadn't closed the Heaven Gate, humans would be caught in a supernatural war that would end in millions, maybe billions, of deaths. As it stood now, when anyone with a decent soul died, angel or human, they could ascend to Heaven through Saint Peter's Gates. I'd been told that it didn't hold the majesty of the Heaven where angels had lived, but it was better than nothing.

Maybe if I tell myself that enough, I'll actually start believing it.

Just as my thought finished, the television and the lights snapped off. We'd closed the blinds in the house to keep prying eyes away, so now we were stuck in complete darkness. My hand immediately went to my hip, my fingers curling around my hatchet.

Aside from Max's muttered cursing in the dark, we couldn't hear a thing. He and Warrick left the room to see if a fuse had blown. I sat up and drifted toward the window. The curtain was dark, but shards of daylight were starting to break through. I pressed my back against the wall and slowly moved the curtain.

The street was isolated, except for the trio of electricians in grey jumpsuits who were smashing a power box with crowbars. It didn't look safe for them, but I wasn't going to stomp out and scold them. Instead, I curled my hand around my hatchet and ran my thumb up and down its hilt. The blade was silver and the handle was wrapped with black leather. Engraved on the handle were the words '*Anima potentis, cor sororis,*' which meant 'Soul of a warrior, heart of a sister,' in Latin. Sephiel made me this weapon after I lost my father's hatchet in a cave-in. He'd also blessed it with his angelic powers, making it even more deadly to demons. Now that he was human, I wasn't sure if the blessing still held. But it killed demons just fine.

The three moronic delinquents became bored with the electric box and decided to run down the left side of the street. I watched them carefully, waiting to see if they would return, or if anyone else would slink out of their houses to assess the damage. When nobody did, my eyes drifted up to catch a glimpse of downtown Juárez.

When we first arrived here, it was in worse condition than I remembered. I was familiar with a muggy, dirty city that smelled like gasoline and salt. Streets that were tightly packed with stone buildings and shops, some of them coated with paint that chipped and faded over the years. Most of the homes were shacks with rusted tin roofs and stucco walls. Smart owners put iron bars over their windows, and cheaper owners left them open and vulnerable.

I recalled shouting vendors, honking horns from cars that belonged in the sixties, and disinterested bystanders walking briskly. I remembered being one of the hungry, homeless girls hiding at night, when the ground was coldest and the gunshots were loudest.

Now it was different. The moment we stepped over the city limits, I saw all that had changed from bad to worse. The sides of the houses had gouges and claw marks scratched along them. Broken glass littered the streets with no one around to pick it up. Gang graffiti painted the worn down shops, some of them missing the padlocks on the doors. Piles of burning tires and barrels sat on every street corner, tinting the streets in dull orange light and making the air smell like scorched rubber and taste like smoke. Fresh, glistening bloodstains covered old ones every hundred feet, some of them no bigger than quarters, some of them the size of tables.

All the people I'd seen were wearing the same ratty clothes they'd worn before, but they carried themselves differently. Before, it was easy to pick out who was cautious, who was in a gang, and who was scared. Now people seemed to have stopped caring. They were citizens in a city of anarchy. I'd watched from the distance as a group of laughing men with knives chased after a woman wearing shredded clothes. Two shadows behind a curtain in an apartment had moved together in violent passion. A trio of little boys had sat in an alley, dipping their fingers in a red smear on the pavement and using it to paint on a store wall. Choking smoke layered the already pitch black sky. Pockets of street were glowing red from the fires underneath them while the rest were dark.

I was amazed at how Ciudad Juárez hadn't just deteriorated. It was destroyed. Even if we closed the Hell Gate, it would take decades to repair the damage. Assuming it ever was. The easier route would be to demolish everything left standing and build over the bad memories.

In the course of the three weeks we'd been here, we'd seen some pretty terrible things as we moved from street to street, block to block. Atrocities I hadn't seen since I'd been with the Blood Thorns, doing exactly what they were doing, but getting paid for it.

Finding out that the *Espanis de Sangre* were

running the city with the demons wasn't hard. They'd never been a gang to hide in the shadows. They liked being loud, upfront, and memorable in their murders. That had been one of Emilio Rocha's staples, after all:

Make them remember you.

I suppressed the shiver that had been building under my skin. Every memory I had of Emilio ended in fear and pain. Similar ones were attached to his son, Mateo. The depths of his betrayal tainted any trace of happiness and love I felt for him.

But damned if I didn't stick to Emilio's rule. Even now, when I stalked the alleys and looked for information, I grabbed any unsuspecting Blood Thorn I could and punched him for answers. I was good at my work, and everyone knew me. I'd been the only female enforcer for Emilio's gang, and I had earned my reputation.

I also got the answers I wanted. I assumed it wouldn't be long before Mateo found out where I was. We had the kind of relationship that would end with only one of us still breathing. Only three days after we arrived did we start to hear about the mass murders.

No, 'mass murder' were the wrong words. 'All out slaughter' fit better.

We came across the site by mistake. We'd heard the gunshots and seen the flames tearing up the night, and thought it had been a demon attack.

Until we saw all the humans tearing into each other.

At first I thought they had been possessed. That was rational, after all. Possessors loved butchering people. But when I had squinted from around the corner, I didn't see the trademark black eyes that came with possession. They were completely human, and completely insane.

People of every age and gender, fuelled by carnal rage and bloodlust, raised crude weapons against each other. Kitchen knives held by housewives were painted crimson when they were yanked from the bodies of dying victims. Crowbars and lead pipes smashed into skulls, pulping brain and bone. A doctor pummeled the life from a construction worker. There were some Blood Thorns that strangled unprotected necks, gouged out eyes, gutted bellies with knives. Even now, I could smell the blood that had been painting the brick walls and sandy streets. No matter how long ago it was, you never forget the smell of death. It haunts you just as surely as the sights of butchery do.

But the worst part had been the smiles. Everyone, whether they were a victim or a killer, had been smiling. Wide, Cheshire smiles with mouths full of blood and broken teeth. The smiles of lunatics and psychopaths.

I hadn't understood what it was until we had left the street. We had all been sickened by what we saw, but I was reasoning it out. I was thinking about the street, the buildings surrounding it.

The slaughter hadn't been random. It had been a message.

A message for me.

I wasn't sure how, but I knew Mateo was trying to tell me that he knew I was here, that he was going to find me and make his move soon. He was going to tear me apart the same way those people had torn themselves apart.

The attacks kept happening. Every few days, there would be one pocket of the city that would explode into violence and sin on a level I never thought possible. I caught the pattern soon after– every slaughter site had been a place where I'd been on a run for the Blood Thorns.

If that wasn't a memorable message, I didn't know what was.

Another knot tied in my stomach. Suddenly I couldn't keep my thoughts to myself.

"Seph," I asked the ex-angel. He was standing across from me on the other side of the curtain, watching the opposite end of the street. "These killings, the major ones... Do you think Lucifer is behind them rather than Mateo?"

Sephiel went very still. Talking about Lucifer

always made him tense, and I had to remind myself not to push him. He was human now, and his emotions weren't so tightly reined anymore. A single snap in battle could get him killed.

"It is likely they are working in collaboration," he finally said. "Perhaps Lucifer is feeding Mateo Rocha's thirst for vengeance, and your former lover is constructing the circumstances for the slaughter. His men are nearly always there, are they not?"

"Yeah," I replied, gripping my hatchet tighter as I thought about the bloodstains that would never wash out of cracks in brick and pavement. "They were. But I don't like how they're dragging this out. Something isn't right."

"I agree with you," Sephiel commented. He turned his eyes from the street to me. "I do not know how I can be of more help."

I glanced at him. Sephiel was looking tired, rumpled, and a little too human. I couldn't imagine how hard it was for him to live nearly an eternity as an angel, only to be reduced to a slower, less divine human. He never complained about anything, so I had no idea how he was handling the situation. He had to miss being able to help us the way he used to.

But if his words were anything to go by, he was desperate to keep going.

"You're doing enough," I told him. "There's no point in sending you off to shakedown demons. Whatever Lucifer and the Blood Thorns are planning, they're going to make sure we know about it soon."

I looked at the street, but Sephiel was still watching me. "You sound certain."

I stilled my hand on my hatchet. "I am."

I pushed away from the window and let the curtain fall back into place. The darkness seemed thicker than I remembered.

"Stay by the window. I'm going to check on Dro and the guys."

Sephiel didn't reply, so I assumed he was going to agree. Deep down, he likely knew that I wasn't actually going to check on Max and Warrick. It had been too long since me and Dro had talked, and I was sick of this fight we were stuck in.

After a couple minutes of squinting until my eyes were sore, I made my way up the stairs to the room Max was sharing with Dro. They'd taken the larger master bedroom, since I didn't care where I slept, and I might have threatened Max with bodily harm if he thought about putting moves on my sister. He'd only flinched once before assuring me he wouldn't touch Dro that way unless she wanted him to.

I felt out with my hand and found the door. I rapped on it gently. After a moment, I heard something shifting beyond the wood. Footsteps padded toward the door and it opened inward.

In the pitch black, I could make out the edges of Dro's snow-white hair, but it was too dark for me to read her face.

"Is the power out?" she asked after a long minute.

"Yeah," I replied. "Can I come in?"

Another long pause, but she pulled open the door and stepped inside the room. I followed and let her close it behind me. I spotted a crevice of light coming from the curtain on the far side of the room. I hurried for it and pulled it open just enough to look out into the backyard. No one was in it, and there were no other peering faces in the windows of the surrounding houses. Hoping that wouldn't change, I drew the curtain back so light from the hazy sun could pour into the room.

Satisfied that we wouldn't be watched, I turned and sat cross-legged on the floor and looked up at my sister.

She was still standing by the door, her long braid tumbling over her chest. Her arms were wrapped around her middle, like she was either nauseated or protecting herself. This didn't bode well for me.

"You might as well just say it," I prompted.

"Say what?" Dro muttered.

"Whatever it is that's keeping you five feet away

from me."

Dro sighed. Her arms circled her elbows. She kept her eyes on the floor. "I don't want to fight, Con."

"Neither do I. That's why I came here. So sit down and let's talk."

She was reluctant at first, but some of her anger must have melted into guilt, because she crossed the distance between us and sat on the floor across from me. I wished she would look me in the eyes.

I waited patiently, not willing to make the first move. Yeah, maybe that was cowardly of me, but anything I'd planned to say evaporated the moment I saw the tired rings under her eyes. I didn't want to drive Dro into more guilt and anger. I just wanted to let her know I was here, and to figure out what was wrong.

"Why aren't you letting me help?" Dro whispered.

"You do help," I countered.

"How?" Her temper was beginning to rise. "By giving you a supernatural bandage when one of you is hurt?"

"And keeping Lucifer off our backs by *not* broadcasting yourself," I defended.

"I'm the only supernatural we have. I'm the only one strong enough to stop Lucifer. You promised to let me fight him on my own."

"And you promised me that you wouldn't strain your powers," I snapped. Dro's eyes turned sharp and tense, like the line of her mouth. I took a deep breath and told myself to calm down.

"Dro, listen to me. Most of your powers are on the demon side now." I paused, then added, "I can't help but think that it's doing something to you."

Telling her that didn't make me feel very spectacular, but the thought must have crossed Dro's mind. I saw the conflict, the understanding, and then the reluctant acceptance. My little sister swept a hand over her head. Her hair had been braided for about three days now, and pieces of it were starting to fall out of the ties.

"I know," she agreed quietly. "But my angel powers

aren't what they used to be, Con." She bowed her head. "I don't know if I'll be able to hear the angels. All I have in my head now is silence, and I'm willing to bet it's the same for them. If I can't get used to it, they must be going insane."

She could have asked Sephiel to find out, but I didn't think Dro would be able to bring herself to ask something so personal of a man whose heartache she probably felt responsible for.

"They're just going to have to learn to be human. There's no way around it."

Her eyes met mine. "That doesn't seem fair."

"Maybe not, but that's just the way it is."

We sat there in silence for a long time, both thinking about the same thing. The tall, luscious trees of the Heaven Gate, its bubbling streams and crisp air, glowing flowers and comforting warmth.

The heat of the fire as we burned it to the ground. The screams of Sephiel and Dro as their angel powers were stripped from their souls.

"Why hasn't he made a move yet?" she asked suddenly. I looked at my sister. "Lucifer was so angry at us for closing the Heaven Gate right in front of him. He could find me if he really, truly wanted to. But he hasn't. Why do you think that is?"

That was a question I wasn't in the mood to answer, since I didn't want to know. Beings like Lucifer were too complicated and dangerous to understand. But Dro had a point. He could have shown up at any time and obliterated us. Instead, we were waiting for him to make a move.

I thought back to the battle we'd been caught in the night we destroyed the Heaven Gate. The angels charging forward to fight the demons spilling out of the portals Lucifer created, despite their rapidly fading powers. The amount of strength Michael had when he started a fight with Lucifer. The way the Devil looked at me before we escaped, his lips mouthing a single, terrifying promise:

I will destroy you.

"We'll worry about it when we cross paths again.

He won't sit back if we walk up to the Hell Gate and shut it." I shrugged, "Who knows, maybe he'll even disappear once we close the Gate."

I wouldn't have been so stupidly optimistic if my sister hadn't needed to hear it.

She didn't believe my statement anymore than I did, but the ghost of a smile crossed her face. I didn't like how weary and depressed it made her look.

"That would be nice and simple, wouldn't it?" The smile widened a little more, then faded away.

"Con, I'm sorry. I know I haven't been myself lately, and you didn't want to come back here. I just... I wasn't thinking, because I'm tired of this. I'm tired of being afraid and running all the time. I just want it to be over."

I couldn't fault her for that, since it was exactly what I wanted too. It had been so long since I'd felt true safety. Sleeping under a roof or having dinner with my sister or being held by Warrick never took away the stress and panic. It merely dulled it. I was ready to leave it all behind, to remember what it meant to feel alive instead of lucky to be breathing.

If wishes were horses...

"Are we okay?"

Dro's voice was tentative, as if she didn't think I would say yes. Truthfully, I could have kicked myself for the bit of hesitation I showed. Dro was a good sister and she would never hurt me, but I hoped she would see that her demon blood was making her slightly aggressive, something she had never willingly been. I knew my sister was growing stronger in every way, but there was a difference between her arguing with me and threatening to immolate a dying man.

"Yeah," I said, shoving the memory of the man she'd tried to interrogate into the back of my mind. "You just have to control yourself. Don't use your powers unless we're seconds away from dying."

"Or if Lucifer shows up."

I bit my tongue. "Or if Lucifer shows up," I

mumbled. I *hated* that promise.

Dro looked at the floor. "Thanks for looking out for me, big sister. I know I'm not... easy."

I reached over to take and squeeze her hand. "You're fine, Dro. You always were."

She nodded, but didn't smile. "I'm gonna go find some food. Max is awake and moving around, so he's probably hungry."

I stifled a laugh and let her get to her feet. Dro walked to the door in the dark, then stopped and half-turned back to me.

"I miss being part angel," she confessed. "It made me feel like a good person."

Before I could tell her she was the best kind of person in the world, she turned and walked out of the room. Dro had never thought very highly of herself, which was something I would have given anything to change. Yet as much as I loved her, I couldn't help but think that Dro's change would make her into something neither of us wanted her to be.

Chapter 5

The rest of the day passed without incident. The power didn't come back on, so we decided to stay in the house for a little longer and move to another one when it was dark. We'd been fortunate in choosing a block of houses that had been mostly empty. Downtown seemed to be the most dangerous area, but I wasn't expecting to go back there any time soon.

Then again, I had a bad habit of expecting anything to go the way I wanted it to...

"I don't get it," I said for the third time, my eyes flicking over the box of black hair dye. "It says it's supposed to be permanent. Why the hell isn't it holding?"

Dro looked at me from the motel's bathroom door, rubbing the strands of her pale hair. The hotel towel was greasy and black, completely ruined from the hair dye that leeched onto it.

"I dunno," she muttered, sounding almost guilty. "But maybe we should stop trying. I don't think we can change how I look."

I sighed and roughly threw the empty dye box into the trashcan by the table. It hit the other five hair dye boxes and tumbled onto the stained carpet. I sighed and flopped down on the bed, running a hand over my face. Dro put the towel into the bathtub and came into the room to sit down on the bed beside me.

"Do you think we should cut it?" Dro asked softly.

I glanced at her. She was toying with the edges of her hair, brushing it with her fingers as if she wasn't going to be able to do so again. For a second, I considered it. Dye wasn't holding and I couldn't spend money on a wig, but cutting Dro's hair wouldn't make her look less unique. She had a look that was all her own. Beautiful, marble pale, snowy hair, icy eyes. She was impossible not to notice, and even harder to forget.

"Nah," I said, turning my face back to the water-spotted ceiling. "We'll just have to find a way to put it up and hide it that way."

I could feel Dro smiling at me. She always thought she looked like a freak, but like all fourteen year old girls, she loved her hair.

"So what are we going to do now?" she asked.

Pray for a fucking miracle. "I dunno. Look for jobs, I guess. We can do that tomorrow. Odessa is pretty big. I'm sure they'll have something."

Though my skills were pretty limited. I helped out around the house with chores, but I damn sure couldn't be a maid. I wasn't very good with people, so retail was out. I was wary around people with knives, so kitchens weren't going to work. The only thing I knew how to do was fight, but that was sketchy, too.

I was a damn good fighter, but I was also a felon. I didn't want to advertise myself by getting into professional boxing or something like that. Being a bodyguard was an option, until I remembered that they required a background check, so I couldn't lie about who I'd worked for last.

That would be an interesting conversation. They'd call up the Blood Thorns and ask to speak to my employer, who they would find out I had killed.

The fallback was the criminal lifestyle. At least I could work underground, assuming another gang would accept me. I didn't want to do that, but nothing else was open to me. And even that was dangerous, and not just for the obvious reasons. News traveled at the speed of sound in the gritty underworld, and the tattoo behind my ear would be a dead giveaway. Someone would know I'd worked for the Blood Thorns. Someone would know I'd killed my boss. Then that same someone would probably tell Mateo, who would put me in the ground faster than a bullet.

My heart ached again. I told myself I wasn't missing him. I was just hurting because he'd chosen to give up Dro to a woman who wanted to use her for God knows what. He assumed I would stop loving him, and had been jealous of Dro. She'd never liked him, but I'd hoped that we would have found a way to live together. I'd loved him, and he'd burned me worse than any fire.

"It'll get easier, Connie," Dro's whisper came from the other bed.

I turned my head. Dro watched me with anxious eyes. She could tell I was deeply wounded from what Mateo and his father had done to me. They'd left scars on me inside and out, tortured me, wanted to see me dead. I would second guess everyone, never let anyone but Dro get close to me. I would jump when someone was too close, have horrible nightmares, and never be able to take a bath again.

"Maybe," I said. My entire being was suddenly exhausted: heart, body, and soul. "We should get some sleep. We have a lot to do tomorrow."

I crawled up to my bed, placing my hatchet and throwing knives on the nightstand. I dragged the covers over my body, too tired to take off my clothes. I put my back to Dro and pretended to sleep, though I felt the weight of her gaze on me for a long time before she followed my lead. In a few minutes, I could hear her steady breathing. The heaviness of sleep eventually came over me, and thought that I might actually be able to rest peacefully for a whole night...

***

The first thing that woke me up was the smell. A thick, smoky smell pushed down my nose and swelled in my throat. Then it was the heat. My clothes and hair were plastered to my body, though the air so dry I was choking on it.

Then it was the screams. The ones that didn't belong to me. I hastily opened my eyes and shot upward. I turned *my head to see why Dro was screaming.*

She was burning.

Blinding white flames were shifting around her body. I squinted like I was looking at the sun. The flames had turned the sheets to dust. They crawled up the cheap wallpaper and incinerated it.

Dro's half of the hotel room was completely destroyed. The walls were curtains of white and orange flame. Smoke curled on the top of the groaning ceiling. The sprinklers were on, but the water was dissolving as soon as it hit the fire.

Dro barely stopped to breathe. It was like she'd turned into a siren that was signaling the end of the world.

I'd seen this once before, and knew I had to move. I tossed the sheets off the bed and went to grab my boots. I yanked them up, just as the carpet caught fire.

Shit shit shit!

I looked back at my sister, who was lying on a bed of white fire. How was I going to wake her up?!

I forced myself to focus. Calming down was impossible, but I pulled on my boots and grabbed my weapons from the nightstand. I glanced at my backpack, which was sitting on the table. Or it was, until the flames engulfed it, cracking the wood and disintegrating everything that had once covered it.

It was getting hard to breathe. I was trapped on the bed. Smoke and heat dried out my eyes and dehydrated my throat. I looked at the window across from me and then at the nightstand. It was still fairly intact, though the bottom was beginning to catch fire. I grabbed the cheap but fairly heavy nightstand and hurled it at the glass. Its half burned shape crashed through the window, flames licking curtains. Smoke flushed out and revealed an exit.

Now we just had to get to it.

"Dro!" I half screamed, half coughed. "Dro!"

Her screams were lessening, but she still wasn't awake.

"Andromeda!"

She stopped howling. Her bright eyes snapped

open, and she saw the disaster around her. Dro tried to scream again, but her voice was too hoarse. Her eyes met mine, wider and more terrified than I'd ever seen them.

"The window!" I managed to yell and point.

Dro nodded and leaped off the bed. I was about to warn her that the floor was burning, but she seemed to be walking around just fine. Dro moved around the beds and crawled out of smoking window, completely gone from my sight. The fire didn't seem to have hurt her at all.

I didn't think I would be as lucky. Before I could think too much about the consequences of what would happen if I failed, I made the jump. My bed was close to the window, so I nearly got out unscathed.

Part of the ceiling collapsed as I was soaring. It landed behind me and singed the back of my leg. I cried out and caught myself in a roll when I went through the window. Heat flared along my back and right side. I landed hard on the metal landing. Someone shrieked and started patting me down. A searing pain filled my body. I smelled something that reminded me of overcooked pork. Whoever was patting me down was probably getting rid of the flames, but they were also slapping raw blisters and burns. I gasped and coughed, tears from smoke and pain blurring my eyes.

I was faintly aware of what was going on around me. The fire must have spread, because other people were screaming.

My arm was grabbed and lifted. I bit my tongue and shifted to get to my feet. I buckled when I put pressure on my right shin. Whoever was carrying me kept me upright.

"Come on, Connie, we need to go."

Hearing Dro's voice calmed me down and got my head back on a swivel. I took my arm off Dro's, though she was reluctant to let me go. I hobbled well enough on my own, taking a long second to make sure we could get away.

We were on the second floor and thankfully close to the stairs, which weren't on fire yet. I could feel the *heat on my back and moved down the creaky metal steps as fast as I could. Dro was beside me, moving at a good pace but never pulling too far ahead. The roaring fire and the terrified cries made her flinch repeatedly.*

We finally got down the stairs when my body chose to remind me of the pain it was in. My leg, back, and right side throbbed violently, like someone was continually smacking me with a yardstick. Sweat beaded down my temples and neck. I looked up as the ambulances and fire trucks arrived. Their sirens blared wildly as the firefighters jumped out. Their eyes widened when they saw the blaze. I knew we had to leave, but I wanted to look back and see what I had survived.

Half the motel was crumbling into flaming rubble, looking like an orange bonfire and nothing else. Another quarter of it had smoke and flames climbing out of every window and door. The last quarter was catching fire quickly. The heat was intense, the light from the torched building strong enough to signal an airplane. Smoke blanketed the night sky, blotting out the stars.

Maybe it would have been beautiful, in its own destructive way, if I'd been able to ignore the people.

Everyone who made it out of the motel was standing in the parking lot panicking. Paramedics and EMTs were running back and forth to help as many people as they could. Firefighters dragged water hoses into the parking lot and hurried to put them to use. The motel residents were huddling together and staring at the blaze with horrified awe. Their shouts were panicked and heartbreaking.

"What are we gonna do?!"

"What happened?!"

"Has anyone seen my son?! Where's my son?!"

There were about seven people who couldn't speak properly because they were in agony. Charred bodies were lifted onto stretchers and hauled away quickly. Others were being tended to on the ground, begging for something to take away the pain. There were a couple of bodies that weren't moving at all. The paramedics walked to them with body bags.

I'd been around burning flesh before. I'd seen the damage fire could do. I was grateful not to be any closer.

Something brushed along my right arm. I jumped from the tingling pain. I looked over my shoulder and immediately regretted my reaction.

Dro was standing behind me, staring at the fire she'd created. She was shaking as she moved closer to me. I'd nearly forgotten she was there. Tears filled her eyes. Dro watched the fire again, breathing in shivers.

Red and blue lights flashed, and I knew the cops had arrived. My mind snapped out of shock, and I was able to concentrate again.

"Come on," I said. My voice still sounded raspy from the smoke I breathed in.

I turned and limped toward the farthest end of the parking lot. I needed to sit down and do something about these fucking burns. I wandered behind a car at the end of the lot and was about to get in when the burning, throbbing pain made itself known again. I had to prop myself against the car to breathe through it.

I looked over the side of the car. The police were out of their vehicles. They were talking to the fire crews and gathering witnesses. I didn't think anyone had seen us yet but it would just be a matter of time. News vans were probably on their way.

"Dro, I need you to heal me," I said.

She'd done so a thousand times in the past without me ever asking. Usually she never even hesitated. Now she wasn't even in arm's length.

"Dro?"

"I don't know what happened," she half whispered. "I don't... I didn't mean it!"

She started gasping instead of breathing. I took a step closer to her. Dro cringed and jumped back a foot.

"No! No, don't come near me!"

I didn't know if anyone could hear us, and I didn't bother to check. Dro's hands began filling with white light, which was quickly turning to flame. She looked at her hands like they were covered in blood.

"Oh no," she whimpered. "No, no, no!"

I took another careful step forward. "Dro, you need to calm down."

I sounded calm myself. Miracles can happen. Not that Dro would believe that right now.

"Don't come any closer, please," she begged.

Tears were streaking her face and sobs cracked her voice. I hadn't seen Dro this upset since our parents were murdered. It broke my heart to see her like this, so I kept moving closer.

"Connie, please," she wept.

I stopped. When she sounded that wretched, it was impossible for me not to listen. The flames curled up to her elbows. She was still hyperventilating.

"It's okay," I told her. "You won't hurt me."

"Yes, I will," she said.

I looked directly into her eyes. "No, little sister. You won't."

She tried to breathe normally. We needed to get out of here, but I couldn't force Dro in this state.

"You can make it stop, just like you did at Owl Creek."

Dro blanched when she heard the name of the camp where our parents had been killed. But the fire was starting to die down from her hands. She was a tiny bit calmer. The fire dwindled until it was gone. She shuddered once and gasped sharply. I walked toward her and put my arms around her. She tensed at first, then relaxed and hugged me tightly. The burns on my body were pulsing and tender, but Dro was more important.

"We'll get through this, Dro," I whispered. "I promise, we'll figure it out."

She stiffened before she pulled away from me. She wiped her eyes and quickly walked to the car. I watched her carefully, my eyes turning back toward the burning motel.

Dro didn't believe me. After seeing what she had done, I could understand. I wouldn't believe myself either.

There are some things you just can't forget...

The smell of smoke was strong when the dream ended. I didn't know why, since in the dream we were leaving the motel...

Wait.

I shot upright from the floor, taking one deep breath.

Smoke.

That was enough to have me moving faster than lightning.

My sudden motion caused Warrick to stir. He was coming out of sleep, moving faster as he realized something was very wrong. I wasn't waiting for him. I was yanking on my clothes, boots, and grabbing a backpack to throw over my shoulder.

It was reflex, but one I hadn't needed to exercise in months. Dro's nightmares had stopped a little while back. She'd had control.

I was stupid to think that luck would last.

I could hear more shouts, and Warrick was trying to tell me something. He was trying to keep up, but I wasn't listening. The moment I had everything I could carry, I darted for the door. I stopped and looked over my shoulder. Warrick was behind me, looking confused yet ready for anything.

"Find Max and Sephiel. Make sure they get out."

His lack of understanding was clear. "What about you and Dro?"

I held his eyes. "Dro's the one causing this."

Before he could reply, before I could even attempt to read his expression, I turned and yanked open the door.

A smothering wave of heat and light crashed into me. Dry smoke curled off the walls and ceiling, dancing away from the red and orange flames shivering on every surface. The fire was unforgiving, dredging sweat out of my pores and making my eyes water. I turned out of the room, coughing and choking as I tried to remember where the stairs were.

Over the crackling roar of angry flames and creaking wood, I caught the sound of screams.

Dro's was only one of them.

Oh no.

I pushed myself harder, barely taking in how close the flames were getting to me. I could feel them peeling off the walls, teasing the edges of my hair and clothes. Through the haze of smoke and fire, I noticed Sephiel climbing the stairs. He held an arm over his mouth and he needed to squint, but I knew he saw us.

I was coming up to the spare bedroom when something tumbled out of it. A body, one arm covered in fire.

I skidded to a stop and fell beside it, automatically batting out the flames without seeing who I was hitting. Their voice was hoarse and filled with pain. They curled in on themselves, clearly never thinking they would be burned so severely. My eyes went to the person's face, and my heart sank.

Max probably never expected Dro would burn him.

Warrick and Sephiel stood over me and the partially burned prophet, carefully lifting him to his feet. Max cried out again, unable to think past all the agony. I made sure Warrick and Sephiel were able to hold him. Between their sets of muscles, I didn't think the men would have a problem carrying Max out.

"Run!" I shouted at them.

Sephiel slung Max's unburned arm over his shoulder and turned for the stairs. It wouldn't be long before the flames reached the bottom and trapped us inside.

Which made my temper flare when Warrick refused to move.

He looked at me desperately, thinking I would come with him.

"I'm getting Dro," I shouted over the clamor.

He hesitated until I gave him a look that said, *Trust me. I can get us both out.*

At least, that's what I hoped my look said.

There wasn't enough time for me to make sure Warrick took my expression seriously. Sephiel would make him move, and if it turned out that I couldn't keep my promise... Well, at least there wouldn't be a way for him to argue with me. Not unless he wanted to yell at a pile of dust.

The second I entered into the spare bedroom where the fire had begun, the temperature ratcheted up at least ten more degrees. It was so hot I could feel blisters starting to grow on my skin. My hair was clinging to the sweat on my face. The clothes and backpack weighed a thousand pounds. Every breath was a struggle, parching my throat and binding my lungs. Scorching light embedded into my retinas, forcing tears from my eyelids.

All three walls I could see were made of fire. It cased the room, growing inward and filling every space it could find. Tornadoes of smoke caught flakes of ash and spun them through the air. The floor was groaning and straining under the heat and pressure. I had to get Dro and leave the room before it collapsed.

She wasn't hard to find.

Ten feet away from me was a silhouette of white flame. It burned like the sun, glowing so brightly I had to raise my hand to my eyes and squint through my fingertips. It was so bright I couldn't even see her outline.

But I knew it was her. Just like I knew this wasn't the way it usually happened. Dro usually had a nightmare and would be woken up from sleep.

This time she was standing, her screams mixing with the tumultuous blaze, as if they were mocking her.

Dro was causing the fire, and she was wide awake this time.

"Dro!" I screamed. It quickly turned into a ragged cough. "*Dro!*"

I wasn't getting through to her. There was no way she could hear me through this storm. She might not have even seen me. That left me with one choice.

I took a step forward. I screamed her name. She

didn't hear me.

So I took another step and screamed again. Then again. And again.

With every stride, I felt the inferno crowding toward me. Tortured wood groaned under my boots. I was gagging each breath. My eyes were blurred with forced tears. Every inch of my body seemed to gain five pounds when I moved.

I only stopped when I looked down and saw the fire snaking its way toward my boots. If I kept walking, I would go up in flames.

"*Andromeda!*"

She was about four feet from me. She should have seen me, should have heard me. But the glowing whiteness stretched and pushed outward, growing like a supernova about to burst. The floor under me began to shiver.

"*Andromeda, plea–*"

The floor couldn't take any more pressure. It collapsed, and took me with it.

It wasn't a far fall, but I wasn't prepared. I didn't bend my knees fast enough, so when I landed, I landed in the worst possible way. My ankle twisted and exploded with a pain so blinding I screamed. My back hit the floor, while splinters of wood clattered beside my head, burning pieces singeing the ends of my hair. My ankle throbbed mercilessly, but I opened my eyes and looked up.

To see the rest of the debris falling fast toward me.

I rolled away, yelping at the sharp torment it put my ankle through. I shifted onto my side and looked around. I was in the kitchen, I think. It was hard to tell from all the smoke. I used my good foot to push further back, whipping my head up to see where I'd fallen through.

The fire wound its way out of the shattered space, splitting off and consuming the walls. The kitchen began to fill with unwelcome light and heat.

I couldn't see Dro, and with a broken ankle, there was no way I could get back up the stairs to her without being set on fire.

The flames wouldn't hurt her, but I couldn't leave her trapped in her nightmare. She wasn't in danger, but she was trapped in a different kind of torture.

A trap that only Lucifer could create for someone like Dro.

I will destroy you.

No. No, he didn't want to hurt Dro. Not after going through so much to find her. I had to believe that. I couldn't imagine he would try to kill her.

But now the thought was there, and it wouldn't fucking leave.

I tore my eyes away from the ceiling and pushed to my feet. My ankle fired up with pain the moment I put the slightest amount of pressure on it, but I concentrated on moving. Sitting on my ass and praying for a miracle would only end with me being torched.

I had just hobbled to the entryway when a huge *whoosh* fell behind me. Light flared at my back, like the fire had gasped in awe. I spun around too quickly, lost my balance and landed on my ass.

The column of white fire that circled my sister was in front of me.

For a moment, I didn't so much as breathe. Not that I could, given the lack of oxygen in the air, but what little I had was locked in my lungs next to a heart ready to break from my chest.

I knew Dro was in there, but I couldn't scream. I couldn't move. Couldn't do anything.

Come on, little sister. I know you're in there. Wake up.

Just as I finished the thought, the blaze began to dull. It receded inward, getting smaller and drawing back to its source.

Dro pitched forward, slapping her hands on the ashy floor and dipping her head. She was shaking. I started crawling toward her, trying to get her to snap out of it.

Dro lifted her head, and I stopped.

Her eyes glowed brighter than I could have ever imagined. Even in the drowning red, orange, and black world around us, there was no avoiding that electrified blue gaze.

Just like there was no missing the anger in it.

"Dro." My lips mouthed her name, though my voice couldn't speak it. Whether that was because it was too cracked, or I was too scared, I couldn't tell.

I had never seen Dro look like this before. For the first time in my life, I couldn't see her as human.

But it only lasted an instant. The glow began to fade, and soon I was looking at my sister again. She blinked, eyes fading back to the shade I knew.

I must have looked awful, because Dro's eyes widened to saucers. She scrambled to her feet, oblivious to the ash peppering her hair or the scorched holes in her clothes. She grabbed my arm and looped it over her shoulder, rocketing to her feet.

I choked on another cry when my broken ankle touched ground, but I limped with Dro anyway. I trusted her to get us out, because I couldn't see a fucking thing. My vision was swimming in tears and ash. Every time I stumbled, Dro tightened her grip and kept me upright.

It seemed like forever before we made it outside. Fresh air rushed into my lungs, fighting against the smoky tar inside them. It was summer, but coming outside after being trapped in a bonfire sent a vicious chill down my spine.

I saw someone running toward us from the corner of my eye. I had barely lifted my head by the time Warrick crushed me into his arms for a backbreaking hug. He wasn't even aware that Dro's arm was tangled in his embrace, or that he was getting soot on his face every time he buried it in my hair.

"I thought you were trapped," he whispered in my ear. "When we heard the house breaking apart..."

I ran my hand up his back, soothing him. He tightened his embrace. I patted him roughly.

"Warrick," I rasped. "I can't breathe."

He backed off instantly, giving Dro the chance to free her arm. She stepped back and gave us space. Warrick took up the rest of it. His hands smoothed down the hair on either side of my head, his thumbs cleaning away grime while his eyes looked for injuries.

"Are you okay?"

Broken ankle says no. "Let me sit down."

He didn't argue. He looped his hand around my waist and eased me onto the ground as gently as possible. I still winced, and he finally pulled off my boot to reveal my fucked up foot. The bone hadn't broken through the skin, but my ankle was ruthlessly swollen and bulging too far left. It looked like I'd been stung by a fat, furious bee. Just looking at it sent a sharp bolt of pain through my entire leg. I rested my hand on my shin and looked up at my sister.

"Dro, can you..."

She was staring at me, but it was like she was looking down at me from the moon. She was completely lost.

"Dro," Warrick tried, barely holding in his anxiety. "Please."

She still stared.

That was when Sephiel took a step forward. His white coat was covered in black dust, his auburn hair rumpled and wild. But as bad as he looked, Max was a million times worse.

He stood frozen a couple of feet behind the ex-angel, clutching his arm to his chest. He wasn't wearing a shirt. It looked like it had been ripped off him and used as a bandage. I couldn't see the extent of damage to his forearm, but the bits I did see were blackened with cracks of red. He looked awful, and I could see him trembling.

Max looked seconds away from screaming.

"Andromeda," Sephiel said, getting my attention. "You must heal your sister. She cannot run, and we do not have long before demons and the corrupted seek out this flame."

My sister snapped out of her trance. Before she

could walk to me, I shook my head.

"Heal Max first," I told Dro.

She whirled around and saw her boyfriend. The gasp that escaped her lips was sharp and hurt. She rushed for him.

Max flinched.

Dro froze in place, looking at her boyfriend like he'd slapped her.

Max backpedaled immediately, guilt crossing his face. But the damage was already done, and we all knew it.

"I just..." he tried. He swallowed nervously. "I need a minute, Dro."

I wanted to sympathize with him, to say I understood his nerves, but the look on Dro's face was too heartbreaking. Max quickly dropped his eyes to his feet.

None of us spoke. We stared at Dro like she was a powder keg. The very thing she always feared she would become. I kicked myself for being so insensitive.

"Thanks for letting me take your place in the waiting line, Max."

He didn't snark or joke. He didn't even look at me. *Shit.*

"Dro," I tried. "I hate nagging, but my ankle really fucking hurts."

Warrick's hand squeezed my shoulder. She turned away from Max, dropping her head. It didn't hide her tears. Dro knelt by my ruined ankle and raised her hands, but didn't touch it. She was scared to.

So I lifted my leg and forced my ankle into her hands.

The moment she touched me, the golden healing light filled her hands. She curled her hands around my ankle and soon the familiar pins and needles sensation filled my foot.

Normally I flinched away when she healed me. It was an uncomfortable prickling that I never liked, but already the swelling was going down and the bones were shifting back together. This time I stayed as still as possible, even when she turned my foot back in the right direction, and my bones were forced to grind together.

In a couple minutes, my foot looked no different than it had earlier tonight. The light faded from Dro's hand and she cowered back. I pushed forward, out of Warrick's hands, and pulled Dro into a tight hug. She stiffened, then began to sob into my shoulder. I stroked her hair, trying to calm her down.

"I'm sor–"

"Don't be," I interrupted. "You didn't know it would happen."

Dro's arms tightened around me. Her next words were a whisper I barely heard, yet would never forget.

"Yes, I did."

Chapter 6

After a fair amount of coaxing, a free jacket from Warrick, and many harsh glares from me, Max finally allowed Dro to touch him.

She healed his arm until the only remains were tiny flakes of ash on his skin. She swayed for a moment, and that was when Max snapped out of his trance. He hugged Dro tight to his chest and repeated how sorry he was.

She forgave him, but would never forget his hesitation.

Neither would I.

As soon as Max and I were fully healed, we started to move. Sephiel had managed to get together some last minute supplies when he smelled the smoke. Smart man, knowing we would need them since we didn't know where our next "safe" place would be.

As we walked on the dusty road lining the edge of the slums, Dro fell out of step with us. She drifted to the side of the group. Sephiel turned his head to look at her, making sure nothing would jump out of the crumbling houses or their shadows to grab her. Warrick, Max, and myself huddled together, unable to think of anything to say.

Max looked the most uncomfortable. Warrick had given him his leather jacket so he wouldn't need to walk around shirtless, and even though it was perfectly fine now, he was clutching his once burned arm to his chest.

There was a lot to say, but no one knew how to start. I wanted to be angry with Max, but that was the first time he'd ever been fully exposed to one of Dro's nightmares, and he had gotten hurt by it. I'd never been burned by Dro's fire. At least not directly.

Then there were the words my sister had whispered in my ear. How she'd known she was going to burst into flame. I glanced over my shoulder at her.

Dro seemed to be slumped and broken. I wanted to respect her privacy, give her space, but Dro had never felt comfortable on her own. And patience was never my strong suit.

Ignoring the stares from Warrick and Max, I crossed from their side to my sister's. Dro turned her head ever so slightly, but didn't lift her eyes from the ground.

"I'm all right," she muttered.

"Okay," I told her. I didn't care if she believed me or not. I just stayed at her side.

Dro sighed and tilted her head back. "What do you want me to say?"

"Nothing," I replied honestly. "I was getting bored with the Testosterone Team."

I looked at her with a stupid grin on my face. It didn't make her smile. I sighed, and gave up on the effort. Dro would talk when she was ready to.

After another hour of silent walking, Sephiel came to a halt in front of us. I had shut off my mind, so I wasn't paying attention as much as I should have.

"Seph? What's up?"

That was when I heard the distant screeches on the main street. We were about twenty feet away from it, still hidden behind the boxy houses. We hadn't seen any demons or Possessors or maniacal citizens, and while I was grateful for that, hoping that they were all checking out the bonfire Dro had made, the lack of monstrosities made me uneasy.

I felt like I was walking into a trap.

"It does not appear the main road is safe," Seph stated.

I looked around the houses. They were all dumpy half painted boxes with torn roofing and shuttered windows. The area we'd stayed in before was a little classier, but anything resembling class seemed to disappear entirely when the demons arrived and started plaguing sin on everyone. There had been good people here. Decent people.

Now they were probably all dead.

Tearing myself away from dark thoughts, I looked at Max.

"Any of these houses safe?"

The kid blinked slowly, letting my words sink in. I'd never thought Max would be able to brood. Shows what I knew about him.

He took another deep breath and closed his eyes. After a long minute, he opened them again and turned around. He pointed to a grim, pale grey stucco house with a dark grey roof.

"Yeah. We'll be good there," he announced, already walking for it.

We followed him off the road and up the concrete path. He stood in front of the screen door and carefully wrapped his hand around the doorknob. Sephiel moved past me to stand by Max, his hands reaching in his coat for the hilts of his short swords. Max pushed the door open and tried to walk inside, but Sephiel got in front of him.

"You know I wouldn't have opened the door if there were monsters or murderers inside, right?" Max told the ex-angel impatiently.

Sephiel didn't turn, his head moving from side to side as he did his own assessment.

"I do not doubt your gifts, Max, but I would prefer to err on the side of caution. Warrick, will you assist me in confirming the security of his location?"

"Sure," was Warrick's simple reply. He didn't look at me, but his presence when he brushed past me was impossible to ignore. I was tempted to follow them, but changed my mind when I realized that would leave Dro alone with Max, something I wasn't sure either of them was ready to be yet.

It doesn't matter what you think, my brain told me in a rare, rational moment. *They need to work it out themselves.*

"I'll check the left side," I said, already moving

into the foyer. I didn't plan on going far, but I was going to give the two kids some space.

The house was a mess. Dirty newspapers and crumpled heaps of clothing were strewn over broken plates in the kitchen. Pictures were knocked off the walls and chairs were tossed over the upturned table. All the destruction looked recent, a raid or a fight gone wrong. When I saw the blood splatter on the tile floor, I was guessing which was more likely.

But there were no screeches or clicking claws of a demon. There were no hooting or hollering sinners. It was eerily quiet, and that made me even tenser. Certain that nothing would jump out of the shadows at me, I stepped back toward the foyer. I stopped when I heard the edges of Dro and Max's conversation beyond the doorframe.

"I wasn't thinking," he said. "I was trying to wake you up."

"You should have run," she told him. "I'm too dangerous when I'm like that."

Max sighed. "I know, and I'm sorry I freaked out after, but... Dro, when I touched you, I saw what you were dreaming."

The silence following that statement was a weight. I edged closer to the corner of the wall.

"I didn't know what I was going to see," Max went on. "I just wanted to know you were okay."

"Well, I'm not," Dro replied. She sounded bitter, but also a little scared.

There were some footsteps. I was betting they were Max's.

"You have to tell Constance. Lucifer must have given you that dream. He must have been manipulating your mind until–"

"Lucifer wasn't doing anything," Dro interrupted. Her voice was sharp, but when she spoke again, the anger was dialed back. "Or if he was, I couldn't tell. I was in control in that nightmare, Max. I was the one standing back while the rest of you were murdered. I was the one who... I was the one who went after Constance. It was all me. Lucifer was never even there."

She took a shuddering breath, the way she did when she was about to cry.

"And the worst part was that I *knew* it wasn't a dream. Not really. It felt too real. I can still taste the smoke. And I just didn't care. I loved how powerful I felt. Like I was actually free, and didn't need to hide anymore. It wasn't a nightmare, Max. It was a premonition."

Max must have moved closer to her, because I couldn't hear his reply. That or I was in denial-laced shock.

Precognition was one of Dro's weaker powers, so I assumed that Lucifer was playing some sort of telepathic role in her nightmare. But my sister wouldn't see it that way. Dro thought she was going to be the death of us all.

Before my heart could strain at the thought, I heard a low thumping noise coming from the back of the house. My senses went on high alert, my hand flipping down to grip my hatchet. I turned around the corner of the wall to check on Dro and Max.

They were standing in front of each other, his hands curling around hers and holding them to his chest. Both of them were looking in the direction the noise had come. I glared at Max.

"I thought you said this place was safe," I whispered angrily. "That there were no monsters or murderers here."

He matched my glare. "There aren't."

The idea didn't relieve me as much as I wanted it to, especially when neither Warrick or Sephiel came back. I spun on my heel, yanked my hatchet from its sheath on my hip, and stormed toward the back of the house. I slowed down when I got to the living room, as there were two square windows that opened to reveal part of the backyard.

It was a two story house, but the sound hadn't come from upstairs, and neither the demon slayer or the ex-angel had gone up that way. The backyard it was.

I slid along the walls, hoping I wouldn't be seen

through the windows. The living room was the same mess as the rest of the house, all the furniture thrown carelessly around the room, making it difficult to maneuver when I finally crossed the room to the back door. Broken plastic crunched under my boots as I moved forward, kicking aside clothes and white padding from the punctured sofa.

Finally, I made it to the back door. It was already open. Just a crevice, like it had forgotten to be locked, but it only worried me more.

There was no way to sneak outside. It was all or nothing now. I pushed open the door with the toe of my boot and stepped outside.

It was definitely a trap, and while it might not have been meant for me, the insult was all the same.

Warrick and Sephiel, looking a bit battered and bruised, were on their knees with their hands behind their heads. Both men were held in place by swords lying across their necks.

Behind them were three men and one woman in long white trench coats. They were human, but still ethereally beautiful and perfect. The two men on the sides stood out more than the others.

One of the angels was a large man with flawless mocha skin and a strong face. His dark eyes were focused on me as he was gripped Warrick's shoulder with one hand and held a curved blade to my lover's throat with the other.

Holding Sephiel in place was an angel even bigger than the dark skinned one. He was impossibly beautiful, like Lucifer, though it wasn't desire mixed with fear that made my pulse pound at the sight of him. Despite the curling golden hair spilling down to his shoulders, the chiseled features of his face, the piercing azure eyes, there was no mistaking the danger he posed. He was wearing a white metal chest plate over his white coat as if he were a saint fighting in Roman armor.

I knew better, just as recognized him the moment I saw him. If I hadn't, the gold sigil engraved on his chest plate would have given him away.

The exact same symbol was tattooed over my heart to protect me from demons.

But there was nothing in the world that would protect me from the archangel Michael.

A wave of panic went through me for a moment. Even without a connection to Heaven, he was strong enough to blast me into a red stain on the walls. Especially since Michael had made it very clear that we would pay for shutting the Heaven Gate and condemning him and the entire Heavenly Host to spend the rest of their lives as humans on earth.

I was terrible when it came to making supernatural allies.

I did my best to look unimpressed. It wasn't the first time I'd been witness to an execution setup, but all those times before, my friends had never been on the chopping block. And I had usually been the one holding the axe.

Dro and Max skidded to a stop behind me. I shoved them back, making sure they were trapped in the doorway and not in a clear shot for Michael.

Somehow I wasn't sure my willingness to be a meat-shield and tendency to mouth off was going to be much help to them. The more I could make this my problem, the safer they might be.

Keep telling yourself that, Constance. Maybe Michael will find you amusing enough not to blow you into a million different pieces.

One hard look at the archangel told me otherwise.

"How did you find us?" I asked. There was no point in asking them to let Warrick and Sephiel go. Anyone who'd ever dealt with serious hostage situations knew that never worked right off the bat.

"I have learned to shield myself from prophets much stronger than yours," Michael said. He had a beautiful voice, just like Lucifer did. Strong, encompassing, and confident. The kind of voice that would make people do anything just to hear it again.

Most people, anyway.

Max knew when to pick his battles when it came to his pride. I was glad he chose to remain silent and lose this one.

"Following the abomination was perhaps simpler," Michael went on.

"So you listened real hard and got lucky. Give yourself a pat on the back, Mike. You earned it."

I don't know why I found it easier to backtalk to angels than demons. Maybe it had something to do with a subconscious hope that they had tiny shreds of morals and decency in them, and wouldn't be so willing to crush me for being so flippant.

When the pain first hit, I thought a boulder had broken a vase into my head. My skull seemed to harden into glass, then begin cracking until the shards were pushing outward to break through my scalp. It hurt so bad that I grabbed my head, dropped to my knees, and screamed.

It wasn't what I wanted to do, something I shouldn't have done, but the pain was blinding and relentless. I couldn't focus on anything else. Whenever I tried to, it only got worse.

There were angry shouts and yelps of pain. I couldn't tell what was going on. I felt heat and thought I heard my name once or twice, but it was a hopeless guess beyond the throbbing, stabbing pain threatening to turn my head into a crushed melon.

One shout was louder than the others. It was Dro's. I would know her voice anywhere, even if I couldn't make out the words she was saying. Her tone, though... That I didn't recognize. It was powerful, demanding, implacable.

It was the exact tone she had once used when she promised to erase Lucifer from the earth after he nearly burned me alive.

The heat remained, but as soon as her voice disappeared, so did the pain. The glass shards were yanked out of my head so fast that I gasped and collapsed onto my side. My head thrummed with remnants of pain, and I couldn't stop shaking. There was a wetness on either side of my ears. I tasted blood on my upper lip, and wondered how long I had been bleeding.

Dro's familiar, delicate hand placed itself on the back of my head. I jumped when her pins-and-needles healing sank into my skull and erased the damage he had done.

"Last time I ever piss off an angel," I muttered.

Dro leaned closer to my ear, but it wasn't just her I felt looming over me.

"I hope you remember that," Dro whispered. A second shadow reached down to grab my arms just as she finished saying, "Because we're going with them."

Chapter 7

It was strange to be willingly kidnapped. While we'd been transported wearing blindfolds in the back of a van, I'd managed to get the gist of what happened before one of our angel captors silenced us.

Warrick and Sephiel had been caught by surprise when Michael tracked Dro and teleported a squad of angels to our location. Warrick and Sephiel had been subdued, and it was inevitable that I would stumble out. While Michael was torturing me, Dro let go of some of her hellfire to warn them. She didn't attack them, but said she would turn them all into ash if they didn't stop. Michael only agreed to do so if we came with them. This was the point where I'd started bleeding out of my ears, so Dro felt no choice but to comply.

Three hours later, the five of us were trapped in a wooden cellar that smelled like sour wine, bound to chairs and stripped of our weapons. Dro and I got special treatment. We were seated across from the guys, with two angels pressing swords to the back of our necks. The theory was that if Dro tried to use her powers to escape, I would be killed in front of her. If I tried to unbind myself, she would be killed in front of me. If the guys tried anything, they would watch us both die.

Their theory seemed pretty sound, and none of us were willing to test it.

We sat there in silence for what seemed like an eternity. We all seemed to come to the same conclusion that talking would lead to throat cutting, so we just stared at the floor like good little hostages. It was infuriating for me because I knew I could get out of the knots. They were rope and loose around my wrists. This time I would have been able to get free and fight easily, since no one was trying to electrocute me in a metal tub.

Yeah, it would be a cakewalk. If it weren't for that damn sword poking into my spinal column.

We might not be allowed to talk, but we were allowed to look. Very carefully, I turned my head toward Dro. She caught me looking at her and tilted her head to meet my stare. Her braid was gone, long, wavy strands of pale hair spilling down her shoulders and half concealing her face. I understood the look in her eyes well enough, though.

I tried.

Try she had, and for now it seemed as though she'd done the best she could. I didn't think Michael would want to sit down for tea and biscuits when he came back, but different circumstances didn't always mean better ones. We were still alive, and that was the most important thing.

Though it seemed like that was going to change when the heavy door creaked open and Michael stomped down the stairs.

I couldn't see him clearly yet, but I knew it was him. The way people stamp their feet is more distinctive than they realize. Michael's footfalls were all about power, certainty, and demanding respect.

If that weren't enough to make people cower in front of him, the heavy silver broadsword he carried at his side would probably do the trick.

It almost looked like Sephiel's short swords, but longer than both of them combined. The hilt was white leather wrapped in gold, the blade looking sharp enough to cut through a tree trunk with a single swing.

Michael took his time marching toward us. The closer he got, the more I could feel his power. He was *strong*. Not as strong as Lucifer, thanks to me and my sister, but as the most formidable archangel, it would only make sense that he would retain some of his gifts even after the Heaven Gate was shut. I didn't drown in his power the way I did with Lucifer, though it was enough to make me think twice about what I said to him. As he eagerly proved earlier, he wasn't above torturing anyone he thought was below him.

I was guessing that was a long list.

Michael stood between us, almost completely blocking the guys from my view thanks to his enormous body structure and the overcompensating sword. I barely caught Max's nervous eyes twitching toward the sword, Sephiel's hanging head, or Warrick's angry, desperate expression as he looked for a way to help us.

I was just about to lift my own head when the tip of a sword kissed my chin. I didn't flinch, but the rest of my body froze in place. Even with this lightest touch, I knew that sword was wickedly sharp. One clean swipe, and my throat would be split in half. My eyes were the only part of me that moved, rising slowly to meet Michael's.

His clear azure eyes were cold and calculating, like he was a vengeful murderer deciding on how he wanted to take apart his enemy.

It seemed like forever before he decided to speak.

"Your allies have been the cause of great trouble for Heaven and Hell." He narrowed his eyes. "Though I presume you are the key orchestrator of it."

I grinned, unable to help myself. "What can I say? I never liked walking a straight line."

Michael, of course, wasn't amused. He pushed the tip of the sword just a little higher, put on just a little more pressure. I felt it bite into my skin just under the bone. I set my jaw but didn't blink or turn away from Michael. He stared at me with no visible emotion, studying my face and ignoring the trail of blood dripping down the front of my throat.

"Why are you here?" he asked, finished with the pleasantries. If he considered holding a broadsword to a woman's throat "pleasant." I clearly didn't know enough about archangels. Maybe this was happy hour for him.

"We're trying to find the Hell Gate," Dro answered for me. Her voice was a little rushed, and since she was closest to me, she could see how the sword was inches from the tender spot of my throat, right where it connected to my head. One push, and I was dead.

"What purpose does the Hell Gate serve the daughter of Lucifer?" Michael asked bitterly. He might have been talking to Dro, might have wanted her dead, but he was completely focused on me. This was probably his way of making sure he had all the answers he wanted before he got bored and started taking literal heads.

I wished it wasn't working so well for the bastard.

"We want to close it," Dro answered. "The same as you."

"Do not presume to know what Heaven desires, half-breed," he spat. Keeping the sword on my neck, he turned his head toward Dro. "It is because of you we are Fallen. It is because of you we shall never see our home again. It is because of you that we shall die."

Dro looked like she was going to apologize, then thought better of it. Saying sorry to the most powerful angel ever known after stripping him of most of that power would add insult to injury. Considering he might be barely containing his anger, the injuries would be of the fatal variety.

"Closing the Hell Gate is not a matter that concerns you. It is the responsibility of Heaven to destroy Lucifer's attempts at corrupting all of mankind. Had you become my vessel, you would have been able to save humanity. We would have purged the unworthy from Hell and created a new prison for the sinful. One that was just and true to its namesake." Michael paused, never moving his eyes from my sister.

"But you chose to abandon faith and rationality. You presumed we were the enemy, and you claimed a responsibility that did not belong to you. You mutilated those with the power to stop the Archfiend. I am now forced to scour this wretched place, recover my broken brothers and sisters in the hope of forming a suitable resistance to combat the minions of Hell and their King. You have not saved the human race, daughter of Lucifer. You have ensured its demise."

The air was so silent it threatened to strangle us. Dro held up her head, trying to show confidence, to defend her actions and reason with Michael.

But she couldn't do it. Like me, she had felt the pain and heartache of burning the Heaven Gate. Like me, she had lain awake and night, asking herself over and over and over if she'd made the right choice. Like me, she had mourned for angels who would never see their home again.

Unlike me, she kept her mouth shut.

"You're so full of shit," I hissed.

Michael looked at me again, pushing the tip of the sword until my head was tilted all the way back. His sword cut me anew, and this time I could feel the blade at the back of my neck poking deeper into my spine.

All of that should have silenced me. None of it actually did.

"You're no fucking innocent, Michael," I forged on. Across from me, I could make out the pleading stares of Warrick, Sephiel, and Max, begging me to stop talking before my mouth got me killed.

I ignored them too.

"Don't pretend you wanted her to live," I continued. "Yeah, you wanted a vessel when you *thought* you knew what she was. But you wanted to kill her the moment you learned she had Lucifer's blood in her. You didn't take the time to consider her offer to fucking *help you.* That maybe she doesn't want to be around Lucifer any more than you do. You and your damn angels refused to give her a chance, which makes Lucifer smarter than you."

For a second, I was sure he was going to kill me. There was so much rage flowing through him that I was nearly positive he was going to cut my smart mouth off my face so it wouldn't offend him anymore.

My head remained on my body when he lowered his sword. I wondered if it was a trick, if he was going to stab me in the chest instead, but he shocked me even further by returning the sword to his side. I stayed tense, knowing how fast angels could be and if he were going to change his mind, nothing would stop him from hacking me in two.

"It would please me to kill you for your disrespect, but I shall allow you to keep your life, as you have provided me with a solution to my current predicament."

Oh, shit. "Good to know we can both be generous," I snarked.

Michael didn't smile or even pretend to be amused. God must have left that piece out when he was creating Heaven's Holiest Hard-Ass.

"It is clear Lucifer currently holds the upper hand, and he is in search of his spawn." I bristled at what he called Dro, but of course he didn't care. "Her powers of manipulation must be greater than I imagined. She has gathered a human," he looked over his shoulder at the guys, "a demon slayer, a prophet, and an angel who was ready to Fall."

I couldn't imagine the look on Sephiel's face right then. He'd never forgiven Michael for refusing to help in the search for his true love, Everiel. The stupid archangel should have listened. If he had, they might have found Everiel before Lucifer impregnated her. This whole disaster would have been avoided.

But then Dro would never have been born.

Would I really want to go back, knowing everything that happened and knowing more horror was on its way? Would I have wished she had never been born to spare myself and those I cared about pain?

No.

Because then I would never have met Manny, Max, or Sephiel. I would never have given myself another chance at being in a relationship with someone like Warrick. I would never have had a sister.

Michael brought me back to the present when he turned and faced Dro directly. "I shall keep your friends alive, provided you do as I ask."

All my senses went on red alert. A supernatural creature asking for a favor was never good.

"What do you want?" she asked hesitantly. Her head was raised again, so there was no missing the shine to her cheeks. Michael saw her tears, and didn't comment on them. I wondered if he found them pitiful, or disgusting. How he saw her right now might determine how much longer she would live.

When Michael gave his request, I had my answer.

"I want you to bring Lucifer to me."

The edge of the sword at the back of my neck scraped through my skin when I jerked in my chair. The angel holding me in place gripped my hair and gave my head a hard yank. It didn't keep me from continuing to lose my shit.

"No!" I shouted. "No fucking way!"

"You are under the assumption that you have a say in the matter," Michael told me without breaking eye contact from Dro. "Or that I would heed you even if you were."

I hated Lucifer. Hated him with every fiber of my being. But right then, I hated Michael more.

"Michael." Sephiel's voice was hesitant and tired. "Forgive me, but this is not a wise idea. A more thorough plan must be devised before engaging Lucifer openly. We have fought him on such grounds, and we barely escaped with our lives. He has spread his influence further than comprehension. No matter how badly he wishes to reclaim what he believes belongs to him, he is working on another plan. Presenting Dro to him would provide him with the final piece of it."

The archangel turned to look at Sephiel. "You fear him so, Sephiel?"

"I have always feared him." The ex-angel didn't bother to lie. "I have seen what he is capable of, and know he will not be defeated if he gains what he wants. He will have plotted for every conceivable outcome."

"Not this," Dro said quietly. We all looked at her. "He can't be expecting us to give in. He knows we aren't the type."

That was directed at me, and it was true as hell,

which is probably what terrified me the most.

Dro looked at me with sad, exhausted blue eyes, and I couldn't see a way of making her change her mind.

"We're going to face him down sooner or later, Con. We don't know how else to close the Hell Gate, so if meeting him this way is what we're supposed to do..." I heard her hesitance. It was tied to her fear. "Then it's what we have to do. It was inevitable."

I didn't want to hear that shit. Nothing was ever written in stone. It couldn't be.

Except sometimes it was. All it took was a little time...

There were a lot of things I hated. People taunting or trying to hurt my sister. Those who disrespected me or disregarded me. Early morning talk shows and a lack of sleep.

Job hunting beat them all.

After the motel burned, I decided it would be smart to get out of Odessa and try somewhere smaller. Dro had silently agreed. The next stop we made was Midland, which was currently in the middle of a blue collar hiring spree. We looked for jobs that needed more than one person, since I refused to leave Dro's side for any reason. As we drove and wandered around the city, dropping by the library to print off resumes filled with B.S., we noticed there weren't a lot of options. Dro was too young and I was too pissy.

"What about here?" Dro asked, pointing at the window of a cafe. There was a chalkboard sign in the window that said, Now Hiring: Full Time Dishwasher and Part Time Barista. I frowned. I had no people skills, so the barista option was out. Which meant I would be going from a badass drug enforcer to an angry-eyed dishwasher.

Then again, this request was the most excited Dro had been about anything all day. She would get the job. She liked people, trusted them to the extent that I taught her to, and she would be able to work with ease knowing I could be out of the back in a flash if need be. How hard was it to wash dishes, anyway? Mom used to heap them on me all the time.

"Sure," I agreed. "Can't hurt."

My little sister gave me a small smile and walked with me into the cafe. It was about 2:30 in the afternoon, so it wasn't very busy. There were three people working behind the counter, one customer waiting in line for her coffee, and two more sitting in the armchairs reading the newspaper. I glanced at them all quickly. Dro would tell me if something was off about them, and we would get the hell out of here.

But she didn't say anything, which meant the coast was clear.

A forty-something barista with thick red hair and brown eyes finished helping her customer. Her smile was pleasant and carefree. I wondered if she really was that blissful, or just putting on an act. She turned that smile on us, and it quickly faded.

My hand dropped to my side. I felt the edge of my father's hatchet under my long T-shirt. I didn't think I would have to draw it in a public place, but this was Texas. If that happy-go-lucky barista had a double-barrel under the cash register, I didn't want to be the first one to meet it.

"Can I get you ladies something?" the barista asked, gliding over to the cash desk. Dro matched her smile and walked forward casually. My sister was shy, but she knew how to talk to people instead of threatening them.

"My friend and I saw the sign in the window," Dro said, pointing to it. "We'd like to apply for the jobs, if they're still open."

"Sure, they are," replied the barista. She looked at me nervously when I walked closer. I was used to people looking at me like I was going to hit them, but I thought I had my disinterested face on instead of my mad face.

"I just need to call my manager," she said.

I narrowed my eyes. She flinched. "Is there a reason we can't give you our résumés?"

"Our manager likes to take them personally," the barista answered a little too quickly. *"I'll be right back."*

She moved to the swinging door that let her into the back. The other baristas glanced at me curiously, then nervously. I looked at Dro.

"We should leave," I whispered.

Dro turned her head. *"Why, what's wrong?"*

I shifted to look at her, stopping when something else caught my eye. One of the men reading the paper was looking at me. He was talking on a cell phone but I couldn't hear the words he said. I was looking at the mirror, my gaze trailing down to the page reflecting in it.

And the picture of my face on it. Reading backward wasn't a talent of mine, but I understood the word *"WANTED"* well enough.

I grabbed my sister's arm and started dragging her toward the door, which was a huge mistake when the police car pulled up on the side of the curb.

The cops were out of their car almost immediately. Their guns came out even quicker.

"Let the hostage go!" one shouted. He was a middle-aged man with cold dark eyes and a hard frown.

"Get on the ground and put your hands on your head!" his partner ordered. She was a Hispanic woman a few years older than me, but she had the same hard eyes and frown as her friend.

"Wait, I'm not a hostage!" Dro pleaded, holding up her hands. *"She's my sister!"*

"Step away from her!"

I didn't know if they were referring to my sister or to me, but I wasn't about to risk Dro's life. I raised my hands and backed away from her.

My sister was horrified when the female cop marched forward. I went down to my knees slowly, until she stepped on the back of them and shoved me onto the ground. She put her knee on my back and pushed my face into the concrete with her free hand. Cold metal circled my wrists tightly and clicked shut.

"Connie! Connie!" Dro cried. *"Please, you have to*

let me go with her! She's my sister!"

I didn't know what the male cop told her because the female cop gripped the handcuffs and jerked me to my feet. She was a lot stronger than she looked.

Dro tried to catch my eyes over the broad shoulders of the cop holding her back. She looked desperate and scared. I returned her stare with grief.

I'm sorry, little sister. *I couldn't have run. If I had, I might have been shot and Dro would have watched me die. On the other hand, I wasn't sure if she was going to be able to see me while I was in prison. We'd never be able to afford a lawyer. We had no money for bail. Whatever I was being arrested for, I was most definitely guilty.*

I could have just condemned her to another kind of loneliness.

The cop slapped her hand on top of my head and pushed me into the backseat, slamming the door closed. I looked out of it as the cops talked to my sister. My back was rigid and my mind wired as I watched Dro shout at them. She didn't get angry often– as in only once when she wanted to leave the Blood Thorns– but when she did, she made an impression.

The cops were trying to calm her down but she kept shouting. Then they gave up, and the male officer took out a set of handcuffs and put them on my little sister.

I blinked, unable to believe what I was seeing. Sure, I knew that one day I would probably be arrested. It's a given when you're a dangerous criminal. But Dro? Innocent, sweet, loving Dro who stepped over ants instead of on them, who hated to lie, cheat, and steal? Who knew right from wrong even when she had blind loyalty to me?

Never thought I'd see the day. Yet sure enough, she was placed in the backseat beside me. I stared at her, eyes wide with surprise. My sister managed to look guilty and defiant at the same time.

"This seemed like a good idea earlier," she said.

I laughed. It was such a Dro thing to say. That was the last laugh we got in before we were driven to the *police station...*

Chapter 8

After Michael left, it was back to silence. This time it felt more self-induced than forced, even though the angels holding swords to my neck and Dro's still hovered incessantly.

No, this time we didn't have anything to say. Nobody wanted Dro to give in to Lucifer, least of all me, but if we couldn't escape, what could the rest of us do but sit back and watch her give herself up in a plan that would likely mean she was killed in the crossfire?

Even if things went his way, Michael would never let Dro live. All he could see was the daughter of Lucifer. If she weren't supposed to exist, he would make sure that she didn't.

As I tried to force my brain to come up with a scenario that wouldn't end with us skewered, I sat slumped in my chair. The cut under my chin was still throbbing dully, and I knew it would scar. The wound on the back of my neck wasn't as bad, but it wasn't letting me forget about it, either.

When the door at the top of the stairs opened, my heart leaped. I was sure it was time, that Michael was ready to take my sister to the creature that wanted to use her and destroy every ounce of goodness in her.

No, I thought with an aching heart. *No, it's too soon. This isn't supposed to happen. It's not supposed to be this way.*

Fuck that the angels behind me had swords. I was getting out of these binds. Nobody was taking Dro. I wasn't letting her go without a fight.

Just as I began to twist my wrists, I heard an angel giving commands.

"You may both take leave," he said.

I stopped struggling. It wasn't Michael. This angel had a deeper voice, almost like a crooning jazz singer. I lifted my head and looked past Dro.

It was the mocha-skinned angel who had shadowed Michael earlier. I got a good look at him again, seeing how he virtually mirrored Michael's mannerisms and posture. He clearly had an idol, and he wanted us to know he was proud of it.

Sephiel tensed a little as the angel drew closer. That was the biggest warning I could have asked for.

The angel stopped in front of us, giving each member of our group a harsh once over. He scrutinized Sephiel, Dro, and me the longest. He was still glaring at me when he spoke.

"Leave us," he told the other angels.

His voice had a deep, baritone quality that soothed me as much as it unnerved me.

"Sir, are you certain?" the angel behind me asked.

The tall angel lifted his eyes from my face to the angel behind me. The sword at the back of my neck twitched.

"They pose no threat to me. Leave us."

There weren't any questions after that. Both angels standing guard behind Dro and me stepped back and started walking up the steps. The angel between us stood completely still, looking from one of us to the other even when the door was closed beyond him.

"Let me guess," I said, when the silence became too long, "Michael wanted us tenderized before the real torture started?"

The angel looked at me, enjoying my humor about as much as the rest of my group did.

"Michael does not know I am here," answered the angel.

"I hope that isn't supposed to make us feel better."

He stared, reaching inside his long white coat. "Perhaps this will."

The angel pulled out a slender golden tube inscribed with words I couldn't read. A *movens caeli,* the tool the Heavenly Host would use to transport a large amount of soldiers to anywhere they wanted. The same tool our old friend/enemy Rorikel had given us so we could escape the battle at the Heaven Gate.

Why was he showing it to us?

The angel turned his back to me to look at Sephiel. "Is it truly your mission to destroy the Hell Gate?"

Sephiel looked directly into his eyes, as if there was nowhere else to look. "Yes, Raphael. It is."

Raphael. As in the archangel, one of the most powerful of Michael's generals. *Shit.*

But if he was on Michael's side, what was he doing down here with the *movens caeli*, and why was he asking about our goal?

Raphael dropped his head to his chest. "He does not understand," he whispered so low I barely heard him. "He does not understand that the rest of us continue to lose our powers. Our soldiers have martial skill and nothing more. We cannot combat Lucifer as Michael expects. Some of us no longer want to."

This time he turned so he could look at all of us. "Some of us have seen past our rage to accept the truth. We cannot return to Heaven through any gate but Saint Peter's. And though we could seek vengeance for that," he directed this to Dro, "it would achieve nothing. Our only hope remains to sever the connection of the Hell Gate, and force Lucifer back into his domain."

My heart skipped a beat. "How do we stop him?" I asked in a rush.

I was hoping for a quick, simple answer that would involve me stabbing Lucifer, but from the heavy look Raphael gave me, it wasn't going to be that easy.

"When he Fell and was locked in Hell, the archangels operated under the belief that he would never be able to return to Earth. We never imagined he would use blood magic to create demons, or that he would gain human followers with enough strength to summon him."

I grimaced, remembering how powerful Isabel, the witch who brought Lucifer from Hell and murdered my father, had been. I recalled how Mateo had been eager and willing to sell his soul to have his dreams turn into reality– a successful, untouchable reign over the crime world, and complete devotion and love from me.

All he had to do was give up my sister.

Neither Isabel's nor Mateo's plans had gone in their favor.

"Tell me he can't give humans his powers," I gritted out.

"No," Raphael answered, offering me at least one consolation. "To manipulate humans and grant them gifts while they are on Earth takes a great deal of power, and it is rarely done. In Hell, Lucifer and his demons are invincible. Anything that bears his blood there cannot be killed. But since Lucifer does not control the mortal realm, his powers are slightly weaker, and his creations can be destroyed. When the Hell Gate was opened, Michael sent some scouts to assess the potency of its power." Raphael's jaw was set tight. "The last survivor informed us that Lucifer spent those first few months binding his essence to the Hell Gate, drawing on the power that leaked from Hell into Earth. It strengthens his abilities here, as well as the strength of his demons.

"Lucifer cannot be killed while the Hell Gate powers him. He is far too powerful with it. Even Michael is not strong enough to stop him, though he refuses to see as such. However, if the Hell Gate is closed, Lucifer and all the demons he has tied to him with blood magic will be forced to return to the Pit from whence they came."

I frowned. "He can't do anything convenient, like die?"

Raphael's grin was weak and mirthless. "Unfortunately, no. While demons continue to escape Hell at alarming rates, many remain behind the Gate. As long as they live, so does Lucifer. Yet, considering how much energy it is taking for him to hold the Gate open, closing it will be a grievous blow. Akin to him losing an arm. Such a loss of power would force him back into Hell to recuperate, and with the angels locked in Heaven or losing their powers on Earth, he would not be able to create another hybrid and repeat his ritual. He would remain in Hell until the End of Days."

That sounded both perfect *and* amazing, especially the part about Lucifer never being able to re-emerge from Hell again and metaphorically losing an arm (I enjoyed that imagine a little too much, to be honest), but a bolt of panic rushed through my brain. If we shut the Hell Gate, did that mean Dro would be taken too? No matter how many times I tried to tell myself otherwise, she had a blood tie to Lucifer. If closing the Hell Gate stripped away a piece of her as closing the Heaven Gate had, would she survive?

Before I could ask that vital question, Raphael continued with information overload.

"You have heard of these sprees of violence and debauchery," he said. It wasn't a question. It was hard to miss it when the streets were painted with blood.

"They are being caused superficially."

I was so stunned that I was sure I'd misheard him.

"What?" Warrick asked in my stead.

"To sustain his hold on it, Lucifer has a Key to Hell," Raphael explained. "The Gate is this place," he waved a hand in the air, indicating the crumbling city above us rather than the stuffy cellar we were held in.

The Hell Gate was an entire place, just as the Heaven Gate had been. Somehow, I didn't think that we'd be able to burn the city down to erase it from the earth. Even if we could, I didn't think I would be able to. Unlike the Heaven Gate, Ciudad Juárez was teeming with people. I was capable of some pretty awful things if I was pushed, but razing an entire city of people wasn't one of them. Even if doing so meant I would protect the rest of the world from Lucifer and his madness.

Raphael started walking behind Sephiel. He put the *movens caeli* in the ex-angel's lap, then began unbinding his wrists from the chair.

"We began obtaining information on Lucifer's plan upon our arrival," Raphael went on. "Through…

unseemly methods, we discovered that Lucifer has shattered a physical Key, likely made from his own blood, since each fragment contains a piece of the Hell Gate's power. Destroying all the fragments, and therefore the Key, shall weaken Lucifer and force him back into Hell, locking the door behind him."

For once, I was glad that angels had to resort to torture to get their answers. They had gotten more information than I ever expected them to get.

"How does this connect to the murder sprees?" I asked.

Raphael had set Sephiel free from the chair and was moving onto Max.

"The fragments must be activated by a soul. Lucifer does not have one, and this kind of dark magic requires the corruption of a powerful spiritual force. They are placed inside a living carrier to keep the Gate open. The fragment causes uncontrollable behavior. The closer the carrier is to sinners, the more violent they become. This in turn amplifies the violence to those who do not carry a fragment."

"So it's a symbiotic relationship," Warrick simplified, rising to his feet and rubbing his wrists when Raphael released him. "One of them feeds the other."

"Precisely. It is a magic that consumes its host entirely. Its effect is far more dangerous, and I fear we cannot obtain the Key without being corrupted ourselves."

"So will it corrupt you if you touch it?" I asked when Raphael moved behind me and began untying me from the chair. I was stiff, not trusting him to be so close to me, but I focused on getting more information rather than how many different ways I could punch him.

"I am not sure," he answered. "No one has ever successfully removed a fragment from a living specimen. I am under the assumption that the carrier would need to be incapacitated to ensure the fragment's removal."

Meaning that killing these carriers was probably the best way of getting a fragment out. It was certainly the easiest way.

"You certainly have a lot of information about this," I said warily, shooting up from my chair so I could face Raphael.

He loomed over me, but there was no aggression in his eyes. He seemed tired, his shoulders slumped way lower than they'd been when he first came downstairs.

"To obtain it, we were forced to do things. Things that Michael commanded us to do, but they have not eased our minds. They were... unpleasant."

Sounds like an understatement, I thought.

"Where do we find these people?" I asked. When Raphael didn't move to free Dro, I went to the back of her chair to do it myself. "The fragment carriers."

"This I do not know," Raphael admitted. "We checked every body we could once we discovered the massacres, but we found nothing. It is likely the carriers retreated before they could die, or the fragment was taken by another."

"What I don't get is why the attacks don't happen all the time," Max said while I stepped back from Dro's chair and let her get to her feet. "I mean, if these people have a literal wildcard in their body, why aren't they playing it all the time? These massacres should be happening on every corner."

I thought back to encountering Drake only days ago, and had a very uncomfortable idea.

"Maybe they're being hidden, and under orders."

All eyes went to me. I folded my arms over my chest. "Drake said he was looking for something in that store. Maybe he was looking for a fragment. Maybe he's a fucking carrier himself."

Warrick's eyes darkened with rage. Max's expression was grim, but more with anxiety than anger.

"I fear that with Lucifer, anything is possible," Sephiel said icily.

"Regardless, you must find these fragments and stop Lucifer by closing the Hell Gate."

I turned to Raphael. "I take it you're not going to be lending a hand."

Raphael almost smiled at my snarky proposition. It would have felt more real if his eyes weren't so sad.

"I fear I cannot be of any more assistance. It shall be challenging enough to explain that you overcame me and escaped." The Not Smile vanished all together. "Michael has been focusing on his efforts on locating Lucifer and destroying him once and for all." Finally, he looked at my sister. "It is why he was prepared to bait you. Normally, I would not be adverse to his idea, but all of us following him have grown weary. We have seen the destruction he has wrought, and we no longer believe we are strong enough to defeat Lucifer. Not when we are assured that we can never return home."

That was what it boiled down to. The only reason Raphael was helping us was because the Heaven Gate was locked for good. If it hadn't been, Sephiel would have been ruthlessly punished, and Dro would have been killed.

We had made an ally here, but not a reliable one and certainly not a friend. I wasn't sure if we'd gotten a short-term blessing or a long-term curse.

Raphael stalked through the chairs toward Sephiel. He placed his hand on the auburn-haired man's shoulder.

"The others shall not inform you, but I believe you ought to know. Rorikel is dead."

We all fell silent at that, but Sephiel looked like he'd been punched in the stomach.

"How? When?" was all he could breathe out.

"Lucifer saw him help you escape at the Heaven Gate. His rage was catastrophic."

Sephiel dropped his head. There had to be more details about the death of Sephiel's former partner, but Sephiel didn't need to hear them. We all knew what Lucifer could do when he was mildly annoyed. Nothing and no one would be able to escape him if his rage was "catastrophic."

I thought about Rorikel. Pale eyed and cranky as hell, we'd never gotten along with the uptight bastard. He had been committed to protecting Dro in the beginning, but his disdain for humans– and me in particular– had been about as bare as the skin on a nude beach. Rorikel thought all humans were bound to sin, and he'd been a huge supporter of Heaven's plan. The moment he learned what Dro *really* was, he went from crotchety asshole to cold-hearted assassin.

But then he saved us at the Heaven Gate. I never knew why Rorikel chose to save us, and now I never would. I hadn't liked the son of a bitch any more than he'd liked me, but now I felt guilty for hating him, and I would never have the chance to thank him for what he did for us.

"You must leave now," Raphael said, stepping back from Sephiel. He walked over to a wine barrel in the corner and pried off the lid. He reached inside and brought out all of our weapons. I practically jumped for joy when I took my hatchet from Raphael's hands.

Once we had all of our belongings intact, we formed a circle. Sephiel took control of the *movens caeli,* his head still bowed down. While he began to manipulate the device, Raphael put his hand on my shoulder.

I jumped under his touch and started baring my teeth. Raphael wisely stepped back. "You must make it seem as though I was attacked," he informed. "It shall make the story of your escape easier to believe."

I stepped out of the circle and shook out my hands. "You sure about this?"

Raphael smiled weakly. "It is not the first time I have received pain in combat."

"I meant about lying to Michael."

That caused Raphael's grin to falter. He sighed. "If there was a way to convince him to join forces with you, I would have found it. But since losing Gabriel and his powers, he has not been in his proper mind. He is filled with venom and hate, though I cannot tell if it is due to his loss of power, or the influence of this city."

Since he seemed to know a lot about what was going on, I was willing to bet he knew the truth, but didn't want to admit it. That was fair. I wouldn't want to admit to either truth if I was him.

"Don't worry," I said. "I won't let you think about

it too long."

I punched him in the face, not caring if he was ready or not. If he wanted to sell this, I would deliver a premiere product. It took another two punches to the head and one solid kick to the temple before Raphael collapsed into a heap on the ground.

I stared down at him, feeling a twinge of guilt. This could all be a ruse, a trick planted by Michael, but then I recalled the sadness in Raphael's eyes. He wanted this over as much as I did. He was willing to let himself be beaten if it meant he could live the rest of his life on earth, die on earth, and return to another realm of Heaven.

Leaving the archangel behind, I took my place in the circle between Dro and Warrick. I glanced at Sephiel across from me. His shoulders were slouched, his hair was limp, and the dark circles under his eyes were trimmed with red. I hadn't known how close he was to Rorikel. They never really seemed like friends, and they'd betrayed each other when Sephiel chose to help Dro instead of siding with Rorikel and Heaven. But I had never asked about their lives before us. For all I knew, Rorikel could have been Sephiel's best friend.

Seeing all that barely hidden emotion suddenly reminded me of how human Sephiel had become.

Without another word, Sephiel unscrewed the top of the *movens caeli.* The world exploded into thunderous golden light. Our bodies were yanked into the light, rocketing us from the cellar to somewhere else in this Hell on earth.

Chapter 9

While I'd been punching up Raphael, Dro had directed Sephiel to a now abandoned, family owned taco restaurant. When we'd been living on the streets, restaurants had been my favorite places to raid. They always threw out unwanted, but perfectly edible food. I'd picked through the garbage, stolen unattended plates from the windowsill, had even broken into this particular restaurant once after they locked up to take an armful of food from their fridge.

Even now, I could remember the taste of their home-cooked food. The juicy pulled pork, hearty beans and rice, crunchy corn and spicy *pico de gallo*, all wrapped up in a warm, soft tortilla.

My stomach reminded me how hungry it was, letting out a quiet snarl, but there was nothing to eat in the restaurant now. That was plain to see, since all the chairs and tables had been removed or taken outside. Broken glass covered the floor. Wallpaper had been stripped from its place, revealing cracked grey drywall. The air smell stale and old, and there wasn't a scrap of food left in the fridge.

While the guys looked for anything salvageable, I wandered to a booth in the corner, the only one that hadn't been ripped off the wall. Most of the leather had been peeled away, but I needed to sit down. At this point I didn't care if I was going to get a splinter in the ass.

I put my face in my hands and started running my hands through my hair. My moment of solitude was quickly interrupted when Dro took the seat across from me, placing her hands on her lap. She lowered her head, and I didn't try to start a conversation with her either. I wasn't sure what to say. She didn't know that I heard her conversation with Max, that she believed she was going to kill me.

To be honest, it wasn't a conversation I wanted to have either.

"He didn't want to touch me," Dro finally said.

I lowered my hands. "Max will get over it–"

"Not Max. Raphael."

She lifted her chin just enough so I could see the sadness welling in her icy blue eyes. "Raphael untied the rest of you, but he wouldn't come near me."

"So? The only angel we've ever met who hasn't had a stick up his ass is Sephiel, and he's a special case in basically every sense of the word."

"It doesn't feel like that. He must see me as a plague or something. Maybe he knows what I'll become."

"You're not going to become anything. You're just Dro."

She lowered her eyes and sighed, shaking her head. "Not anymore. I used to be, but I'm different now, Connie. I can feel it. That nightmare..." She opened her mouth to speak again, but couldn't get out the words.

"It won't happen, little sister."

Dro looked at me. "You don't know what I dreamed."

"Doesn't matter. If you don't want it to happen, then it won't."

She held the stare for a long time, then said, "Back at the house, I told you that I knew it was going to happen. I knew that I was going to lose control. I wanted to just let it all go. I can't stop what's happening to me, Constance. It's just going to get worse."

That gave me pause. "What are you trying to say?"

Dro hesitated, biting her lip. "You would save me from anything, right?"

We both knew it wasn't a question, but she was waiting for an answer anyway. "Of course."

"Even myself?"

Any other coherent thought I had stopped. "You'd better not be suggesting what I think you're suggesting," I warned.

"Constance–"

"No. I'm not going to entertain that thought because it will not happen, do you understand me?"

There was no room for negotiation. Not this time. There was nothing I wouldn't do for Dro.

Except what she was asking for.

"I nearly got everyone killed," Dro pleaded. "I burned Max, and you would have died if I didn't find you."

"But you did," I pointed out. "You found me, and you saved me."

I was proud of the small grin I managed, but Dro was still too upset. I reached across the scarred table and held out my upturned hand. Dro stared uncertainly at it, like she wasn't sure she could touch me. I kept waiting, and she finally put her hand in mine.

"We'll figure this out, little sister," I promised. "The best thing we can do right now is find the fragment carriers." I twisted my face into a grimace. "Ugh. Kinda sounds like an STD, doesn't it?"

Dro's laugh was so unexpected that I was sure I was hearing things. And while it was a small laugh, it was her through and through. I missed the sound so much that it almost hurt to hear again. Thankfully, I wasn't the only one who did.

"What did we miss?" Max asked, slowly taking his seat next to Dro. He distanced himself at first, then started shuffling closer until his arm was touching hers. It was a slow start, but it was progress.

"Nothing I want to repeat," I told him, glancing over my shoulder as Warrick slipped into the booth next to me. His arm stretched along the edge of the seat behind me, like it was the most casual thing in the world for him. Damned if it didn't relax me.

"We've got bigger problems now," I said, getting back on track. "We need to find those fragments."

I turned my head to Sephiel, who was standing in front of the booth like a waiter about to take our orders.

He was paying attention, but his eyes were more distant than usual. The news of Rorikel's death must have been hitting him harder than I realized. Usually he was jumping at the chance to put a wrench in Lucifer's plots.

"You think Raphael was telling us the truth?" I asked him.

Sephiel didn't look up when he responded. "Angels see little use in lying, especially archangels. I cannot confirm what he shall tell Michael upon waking, but his theory is sound. Lucifer is fond of these sorts of games."

Ah. There was the bitterness he thought he was hiding.

"So how the hell are we supposed to find these people? It isn't like they organize Bring Your Own Knife block parties." Max suddenly looked uncomfortable with his comment. "Do they?"

"Doubt it," I responded, not liking where this was going to go. "But I do think they're under orders from someone. Not just Lucifer."

"Drake is the kind of guy willing to take orders for money," Warrick said, barely masking his own anger. "Which leaves..."

"Yup," I sighed. "Mateo and the Blood Thorns."

The table went silent at the mention of my ex-lover. I always knew I would cross paths with him sooner or later, but I was seriously hoping for the later option. He'd never forgive me for the depths of my betrayal, just as I wouldn't forgive him for his. The next time we met, one of us was going to be bleeding.

"Are you positive it's him and not just some random guys?" Dro asked. She had never trusted Mateo when we were together, and I had just brushed it off as jealousy at the time.

Now I wished I had listened.

"I'm very sure," I told her. "Think about what Drake said."

"He could have just been saying that to freak you out..."

I was shaking my head. "No. He knew what he was saying. Then think about where the attacks have been taking place, and in what order." I looked deep into my little sister's eyes. "Every single attack has been in a spot where I did a run. He started at the beginning, at the warehouse."

I held back my shiver as the memory threatened to surface. Dozens of bodies, riddled with holes that still dripped blood, sightless eyes staring at me, a man's tongue being cut out before a bullet shattered his brain.

We send messages, Constance, Emilio recited in my head. *You will never be respected if you do not make them remember you.*

My shoulders stiffened when Warrick's hand rested on my shoulder. He rubbed his thumb along the side of my neck, the slow, tender motion drawing me back to reality.

"I know where the next attack will be," I said. "Simon is next."

Dro winced. The night I helped Mateo kill the stupid thief was also the night I promised Dro that we'd find a way out.

We did, but only barely. This time I wasn't sure we'd be so lucky.

"No offence, Constance," Max said warily. "But how do you know they're even involved? I mean, they were with Lucifer last time, but why would he trust them with the Key to Hell?"

"Anarchy strengthens the Gate," Sephiel reminded us. "Causing chaos while sending a message to Constance would be efficient on many levels."

I wasn't about to argue that. "Mateo has enough control over the Blood Thorns to make sure they know where to go and when. Maybe he holds all the fragments and is giving them to a Thorn when he wants to use them. I'll ask him after we have a nice reunion."

A nice reunion being when I buried my hatchet in his heart. If he didn't have the fragments, he would know where they were. Blood Thorns always had ears to the ground. Besides, the sooner he was dead, the less I would have to look over my shoulder.

"Okay, let's assume he does have them, and these are messages to you," Warrick said. "We don't know when the next massacre is going to take place. We won't have time to just wait for it."

"What's the date?"

Warrick looked at me curiously, then glanced at his watch. "August 19."

I sighed. "We won't have to wait long. The attack will be tomorrow night."

The room fell silent. I could feel Warrick and Dro's worried eyes on me, but instead of meeting either, I slouched in my seat and crossed my arms over my chest. Warrick turned his head.

"Max?"

The psychic exhaled and closed his eyes. After a couple moments of concentration, he blinked open his eyes and gave Warrick a pitying look.

"She's right. I saw an attack and..." he glanced at me nervously, "and Constance got hurt, but that was it. Everything in this damn city is blocking my precognition." He put his elbows on the table and lowered his chin into his cupped hands. "This frigging sucks."

Dro paused, then reached out and touched Max's arm. He glanced at her, but didn't flinch. They smiled cautiously at each other, and then Max lowered his far hand to slide it across the table and take hers.

I was glad Dro was working things out with her boyfriend. She would need someone to talk to when I was finished telling them my plan.

"Mateo has got to be running out of patience. If we don't move now, he's going to turn the city upside down to find me." I shook my head absently. "It's a fucking wonder he's waited this long. But I know him. If we don't give him what he wants, he'll find another way to take it. He'll burn down every building in sight if he has to."

And, here comes the tricky part.

"We need to draw him out," I said. "Bait him and

trick him. There's only one way to do that."

Max and Sephiel were waiting for my answer, but Dro and Warrick already knew.

"Con, you can't," Dro protested and the same time Warrick said, "No fucking way."

"It's the best way to make sure they have the fragments. It's me he wants, anyway."

"Which is exactly why you shouldn't go," Warrick said aggressively.

"It isn't like we have a lot of options right now," I defended. "I know that street and building just as well as Mateo does. I can hold my own against him."

"He tried to cut off your head last time." Warrick was getting riled. "Mateo has Drake with him now. They have the Blood Thorns. They'll swarm you with demons. You are not going alone."

I shoved his arm off my shoulder, then turned to face him. "What do you think is going to happen if you show up with me? If something goes down–"

"When," he interrupted, green eyes blazing.

"–then I can't protect you."

I skipped over what I was really trying to say: that if Warrick got into another fight with Drake, it would be to the death. Warrick had fought him before and barely walked away. If he was losing his fight, I wouldn't be able to help him. I would only be able to watch him die.

"I've never been the one who needed protecting," he shot back.

I almost wanted to slap him. I might have, if Dro hadn't intervened.

"He's right, Constance. This is too dangerous for you to do alone. I know you don't want to risk any of us, but it isn't fair to ask us that for you. We've always been stronger together. So you can face Mateo and Drake on your own at first, but we aren't staying behind."

And that was that.

Even though I wanted to keep arguing, even though I wanted to dive across the table and make a mad dash for the door, it wasn't going to happen. Warrick would yank me back into my seat, and even if I could escape him, Dro would be on my heels before I hit the door. I looked at Max and Sephiel for help, but their expressions told me I wasn't going to find allies there, either.

"It is not wise for you to engage these enemies alone," Sephiel told me.

I glanced at Max, who held his hands up in defense.

"Hey, even if I wasn't a psychic, I'd say this is a bad idea," Max confessed.

Damn it. These people are going to get me killed. Or I'm going to get them killed.

But they weren't giving me a choice.

"Fine," I grumped, tightening my arms across my chest. I would keep the cranky act up for as long as I could.

If I didn't, I would end up thinking about what it would mean if something went wrong. Given what we were taking a risk for, there was too much to lose if we failed.

Chapter 10

The group wanted to ease my crankiness, so we decided the best remedy was to find some food. I wasn't going to complain, since I was starving, but it also gave me an excuse to walk and think. I had more on my mind than I cared to admit. Stalking ahead of the group on my own wasn't really helping matters, but I wasn't in the mood to talk.

I looked back and forth, trying to get a sense of the place I used to call home. We were clinging to the sidewalk, drawing up our hoodies and shirt collars to move attention away from us. We hadn't seen any demons yet, and their lack of presence was making me uneasy. Demons used to find us the way wolves found a bleeding animal. It was just a matter of time, and before you knew it, your insides were leaking on your outsides.

But all I could see were boarded up windows covered in graffiti and sharply curved demonic symbols, broken glass and trash skittering along the cracked gravel. The buildings had taken on an ominous red glow from the fires set in oil drums, their heavy red lights flickering through the alleys. Over our heads, smoke hung like a storm cloud that refused to rain. Every breath tasted dirty, like my throat was being coated with smoke and sand.

The streets weren't empty. Lying in the middle of the street on my left were three men. I thought they were passed out, until I saw the dried pool of crimson underneath them. A few blocks down, a man was slumped half in, half out of a shop window. His head hung over the windowsill, thin streaks of blood tracing down the brick wall. Over my head, I could hear a woman screaming past an illuminated apartment window. I couldn't tell if it was a scream of earth-shattering pleasure, or soul-crushing pain. I stopped and listened to it, staring at the apartment window and feeling torn about running to find out what was happening.

"Constance?" I heard Warrick's voice, felt him stand beside me.

The scream came again, and I made up my mind. My hand went to my belt and curled around my hatchet. I marched toward the apartment–

A new scream pierced my ears and my heart, only to be cut off a split second later, after a fountain of blood exploded across the glass window. I halted in my tracks, staring at the bloodstain and feeling my heart squeeze. A man stalked into sight, slightly obscured by the bloodstains. His hand swiped along the blood, removing it from the window. He licked the gore from his fingers, his eyes finding me. He smiled and raised his other hand, displaying a crimson-coated knife. He waggled his fingers around the blade, and kept licking the blood off his hand.

Warrick gripped my elbow and drew me away. I struggled at first, wanting to storm the apartment and cut that devious fucking smile off his face, but a glance at Warrick stopped me. His eyes were grim and shadowed, haunted. He shook his head slowly, and I understood.

There was no way we could save everyone. The whole city was drowning in violence, and it wasn't going to change unless we shut the Hell Gate. That was just the way it was.

Didn't mean I had to like it.

I pried my arm free of Warrick's grip and kept walking. More screams carried through the darkened alleys and burned out buildings, and I couldn't get them out of my head. It took all my will to remain in control and walk away.

But walking the streets I used to be so familiar with, I got the uneasy feeling that I wasn't as in control as I wanted to be. It wouldn't be the first time I had been helpless in the face of overwhelming obstacles...

They threw us in lockup without telling us what

we'd been arrested for. We were kept in separate cells but at least we were across from each other.

Dro was sitting on the bench in her cell with her head in her hands. She was obviously ashamed and embarrassed for both of us. I was on the bench as well with my legs pulled up to my chest and my elbows on my knees. I was pissed that this was taking so long, that no one was telling us shit, and that they'd taken my father's hatchet. That was what infuriated me the most. They were holding the last reminder of my dead parents. I wanted it back.

We were stuck there for hours before the cops finally came back. Two men with biceps the size of cantaloupes marched in with them. Dro lifted her head from her hands. I brought my feet off the bench and set them on the concrete floor so I could stand.

The cops were the same ones who had arrested us, and they harshly clashed with the two men behind them. The new guys were dressed in black jeans, black shirts, heavy boots, and leather jackets. My eyes went down to the black gloves on their hands. Instinct told me they were armed with guns and knives. I looked at their faces as I walked closer to the bars. They were both Hispanic, like me. One of the men had a face that reminded me of a pug, all squashed in and flat with beady dark eyes. A black teardrop was tattooed under the corner of his left eye, as if this guy was crying on the inside all the time. Yeah, right.

The second man was even bigger. He was a head taller than his friend and almost twice as wide, and Teardrop wasn't a small guy. The Monster Man had thick black hair tied in a ponytail at the nape of his neck and bushy eyebrows. His lips were curled in an ugly scowl. He seemed to really hate me, though I wasn't sure why. Both of them seemed familiar, and I couldn't understand that, either.

"These are the two you want?" the male cop asked.

Teardrop nodded slowly, his eyes never leaving mine. Monster Man clenched his fists so tightly I thought he was going to crack his leather gloves open at the knuckles.

"Tell your brother at the border that he'll get his share," Teardrop said.

Fuck fuck fuck. *I should have known there was a reason that the other border guard was looking at me so much. He must have recognized me and called the cops, and those cops called these guys. My stomach dropped. I watched both men, even though I was trapped behind the bars and unable to get close to them.*

"You got the keys?" Teardrop asked. His Mexican accent was thick and he sounded like he'd been smoking for thirty years.

The male cop fumbled around his belt, unhooking a ring of silver keys. Teardrop held out his hand, but the cop didn't give up the keys just yet.

"You got our money?"

Teardrop stared blankly. "He does," the man replied, jerking his thumb at Monster Man.

The big thug reached into his jacket, and pulled out a gun. With no hesitation, he raised the weapon and fired a bullet into the cop's throat.

The silencer on the end of the pistol muffled the blast, but only just. Dro's scream echoed off the walls as blood sprayed between our cells. The female cop shrieked and slapped her waist, looking for her gun. The Monster Man turned his gun to the right and fired another muffled round. The female cop's head snapped back as blood, brain and bone exploded out of the back of her skull.

I waited for more cops to come running. Silencers made it harder to hear a gunshot, but couldn't drown out the sound completely.

No one came in.

Teardrop stalked toward my cell. He stared like he could intimidate me. I'd stared down worse assholes than him, seen the faces of monsters. I flicked my eyes to the dead cops. A twinge of pity went through my heart. Yeah, they'd arrested us and been bribed, but that didn't mean they deserved to die.

Teardrop took a step forward and smiled at me. It was a horrible, yellow smile that promised pain.

"Don't worry. They were the only ones in the station. By the time the next pigs come in, you'll be well on your way home, puta."

My chest tightened and my gut flipped. Without even needing to see their tattoos, I knew who these men were.

Teardrop smiled when he saw the realization hit me. I wanted to punch every tooth down that smug bastard's throat, but those damn bars were in my way. Not to mention that Monster Man was looming behind his friend, looking even larger than before. I scanned his face, trying to figure out why he was so familiar.

"I don't think you ever met Enrique," Teardrop said casually, like he was talking about the seven day forecast and not a coldblooded murderer. "But maybe you remember his brother. Hernandez."

Oh, fuck.

Hernandez, Emilio and Mateo's most trusted and loyal bodyguard. The man I stabbed to help Dro escape the hacienda.

Yeah. I remembered him, all right. He'd never been a friend so I didn't know he had a brother, but Enrique was almost a twin of his sibling.

Enrique was also triple my size and catatonic with fury. I was in serious trouble.

"We're supposed to bring you back in one piece," Teardrop droned on. "You and your sister. But we'll hurt you if we have to." He tilted his head to make his beady eyes more intense. "And Enrique really, really wants to hurt you."

I kept my movements slow and controlled. I needed a plan, needed it fast. 'One piece' was a pretty broad term for the Blood Thorns. It could mean whole, but shot, stabbed, beaten, strangled, burned, drowned, or worse.

We couldn't go back. Dro would be given up to the witch who made a deal with Mateo. My old flame would torture me to the point of death, revive me, then do it over and over again until I shattered. Until I suffered in every way he could imagine, begged for mercy at his feet, and was reduced to something worse than death.

Mateo's father had taught him well.

Teardrop took the keys from the body of the dead cop. He opened the lock on my door, but didn't pull it open.

"Get her out," Teardrop said to Enrique. "I'll get the other one."

The huge thug blocked my view of my sister. I had to crane my neck to see him properly. I backed away from the door as Enrique yanked it open. I heard the other cell opening and Dro crying my name. I didn't answer her, still trying to figure out the massive Enrique problem. I had fought big men before, but never one looking for revenge. Big men looking for revenge were always the most dangerous.

His swing at my head was so heavy I could practically hear the air splitting. I ducked the punch, grateful I was smaller and quicker. If I could get out of the cell and lock the guy in, that would be one problem solved. I drove my fist into Enrique's ribs. He jerked, but didn't even let out a grunt. If turned into the key word.

Enrique grabbed the back of my neck and pulled me away from him. His fist pounded into my stomach. It hurt so bad I thought I was going to throw up my lungs. They burned, working hard to regain the oxygen they'd lost. I was just recovering when Enrique punched me in the cheek.

Stars burst behind my eyes and the world went black for a half a second. His fist might as well have been a sledgehammer. I pitched to the side, trying to right myself before I collapsed. Another blow struck me in the middle, crushing the air out of me. I stumbled back again, his hand clamping on my hair. He twisted it in his fist, and I grimaced. He pulled and pulled until I thought he was going to scalp me. Dro was shouting my name. I heard a loud crack that could only be from a slap, followed by Teardrop yelling at her to shut the fuck up.

Before I could see what was happening, Enrique slugged me in the jaw. My teeth dug into my lip and I tasted blood. When my head twisted under Enrique's grip, I could feel a small clump of my hair wrench out of my head. He finally released me and locked his hands around my throat. He shoved me toward the back of the cell. My heels skidded along the stone floor, desperate to find traction. Enrique slammed me into the bars on the left side of the cell, a sharp pain cracking through my head.

He used both hands to squeeze the air out of my lungs. I wheezed and gasped as my lungs tightened, an invisible noose of agony coiling around them and constricting until I thought they would cave inward.

Enrique lifted me until my feet were off the ground. I got one good look at the hatred on his face before he slammed my head into the bars again. I gasped as much as I could when I felt the spike of pain and something warm matting my hair.

My body felt like lead and I couldn't breathe. I was awake enough to kick pathetically, barely even brushing his shins. He pinned my throat with one enormous hand, then used the other one to beat the life out of me. His blows didn't have a single point in mind. After what I had done to his brother, he wanted everything in me to hurt. He couldn't kill me, couldn't chop me to pieces, but anything else was fair game.

Getting hit by a meat tenderizer would hurt less than this. Blows pounded into me without mercy. My ribs stung as they began to crack. All of my organs were being turned to mush. My face felt like it had been smashed into an anvil. I couldn't see, couldn't move, couldn't breathe. It was the worst beating I'd taken since Mateo had beaten me weeks ago.

Though my head was pounding, I could hear voices in the background. They sounded like they were coming through a thin wall, but I knew one of them was Dro. Her scream was angrier than before. I heard Teardrop shouting, and then he was screaming.

At the same time his terrified cry started, I felt the

temperature in the cell increase rapidly. The air shriveled and parched my throat. A huge white light filled the corner of my vision. Before I could turn my head and see what was going on, Enrique unlatched his grip on my neck. I collapsed in a painful heap, wincing as my knees and palms slapped the concrete floor.

The smell of burning meat and the sound of agonized screams told me all I needed to know. Enrique was swearing in Spanish and trying to get out of the cell. My head was spinning, but I pulled myself up and looked at the cell across from me.

Dro's cell was filled with that terrifying, white flame. It burned like a bonfire, and I was barely able to see her outline in the middle of it. There was a blackened heap on the floor in front of her, which had to have been Teardrop. The fire licked the outside of the bars of Dro's cell, beginning to melt them away. Enrique grabbed my cell door and yanked it open with one hand. He used the other to fumble for his gun.

I brought one knee to my chest and put one hand on my leg, then used it to push myself up. I swayed but got to my feet. My entire body thrummed with pain, yet I kept standing. The whole world was swirling in front of me as I put on foot in front of the other. Enrique almost had his gun. The fire coming off Dro's silhouette was powerful, but I didn't know if it would stop a bullet. I wasn't going to take the chance.

No matter how hard I tried, my legs just wouldn't move fast enough. The white inferno consumed the hall between the cells. I couldn't see Dro at all now past the fire. Enrique lifted his gun, aimed it at the center of the blaze, and pulled the trigger.

Everything around me seemed to stop. My feet anchored to the concrete. I couldn't draw a single breath. The beating of my heart seemed to disappear. I was barely aware of the entire lockup scorching around me, the water building in my eyes, the pulsing, bruising pain in my body. I didn't hear the shot, but I saw the gun buck in Enrique's hand. There was no way he could have missed.

The blaze continued to burn, stretching across the cell like a rushing tide. The bars turned red hot and shimmered as they began to melt. Enrique backed up, dropping the gun and panting harshly. The fire coiled around him. He raised his hand and screamed one last time. His clothes turned to ash, flaking off his body. Hair turned to cinder and flesh boiled. It smelled horrible, and nearly made me throw up.

Enrique's body dropped when his screaming ended. Soon I wasn't looking at a dead man, but a blackened heap at my feet. I kept my eyes on the fire, still not able to see my sister. The bullet might have hit her, and the fire was now just out of control. If that were the case, then I wouldn't even try to escape the flames. There would be no point. It would be over quickly, a few moments of searing pain, and that was it. Better than living without Dro at my side.

The light from the fire blinded me, preventing me from finding an escape I coughed, inhaled smoke, and waited.

Then the flames pulled back. They curled over themselves, drawing out of the ruined cell and darkening the world around me. The air smelled and tasted charred and dusty, but I wasn't going to swallow fire. The fire continued retreating until it was back in Dro's cell, turning to a smaller shape, one with arms and legs. It drew back into her body, and she buckled forward.

I lurched toward her, mindful of the melted bars and burned corpses on the floor. I shouldn't have been running in my condition, but I had to know she was all right. That the bullet had missed and she wasn't going to die. I dropped to my knees at the same time Dro fell. I wrapped my arms around my sister. Her clothes were still intact but her skin was burning. I couldn't feel any blood sticking to my clothes, so I pushed her back to get a better look at her.

Dro's face was covered in dust and grime, her hair a tangled mess around her head, shoulders, and back, and there was a red mark on her left cheek. No gunshot *wounds. Either the bullet missed her, or the fire had been so hot that it melted the deadly piece of metal.*

But she wasn't bleeding. She was alive. That was all I needed to know.

Relief, pain, or both made me slump. Her dainty arms curled around me so I didn't land on the floor. I'd pushed myself too hard and too fast yet again. I fought against the exhaustion creeping toward my skull, but it was stronger than I was. The last thing I heard was Dro's anguished cries that she was going to get me somewhere safe, and that she was sorry...

"Con?"

I jumped out of the memory and looked at my sister. I hadn't even heard her come up. *Stupid, pay attention. Someone could have leaped out of the alley and stabbed you and you never would have known.*

"Con? Are you okay?"

I shook myself mentally and focused on my sister. "Yeah, I'm okay," I told her.

Dro frowned. "You don't look okay."

I raised my hands and gave her a half smile. "Guilty as charged, then."

As predicted, my sister's expression never changed. I sighed. "What do you want me to say?"

My sister paused, like she didn't trust herself to speak. If I didn't know better, it would be like she didn't trust me. So I relaxed, and let her speak.

"None of us doubt you, Con. But this is the best option. Nothing we do will be safe, but at least this way we have each other's backs."

She was right, though I was too stubborn to admit it. I grunted instead.

Out of the corner of my eye, I saw Dro shaking her head and hiding a tiny smile. She didn't notice when the gesture wasn't returned. I wanted to smile, or at least fake it, but I couldn't. Yeah, Dro was right. No matter how bad things got, we always had each other's backs. But there had been times when it wasn't enough...

The sirens woke me up. I lurched off the ground, tossing away the blankets and jackets that had been covering me. I whipped my head back and forth, trying to figure out where I was and if the sirens were meant for me. I was in an alley near a dumpster. This must have been as far as Dro had carried me. It was amazing, considering how small she was. Desperate times, desperate measures, I guess. I didn't see her, but she wouldn't be far. I'd check on the cops, and then I would draw her out of wherever she'd stashed herself. She needed someone to talk to about what happened.

I stretched my body out as I stood up. All of my injuries seemed to have been healed. That must have been something Dro did when she got me here. As I felt around my body, I found that I had my lucky jacket, hatchet, and throwing knives again. I curled my hand around the hatchet, comforted by its familiar handle. I pressed my back to the brick wall and carefully edged toward the mouth of the alley.

We were a couple blocks from the police station, which looked like a bomb had gone off at one end. Fire trucks, police cars, and ambulances were parked outside of it. Their red and blue lights flickered wildly, painting the smoke rising off the ruined building. There were news vans cordoned away from the scene, though the reporters were shouting for answers and giving early opinions on what had gone wrong.

I stepped back into the alley. The cops were going to have their hands full for a while, so me and Dro had to take advantage of it to escape. I turned my back on the destruction my sister had caused and started walking back to the pile of blankets and jackets on the dirty alley ground.

I stopped suddenly. Dro had destroyed two buildings with a fire that came from her. It wasn't the first time I'd seen it and I had always known that she had powers, but I'd never seen anything like what she had done over the last week. What had set it off? How was it *out of control at the motel, but in control at the police station? She must have known she'd done it. She must be able to control it. If not...*

I shook myself. I couldn't think too much about it. The more I did, the more hesitant I would be. I couldn't be afraid of my little sister. She kept me from falling apart, and needed to be protected from the monsters. Maybe when things settled down, we could sit down and have a long talk about what was happening to her. There were proper times and places for that conversation, and this wasn't one of them.

Especially since I couldn't find her.

I searched every crack and dark corner of the alley, but she wasn't in any of them. Not even a trail to let me know where she'd gone. I couldn't see her on any of the other streets, and all the shops were closed.

Confusion mixed with dread in my chest and left me gasping. Had she been taken while I was asleep? That had to be the answer. She would never leave me. But who had taken her? Cops? Blood Thorns? The monsters?

I had to stop because I was hyperventilating. I staggered back against the wall, sliding down the rough brick. I dropped onto my ass and drew my knees up to my chest. I took deep breaths, as if they would calm me down. As if they would make me forget that my little sister had been kidnapped while I'd been unconscious for who knew how long.

The cops could be shouting questions at her right now. The Blood Thorns could be torturing her. The monsters could be...

A lump grew in my throat. Tears pricked my eyes. I'd never been without Dro. I felt more than alone. I felt lost.

The cold wind brushed through my jacket. I tugged the edges closer to my body, putting my hands under my armpits to keep them warm. I couldn't think about what might be happening to her, only on how to find her...

The back of my hand brushed against something. Paper, near the knife holsters sewn into my coat. I reached inside and yanked it out. The cops would have arrested me and the monsters probably couldn't write very well, which left the Blood Thorns. Anger burned away the cold as I unfolded the paper. I don't know why the Blood Thorns wouldn't have taken us both, unless they wanted to use Dro as some awful torture to punish me. That seemed like their style.

But when I opened the note, my heart sank even further.

It wasn't from the cops or the monsters. It wasn't even from the Blood Thorns.

It was from Dro.

My eyes traced over the words again and again and again, knowing they had to be a mistake. It was there, in her shaky writing from the drying out pen she had found to use. There were tear stains on the paper. She hadn't wanted to write this. She couldn't have meant it.

But deep down, I knew better.

I dropped the note, watching it blow away in a wind that felt colder than the last. I didn't want it. The words were etched into my brain forever.

Connie,

I had to write this while you were asleep because I knew you would argue with me when you woke up, and I'm too tired for that. I'm too tired for all of this. No matter what you do, how hard you try or how hard you fight, you can't protect me. I nearly got you killed twice this week. I don't know what's wrong with me, but it will get you killed. And I can't live with that. You'll be safer without me. If you keep moving north, the Blood Thorns will lose you. The monsters will never come after you again. Please don't look for me, Connie. I don't want you to find me.

I'm sorry for ruining your life. I hope you can forgive me.

Always your sister,
Dro.

Tears flowed down my cheeks, but my determination was fired up like never before. I would promise my sister anything, except for abandoning her.

Good sisters didn't break each other's hearts...

"Do you hear that?"

Warrick's voice cut me back to the present. I was about to say no, that I didn't hear anything, but then I listened carefully, and caught the sound of raised voices and wicked laughter.

My heart began beating faster. It was too soon for another attack, and we weren't anywhere near the right location. Whatever was happening couldn't be related to the fragments.

The first thought that crossed my mind was walking away. Take any other street or alley and get the hell away from whatever was causing the commotion.

Then I heard a woman's sharp cry of pain, and knew I couldn't run. Not this time. Not with that other woman's scream ringing in my head, and the sight of her murderer's bloody smile and wave burned into the back of my mind.

So I took off running, hearing my friends curse before they followed me.

Two blocks is nothing when you're running at a full tilt. The closer I got, the louder the battle cries were. I was hearing snarls and shouts, and it wasn't long before I smelled blood. I swung around the last corner in the direction of the fight, winding up in a dirty alley behind a brown-brick building.

Four men were pinning a woman to a wall, beating the life from her. I couldn't tell who she was, but she was fighting back with all her strength. The thugs didn't see me coming, which made it easy for me to run up to the one closest to me and kick him in the side.

He grunted and turned around, sneering at me. I spun my leg in a wide arc, and kicked that look right off his face.

This was when the rest of his heavyset pals noticed

me. I was hoping they would be stupid and come at me one at a time. Unfortunately, the dirty hulks had some intelligence in their thick skulls. They rushed me at the same time.

I stepped back and snapped out a kick into the ribs of the closest man. It made him stagger and bought me seconds, which is when his last two friends pounced. I ducked under a fist and drove my fist into the third man's stomach. Just as my hit connected, the fourth man punched me in the head. My neck twisted to the side and I backed up, blocking the next hit from the third man. I saw the fourth man's fist moving for me again, but I leaned away and grabbed his outstretched arm. I socked him in the jaw and kicked him in the chin, then whirled around him. I kicked forward as hard as I could, knocking him back into his friend.

Just as I was stepping back, heavy arms looped around my chest and locked me to someone's chest. *Damn. Forgot about the other two guys.*

The one rushing my front was the second man I had kicked. My arms were still free, so I reacted fast, reaching into my jacket and grabbing a silver knife. As the second man approached, I slammed the back of my head into the nose of my captor. He cursed as I shattered his nose, loosening his hold on me. I kicked the knee of the second man when he was in range, causing him to stumble. Before he could regain himself, I stabbed him in the side of the head.

My knife shuddered when it struck the bone, and it wasn't easy to pull back. The man behind me drove his fist into my ribs, making me wince. I repaid him by sending my elbow into his cheek. Dazing him again, I twirled the knife in my hands, then stabbed it back into his ribs.

The man screamed in pain, making my ears ring. I twisted the blade and he was forced to release me. I stumbled forward, barely getting to my feet when the third and fourth man charged me. This time, they had knives, too. I wasn't ready, and there was no way I could avoid being hit and stabbed.

But they assumed I was alone. The third man was caught completely off-guard when Warrick shot into the alley and delivered a powerful uppercut to his chin. The man skidded back, head tilted skyward and his throat exposed. Warrick planted a sidekick into his stomach and sent him into the wall.

The fourth man suddenly realized what was happening, curving his knife wrist toward Warrick, but Sephiel had slipped behind him. He snared the man's arm and wrenched it upward, almost to the point of breaking it. As the man cried out, Sephiel drove his knee into his back. Then he lifted him up, stepped back, and slammed him into the ground. One solid kick to the face, and the man was out.

My hand moved subconsciously to my middle, carefully prodding my ribs. None of them seemed broken and my face was going to have a bruise. All things considered, I'd gotten away lucky.

While Sephiel made sure that none of the four thugs would be getting back up, Warrick marched over to me. His hands cupped my chin and gently lifted my face.

After frowning at the bruise forming on my face, Warrick looked in my eyes.

"That was reckless, stupid, and extremely brave," he told me.

I couldn't hide my grin any more than he could. "Glad you're impressed," I said.

Warrick stifled a laugh and pressed his lips to my forehead. When he pulled back, Dro appeared at our side. Her icy blue eyes traced down my body, searching for injuries. I waved her off.

"I'm fine, Dro," I promised her. I nodded at the woman who was pushing herself up from the ground. "Let's go make sure she's okay."

Just as I said that, the woman turned and looked at us. She had a bloody lip and a blackening eye, which made her hate-filled scowl even more ferocious.

"*You*," she spat.

I made a face that was somewhere between a smirk and a snarl.

"Hello, Elle."

Chapter 11

Elle and I had two things in common. We were both fighters, and we hated each other.

It was inevitable, really. I had an attitude that would make any nun faint, and Elle was about as friendly as an agitated pit viper.

But I believed she was loyal to the demon slayers. They lived by a loose but ever present code, and she was adamant when it came to killing demons. She and the other slayers had been ready to destroy Dro, regardless of her angel half.

Needless to say, we didn't get along.

"What the fuck are you doing here?" she demanded.

I stared at Elle blankly. Aside from the bruises and blood, she looked exactly as I remembered her; blonde hair falling out of a loose ponytail, nice cheekbones, full lips, perfected eyebrows, and bright blue eyes. She could have been a supermodel if she weren't dressed in black combat clothes and carrying a knife on her hip.

"I could ask you the same question," I shot back, pushing myself away from Warrick. "You're welcome, by the way."

Her scowl intensified, nearly twisting off her face. I didn't move my eyes from her face, but Warrick stepped in front of me.

"Where are the others?" he asked. "Where are Carver and Jackson?"

I was pretty sure he only really cared about Jackson. Carver was Elle's father, and she had obviously inherited his callousness and frigid attitude. Jackson, however, actually had kindness in him. He was Warrick's friend, and he didn't immediately want to kill my sister when he met her, which put him in my good book.

"What does it matter to you?" Elle spat. "You made it clear where your loyalties lie."

Ouch. That's low. So low I thought about punching her for it. Warrick might have chosen us over his fellow demon slayers, but I had no doubt that he would help them however he could. He was happy to play the White Knight whenever he had the chance.

Though the moment the words left her mouth, I heard boots stomping against pavement behind me. I turned around, tightening the grip on my knife. Dro and Max backed up while Sephiel slipped in front of them.

Elle must have been wearing some kind of earpiece or microphone. It was the only way Carver and Jackson could have gotten here so fast.

Jackson was a tall, muscular dark-skinned man with large lips and dark eyes. He wore the same black, tactical outfit Elle was wearing, but he was carrying a large automatic rifle over his shoulder.

Next to him was a brawny middle-aged man wearing a black shirt and cargo pants. He was carrying a rifle as well, but also had a riot shotgun slung over his back. The short grey hair on his head was starting to grow longer, and sharp stubble was now circling his mouth. His face was hard and his eyes were cold. There was no mistaking that he was Elle's father.

His eyes flicked back and forth, taking in the whole scene and all the people in it. He glared at Warrick, Dro, and me the hardest. He didn't like me– shocker– and felt that Warrick had irreparably betrayed him. He wanted Dro dead simply because she existed.

This was not going to go well.

"Jackson," Warrick said, nodding to his friend. The large, onyx-skinned man nodded back. Warrick's eyes slid back to Carver, and he sighed. "Carver."

"What the hell are you doing here, Warrick?" he demanded, the same way Elle had moments ago. They were cut from a freakishly similar cloth.

"We heard someone being attacked," he explained.

"We wanted to help." Warrick looked at me with some pride. "Constance saved Elle."

I didn't react. Carver would care about my saving his daughter about as much as he cared about the beetle he crushed under his boot.

Still, the man did have some emotion beneath his self-righteous mask. He turned his eyes to Elle and started shoving us aside so he could get to her. He stopped in front of Elle and cupped the back of her neck. Warrick stepped away to give them space, glancing at me to make sure I wouldn't start a fight.

I didn't plan on starting one, but if they gave me a reason... Well, it wasn't the first time I'd butted heads with the demon slayers.

After assuring himself that Elle was all right, Carver turned back to Warrick. "You didn't answer my question. What the hell are you doing here?"

Warrick hesitated, but only barely. "The same as you. We're trying to stop the demons."

"You should have let us handle it," Elle said over her father's shoulder. "We had a lead, and you fucked it up."

"I'm sorry," I interjected. "Was getting the shit kicked out of you part of your plan?"

Elle practically snarled at me. I had to hold back my laughter.

"I was waiting to get information from my contacts, you bitch," Elle snapped. "Now they're dead, and it's your fucking fault!"

I looked at the bodies, really seeing them this time. Any attitude I had disappeared when I saw the tattoos on their bodies. I was suddenly very still, and very, very serious.

"These were your contacts?" I asked.

"Yes." Elle's reply was exasperated, but I didn't care.

My blood went cold. "They're Blood Thorns," I stated.

The tattoos on their arms and necks gave them

away, the mark of a thorn weaving in and out of their skin, with drops of inked on blood hidden behind real blood.

"We know who they are," Carver said.

I stared at him, unbelieving. "You know?! And you still wanted to deal with them?!"

"We were doing a recon mission," the older slayer defended. "We know the Blood Thorns are working with the demons. Offering to help them was the best way of understanding their operation. The enemy of my enemy is my friend, as the saying goes."

He explained it perfectly, but I still couldn't understand what he said.

"What the hell kind of deal did you make?" Warrick burst.

"I don't see how that matters–"

"Of course it fucking matters!" I shouted. "If you think for one second that they won't feed you to hellhounds the second they have a chance, you're even stupider than I thought."

When Carver glared at me, I could practically feel the hate wafting off him. I was too pissed to care. They had no idea what they were getting themselves into. By the time the Blood Thorns were done with the slayers, there wouldn't be enough left of them to scrape off the pavement.

"How did this even happen?" Warrick asked, turning his head to look at Jackson.

The big man hesitated, then sighed. "After that fight in Washington, when you guys disappeared, things went to shit, John. The entire country was falling apart, and we couldn't fight back. We had to come up with another plan. So we grabbed whatever Possessors we could find and made them talk."

Jackson didn't sound pleased with the methods they must have used. I remembered Gabriel's pulped face, trapped in chains in a circle. I gave Carver another dark look. Yet another person who wasn't beyond torturing anyone if he wanted information.

"Eventually we learned that all the demonic activity

was coming from here," Jackson continued. "We came into town, learned that the Blood Thorns were working with the demons, and that their leader was connected to Lucifer. They didn't know who we were, so they let us join up. We've been acting as messengers for them, trying to get as much intel as possible. But we're not getting as much as we hoped for."

"Because Mateo's using you," I snapped. "That's what he does. You're never going to learn anything from him."

"Do you know about the fragments?" Elle asked.

I glared at her. "Yes. And I did it without taking the side of the fucking King of Hell."

Elle's lip curled into an ugly sneer. I laughed at it before, but now it made me want to smack her.

"And how close are you to obtaining those fragments?" Carver asked me.

I wish I'd spoken, even if it would have been a lie. It would have been better than letting him know that we didn't have anything except information on the fragments, and that they were dangerously out of our reach. I couldn't get them until tomorrow, but if the slayers tried hard enough, they'd find a way to get them sooner than that.

Is that such a bad thing, Constance? Letting someone else do the hard work? This way you don't have to get anywhere near Mateo, Drake, or Lucifer.

But there was a nagging in the back of my head. This situation didn't feel right, the obvious traitors aside, and I had no idea what Mateo or Drake might have told them, if they'd mentioned anything about capturing me or why. I could have asked, but there was no guarantee they would tell me the truth. I generally placed anyone associated with the Blood Thorns in untrustworthy categories.

My hand went to the hilt of my hatchet and I stepped to the side to keep all three demon slayers in my line of sight. Even Jackson. I liked him, but I didn't trust him.

"Can you get them?" Warrick inquired. "Have you seen them?"

Carver shook his head lightly. "We've tried to find out where their location is, but Mr. Rocha is keeping them well hidden. He brushes off our questions like we'd never asked them."

He called him Mr. Rocha. That was my first signal that something was very wrong. More to the point, why were the slayers still waiting here out in the open? Sure, we'd stopped to burden them with questions, but honest slayers secretly working against their employers would want to get off the streets in case unfriendly eyes turned their way.

But here we were, in the middle of an alley in mid-afternoon.

"Drake is on their side," Max said from behind us, yanking me from my thoughts. "You can't possibly think being around them is a good idea."

At the mention of Drake's name, Warrick bristled. He fixed a stony look onto his former boss and clenched his fists. Betrayal was going both ways now.

"You're making a huge mistake," Warrick growled.

Carver's cold blue eyes locked on Warrick's furious green ones. "You aren't in a position to tell right from wrong, Warrick. You make your own mistakes every time you do."

If I hadn't been suspicious of the whole situation, I would have let Warrick hit him. I would have stood back and smiled as my lover beat the callous disregard out of his former boss. But the sense of wrongness had clamped itself over my heart, and I knew we were out of time.

Warrick took a step closer to Carver, about to raise his fist, but I grabbed his wrist and held it down. Warrick's outraged stare turned on me.

"Fuck them," I said. "If they want to dick around with a bunch of demon-loving thugs, they can suffer the consequences. We don't need their help."

Warrick read my eyes carefully, picking out the underlying meaning I had.

Drop it. Something isn't right. We need to go.

He relaxed just enough. Casting one more deadly

glare at Carver, Warrick pulled himself back and started walking down the alley with me. He lowered his eyes so he wouldn't have to look at Jackson, but I could see that the big demon slayer was sad about what happened. Why Jackson stayed with Carver and Elle was beyond me.

Dro and Max watched us. Sephiel looked over my shoulder, watching the demon slayers carefully. He had a bone or two to pick with them since they'd tortured his brother, Gabriel.

"What do you sense, Constance?" Sephiel asked as we passed him.

"I don't know," I muttered under my breath. "Something just felt off."

My word seemed good enough. Without waiting to say goodbye, we left the demon slayers in the alley. I assumed that once we were back on the street, we would be able to make our way to a new hiding spot and wait out the night so I could hunt down Mateo and Drake.

God, was I ever wrong.

Chapter 12

I'd been moving quickly with Warrick's hand in mine. Both of us were on edge and wanting some kind of comfort. He was tense because his former allies and employer had shown up and were acting as double agents for the most conniving enemies he could imagine. I was booking it because I felt like the walls of a trap were closing in.

Dro, Max, and Sephiel were all but running to keep up with us. Finally, Dro broke away from them and jogged to my side. She looked at me as I stomped through the dusty streets.

"Con? Where are we going?"

Guess I should have thought of that. "I don't know. There has to be somewhere close where we can lay low for a bit."

Killing time before I possibly get killed by my ex. Wonderful.

We were just coming up to a main intersection when an ugly screech cut through the night. I skidded to a stop, knowing only one thing could make that sound.

"Demons," Warrick grunted. He let go of my hand and drew the sawed-off shotgun from his back. The blessed rock salt and sage shells would put down a demon for good, and for once I was glad that any gunfire in public view would go completely unnoticed. Even now I was hearing distant pops of guns being fired at who knew what.

It had been weeks since I'd had to fight a demon, and I had been content with that. Somehow I knew I was about to pay the price for all those days of staying under their radar.

They were too far away for me to tell what type of

demon they were, and I wasn't about to ask Dro or Max to find out. Max's foresight was muddled and Dro was the prize the minions of Hell wanted to claim for their master. The best option was to get out of sight and avoid a confrontation all together.

Not the tactic I usually took, but desperate times, and all that.

"We need to get off the street," I said, dragging Warrick behind me and looking for anything that resembled shelter. Most of the shops and apartments had been boarded up. Some of the boards on the windows had been splintered, but the spaces between them weren't big enough for us to fit through.

Another inhuman shriek echoed from the streets on my right, closer than before. Way closer. We were running out of time.

Finally, my eyes locked on a brick shop with a sign reading *Farmacia*. The pharmacy was about twenty feet away. We had seconds, maybe a minute if we were lucky. I bolted for the store, knowing my sister and my friends were right behind me.

I thought we were going to make it. The shop was right there, less than fifteen feet away from us. But it was on the corner of the street, right next to a main road.

By the time I saw them out of the corner of my eye, it was too late to stop. The demons had found us.

I grabbed a silver throwing knife from inside my jacket and stopped, taking a second to position myself and get aim. Then I hurled the silver blade at the Red demon speeding toward us.

My aim was perfect, the weapon slamming into its tough red skin on its chest. The metal caused it to howl and buckle backward.

But it wasn't alone. Dashing out of the side streets and corners of the main streets were at least twelve other demons, none of which were the same. There were two red-skinned, oily haired, humanoid Reds gnashing their teeth and revealing their pointed black claws. A scarred, half-blind Shredder lumbered behind them, dragging its thick, bony claws almost on the ground. A couple of wailing Wretches trailed after it, the limbs of their tortured angelic bodies clumped together like twigs in putty. At the rear were seven grey ghouls limping toward us, hungry for our flesh.

That wasn't even counting the two Reds that sprang out of the alley behind us. Sephiel must have heard them coming, because he spun on his heel while drawing his short swords, and sliced the throats of both Reds at the same time. Black blood squirted onto his white leather coat, but the ex-angel refused to move until he saw the demons collapse onto the dirty pavement and dissolve into piles of dark ash.

I yanked the hatchet off my hip and faced the demons head-on. Warrick was at my side instantly, firing rock salt at the horde of monsters. Some of them cringed and collapsed back as the salt shredded their bodies and started to destroy them, but they were far from dead.

I couldn't warn Dro and Max to run. All I could do was shield them, trust Sephiel to have our backs, and fight with Warrick. Dro knew how to defend herself, and Max was going to have to focus long enough to foresee an escape route, or find a way to use the *movens caeli.* That was all the time I had to worry before the first Wretch shouldered past the Shredder, and launched itself at me.

I stepped back so it didn't slam into me, and kicked it in the face when it landed in a crouch. The angel-turned-demon howled furiously, swiping its hooked nails at my legs. I danced back and crashed my hatchet down onto its head. The Wretch twisted away, the blade sinking into its shoulder instead of managing a killing blow. The Wretch still screamed angrily, but now it was trying to get to its feet. I backed up again, taking out another knife from inside my jacket.

The Wretch unquestionably lived up to its name. It was a hunchbacked monstrosity with broken stumps of bone protruding from the backs of its shoulders. The creature's thin skin was pasty and beaded with sweat that oiled the thin strips of hair on its head. Blue veins were visible all over its body, at least the parts that weren't covered in whip marks and patchy scars. Decaying yellow nails became uneven claws on the ends of its bony fingers. The whites of the insane angel's eyes had become yellow, the irises half purple from being filled with blood. Combined with their unstoppable madness, it was hard to believe that this creature had once been considered holy.

It howled at me, its voice reduced to a tortured rasp from centuries of screaming. Then it leaped for me.

I twisted to the side at the last second, missing its outstretched arms. I shoved my knife up until it drove into the Wretch's chest. I used my other hand to slam the hatchet into the back of its neck.

The Wretch bucked and twitched against the silver, its scrawny limbs slapping at my stomach. I grimaced and struck down with the hatchet. The Wretch jerked and demon blood sprayed, but it wasn't dead yet.

Something big moved on my right. I turned my head just as the Shredder lunged with its bone claws extended.

I pushed away from the Wretch, trying to shield myself behind it. The bone claws punched through the Wretch's back, splashing me with dark, hot blood. I leaned back, my eyes widening when I saw the demon's blood-covered claws just half an inch from my face.

The Shredder yanked its claws out of the Wretch, which had begun to collapse in on itself, turning into nothing but ash. I looked up at the Shredder, then kept looking up.

It was easily double my size and stood an extra two feet over me. Like the Wretch, its pale skin was covered in ragged scars. Strips of tar black hair hung to its shoulders. The face resembled a concrete block with glazed white eyes that gave it a blind appearance. Like most demons, this monster had jagged teeth behind its lips, but that wasn't its primary weapon. On the end of each finger was a foot long bone-claw. I didn't think I'd ever look at those claws and not be terrified of how easily they could rip me in half.

The Shredder swung its claws at me and forced me to jump back. The claws just barely snagged my shirt, and I winced at how lucky I'd been.

Shredders were big, but they were remarkably fast. The moment I backed away, the demon was rushing forward and striking down at me. I feinted to the side, staying away from its front. My back brushed the brick wall, though I still had enough room to toss my knife into the Shredder's face.

It was an awkward angle, but I managed to send the blade into the Shredder's cheek. It roared furiously, swinging its body around as it tried to catch me with its far claws. I dashed out into the main street, hoping I'd be fast enough to avoid the claws. My luck held, and the claws smashed into the corner of the shop. The Shredder's blow had so much force behind it that chunks of brick were torn off when the claws connected.

I kept running, knowing it would chase me no matter what I did.

Staying ahead of it gave me the stupid idea that my luck would hold out. That completely changed when a grey shape shot out from the alley and tackled me.

I went down fast and hard, landing roughly on my ribs. The smell of rotting flesh and sour breath nearly gagged me. A damn *ghoul* had taken me down?

Angry, I drove my elbow back. It connected with the ghoul's face and knocked it away from me. I rolled onto my front and shot to my feet, glaring at the demon. Ghouls were thin, humanoid creatures with enlarged heads and almond eyes the shade of spoiled milk. Their flesh was made of rough scales and their teeth were as sharp and yellow as their claws.

I raised my hatchet to strike the ghoul, but the Shredder had caught up to me. It lumbered forward, batting the ghoul aside with the back of its fist. The smaller demon flew through the air like a piece of paper on the wind. I might have laughed if I wasn't the Shredder's next target.

I turned and started running again, making my way

back to the group. They'd spread out, trying to keep the demons from surrounding them. But it wasn't enough. There were too many, and I could see that everyone was tired. Dro was slashing and kicking the Reds with her silver knives. Warrick and Sephiel were in front of her and Max, the demon slayer shooting any demons that got too close while the ex-angel cut down anything that came near him.

But there was blood on their clothes and bruises on their faces, and the demons weren't afraid of dying. They wouldn't be able to hang on much longer, and I still hadn't killed the Shredder chasing after me.

Max fiddled with the *movens caeli,* waiting for me to get in range to use it. The group might be able to kill the rest of the demons, but the Shredder would be more than they could handle right now.

They needed time to escape, and I couldn't stop running.

"Dro!" I screamed, dodging to the left and letting the Shredder swing wide. I could still see my sister out of the corner of my eye, but I was backing away into another alley with the large beast looming over me.

"Last week's house!" was the most I could manage before the Shredder swung wide and nearly took my head off with its claws.

"Constance! Come on!" she screamed back.

I didn't look at her, moving into the narrow alley behind me.

"Go! I'll catch up!"

The Shredder rushed the alley before I could hear her reply. I turned and ran faster than I thought I could.

The Shredder struggled to fit its bulk into the alley. I risked a glance back, seeing a flash of gold light. They'd used the *movens caeli.* I wanted to cry with relief, but I still had six more blocks to run to before I met up with them again. I had to lose the Shredder before then.

As I tore through the alley, I drew on memory. I knew all the streets and alleys downtown. I'd had to run them all when rival gangs were chasing me. I'd been good at giving them the slip, and this demon probably wasn't half as smart as they'd been.

I took a sharp left and heard the Shredder roar in frustration when it lost sight of me. It turned and squeezed itself through the exit I had already taken, barely able to force its mass through the narrow corridor. Up ahead of me was a wire fence acting as a block for parking. I turned toward the wall and jumped, pushing off of it to get a little more height. I slammed into the wire and glanced over my shoulder.

The Shredder was still stuck, but it was determined to force its way toward me. It rolled its shoulders to help itself move across the brick, snarling hideously and glaring at me with blind eyes. I turned back to the fence and started climbing.

It wasn't difficult, but the top of the fence was uncut wire that scratched along my arms as I dragged myself over it. I slipped onto the other side and dropped down. The Shredder was about halfway through the alley, bellowing furiously, but I still had the advantage. I turned to the left and dashed down another alley.

I wondered if the Shredder could track my scent, or if other demons would be following it now that my sister and my friends had escaped them. I slowed down and took off my lucky jacket, grabbing all the weapons from it and sliding them into my belt. I stopped by a dumpster and threw open the lid, about to toss my jacket down.

I hesitated.

It was stupid, but I still thought of it as my lucky jacket. Granted I wasn't superstitious, but I was still alive. Wearing a reminder of the first man I'd killed had brought me some kind of strength. What did it mean to throw it away?

Nothing, you idiot. It means you give the demons a false trail. It's just a jacket. Get rid of it.

Before I could think about it any further, I threw my lucky jacket into the dumpster and slammed down the lid. Then I turned and headed for the main street.

I was glad that it was empty, and started jogging to the left to turn into the market. I looked over my shoulder again, hearing the Shredder roar and hoping it would take my false trail and lose me completely. I couldn't see it behind me, so I figured I'd be safe for a few minutes. I got off the road and onto the sidewalk, wedging myself between two fly-infested taco carts to catch my breath.

My heart pounded against my ribcage, and it was a huge effort to raise my head. The scratches and bruises I'd gotten were tender, but I could still run with them. I looked over my shoulder one more time, and still wasn't seeing the Shredder.

Once I caught my breath, I focused on where I was.

Okay, so I can't go back the way I came, and with the false trail across the street, I can't double-back in case other demons show up. I have to cut through the market and make my way through the square to get to the house.

Which means I just turned a six block run into twelve.

I should have kept my damn jacket.

I took a moment to rearrange the weapons on my body, sliding two of the knives into my shoulder holsters and putting another one on my belt. I gripped the last knife in one hand and my hatchet in the other, and stated walking.

I tried to focus on the shadows behind the windows of each shop I passed, but my eyes always went back to the wooden and metal carts. They'd once been bursting with fresh fruit, food, jewelry, hand-made clothes and ornaments, anything tourists and bargain-hunters would want to find.

It didn't look like any of the carts had been used in months, each one stripped of its contents and dented near the front. Some of them were missing their wheels, umbrellas, and even grills. I stared at them, unable to remember the last time I'd eaten. I pulled my eyes away from the carts and looked straight ahead. That didn't keep my stomach from rumbling angrily. I'd just used up a lot of energy running and fighting for my life. We'd been on the hunt for food when we left, and now I was determined to—

"Fancy seeing you again."

I froze the second I heard his voice, then spun and planted my feet in a fighting stance. Drake was standing in the alley on my right, leaning against the wall with his arms folded across his chest, smiling like he didn't have a care in the world.

"I was wondering when I'd run into you next, *chica*. Been thinking a lot about you."

"Me too," I replied. "I've been thinking about how much you'll scream when I cut you to pieces."

"Ooo," he said, edging off the wall and slowly walking toward me. "Someone's feeling nasty. Is that 'cause you're missing your little gang? Where oh where could they be, I wonder?"

I tensed, watching him get closer and thinking about how I could attack him. Throwing my knife would be the best way. I had extremely good aim, and could hit him from here.

But Drake was a chatty bastard. If I kept him talking, I might be able to figure out what he wanted me for.

And maybe he would let down his guard so I could kill him.

"They can't be far," he said through his smile. "You never let your sister out of your sight any more than that scrawny brat or that uptight angel do, and Johnny-boy would probably tear the city apart if he knew you and me were having a chat. So where did they go?"

"What do you care? They aren't your targets right now. I am."

Drake grinned. "Bet you feel pretty special, don't you?"

I glared in reply, trudging past his words. "You said Lucifer has plans for me. Things that even Mateo can't get between. What does that mean?"

Drake shrugged. "I never was good with the

details. Your old boy toy knows. He can tell you more, but I think he needs to vent a little first."

It took me a second too long to understand what he meant. That second was when I felt hands snare the back of my shirt and yank me onto the ground.

I hit it with a jolt, rolling to the left and getting up on one knee. I was almost kicked in the face, but leaned away and brought up my hatchet. The booted foot knocked against my wrist, sending the hatchet flying out of my grasp.

Cursing under my breath, I slid back to get distance and got onto my feet. He was on me just as I stood up.

I blocked his furious punches and kicks, trying to get in some shots, but his defense was as good as mine. Maybe even better.

But I still had a knife.

He threw a punch toward my chest that I batted down. I held his arm and stabbed for his neck. He caught my wrist and twisted it until I was forced to drop the blade.

So much for the knife.

I kicked for his knee, but he stepped back and jerked me against his chest.

"You're so fucking predictable," Mateo snarled.

He slammed his forehead into mine. Stars exploded behind my eyes and the world spun. I tried to get my bearings, but Mateo was at the top of his game. He shoved me away so hard I stumbled, unable to stop the powerful kick that slammed into my chest. I landed on the road hard, my head cracking against the concrete and nearly blacking me out.

"That was disappointing, *chica*," Drake's voice said from...somewhere. "Thought you had more fight in you than that."

Even while the asshole had been talking, I was reaching for another knife. I was just about to grab one when Mateo appeared over top of me and raised his foot above my chest. I crossed my arms at the last second, keeping the full weight of his foot away from my body. My arms were still crushed into my chest, but nothing had been broken. He stepped off my arm and aimed another kick for my head. I rolled away and reached for a knife. I got to my feet and aimed another stab at him. Mateo grabbed my wrist and turned it around my back, launching my arm up and exposing my side. He punched my vulnerable ribs and kidney. Every hit was filled with anger, and if I couldn't stop him soon, he would break every bone in my body, promise to Lucifer or not.

I threw back my far elbow, managing to catch Mateo in the side of the head. He let me go and I spun my recently freed arm in a loose backward punch. It was a sloppy strike, but the back of my fist still crashed into Mateo's cheek. His head snapped to the side, giving me the chance to kick him in the stomach. I still had my knife, so I dove in for the kill—

Just as huge arms looped around my chest and pulled me off the ground. I screamed furiously, lashing and kicking back. The arms tightened and squeezed air out of my lungs. I reversed the grip on my knife and stabbed back, aiming for whatever I could hit.

The knife sank into my captor's bicep. Not a lethal stab like I wanted, but I still got a bark of pain and one of the arms on my chest loosened. I was dropped onto the ground, my fingers slipping from the knife as the big man thrashed. I grabbed the far fingers of his other hand and pulled them away from my chest. I spun under the man's arm while holding it away from me. Drake snarled at me, but I started kicking him in the ribs as hard as I could. He was a huge man, so his body absorbed the kicks pretty well, but it was better than nothing.

At least until I was kicked in the back.

I stumbled from the unexpected hit, and barely had time to lift my head when Drake's fist sailed toward me. The punch connected with my collarbone, sending a fierce wave of pain through it. I lurched back, someone coming up behind me and looping their arms through mine. I tried to slip away, but his grip was too tight. He lifted his arms, bending my shoulders back until they strained in they sockets. I winced and arched my back to relieve the pressure, but it didn't matter.

I was trapped regardless.

Drake's face was contorted in a horrible scowl. I'd never seen him so angry before.

"You fucking bitch," he spat, drawing his fist back.

He practically knocked my head off when the punch hit. I felt my nose break, sharp pain swelling in my face and forcing tears into my eyes. My head lolled forward, but Drake still didn't stop. He pounded hits into my stomach, ribs, chest and face. He was relentless and merciless, each blow hurting more than the last. At first I tried to kick him, tried to break free from Mateo, but soon I was in too much pain to move.

By the time it was over, there wasn't an inch of my front that wasn't battered. Drake finally stepped back, my blood dripping off his knuckles. I slumped forward, watching the ground spin under me. Mateo released my arms and let me collapse onto the ground.

I barely caught myself. My skull felt like it had been covered in cement. My chest might as well have been run over by a tank. My stomach ached every time I breathed, and I felt sick.

Get up, Constance, I told myself. *If you can't fight, you have to run. You barely touched them.*

I bent my knee and tried to get up, but my body just wouldn't respond at the speed I needed it to.

"Sorry you didn't get more shots in," Drake said from behind me. "Kinda got carried away."

"That's fine. I'll do the last bit."

I pushed upward, but a hand clamped onto my shoulder and shoved me back onto the ground. Mateo stepped over me and sat down on my hips. I hissed as the move pulled on the muscles my throbbing stomach, swatting at him weakly. Mateo brushed my hands away and backhanded me across the face. It wasn't as bad as Drake's punches, but pain still flashed through my face as my head twisted to the side.

"Hold her arms," Mateo commanded.

Drake dropped to his knees behind my head, grabbing my arms and pulling them away from my body. I growled and tried to kick and throw Mateo off me, but he positioned himself perfectly to keep that from happening. He just sat there and reached for something on his belt.

I stopped moving completely when he held the knife in front of my face.

This was the first time I fully registered his face. He was as painfully handsome as I remembered.

The last time I saw him, he'd had short hair and stubble, looking more like a soldier than a gangster. He still wore a black t-shirt and dark cargo pants, but his jet-black hair was stylishly smoothed. The stubble was gone, making him look like a bronzed male model until you saw his eyes. They were dark, distant, and hateful. Just as his father's had been. A solid gold chain hung around his neck. A black leather belt looped through his pants, showing off a gold buckle in the shape of a rose. Both had once belonged to Emilio.

I tried to glare at Mateo, but my eyes kept flicking back to the knife. It was so close I could see my breath misting on the silver blade.

"How does it feel, Constance?" he asked coldly. "How do you like being trapped? Knowing something terrible is going to happen to you, and there isn't a fucking thing you can do to stop it?"

He must have been thinking about his father, remembering the fight we'd had before I blew Emilio's brains out. Mateo had watched the whole thing, unable to save someone he loved. His hatred had been growing ever since.

"You didn't ask last time you tortured me," I said bitterly, but quickly. It was the best I could come up with.

Truthfully, I couldn't remember being this scared of Mateo before. Yes, he'd been heartless when he turned me into a punching bag in his father's basement. Yes, he'd been a barbarian when I'd crossed paths with him a month ago and he tried to walk away with my head.

But he'd still loved me when he'd been "forced" to torture me. Adrenaline had been fuelling both of us when we fought last time.

Now I was defenseless against him. Now he loathed me. Now I couldn't fight back, and he had nothing but time on his hands.

"I worked hard for this," Mateo went on, slowly lowering the blade toward my face. "I sent the Blood Thorns to find you. I bribed border guards and cops. I hired the best bounty hunter on the continent. I sided with demons. Now I have you, and you know what the twist is?"

The flat of the knife pressed under my face, just below my eye. I tensed all my muscles, praying that I wouldn't shake and he wouldn't be able to see the fear on my face.

"I don't get to kill you."

Mateo drew the knife back, leaving just a shallow, stinging cut under my eye. I would have slumped with relief, if Drake hadn't been holding my arms.

"But he promised to make you suffer," Mateo continued, reaching into the pocket of his cargo pants. "He said it would take time, and it wouldn't happen the way I wanted it to, but he promised that you'd endure more pain than you could ever imagine."

He held something up between his thumb and middle finger. At first I thought it was a piece of obsidian. It didn't seem that impressive, just a jagged black piece of rock no longer than my pinky finger.

But then I looked closer, and saw that it was nothing that could have been made on earth.

The gleaming black stone had chipped edges, like it had been sawn off a larger rock. Both tips were pointed, sharp enough to stab. Thin red lines creased the shard like broken veins.

Those broken veins were glowing red, as if the obsidian contained a fire so hot it was breaking its casing.

Somehow I knew that's exactly what was

happening. Just as I was pretty sure of where the fire had come from.

"Get that fucking thing away from me," I hissed at my ex-lover, praying he wouldn't hear the tremble in my voice.

"What's wrong, *chica*?" Drake taunted over my head. "You don't like Operation?"

I started twisting and wrenching, my flight or fight instincts kicking in even though my brain knew it was pointless. These two men had me perfectly pinned, and there was no one nearby to help me. If anyone saw what was happening, they would either run for cover, or stand back and watch.

Mateo flipped up the bottom of my shirt with the knife until my stomach was exposed. I started thrashing around worse than ever. I pulled my arms in, hoping the sweat coating my palms would be enough to let me slip out of Drake's grasp. But his hands were iron vices, and he crushed my wrists until I thought he would break the bones inside them.

I hissed when knife sliced a line under my ribcage. This time the cut wasn't shallow. It burned along my upper abdomen, blood sliding around as my body trembled. There was no point in pretending I wasn't terrified. If that was a fragment, whatever it was going to do to me was going to be awful. It was going to hurt.

I wasn't entirely sure it wouldn't kill me.

"You brought this on yourself," Mateo said in a voice dead of emotion.

He pushed the fragment into the open wound.

It was a tiny rock. Small enough that it shouldn't have mattered. A fragment.

Yet it hurt me worse than I could have imagined.

It was like being burned by Lucifer's fire again, but this time I wasn't burning on the outside.

No, all this pain was coming from inside me.

The fragment exploded like a bomb under my ribs, tearing through my body like lightning. Blood turned to lava in my veins and torched my bones. My lungs shriveled inward, crushing to protect themselves rather than let me breathe. My throat was cracked and parched, saliva drying in my mouth. The fire ripped up my spine, so hot I thought it would splinter. My nerves were alight with agony, an enormous pain thrashing through my skull and trying to punch out of my eyes.

I knew I was screaming, but I couldn't hear anything. I thought I would erupt into flames.

The incendiary heat continued to swell and burn, expanding through my body like one giant balloon. Screams choked any attempt at begging for mercy. I couldn't stop crying.

Then the flames curled around my bones like live wires, taking control of me. My skin was hot and wet, as if it was beginning to melt. I tasted smoke in my mouth. Every time I thought I couldn't take any more pain, the fragment burst again and filled me with devastating agony.

I prayed that someone would kill me. Mateo could stab me in the heart or Drake could smash open my head on the concrete, and I would welcome it. Anything would be better than this unbearable torture.

A third wave of anguish rolled through me like a burning tide. My body convulsed violently as the pain redoubled, threatening to turn my entire body into a cinder.

Then the inferno scorched its way through my skull and branded my brain. It was like a burning sword had sliced into my skull. I went blind from the pain, and that was when I started to feel…

… better.

All the pain began to ebb way, each beat of my heart absorbing the torture. Embracing it, accepting it as part of me.

Soon it was gone, and I could breathe again.

I sighed, swallowing deep to drag the smoke back into my lungs. It took my body a long time to relax, but eventually it did. I couldn't feel anything anymore.

I was aware of two men standing over me, but at

the moment, I didn't remember who they were. I didn't care either. They could do whatever they wanted to me, and I'd let them.

Depending on what they had in mind, I might even enjoy it.

"We'll see you again, *chica*," one of them said. "Try not to have too much fun until then."

Sleep was coming heavily over my mind. I still managed a small smile and a slurred response.

"No promises."

Chapter 13

When I woke up, I felt better than I'd ever felt in my whole life.

Sure, I was a little beat up and there was something poking into my ribs, but I focused on the positives.

I was alive, I was awake, and I was ready to do something fun.

I sucked in a breath and sat up. I stretched my legs and stretched my arms behind my back, pulling them together over my head. It hurt a little bit, but pain was okay. I didn't like the itching burn under my ribs though. I dropped my arms to see what was happening there.

There was some blood on the outside of my shirt, but I ignored it and raised my shirt to see where it was coming from.

An angry red line had been zippered just under my ribcage. The skin around it was a disgusting shade of black, and it looked like something was stuck in the cut. I prodded the skin around it with my finger. The injury flashed with heat and pain, and I yanked my hand back.

Okay. Not touching that again.

I dropped my shirt and pushed myself to my feet. More bruises made themselves known as I moved, but I ignored the pain and started dusting down my jeans.

That was when I noticed someone watching me. I looked to my right and saw three people standing in the intersection at the front of the market. Two middle-aged men and a woman. They didn't seem to have any expression that I could register. They were just staring at me.

"You got a problem?" I called to them.

They didn't move. I don't think they even blinked.

"Whatever," I muttered, turning and walking away.

If they wanted to be zombies, they could be zombies. I had better things to do with my time. I had to go... somewhere. Meet up with my sister. I think. Maybe. I didn't really care.

As I walked through the center of the market, I saw the weapons I had dropped during my fight with Drake and Mateo. Drake. Still hated that beef-headed prick. Mateo was a thorn in my side too, no pun intended, but it had been a rush to see him again. No matter how badly I wanted to kill him, I couldn't deny that he still looked as sexy as the first moment I saw him.

Wait, didn't I have a new boyfriend? Why was I thinking about my ex?

I mentally shrugged again. Another thing in my life that didn't matter.

I stopped to pick the weapons up. As I started to lift my head, I noticed five more people approaching from the opposite side of the market. They had the same blank stares as the morons behind me. I tucked my blades away until I was holding only my hatchet and one throwing knife. More figures started revealing themselves from the alleys, some of them even crawling down from apartment windows.

They edged closer, moving with caution but curiosity, the same way they would move if they saw a wounded animal and were debating on putting it out of its misery.

I spun the hatchet lazily in my hand. They continued to close in around me.

"Looks like the market's closed today, folks," I told them. "I don't know why for sure, but let's just assume that all the vendors are dead."

Nobody in the zombie crowd flinched when I said that. I'm not sure if a collective shiver would have been more disturbing than the lifeless eyes boring into my skull at every conceivable angle. And I wasn't going to stick around to find out.

"Okay, my creepiness scale has officially gone off the charts. You all take care now."

I turned and started walking for the spot where the crowd was still semi-spaced out. I shouldered between two construction workers and actually broke away from the circle, until one of them grabbed my wrist.

I jerked to a stop and glared at his hand. Rage burned in my heart. Who the fuck did this asshole think he was, touching me as if he could own me? I didn't belong to him. I didn't belong to anyone.

"If you want to keep that hand, you better take it off me," I warned him.

His hand remained in place.

"You have it," he whispered.

I looked up. He stared at me with the same dead eyes, though they had begun to widen.

"Last chance," I told him.

"You were chosen. You have it."

You can't say I didn't warn him.

I raised my arm and hacked the hatchet down onto his wrist. It was a strong, powerful strike that split apart his skin all the way to the bone. His half-severed hand fell from mine while his scream rang in my ears.

I grinned.

The crowd exploded into chaos.

I turned and bolted, moving onto the sidewalk and running behind the carts. The heavier, clumsier people stumbled and tripped over each other. Sometimes they even dragged the faster runners down with them. Unlucky tumblers were trampled by the rest of the horde.

I laughed.

All two dozen of us ended up in the middle of the main street. I spun on my heel and waited for the first person to reach me. She was a speedy, scrawny little girl who couldn't have been more than sixteen. Maybe she played soccer or ran track in high school.

She damn sure wasn't involved in martial arts. She practically walked into my kick.

Her body crumpled in half and flew back into the

crowd. The effect reminded me of bowling pins. I smiled again. *I'll count that as a strike.*

The crowd turned against the girl, furious that she'd been pushed into them. They started hitting her and pulling her hair. She screamed defiantly and fought back, but she was just skin and bones. No fighting experience would save her from the three men and two women who swarmed her. It wasn't long before her screams of anger turned into screams of fear. It wasn't long before she stopped screaming all together.

One down, twenty-three to go.

The girl wasn't the only one who suffered from accidently bumping into someone. She was just the powder to the keg. Anyone who was shoved would push back twice as hard, and it took seconds for the rest of the crowd to erupt into violence.

Fists flew, bones cracked, and blood sprayed. I could feel my heart pumping with adrenaline, watching the chaos and loving every second of it. I hoped the crowd hadn't forgotten about me.

A man in a suit twisted his head in my direction and left himself open to a strike in the side of the head. Rather than go back at his attacker, he locked eyes with me. I was smaller than him, so he probably thought he had a better chance. I smiled and tucked my knife and hatchet into my belt, then beckoned him. He didn't need a lot of encouragement.

He flew out of the crowd and darted for me, pulling his right fist back way too early. I stood there and smiled until the last possible moment, then twisted around his left side. I curled my arm around his throat while he skidded to a stop, then used his momentum to drag him onto the ground. His head cracked loudly against the pavement, but he was still alive.

For now, at least.

I would have kept going at him, but someone was coming up behind me. I spun around and rocketed my fist into the chin of the woman thinking she had me. Her head snapped back, making it easy to punch her in the throat and kick her away.

The crowd started to realize that I was the real danger here, and began splitting off from their pathetic scuffles to try their luck against a true predator.

The next two that came at me held knives in their bloody hands. I drew my own knife and waited. The smile was still plastered on my face.

The first man who reached me was wearing a grubby shirt and sweats. He must have been homeless once upon a time. His knife looked more like a shank. He stabbed the weapon toward my face. I leaned away, grabbing his wrist and slashing it. He yelped and dropped the weapon.

I turned to his front and kicked his knee, making him stumble forward. He grunted and swung an awkward punch that I smoothly ducked. I ripped the shank from his hand and drove it into his stomach. As he crumpled in pain and shock, I used my knife to stab him in the back of the neck.

He jerked once, then stopped moving all together. I pulled the knife and shank free and flipped both into a reversed grip. The second man was a teenager wearing a flat baseball hat and clothes two sizes too big for him. Maybe he thought dressing like a gangster would make him one. Maybe he thought killing me would prove his toughness.

In the end, it didn't matter. He was still pulling back his knife when I bent my knees and shouldered close. I stabbed both knives into his chest and pulled them down to his ribs. His blood sprayed onto my face as he fell back screaming.

I took a step back and was ready for the next fight when a heavy body slammed into me. I tried to roll away, but my attacker refused to release me. His weight finally turned into his advantage when he pinned me underneath him.

He locked eyes with me, and I noticed that he wasn't that unattractive. Dark hair, dark eyes, nice lips, nice skin. Sure, he wasn't a closet male model like Mateo, and he wasn't even close to the realm of sexiness that Warrick conquered...

But I still wanted him.

And he wanted me.

With my arms pinned at my side, I couldn't stop him from snapping his head down and kissing me. He forced his tongue into my mouth, pushing it around like he was looking for hidden treasure. I let him play around my mouth for a couple seconds before I decided to get rough. I caught his bottom lip in my teeth and bit down hard.

He yelped and pulled back, and I just bit down harder. Soon I could taste his blood.

The man finally tore away from me. Blood dribbled down his chin as he scowled menacingly at me. Somehow I was *still* smiling, even when he pulled back his fist to hit me.

The strike never connected, because the man's arm was grabbed. He whipped his head around, and had his face punched so hard I swore I heard every bone in it crack. The man toppled off me, completely unconscious. Another man knelt down beside me, reaching down to cup my face in his hands.

I smiled seductively at Warrick and looped my arms around his neck.

"Hey, handsome."

He seemed torn, like he was fighting every urge he ever knew. "We need to get out of here." Instead of draping himself over me like I wanted, he scooped me up and pulled me to my feet. I staggered onto my feet and looked over his shoulder to the riot.

The crowd was pushing forward, aiming for his back. Aiming for me.

I unwrapped myself from Warrick and shoved him away, rushing the crowd. I heard him shouting my name, him and other voices I knew, but I ignored them and threw myself at the crowd.

The first woman to reach me had a butcher knife, oblivious to the two blades I was holding. She shoved the wide knife at my face, but I spun around her back. I kicked the chest of the man behind her to get more space, then turned to her and stabbed the tops of her shoulders. She stiffened and screamed, but I was still moving. I swung around and drove both of my knives into her throat. Blood sprayed and when I pulled my knives back. She dropped to the ground and stopped moving.

It was impossible to keep track of the people I was stabbing. Every time I saw a hand curled around a weapon, I struck first. Shallow cuts traced along my lower back and arms and ribs, but they were paper cuts compared to what I was doing. The occasional fist caught me off balance, but I wasn't feeling any pain.

I was fighting, I was killing, and I was having the time of my life.

Two more bodies threw themselves into the remaining crush, using their hands and feet to push attackers away from me. I stopped smiling as I saw Sephiel glide in front of me, knocking away punches with ease. Once he had the space, he whirled a powerful roundhouse kick that took down two men at once. Warrick was at my right side, forcing people back with single, powerful hits. Before I could figure out why they weren't killing anyone, he spun on his heel, grabbed my waist, and started taking me out of the crowd.

It took effort not to stab him. I screamed and kicked, desperate to get back in the fight and get more blood on my knives. The only reason I wasn't attacking Warrick was because deep down, something told me that he mattered to me.

But God, was I ever tempted to ignore those feelings.

"Seph!" Warrick shouted. "Get back here!"

The red-haired angel obeyed, turning toward us. Half of the crowd collapsed behind him, and the rest were fighting each other without restraint. Warrick's grip loosened just enough for me to slip out of his arms. I tried to run, but he spun around and caught me again.

"Constance! Stop!"

"Fuck you!" I screamed back. "Let me go!"

"Con!"

Her voice cut through the violent haze that had taken over my mind. I looked over my shoulder and saw the only person I ever really listened to.

Dro stood a couple feet back with Max, who was holding the *movens caeli* in his hands. He stared at the crowd with wide, horrified eyes, but my sister was entirely focused on me. There was something different about her. Physically, there was nothing out of place. She was still wearing the same oversize green sweater, dirty jeans, and ratty boots. Her skin and hair were still paper white, and she still held her regal beauty.

But her eyes were maelstroms, wide with horror and shock, glistening with disbelief and sadness.

The urge to kill was still threatening to overwhelm me, but now something else was breaking through. Slowly, I was beginning to realize what was happening, and that was when the pain hit again.

I dropped the knife and the shank and doubled over to clutch my upper abdomen, a crippling burn slicing through it and leaving me breathless. I dug my fingers into Warrick's arm so hard that my nails broke his skin.

"Constance?" his hand smoothed over my back. Either he didn't notice that I was hurting him, or he didn't care. "What's wrong?"

Before I could tell him that my body was burning from the inside out, Sephiel shouted in pain.

It caught all our attention. He almost always avoided injury in battle. With a few exceptions when the pain was too horrific for even us to comprehend, Sephiel almost never made any sound to suggest that he was in pain.

But that had been when he was an angel. Now he's human.

I couldn't see what was wrong until he turned around. That was when I noticed the blood spreading from the wound on his side. He'd been stabbed.

Warrick shouted something to Max. I was too stunned and in too much pain to hear what it was. Soon I was being moved into Max's arms while Warrick ran for the fight to rescue Sephiel. I looked around frantically, seeing that the crowd had begun to grow. People had been hearing the fight from other areas of the city, and were being drawn to the commotion. The excitement of a fight was beginning to grow in their eyes. As they moved closer, they weren't just staring at Warrick, who had managed to grab Sephiel and was dragging him back.

They were looking at me.

Warrick and Sephiel stopped beside us. Both men were breathing heavily, and Sephiel was grimacing in pain.

"Get us out of here Max," Warrick commanded, reaching into his leather jacket to take out a handgun.

"I'm trying," insisted the prophet. "It's not working; we must have used the last of its power when we came back here." He tightened his grip on me. "We're trapped."

He was right. Everywhere I looked, there were hungry eyes locked on us. Eventually all of the stares turned in my direction, and their brisk walk turned into a jog. There had to be at least forty people in this sudden flash-mob, and they were literally tripping over themselves to get to us.

There was no way we could escape. Not unless they had what they wanted.

The fragment lodged inside of me.

Just thinking about it sent another wave of pain through me. I choked on a scream and dropped to my knees, gasping for breath. Max fell with me, putting his hand on the back of my neck. He must have sensed something with his gift, because he suddenly recoiled.

"Oh my God," he breathed.

I hunched over and grabbed my stomach, wishing I could drown out the roar of the crowd. Warrick's arms curled around my back and pulled me into an embrace. I rested my head against his chest and breathed in his pine scent.

The pain worsened, and I nearly screamed again.

The footsteps were getting closer. I couldn't fight. I couldn't even fucking stand. I was going to be torn apart by this crowd, and my friends were going to die trying to save me. Even against the agony scorching through my veins, I could still feel my heart breaking at the thought.

That was when someone stepped forward, brushing past me and standing in front of the crowd.

"Please," Dro begged them. "Don't do this."

For a single, perfect second, I thought the crowd was going to listen to her. They had all gone silent, all of them looking at Dro. I thought she had gotten through to them, that they'd heard the tender pleading of her voice, or seen the desperation on her eyes. I thought they had forgotten about me, and the horrible power I was carrying inside my body.

Then the fire surged through me in one violent burst. The pain covered my body in one savage rush, so hot I could feel it splintering my bones and melting over my heart. I clutched my chest and screamed.

The crowd broke into a run.

I didn't see it all. I was fading in and out of consciousness, unable to take the torture the fragment was putting me through. But I heard Max shout in alarm. I felt heat outside of my body. I saw the blast of light coming from my sister. I smelled the scorched hair and burned flesh.

In seconds, it was over. The light faded and the heat dulled. The next sounds were screams and moans of pain. The group surrounding me was silent.

I was burning, Warrick holding me as tightly as he could, as if it would shield me from pain, but I managed to turn my head just enough to see what had happened.

Blackened bodies lay on the ground in front of Dro, smoke still rising from their torched flesh. Some of them writhed and shivered. Others didn't move at all. Dro stood above them all, dropping her hands to her side. I blinked, certain that I was imagining it. My little sister would never do this, not even pushed. Hurting people was involuntary for her. She never meant it, and would never initiate it.

Yet every time I opened my eyes, there she was, standing over her destruction with a straight back and a seemingly calm demeanor.

What has she done?

It seemed like forever before Dro turned around. When she did, it was a fast motion that startled Warrick. He jumped once, sending another jolt of pain through me. Dro didn't seem to notice. She dropped to her knees in front of me and reached out to touch me.

Warrick's arms tensed around me, as if he didn't trust her hands now that she'd used them so violently. But her hands lit up with their familiar gold glow, and she touched my arm.

I'd always hated the pins and needles feeling that came with her healing. This was a thousand times worse.

The sensation amplified a hundred fold, every tingle becoming a drill. My nerves practically started exploding, piercing each cell and splitting my skull.

I had a twisted talent for being able to take a lot of pain. But all of this– the bruises, the broken bones, the stabs, the heartache, the flaming fragment– was too much.

"*Stop stop stop!*" I screamed.

It was a hoarse, choking sound that barely escaped my throat, but made Dro recoil as if she'd been bitten by a snake.

"Can't..." was the only other word I could get out.

The group sat around me, breathing in the sour smell of burned flesh. I just lay there in Warrick's arms, wishing I would die.

"Lift up her shirt," Max whispered. His voice trembled.

"What the fuck did you just say?" Warrick snapped.

"I felt it... I felt... Just trust me. Dro can't help her, because of..."

Max knows.

Sephiel, still clutching his wounded side, knelt down in front of me. He lifted the bottom of my shirt, drawing it up to the edge of my bra.

"What..." Warrick choked out. He held me tighter.

"It cannot be..." Sephiel breathed.

Dro started crying.

I shouldn't have looked down, but I did. I regretted it immediately.

The blackness surrounding the cut along my middle had spread like a cancer, stretching from the wound to my belly button and the underside of my breasts. It was like a layer of my skin had been replaced with poisonous smoke.

The wound itself had somehow cauterized, the scar glowing like a burning ember.

"Sephiel," Dro sobbed. "What do we do?"

The ex-angel shook his head. "I do not know," he said grimly. "I have never seen anything like this."

"There has to be something," Warrick said. His voice sounded weak, nothing like him.

"Only Andromeda has the ability to heal her, and I am not sure either of their bodies will be able to handle the pressure that healing this wound requires."

Warrick held me closer. Dro cried beside him.

Max hissed sharply. Out of the corner of my eye, I could see him clutching his head. He took a couple deep breaths, then relaxed. He stared at me again with wide, hopeful eyes.

"Wait," he said. "I got a flash. I think someone else can help us."

"Who?" Dro demanded, getting to her feet. "Who?!"

"There's a woman with an herb shop nearby who saw the..." he cast a nervous glance at Dro, "the riot. She knows about this stuff. I saw her helping Constance."

"Then let's go," Warrick said. He was already picking me up. I was too weak to stand on my own.

"Max, I do not doubt your sixth sense, but is it wise to bring something as dangerous as the fragment to a woman who could know of it?"

"Fuck wisdom, Sephiel!" Warrick shouted. "She's

dying!" The demon slayer snapped his head at Max. "Which way?"

Max closed his eyes and concentrated for a moment. He opened his eyes and looked at Dro.

"Do you know where *Heirbas de María* is?"

I couldn't see Dro, but I assumed she nodded because Warrick began moving. The sudden sharp motions were too much for my tortured body to handle, and I could feel darkness creeping over my mind. I closed my eyes and tried to breathe in Warrick's smell, but all I could think about was the burning flesh we were leaving behind.

What did she do?

Chapter 14

The angry, snapping sound of a fist on a screen door jolted me awake. I hated myself for moving, because it meant a fresh wave of agony rushing through my body. I'd passed out on the way to this herb shop, so I had forgotten how brutal the fire corroding my insides was.

Now the pain was back, and it was making me pay for forgetting about it.

The second I opened my eyes, the fragment lodged under my ribcage burst with merciless heat, as if someone had lit a flare under my ribs. I choked on a scream and squeezed my eyes shut again. Sweat was plastered to my face, and something warm leaked from my eyes. I hoped it was tears.

"Open up! Please, we need help!" Dro was screaming. She was the one pounding on the door.

"She's burning up," Warrick muttered. "Are you sure this is the place?"

"Positive," Max replied.

"We must enter the premises before attention is drawn to us," Sephiel said. His voice was obscured, as if he was talking with his back to me. "Our location lacks anything resembling cover. I suspect it shall not be long before demons or corrupted are alerted to our presence."

Dro must have heard what Sephiel said, because she began slamming on the door harder than ever.

"Please open up! *Please!*"

Finally, the door creaked open. I rolled my head just enough to see who was standing behind the screen door.

The woman was old, in her sixties. She wore a loose grey sweater and a flowing black skirt. Her hair was mousy and mostly grey, though I could still see some streaks of black in it. Wrinkles creased around her eyes and the corners of her thin mouth. She looked like a frail, thin woman, but her eyes were sharp and intelligent. Those eyes scanned our entire group with alarm and mistrust. She stared at me, her eyes narrowing.

"I'm not a doctor," the old woman said, her voice rasped from age and perhaps too many cigarettes, "which is what she needs."

The old woman began closing the door, but Dro slammed her hand on it again.

"She has a fragment inside her!"

I hated that Dro was so forward about it, but damned if it didn't make the woman pause. She stared at Dro, then looked at me again. This time her eyes were filled with curiosity, and unease.

"Then you know what that means, and you can't bring her here. I'm not risking my life for someone with the ultimate corruption stuck in her."

The woman's voice was tough, but I heard the fear underneath it. Anyone who knew about the fragment would understand how deadly it was to have around, and would want to be as far from it as humanly possible.

She started closing the door again, but Dro suddenly grabbed the handle on the screen door and yanked it open sharply. The woman stepped back.

"You're the only chance she has," Dro pleaded. "We don't have anywhere else to go, and I... I can't help her." Dro's voice trembled. "Please! Please, I'll do anything!"

"It doesn't matter what you will or won't do," the woman said reasonably. "If you had any idea what a fragment does to a person, you'd know that I don't want to touch it at all. I don't know how you found me or why you came here, but I can't help you. I'm sorry."

She started to close the door in Dro's face. Dro's hand shot out and forced it open again. The woman stared at her with surprised eyes. No one would look at Dro and expect such aggression from her.

I certainly hadn't.

"I'm asking nicely," Dro told her, "but I killed over forty people to bring her here. One more won't make a difference to me."

I had to be hearing things. There was no way my little sister would say anything like that, even if I were dying. She was a saint, all about kindness and compassion, she was...

She's part demon. She's Lucifer's daughter.

No. That didn't matter. She was still Dro. She was just desperate. When she was desperate, she lost control. That was all this was, desperation turning itself into anger. At least she had the decency to try reason. I would have skipped the pleasantries and gone straight for the demands.

But those people in the square, she killed them without making more pleas. She just stood there and stared at them, then moved on like it didn't matter. Like dozens of people aren't dead on the street because of her.

What's happened to her?

Fire lanced through my blood, shocking my nerves and igniting every pain receptor I had. I shivered and curled into Warrick. His arms must have been aching from carrying me for so long, but he refused to put me down. All he did was shift his weight, and hold me closer.

I blinked past the blur of agony swimming through my head, and looked at the old woman standing in the doorway. She was staring at my sister with nervous eyes. That could only mean that Dro's face was gravely serious. She wouldn't let this stranger question her power, and we must have been close enough for her to see the remnants of Dro's fire in the square. If the wind got strong enough, she'd be able to smell the death just down the street.

Everyone knew Dro was different when they looked at her. When you lived in a city full of demons and murderers, different wasn't something to be trusted.

It was something to be feared.

The old woman took a deep breath and sighed it out.

"Fine," she said. She stepped back and pulled

away the door. "But hurry up. The sooner I get this over with, the better. It's not going to be pretty."

Warrick was the first person through the door with me. Dro, Max and Sephiel followed quickly so the woman could close and lock the door. Max was the only one who thanked her.

"Take her to the back room and put her on the couch."

Warrick obeyed, and I felt my legs pushing aside a thin, fabric curtain. Even that single, tiny brush sent a painful tingle through my legs to my stomach and chest. Warrick gently laid me down onto a fabric couch that felt hard and smelled musty. My body naturally stretched out, and I felt like I was being pulled apart on a medieval rack.

Warrick moved around to the top of my head. Dro knelt by my right shoulder. I couldn't see Sephiel or Max, but I thought they were standing by the door.

The woman scurried around the room. Bottles and jars clinked together. Something that sounded like cutlery scraped across wood. I wasn't able to see what she was doing, and it was driving me insane. I stared at the ceiling, trying to get a better idea of where I was.

The area reminded me of a storage room. Stained and pockmarked tiles covered the ceiling with yellow spotlights stuck in every other one. The walls were peeling egg white plaster that met a cold concrete floor smothered by a burgundy shag rug.

When the woman came back, her arms were draped with gauze. She had a shallow bowl in one hand, a scalpel and two sets of forceps in the other.

"What are those for?" Warrick asked. His voice was tight with mistrust.

"The skin over the fragment has healed over," the woman said, kneeling beside Dro. "It needs to be cut out of her. She's resisting, so it hasn't been completely fused into her blood, but it's breaking down and trying to force its way into her bloodstream. If we don't get it out now and she keeps fighting its influence, it's going to rip her insides to literal shreds."

"How do you know this?" Max asked.

The woman paused. "I knew someone who had a fragment in them. I saw what it did to their body afterward."

From the way she sounded, it had been someone she loved. She wasn't going to give us any more information than that, and I couldn't say I blamed her.

"Do you have some kind of anesthetic?" Dro asked. Her hand was close to my body, but she wasn't touching me. She was probably afraid to.

"It's too risky. The fragment is a parasite, and any kind of sedative risks provoking it." The woman looked directly into my eyes. "It truly is amazing she's resisted this long."

As she was staring at me, a blast of pain shot through me. I winced and twisted on the couch. I could feel the fragment beginning to splinter inside me, cutting into my organs and slicing open my veins.

"Just get it out!" I screamed.

"Hold her down," the woman said.

Warrick put his hands on my shoulders. Someone else pinned my legs to the couch. They were strong, so I assumed it was Sephiel. Max wouldn't have the stomach for this.

I felt the cool air on my skin as my shirt was lifted to my chest. There was a dull swish of water, and then the woman was pressing her hand onto my stomach. I hissed and bit back another scream.

"Keep her as still as possible."

That was the last thing the woman said before the scalpel cut open my newest scar.

The blade was freezing against my burning body, and I bucked reflexively. Warrick and Sephiel were still strong enough to hold me onto the couch until the wound was open. I didn't scream again until she placed the icy forceps in the wound and pushed it apart. The smell of copper and sulfur slipped into the air.

"It hasn't gotten very far," the woman said. "But I

can't reach it with her shaking like this. Someone else has to do it."

"I will," Dro volunteered without hesitation.

Dro's long hair tickled my stomach as she leaned over me. "I'm sorry about this, big sister."

The fingers of her free hand hesitantly touched mine. I grabbed her hand desperately, and that was when she dug the medical tweezers inside my wound. The pain coursing through me was too much, and I blacked out. The welcoming darkness didn't last, because I woke up what must have been a couple seconds later.

Dro was still leaning over me, pulling the bloody forceps out of my abdomen. She held the fragment in between them. The blood made the black, red-veined shard slippery, and the piece of Hell slipped out of the metal grip.

She acted reflexively, before I could tell her not to. Dro's hand shot out and cupped the fragment as it fell.

It stayed in her hands for only a couple seconds. She stared at it with wide eyes, turning even paler than usual. I squeezed her hand so sharply I swore her bones creaked. Dro jumped and dropped the fragment onto the ground. As it fell, I was certain it began to disintegrate into ash.

"I'm going to clean the wound," the woman said, lifting the shallow bowl. "This is going to make her pass out, and then we can work from there."

I wasn't sure what she meant until she took the bowl and poured it over my stomach.

The fire was replaced with a cold so intense I was certain it was freezing my blood. The water had to have been holy water, because the raw chill clashed into the fragment's damage and extinguished it. I felt like a candle being snuffed out between someone's fingertips.

The woman was right. I couldn't handle any more pain. The last sparks of pain snapped across my body, and dragged me into inescapable blackness.

***

The world was a hazy dream when I woke up. I didn't know where I was or how I'd gotten here. My entire body felt like a bruise. I wondered if my outside looked as bad as my inside.

"I'm sorry, Constance."

My little sister was close to me, her hand still tightly clasping mine. I wanted to speak, to move, to open my eyes, but my body refused to do any of those things. All I could do was listen.

"For everything," she went on. "Max didn't see what was happening to you until it was too late, and by the time we got there…" She took a deep breath. I could almost see the tears on her face.

"I made a huge mistake. When those people rushed us, I knew we wouldn't escape. I didn't know what else to do, so I… I let him in Con. I thought about what Lucifer would do, and that's what I did."

Even though I was virtually comatose, the ramifications of that slammed into me like a truck. Sending out that kind of energy, killing that many people, was a gateway for Lucifer. Finding Dro would be easy for him now.

But worse than that, was knowing she'd assumed there was no other choice. She hadn't thought about giving Max a little more time, or having Sephiel cut a path through the crowd to get us to safety. She hadn't even considered my warnings or tried using her fading angel powers.

She went straight for the kill, like a lion going for a gazelle's throat.

Over forty people were dead because my sister wasn't able to resist the devil on her shoulder.

That was the thought that gave my body strength. That was the reason my hand twitched, why my elbow bent, and why my shoulder swung just enough to take my hand from Dro's.

I wished I would wake up. I didn't hate Dro for what she'd done, but we needed to talk about it face to face. I tried to focus some of that strength back into my body so I could sit up, but it refused to co-operate. I couldn't even get my jaw moving so I could tell her to stay.

"I'm sorry," she whispered again with cracks in her voice. It wouldn't be long before she broke completely.

"I want this to be over. I'm tired of these powers controlling me, tired of the pain they bring you and everyone else. I'm tired of being a burden. But I can't even blame Lucifer for this, because it's my fault. I was conscious of everything I was doing, and I didn't try to stop it. I can't fight this anymore, Connie. I couldn't even save you."

The paralysis clouding my mind weighed on me like cement, pinning me to the couch and forcing me to listen to my sister cry. I tried to move my hanging arm, to touch her hand and let her know that I was still here, that I always would be. We'd find a way to deal with this, and eventually move past it. We'd find a way to beat Lucifer. We'd overcome this like we did everything else.

But I couldn't move. I couldn't speak. I couldn't see. I might as well have been a corpse in a casket at a funeral viewing.

It was too long before Dro stopped crying. She breathed heavily, gasping until air flowed steadily into her. I heard her rise from the chair beside me.

"I'm so sorry, Constance. I don't know if you can forgive me for this, and if you don't... then I'll understand."

Light footsteps padded toward the door. It creaked open, then clicked shut, and I was left in silence.

I felt nothing but heartache until sleep took me over, and I dreamed of Lucifer.

There wasn't much to the dream. There was no blood or fire or torture or death. It was just me standing on the hilltop by the Heaven Gate. I looked down to see two figures standing in front of the blazing forest. The flames stretched across the entire horizon while smoke poisoned the sky. But all I could focus on was the two people in front of it, standing hand in hand.

Lucifer and Dro.

Lucifer spoke four words to me before everything went black again. Four simple words that pierced my soul sharper than any blade.

You have lost her.

Chapter 15

My next dream was a million times better than the previous one.

I was lying on comfortable couch, relieved of pain, a warm blanket and a strong arm resting over my chest. I turned my head and saw Warrick sleeping heavily beside me. I smiled and touched his hand as it rested on my shoulder. I clasped it and rolled onto my side, watching him sleep peacefully. I reached over and moved some of his hair away from his eyebrows. It was getting long.

Warrick stirred at my touch, shifting his face against the couch and sighing once before opening his eyes. They began to widen when he saw that I was awake. It made me smile.

"Hey–"

The word was barely past my lips before Warrick leaned in and kissed me.

I breathed out against him, letting his kiss blot out the rest of the world as his strong arms circled me. Warrick pressed me to his chest and deepened the kiss. I inhaled the scent of pine needles and manliness, and felt his heart beating against my chest.

He finally pulled away to breathe, though I nearly tugged him back. One of Warrick's hands smoothed down the side of my face. He looked lost and worried.

"Are you okay?"

"Much better now," I replied with a smirk.

Warrick's expression never changed.

"When we found you..." he trailed off. His hand moved through my hair. "We didn't know what to do. We thought we were going to lose you."

I snuggled closer to him, resting my head on his shoulder. "Why do you keep saying 'we'? You're the only person here."

His hand paused. "What are you talking about?"

"This dream," I clarified. "You're the only one in it."

Warrick pushed back so he could look in my eyes. "You're not dreaming, Constance."

I stopped smiling. I should have known that. Warrick had felt too warm and too real to be a dream, and it was wonderful to be back in reality with him.

Except... I was back in reality. That meant bloodthirsty demons and vengeful angels. That meant a sadistic bounty hunter and a murderous ex-boyfriend.

That meant a dangerous sister I was likely going to end up dying for.

That meant three innocent people dead at my hand.

I pushed away from Warrick and sat up on the couch. He sat up slowly and watched me carefully.

"What's wrong?"

I couldn't stop the memories from flooding back into my mind. Being attacked by Mateo and Drake. The unbearable pain of the fragment. I slapped my hand to my stomach, then pulled up my shirt. There was an angry red line across my abdomen. My pulse quickened.

"Where is it?" I whispered shakily. "Is it still in me?"

Warrick took my hand away from my stomach. I hated that it was trembling. His free hand cupped my chin and lifted my head so I could meet his eyes.

"No, Constance. They took it out, remember?"

Warrick was being honest, but my brain refused to believe him. I pulled away from his hands and pulled my shirt up again. I felt the red, rigid line. It was still tender, but the only lump I felt was from the scarring tissue. There was no hard fragment embedded under my skin. Nothing to manipulate my mind and make me do unspeakable things.

I pulled my knees up to my chest and wrapped my arms around them. I didn't look at Warrick.

"Tell me what happened," I said. "Tell me every

fucking thing."

He watched me for another moment, then drew his legs up onto the cushions and rested his forearms on his knees.

"We went to the last house we stayed in. We weren't there for more than five minutes before Max had a vision. He saw you being attacked, and said we had to go back. The *movens caeli* wasn't working properly, and Sephiel said it wasn't charged enough, but Dro refused to take no for an answer. We got it working and went back to the street the demons attacked us." He looked uncomfortable, and angry. "That was when we heard the riot. We followed the noise, and found you."

I tightened my arms around my legs. It all flashed back to me. The adrenaline rush from the madness, the pleasure I felt knowing that I had something they all wanted, and they couldn't take it from me. Feeling the knives in my hands and the warm blood on my face, and wondering where I could find my next victim.

"The rest you know," he said. "But you've been asleep for a couple days. The fragment took a lot out of you, and Maria's allowed us to stay here."

I looked at Warrick. "What's happened?"

He sighed. "No one's seen or heard anything of Carver, Elle, or Jackson, but Michael and his archangels are moving through the city. Sephiel's seen them on scouting missions. He says they're looking for any place populated with demons or corrupted, and trying to find the fragments."

I shivered just from hearing the stupid word. Warrick shifted closer to me.

"They can't touch the fragment," I said. "I don't know what kind of damage it could do if they just put their hands on it, and if it gets inside them…"

I couldn't imagine what sort of slaughter an angel was capable of if a piece of the Hell Key as placed inside them. I didn't want to.

"How did it get inside you?" Warrick asked carefully. I could tell from his voice that he didn't want to prod me, but the truth was going to come out sooner or later. If he knew now, at least he'd be prepared.

"Drake and Mateo found me. They have the fragments."

Warrick went completely still. "They did this to you?" His whisper was laced with fury.

"They put the fragment in me, but they didn't force me to go berserk. I did that on my own. I killed three innocent people."

Saying it made it true, and I needed it to be. It felt like a kick in the stomach, but I deserved to feel the guilt and the pain. Those people had their minds twisted by the demonic presence corroding the city, but I was the one who held the knife. I'd been possessed before, and while it had been agonizing, I'd at least had the strength to fight back. I might not have been able to beat that demon, but my will had been there.

The will had been there this time, but it had made me do terrible things. My hands had never been clean, never would be clean, but I had a line that I built when I started with the Blood Thorns. No pets, children, pregnant women, and no innocents. The rules wouldn't save my soul, but they'd been enough for me to sleep at night.

Now someone's father was dead. A mother was never going to see her son again. I stabbed without remorse or regret. I'd sent a teenage girl into a crowd to be torn apart by savages. And I'd smiled through the whole fucking thing.

I didn't know I was shaking until Warrick put his arm around my shoulder and drew me closer.

"Constance, listen to me. The fragment took you over. That's what it does. Nobody could resist it. What happened wasn't your fault–"

I pushed him away roughly. "Don't give me that shit," I snapped. "This wasn't like when I was possessed and knew something else was controlling me. I knew what I was doing, and I didn't care!"

"Because the fragment was screwing with your head–"

"Is that supposed to make it better?!" I was shouting now. "I killed those people, started that damn riot, and provoked Dro to–"

I stopped when I realized that was something else I was going to have to live with. I drew the crowd to me, welcomed them, and let them surround me. That was when Dro gave up on control and killed them. If I'd resisted, if I'd tried, I would have been able to save even some of them. Even one...

"Every time you resisted, the fragment started to kill you," Warrick said softly. I wasn't sure if I'd spoken my last thoughts aloud, or if he'd simply become too good at reading me. Warrick was the only man I knew who could look both angry and depressed at the same time.

"I would rather have you alive and feeling guilty than not having you alive at all."

"That's sweet," I said bitterly. "Tell that to the families of the three people I butchered."

The shock on his face was so vivid that I couldn't look at him any longer. I turned my head away so he wouldn't see the tears growing in my eyes. Warrick had seen me break down before, and I didn't want him to see it again.

But I couldn't hold it in.

The fear and guilt, the things Dro had said to me, the dream of Lucifer, knowing Mateo and Drake had violated me in the worst possible way... It was too much to bear. I was a ship being dashed on the rocks, breaking apart and taking on too much water. I cursed the tears that slid down my cheeks when I blinked.

Warrick stared at me for a long time, still wearing his angry/sad expression. Then out of the corner of my eye, I saw his arm lift and move toward my back. I started edging away.

"Don't," I warned.

Warrick didn't listen. He slowly circled his arms around my body. I pressed my hands against his chest, trying to shove him back. Either his arms were made of iron, or I wasn't as strong as I should have been.

"Stop it," I tried again, my voice faltering the closer I got to him.

Finally, he cupped the back of my neck and dipped my head to his chest.

"That's enough."

If he'd shouted at me, sounded aggressive, or started a fight, I wouldn't have listened. I would have bolted from the bed and sulked on my own. But right now I knew I was safe, that someone cared about me despite all the horrible things I had just done.

He kissed the top of my head, then left his lips there and sighed.

"I love you," he whispered.

My heart skipped a beat, and I lifted my head to look into Warrick's eyes. They were bright and sparkling, green stars in the dark room. It had been so long since someone had said those words to me that I nearly forgot what they meant. I couldn't think of anything to say, so Warrick continued.

"I loved you from the moment I met you."

My pulse was still racing, and it was hard for me to think of a reply. All I came up with was, "I was possessed when you met me."

Warrick chuckled, a deep warm sound that relaxed my muscles and filled my chest with something other than pain.

"I meant when I met the real you. All attitude and sarcasm, refusing to let anyone stand in your way and running over them when they did. Never giving up and willing to take on the world alone. Fighting for us and trying to convince us you weren't a good person."

"I'm not," I muttered.

Warrick's hand stroked my hair. "Yes, you are." His eyes were filled with trust, admiration, and love. Everything I didn't deserve, he was willingly giving to me.

"You're just a darker kind of good."

I let myself fall under his spell. I let myself believe that everything would be all right. I was here with

Warrick, and the world was locked behind the back room's door.

I kissed Warrick a little harder than I intended, but he responded eagerly. I opened his mouth with mine to taste him, desperate to keep him close. I'd pushed him away before, and now I wondered what could have possibly made me do so.

You love him, and that means you're going to lose him. Just like you lost Dro.

I faltered during the kiss, and Warrick noticed. Before he could ask what was wrong, I grabbed his shirt collar and pulled him on top of me. By the time he steadied himself, I was kissing him again. I threaded my fingers through his shaggy hair, pulling his head closer to mine. It was an effort for him to pull his head back so he could breathe.

Anything he was going to say was cut off when I started grabbing at his shirt. He got the hint and pulled it off, pushing mine over my head. He pressed his muscular chest against mine, his skin hot with desire. Warrick's lips trailed down from my mouth to my neck, to my chest, to the scar on my abdomen. I tensed when he touched it, but the gentle kiss he placed on it took away my unease. He pulled back and I sat up, pressing my body against his and wrapping my legs around his hips. Warrick's hand brushed through my hair.

"You're so beautiful," he breathed.

"Less talk, more action," I sighed.

Warrick grinned, as if he expected me to say that.

I didn't have time to be surprised. Soon there was nothing between us but skin, and pleasure so intense I thought my brain would explode from it. Everything melted away, leaving only my lips on Warrick's, his hands on my body, the two of us pressed together.

It was too soon before we were both spent, Warrick lying on top of me while I wrapped my arms around his back and clung to his warmth. I would have stayed there forever, holding the man I was falling in love with and never worrying about anything else.

But then I looked over and saw the door, and remembered all my problems would break it down sooner or later.

***

I left Warrick sleeping in the back room. He would be awake soon enough. We couldn't stay here and endanger the makeshift doctor, Maria. We had to find the rest of the fragments to destroy them.

How we were going to do that was beyond me, but that was why I was awake, and looking for her.

I pushed aside cheap red drapes and finally figured out where I was. It wasn't just an herbalist's shop. It was an occult shop.

The shelves that lined the walls of the storefront were cluttered with bottles. They seemed fairly organized– there was a shelf for powders, another for herbs, and another filled with bottled liquids. Dream catchers hung from tacks on another shelf, books forming a crooked peak next to them. Under the glass of the front counter were dozens of charms and *calavera* skulls.

The woman stood behind the counter, furiously rearranging her books. She looked like she was moving for the sake of motion, though I wasn't going to judge her. She helped save my life.

My thoughts went back to Dro, and the awful mess I'd made with her while I was half-awake. I needed to fix that soon. But first I needed to know more about the fragment.

I reached out to rap the doorframe with my knuckles.

"I know you're there," said Maria. "Might as well skip the knock and come in."

I did as she said, stifling a laugh.

"Guess you found the food and clothes and cleaned yourself up?"

"Yeah," I replied. When I left the back room to use the bathroom, there had been a collection of protein bars, a bottle of water, and clothes on top of the sink. I almost choked on the protein bars, I inhaled them so fast.

I plucked at the hem of the black, form-fitting V-neck shirt, glancing down at the skinny black pants and dark grey, lace up boots that went to my knees. I was also wearing a slate grey leather moto jacket. It looked sleeker than my tattered lucky jacket, but it was tighter in the shoulders and would have to be cut so I could fight in it. I had liked my lucky jacket because it was bigger, and gave me more flexibility and movement.

Stupid that I missed something so small, but that jacket had seen me through some wretched times. Given how most of my clothes ended up, I doubted this one would be able to withstand the damage I'd be bringing it.

Before dressing, I'd taken a quick shower to wash off all the blood and dirt from my fights. Dro had healed me while I was asleep/unconscious, so the only mark that remained on my body was the scar on my abdomen where the fragment had gone in. My weapons had been recovered and were back on my body– four knives sheathed to a harness at my ribs, two in my boots, and my hatchet on my hip. It felt good to be clean, dressed, healed, and armed again.

"Thanks," I added.

Maria nodded, but still didn't look at me. "They belonged to my daughter. She was about the same size as you."

The hint of sadness in her voice reminded me of the way she'd sounded on her doorstep, when she learned I had the fragment in my stomach. I couldn't help but wonder if her daughter was the reason she knew so much about the fragments.

Then again, maybe her daughter was the person I tossed into a murderous crowd. I knew better than to ask.

"Pretty neat shop you have," I said, glancing around it again. "Where did you get all this stuff?"

"My family has dealt with the supernatural since before you were born," she told me, sliding books onto the shelf over her head. "This shop belonged to them."

"Were they demon slayers?" Warrick and Carver's slayer team was the only ones I knew of, but there had to be more.

"Some of my uncles were," she said. "Most of the women in my family focused on learning and the spiritual aspects of it all." Maria placed the last book on the shelf then turned to look at me. "But we both know you didn't come out here to talk about my family history, so why don't you get to the point?"

I raised my eyebrows at her, not sure what switch I flicked to make her so snarly. Maria put her hands on her hips and gave me a curt look.

"While you were passed out, your friends filled me in on what was happening. I know all about you and your situation." Her eyes were stormy. "I know what your sister is running from."

My blood went cold. I was going to have a serious talk with whoever spilled our secrets to this stranger.

"Fine," I said, folding my arms over my chest. "Tell me everything you know about the fragments, and how to destroy them."

Maria's dark eyes held mine as if to judge how serious I was. Then she turned to the shelf and picked out a notebook from it. She flipped through the pages until she found what she was looking for, then rested it on the counter facing me.

I took a step closer and looked at a picture sketched on the lined paper. A quick spike of fear went down my spine as I stared at the drawing. The text on the page was scratchy and hard to read, but I was too focused on the drawing anyway. It was all of the fragments, each spread out along the page. Even though they were separated from each other, I could make out the image of them fitting together to become a skeleton key. Each piece was the same pitch-black stone with bright red veins scattered around it like lightning.

I recognized the one that had been shoved inside my belly to burn me alive.

Even now I could feel the blistering pain pulsing

through me like an electric shock, and I was just looking at a fucking sketch. I kept my face blank and looked at the other shards. The other five pieces were different– three were the curves from the top of the key, two were splinters of the blade and the cuts, and the final one was a sharp, triangular tip.

There are five more of these things out there, each one inside of a person. How the hell are we supposed to find them all?

"I take it you know what the fragments make a person do," Maria said.

Images flashed through my mind. Mind-numbing agony, sharp stares, blood flying in every direction. Three people dying because of me.

"It kind of possesses you," I said. "It acts like a trigger for your darkest emotions and desires. The worse the desire, the more likely you are to do it. You want to, and it draws other people to do the same."

Maria nodded. "The fragments taint your soul. Human eyes can't see it, but it draws people in like a drug. The closer they are to you, the more corrupted their minds become until the smallest trigger sets them off. Think of it like a poison gas with a sweet scent. You love the smell and wander toward it, only realizing too late that it's killing you."

"Yeah. That sounds about right." I tore my eyes away from the page. "So how do we destroy them?"

"I don't know."

I blinked, confused. "But the one Dro took from me turned to ash," I reminded her. "I saw it. What happened to the ash?"

Maria pulled a key from the chain around her neck and used it to open the drawer beside her. She lifted up a hidden compartment, took out a clear vial no bigger than my pinky finger and placed it on the counter. It was filled with mostly black ash, though there were a few specks that glowed bright red behind the glass.

"That was all I could recover," she said. "I don't know how it was destroyed. If you're going after the fragments like your friend Max said you planned to, then you're going to have to find another way to get them out of the carriers."

Damn it, Max. "Finding them might not be too hard since they're so interested in causing trouble," I grumbled. "But why would we need to find another way? You got this one out of me easy enough." Though it was excruciatingly painful.

"Because the fragment was still intact. Most people would refuse to resist the fragment's influence, whether they couldn't tolerate the pain, or because they didn't want to. You're the only exception I've ever heard of, and so when the fragment was inside you, it was taking its revenge by brutalizing you. For people who embrace the fragment's influence, they feel nothing when it splits apart. Once it breaks down into their bloodstream, you have no hope of getting it out. The only way to destroy the fragment is to destroy the person."

"Then how does it move around? These attacks have never been in one place."

"I seriously doubt the fragments are moving from person to person. Whoever is holding them is probably keeping them, and escaping the chaos while everyone else kills each other." Maria's face was disturbingly serious. "The carriers are probably sided with the demons."

No matter how many times I heard that, it still hit me like a punch to the gut. Drake and Mateo were unquestionably allied with Lucifer and obviously had a couple of fragments, but what about the slayers? Had they become carriers by accident? I didn't think Carver would go that far into deception, but the man was a fanatic hell-bent on stopping the demons, no matter what he had to do to himself or his colleagues. The thought of Jackson having a fragment in him made me sick. He didn't deserve that kind of pain.

We had to find them again and get our answers more aggressively.

"You're thinking about trying to save someone," Maria said. "Don't. You can't. If someone wants the fragment inside of them, they'll keep it there, and there is nothing you can do to help them."

I listened to her voice rise in pitch, watched the tears grow in her eyes. When her rant was finally over, I saw how deep her sorrow was. I looked down at my clothes guiltily. Did I look like her daughter?

Maria took a deep breath. "The people with the fragments can't be saved. Your best bet is to survive."

"And let Lucifer and his minions ruin everyone in the world? I don't think so. He's hunting us, and we need to find a way to stop him."

Her pain turned into anger. "I bet you've told that to yourself before, haven't you? How many more times are you going to say it before you realize you can't stop Lucifer? He's going to take whatever he wants from you in a way you'll never know about. He's the Lord of Deception and Lies. He can take any shape he wants, whenever he wants."

She looked away, weariness wrapping around her like a smothering blanket. "I've been here since the beginning, since the fragments started doing their worst damage. I watched my daughter succumb to their influence and be torn apart by it before I could save her. I scoured every inch of this damned city looking for a way to stop him, and do you know what I found?"

Maria's eyes were as sharp as knives.

"Nothing."

I didn't dare speak. Had I ever thought that stopping Lucifer was impossible? Yes. Did that mean I was going to give up? No. Not with Dro's life in the balance. As long as Lucifer thought he was King of the Universe, he was going to try and bring her under his wing. I refused to let that happen.

It must have showed on my face, because Maria stepped closer to me.

"I know what your sister is," she whispered. "I know who she was born from, and I'm telling you that you can't save her from him. If he wants her, he'll find a way to take her. You need to be ready to deal with that when it happens."

I tightened my arms around my chest. "You better not be telling me to abandon my sister," I warned.

"I'm telling you that she threatened me. I'm telling you that I could see the power she used from my front window. I'm telling you that she's going to be the death of you."

My first impulse was to slap her. Maria wasn't "telling me" anything I didn't already know. She wasn't preparing me for something I didn't wasn't ready to deal with. She was just saying things I didn't want to hear, because I wasn't going to let them come true. Dro had made some mistakes, just as bad as the ones I had made, but she was still herself.

I can't fight this anymore, Connie.

You have lost her.

I inhaled slowly, soothing the storm building in my chest. I didn't need to talk to Maria. I needed to talk to my sister.

"Thanks for the operation, the food, the clothes, and the advice," I said, biting out the last word. "We'll leave right away."

I turned and walked away, shoving the curtains aside. Warrick came out of the bathroom, shaking a hand through his wet hair. He looked clean even in his dirty clothes, but his eyes were still tired. He smiled at me, though it quickly faded when he saw the look on my face.

"Hey, are you okay?"

"Fine," I answered sharply. "We're leaving. Where's everybody else?"

Warrick didn't ask what had set me off. Maybe he was getting used to my moodiness. "There's an apartment upstairs with two spare rooms. Maria let Dro and Max borrow one, and Sephiel took the other."

"Pack up whatever you can," I told him. "I'll get everybody up."

I started walking for the stairs on the left, then stopped. I turned around and grabbed Warrick's hand. When he twisted to face me, I kissed him. He seemed surprised, but melted into the kiss easily. I reluctantly pulled away and touched his face.

"Thank you." I didn't need to say what for.

Warrick smiled. "Any time, beautiful. I'll be down here when you're ready."

I gave him a small nod and an even smaller smile before turning and jogging up the stairs. There weren't many, so I was on the second level in no time. It was narrow and wooden with one door for a kitchen and two for the spare rooms. I turned to the one on my right and knocked on it.

Sephiel opened the door. He wasn't wearing his white trench coat for once, and his white dress shirt had been replaced with a new, clean one that was shorter around the cuffs. With the jeans and sleep-tousled hair, Sephiel looked like a rushed businessman who fell asleep at the office.

"Hey, how's your side?" I asked.

Sephiel turned and prodded the spot where he'd been stabbed. "Andromenda healed it after caring for you. I am no longer in pain, but…" He stared at his side. "It is strange to feel such a small amount of pain for so long."

I set my jaw, not wanting to say anything that might suggest I thought of him as a weak human. He was far from weak. Hell, he was one of the strongest men I knew.

Before I could tell him that, Sephiel turned his head up to me. "You look well," he told me with a smile.

"Thanks. I feel better. Which means it's time to go."

His smile dropped like a rock. "Is everything all right?"

"Well, no one's tried to kill us yet, but we need to get those fragments. Now that we know exactly what they can do to someone…" I shook my head. "We can't let anyone else near them."

Sephiel nodded slowly. The door behind me opened, and I spun around to see Max rubbing his eyes in the doorway of the second room.

"I slept like a rock," he mumbled, "and I still don't think it was enough."

"I'll let you have a nap when we find another safe-house." I started moving for the staircase. "Tell Dro to get her stuff ready and come downstairs."

"She's already downstairs."

I halted in mid step, then turned on my heel. "What?"

"Dro's already downstairs," Max repeated. "She told me she was having trouble sleeping, so she was going down to talk to Maria. Why?"

I didn't answer him. I rushed down the steps and swung around the doorframe into the middle of the shop. Warrick was there, waiting by the door with backpacks in his hand. He straightened up and looked at me anxiously. Maria stared at me from behind the counter with a curious expression. I walked straight to her.

"Did you see her?" I demanded. My heart was in my throat.

Maria nodded slowly, as if she was having trouble understanding the problem. "She came down about an hour ago said she was going to get some air."

My nails dug into the counter. I could feel my body beginning to tremble.

"Constance? What's wrong?"

I barely heard Warrick's voice. All I could hear was two people repeating two phrases in my head.

I can't fight this anymore, Connie.

You have lost her.

"Constance? What happened?"

I didn't have the heart to look at Max when I heard him call my name. I closed my eyes and hid my tears, forcing the words out.

"It's Dro. She's gone."

Chapter 16

It wasn't the first time Dro had left me. It wasn't the first time I had lost her.

But this was worse than all the other times, even when I was certain she had left and would never return…

For nearly three days, I did nothing but search. I barely ate. I barely slept. I started at bus stations and cab corners, keeping my head down and quickly asking if anyone had seen a pale girl with white hair and bright blue eyes. Nobody had, and the moment they eyed me suspiciously was the same moment I left. They probably thought I was crazy.

I hadn't gotten to the crazy phase yet, but I was desperate, so I was coming close. I went to the homeless shelter and talked to them as calmly as possible, but they could offer me nothing but pity and free food.

My next stop was hotels and bed and breakfasts. Dro didn't have a lot of money, but she would appeal to the goodness in people with the hopes that they'd help her. I was less optimistic, and much more aggressive. I made the owners talk, but they hadn't seen her either.

It wasn't long before I hit the alleys and the dark streets. Dro and I had been homeless before, so living under cardboard and dirty blankets wouldn't be new to her. I grilled every sickly addict, threatened every hooker, punched every thief, and came up with nothing.

Fucking, goddamn nothing.

That meant she didn't want to be found. Not even by me.

I cursed myself for protecting us the way I did. She would know how to stay hidden and how to survive on her own. She would know how to disappear completely.

The rain was soaking through my hoodie, the cloth over my head dampening the greasy hair beneath. My hands were tucked under my armpits for warmth, but it didn't help. I was freezing, walking on a road that would lead to somewhere. I could only hope that it would take me to my sister.

You won't find her, *the realistic voice in my head told me.* If she doesn't want to be found, she won't be. You taught her everything she knows. She'll live.

But what about the monsters? *Another part of my brain argued.* They'll be looking for her.

That's what she wants. She left because she doesn't think you're strong enough to protect her from them. She left to keep you alive.

She left because she thinks she'll be the reason you die.

Eventually my body couldn't handle the cold anymore. The rain was pounding on my head now, and I needed a place to get out of the storm. To my right, I could see the lights of a gas station shining in the distance. It was the only place I'd seen for miles. If Dro had gone this way, she would have needed to stop.

If she went this way. She could be anywhere by now.

I was too damn tired to keep thinking about what my sister did or didn't do. I shut off my mind and walked into the gas station.

I must have looked like a drowned rat, because the cashier stared at me with wide-eyed disgust. I ignored him and walked through the store. My eyes picked up everything, but registered nothing.

While I continued to wander aimlessly around the store, the door opened and a man came through. He shivered loudly and shook off the water on his sport jacket.

"Hey, Sam," the new man said. I glanced at the newcomer out of the corner of my eye. He was a trucker. "Hell of a storm, isn't it?"

"Yeah, not a good night to be out. I tried to tell

that to the girl I just dropped off."

My head twitched ever so slightly toward the cash desk. I edged closer to them as inconspicuously as possible.

"You picked up another stray? That's going to get you into trouble one day, Matt."

"What was I supposed to do? Let her walk alone in the dark? You should have seen her, Sam. Pretty little thing, pale as snow, weird white hair, sad smile. I couldn't leave her out there. She wouldn't have made it. Can I get some Marlboros?"

"I don't have any stocked yet. They're in the back. Give me a second."

Sam the cashier walked out from behind the counter toward the back room. I had seconds before he came back. I walked to Matt's back.

"You picked up a girl with white hair?" I asked.

Matt jumped at the sound of my voice, turning sharply. "Whoa, you scared the hell out of me, sweetheart."

I ignored his outburst. "I overheard you. Did you pick up a girl with white hair?"

He looked at me curiously. "What's it to you?"

"I'm looking for her. She's my sister."

"Your sister." His raised eyebrows proved that he didn't believe me. "Sorry, honey, but you don't look anything like the girl I picked up."

"She's adopted, and you're going to take me to the place you dropped her off."

"And why would I do that?"

I turned my eyes into slits and walked closer to him. I moved my hands to my hips, pulling up the hoodie just enough for him to see the hatchet I was carrying. He backed up instinctively. "Because I'm in a very bad mood right now, and if you care about your well being, you're going to do me this simple favor."

Matt wasn't much bigger than me, and he was probably wondering if he could run or call the cops before I caught him.

Then he looked at the hatchet on my belt, and decided not to test the theory out. He turned and walked out of the gas station with me hot on his heels. When we walked back into the rain, I put my hand on my hatchet in case Matt got it in his head to be brave. He swung into the cab and opened it for me. I hopped in the passenger side, glanced at the radio, and switched it off. Matt looked at me nervously.

"I figured Sam would be right one of these days," he muttered, turning the ignition and starting the truck. He put his hands on the wheel and looked at me nervously. "How much trouble am I going to get into?"

"As long as you take me to my sister and don't try any tricks, none."

Matt pulled out of the parking lot slowly. He avoided looking at me as much as possible.

"You're not a liar, right? You're not going to kill me?"

"No," I told him. "But I do have a very short temper."

The trucker gritted his teeth, and didn't say anything else.

I was grateful for that, because I had other things to think about. Like what I was going to say to my little sister when I found her again...

"I still haven't seen anything," Max said. "She might be trying to block me."

The grief in his voice pierced my memory, bringing me back to the harsh reality of Dro disappearing.

I'd been so lost that I wasn't able to concentrate on where we were walking. I blinked, and let the world settle around me. We were moving briskly from the *Mercado Juárez* market district toward the *Colegio Latino Américano,* one of the colleges. The street on the left was lined with brightly colored shops and hole-in-the-wall diners, which contradicted the massive stone and wrought iron fence on the right that guarded the college.

This street, like so many others, was empty of any

living person. Scattered corpses lay in pools of blood. Some of the pools had been turned into smudges, like the bodies had been dragged away by hungry demons for food.

I should have been grateful that there wasn't anyone to confront us. Except that I didn't want to avoid a confrontation. I wanted to find someone, and beat answers out of them. I wanted to find a demon and make it scream. I wanted to find one of Mateo's Blood Thorns and send a message to my sadistic ex.

I wanted to do anything to ease the ache in my chest.

The guys were struggling to keep up with me, and none of them were telling me to slow down. They knew better than to get in my way.

"Constance," Max said warily.

"I heard you," I snapped.

He paused. "I wasn't going to repeat myself," he told me quietly. "I was going to ask where we're going. It has to be somewhere Dro is headed, right?"

I slowed down just long enough to think. I didn't actually know how to answer him. My original plan had been to scour old hideouts and places I'd worked to find Dro, but she knew I'd come looking for her, and she wasn't going to make it easy. There weren't going to be any convenient truck drivers to take me to her. Dro was going to stay away from anywhere she assumed I would look.

But she had to have gone somewhere. She wanted to end this as much as I did, and the only way to do that was…

I stopped walking, staring ahead and seeing nothing.

"Constance?" Warrick's hand touched my shoulder, but I didn't feel it.

"No," I whispered. Horror strangled around my throat like a noose. "No, she wouldn't."

"Wouldn't what?" Warrick moved in front of me, gripping my shoulders and trying to get me out of my trance.

I hated that all three of my friends were staring at me, waiting for me to tell them what I couldn't doubt now. But I didn't want to say it. Saying it would make it true.

Then you might as well face it. The sooner you do, the sooner you can find her before it's too late.

I closed my eyes and sighed. "Dro won't be in any place familiar to her or me. She's not going to hide. She's trying to find him. She's looking for Lucifer."

I heard Max's sharp intake of breath and watched Sephiel's face pale. Warrick squeezed my shoulders and looked at me sadly. I twisted out of his arms before he could hold me and watch me break down again. I turned to Max, who looked completely crushed.

"Why?" he asked. His eyes were glistening. "Why would she do that?"

"Because she wants to stop him," I said. "It's the only thing that makes sense." And I was too afraid to think of any other outcomes.

Max swallowed. "Then I won't be able to find her," he said quietly. "Lucifer will block everything I see."

"What about Mateo, Drake, or the slayers? Can you still see them?"

Max's eyes lit up briefly. "You think they'll have seen her?"

"I'm not sure. But if they have, I'll make them tell us. And if not, we can find out where the fragments are. Maybe if we destroy enough of them, we can draw Lucifer's attention away from finding Dro, and keep her safe for a little bit longer."

Max nodded. He closed his eyes and took a deep breath to concentrate.

"Attacking Lucifer and his sycophants directly is by far your most dangerous plan yet," Sephiel remarked from my left.

I looked at him. "How else are we supposed to do it? We can't keep running and hoping we'll get lucky potshots. We were going to be in this position sooner or later, Seph. You knew that."

His blue eyes were impatient and dark. "I did. But that was also before I knew Michael and his Seraphim were seeking to cleanse the city of its evil."

I faced him directly. "You think they're going to be a problem?"

Sephiel's impatience turned into unease. This didn't seem like a conversation he wanted to have.

"I think Michael will be closer to locating Lucifer than Andromeda will be. He still retains incredible power, and if she crosses his path, he will use her to provoke the King of Hell." He dropped his head. "And he shall not be gentle about it."

The memory of Michael's cold, hard eyes flashed through me. He would have killed me with a flick of his wrist, and only kept us alive to keep Dro in compliance. If he got his hands on her…

"We'll deal with them if we find them," I said. It was the only truth I could believe in. "If it turns out that Michael has her, then we'll take her from him." Yet another truth, but one that I was going to have a difficult time keeping.

Max's sudden, heavy sigh drew my attention. He blinked to register his surroundings, then looked at me grimly.

"We're not far from the slayers," he announced. He pointed to a red apartment building about five blocks away next to a back road. "They're doing something there with some Blood Thorns. Drake and Mateo aren't there, but I could see them arguing. They're planning to draw a crowd and start a fight."

"They wouldn't do that if they were trying to stay under the Thorn's radar," Warrick pointed out.

"Unless they were carrying fragments," I countered.

No one wanted to believe that might be a scenario, but no one disagreed either. I started walking toward the red apartment. The closer I got, the faster I moved. By the time I reached the stop sign in the corner, I was nearly sprinting. I slowed down when I heard raised voices. I crossed the street to an empty strip mall parking lot, knowing the slayers and Thorns were behind it. I pressed myself to the wall of the motel and listened. I couldn't hear most of the conversation, but I picked out certain words.

"… sick of waiting." That was Elle's voice.

"Is this even gonna work?" Jackson said. "We should just…"

"Boss said it should be here," a Blood Thorn mumbled.

I carefully turned my head around the corner of the motel. Seven black clad Blood Thorns were standing with the three demon slayers. All their eyes were on the two story brick condos in front of them.

"Just pick one," Elle said impatiently.

Carver lifted a finger and pointed to the house across from him. "That one. The dust looks like it's been cleared away recently. There are probably people inside."

I didn't know why the Blood Thorns would want anyone who wasn't Dro or me, but it couldn't be for anything good. I glanced back at the guys and held up all ten of my fingers. Max winced, but Warrick and Sephiel silently drew their blades. I took out my hatchet and a throwing knife.

Three of the Blood Thorns marched up the front porch steps of the condo. They started picking the lock to the house.

I looked around for cover, and saw nothing. Open ground was the only way to meet them. I wasn't happy about it, but if there were innocent people in that condo, they were the ones who deserved to be hidden.

And I really, *really* needed to hit something.

I turned around the corner and started jogging down the alley. Most of the Blood Thorns were watching the house, but it was the slayers who noticed me first. Carver turned his head and locked eyes with me. He shoved aside the men in his way and stood in front of them. Eventually the attention on the condo shifted to me.

"What are you doing here?" Carver demanded.

"You're supposed to be dead!"

I slowed to a steady walk and grinned at him. "What's that saying about bad pennies? You're old enough to know it, Carver."

He snarled at me, and then something about his face changed. His snarling mouth curved upward, and the anger in his eyes glittered with cruelty.

I never thought I would see Carver smile. Now that I was, I wanted to see him do anything else.

"Forget the house," Carver shouted, never looking away from me. "This bitch will do."

Three of the Blood Thorns standing next to Carver marched toward me, ready to converge left, right, and center. As they got closer, I began to feel something. It wasn't just the adrenaline beginning to build in my veins. It went deeper, sliding over my skin like oil and sinking toward my bones. I wasn't just looking to the release a fight would give me. I was looking forward to spilling the blood of my enemies, listening to their screams and laughing at them. I was…

My head turned back to Carver, Elle, and Jackson. They were standing back, their fingers itching for weapons. They each had the same, sadistic expression on their faces.

I imagined my face had looked like that back when I lost my mind.

It was too late for me to warn the guys, because the Blood Thorns attacked me at the same time.

Left Guy swung a punch at my head first, hoping to down me with one strike. I ducked and stepped back, seeing Right Guy's boot flying toward my chest. I sliced down with my hatchet, catching him along the shin. He cursed and recoiled while Center Guy punched for my chest. I leaned to the side and stabbed my knife up into his forearm. As he screamed in pain, I ducked under his arm, twisting the knife to keep him subdued. I slashed my hatchet across Left Guy's stomach. He clutched his belly, too shocked to stop me from driving the blade of my hatchet into his chin in a fatal strike.

Center Guy's uninjured hand shot forward to grab my throat. I staggered back and pulled my knife free to get out of his reach. It worked, but it also gave Right Guy the chance to swing at me with a knife of his own. It grazed the leather jacket on my shoulders, just barely missing my skin as I twisted away. I grabbed his outstretched hand, spinning low to drive my elbow into his gut. Center Guy was coming up behind me, a savage roar bursting from his throat.

I flipped my knife and drove it into Right Guy's chest with a heavy *thunk*. I felt him go rigid under my hand, twitching once when I twisted the blade in his heart. Center Guy's shadow grew behind me, and I snapped my elbow back into his throat. He skidded to a stop and clutched his neck, trying to breathe but unable to do anything except cough.

I kicked him in the chest to get him back, then ripped my knife from my latest victim and spun on my heel, launching the throwing knife and hitting the middle of Center Guy's chest perfectly. He tried to reach for the knife, but he was already dead.

Power and excitement surged through me. I felt strong and unstoppable, just as I had when the fragment was embedded under my skin. I looked over my shoulder, and saw the slayers were moving closer.

But they didn't see the group coming up behind them. I did, and noticed they were wearing an alarming amount of white.

Someone appeared in my peripheral, and I didn't have time to react. I raised my hand to block whatever was coming, only to watch Warrick jump into sight, grab the Blood Thorn's wrist, and snap it. The big man screamed in pain, silenced when Warrick slashed his knife across his throat.

On my right, Sephiel stalked forward with both of his short swords drawn. He stopped and watched the last three Blood Thorns run for him. He waited until the last second, then spun his swords in two large rotations. The blades sliced through the faces of the Blood Thorns, spraying blood and making them scream. The last Blood Thorn wasn't deterred; at least not until Sephiel lunged forward and stabbed both swords into the man's chest. He stood there, impaled on the blades until Sephiel tore them out. The two half-blind Blood Thorns rushed him stupidly, and he destroyed them by striking his blades along both of their throats in one fluid motion.

We faced off with the remaining Blood Thorn and the three slayers. They were all smiling. I could feel a haze drifting into my mind. A comforting shadow that whispered in my ear and told me to let go. I needed it. I'd earned it.

I looked away from the slayers, and saw a few people peeking out of the condos. Survivors making themselves known, curious about the fight, and wondering when they could become part of it.

No, I thought. *No, this isn't right. This can't be happening unless...*

I looked at the slayers again, and I knew, without a doubt, what was causing these dark impulses. Why the crowd was moving quickly, why Warrick was chuckling under his breath and walking toward a smiling Jackson with a knife.

But I didn't know what it would do to the group storming toward the backs of the slayers. They were the only reason Sephiel stayed in place. We shared one short, terrified glance at each other before he tightened his hands around his swords, and I held my hatchet like a lifeline.

The angels had arrived.

Chapter 17

The first thing I tried to do was warn Warrick, but the moment I opened my mouth was the moment he charged his friend.

The two of them erupted into a fierce battle that sparked the rest of the observing crowd into action. The people living in the condos raced forward with a short battle cry, clenching their fists or clutching makeshift knives and weapons. I started moving for Warrick, desperate to protect him, but Carver got in front of me.

He swung a massive combat knife at my throat. I leaned back before it could cut me. Carver kicked my stomach and knocked me back, driving in for the kill. All around me I could hear the crowd shouting and screaming and punching each other. It wasn't long before I smelled blood. I lost sight of Warrick as Carver lashed out at me.

He was nearly twice my age, but he was stronger and faster than I expected. I was struggling to keep up, knowing the angels were going to be here any second. I had to get Carver away from me and take the others to safety. I had screwed this up royally, not knowing that I had walked into yet another trap until it snapped closed over me.

But when I came out of a block and slugged Carver in the jaw, it felt good. I'd wanted to punch the asshole in the face for so long that I didn't bother holding back my smile. He fought furiously, reversing his knife and aiming it for my ribs. I hooked the blade with the curve of my hatchet and swung it away from my body. The knife flew from his grip and clattered onto the ground.

Carver growled and punched me in the cheek. Stars exploded in my vision and I swayed on my feet.

Carver placed his hands on either side of my head and began to twist.

I panicked, feeling sharp pain in my neck as it was wrenched to the side. I reacted fast, stomping on his foot and driving my fist into his chin. He released me and I whirled around, slamming a roundhouse kick into his temple.

Carver dropped to one hand and one knee to catch himself. He spat blood and glared at me furiously. I smiled down on him, welcoming the darkness ebbing off him like a pulse. I breathed it in, craved it even though my soul knew how wrong it was.

Carver tried to get up too quickly, unprepared when I kicked him in the face. His nose crunched under my boot and he toppled back onto the ground.

"Didn't think you'd ever get beat up by a girl, did you Carve?" I laughed.

His face was furious, and this time I knew he was going to kill me when he stood up.

Or he would have, if a scream hadn't cut through the air like a knife.

It was an ear-piercing wail of agony that rippled through the entire crowd, silencing them just for a moment. We all looked in its direction.

Elle was in the grip of an angel, her back arched as she stared at the sword shoved clean through her, blood slicking and dripping from the tip protruding out her back. Michael stood in front of her, watching her scream with dead eyes. His wrist twisted violently, and Elle slipped off the blade, dropping into a motionless heap.

"*No!*" Carver screamed from in front of me.

Michael didn't even seem to hear him. He watched Elle's body begin to corrode and blacken, as if she had been a demon herself.

Or if a fragment had been fused with her bloodstream.

Carver rushed Michael, oblivious to the other angels fending off the humans stupid enough to attack them, though I didn't see Raphael anywhere.

Jackson must have escaped Warrick, because he was rushing the archangel with a knife in his hands. I thought for a second that Michael didn't see him coming, and debated on warning him.

Then Michael turned and slammed the palm of his free hand into Jackson's chest. The heavyset man flew back like a tossed ragdoll, landing hard on the unforgiving pavement.

The rest of the crowd began to disperse, either realizing the angels were unstoppable, or that they were killing people with fragments inside of them. Warrick rushed to help his friend, stopping only when an angel appeared in front of him and pressed the tip of her sword at his chest.

Carver was running toward one of the fences between two of the condos, so I chased after him. At least until an angel got in my way and pointed a dagger at my throat. Over the stern bastard's shoulder, I watched Carver vault the fence and disappear from sight.

"Shit," I hissed. I glared at the angel. "You have no idea what you let get away, asshole."

The angel didn't respond. I turned around and watched an angel drag Max over by his arm. Sephiel faced two angels, gripping his short swords tightly and looking between them as if deciding who to take on first.

But we weren't going to be fighting anyone anytime soon. The angels outnumbered us two to one, and even though they were human now, they were still top-notch warriors. And that wasn't taking into account that Michael, the leader of the Heavenly Host and strongest of the archangels, could still crush me between his fingers if I pissed him off enough.

Which was a likely scenario.

Michael looked at Jackson, who was starting to get to his feet. Warrick tried to step around the angel to his friend, but Jackson snarled angrily. Warrick froze in place. He looked stunned, and distraught.

"You have a fragment inside of you," Michael said.

Jackson turned to look at him. "How'd you know, goose?"

Michael didn't flinch at the insult, but some of the other angels scowled.

"I sensed it in you as I sensed it in her," he said, nudging the pile of ash with the tip of his shoe.

I looked down at the remains of Elle Carver. I'd gotten along with her worse than I had with Rorikel. I don't know what it was about me that set her off, but it was insignificant now. I thought about her scream, the horrific way she'd died with Michael crushing her heart. I knew how the fragment would have affected her, that she must have given into it to spare herself pain. I couldn't say I blamed her.

"It was a gift from Lucifer," Jackson said. I looked up and saw the wicked smile on his face. There was no trace of the kind, gentle man I had met only weeks earlier.

"Lucifer does not give gifts," Michael corrected. "He causes pain and chaos through elaborate deceits. You are a victim of one such deception."

Jackson was shaking his head. "No," he told the archangel. "It hurt at first, but then he took away the pain and gave us a purpose. He made us stronger, and gave us a chance to fulfill his plan." He met my eyes, and smiled coldly. "It's coming together exactly the way he wants it to."

I forced myself not to be disturbed by what he said. "What was your plan?" I asked.

Jackson grinned. "Start trouble in places you knew. Send you a sign. Make you one of us. Then take away the one thing you love most."

My mask slipped for a fraction of a second. It was the only opening Jackson needed to taunt me.

"Did you really think she'd stay with you? After everything she's done, after fighting her nature for so long, she gave in to what she really was. I saw it happen with my own eyes. Your sister stood in front of Lucifer and begged– *begged*– to be at his side. All she asked for in return was that you and your band of misfits live."

It took every ounce of my strength to keep the mask on my face. Inside, I was crumbling. Betrayal chipped away at my heart, each piece splintering inside of me like broken glass. I tried to tell myself that Jackson was lying. The Dro I knew and loved would never give up. She would never quit. She was drawing Lucifer away from me to take a shot at him herself.

I can't fight this anymore, Connie.

The moment my hand slipped from hers, I should have known that I was doing irreparable damage. Dro needed me to anchor her, to let her know that she would still be loved no matter what horrible things she had done.

And I took my hand away from hers.

I stood there and stared at Jackson, inches away from the edge. I didn't dare speak. I didn't trust whatever would come out of my mouth.

Thankfully, Michael was eager to talk.

"Why did Lucifer choose you?"

Jackson sneered at him. "You jealous, goose?"

Michael's followers bristled at the remark. Even Sephiel shot Jackson a dirty look. But the archangel didn't even blink.

He narrowed his eyes, and Jackson suddenly grimaced. Michael must have been digging into his mind, going straight for the truth instead of bothering to ask more questions. When Jackson hissed sharply, Warrick tried to run to help him. Two angels grabbed his arms and pulled him back. He glowered at them, but they refused to let him go.

After about a minute, Michael relaxed. Jackson nearly collapsed.

"Your plan was to deceive Lucifer," Michael said. "You believed that infiltrating the ranks of the Antichrist's inner circle would provide you with a method of defeating him. So you and the other humans got close. You warned them it was becoming too dangerous, but they did not heed you. Then one day you got too close. Two humans obeying Lucifer's orders tricked you and placed the fragment inside of you. At first you fought the pain, but then it became unbearable, and you succumbed to it. You were instructed to disperse around the city and draw sinners to their deaths. You became the device of his corruption, spreading it like a disease while targeting this group."

I forgot my heartache momentarily. The old Jackson said the slayers had come here around the time the Heaven Gate was burned. That was more than enough time to infiltrate the Blood Thorns, think they were earning their trust, then have it turned on them to become puppets. Meeting Elle a few days ago no longer seemed like a coincidence. Did she have a fragment inside her then? Did she give a signal to have the demons appear and attack us? Did they have any idea what would happen to me, or was that a plan to be played fast and loose?

It didn't matter. From the look on Jackson's face, it was all true.

Michael took a step closer to the demon slayer. "Your soul is being tainted, Jackson Argyle. But it can be saved." Michael lifted his huge silver broadsword, still stained with Elle's blood. Warrick rushed for his friend again, but two more angels hurried over and grabbed his arms. He shook them and tried to break free, but they were too strong. I took a step forward, but the angel carefully poked me in the neck with his dagger.

Jackson looked at the massive, bloody sword in the archangel's hand. "I think we have different definitions of being saved."

"Your death will have meaning, "Michael promised. "You shall eliminate a piece of Lucifer's Key. You shall help in closing the Hell Gate and saving your race."

"You can't be serious about this," I burst.

Michael snapped his head at me and glared murderously. "The fragment has diluted into his bloodstream. There is no retrieving it now."

"You don't know that," I insisted. "I had a fragment inside of me. It was taken out, and turned to ash, and I'm still standing here."

"You lie."

"No, Commander Michael," Sephiel backed me up. "Constance speaks the truth. I saw it with my own eyes." He looked at Jackson. "It was… unpleasant for her, yet she managed to survive."

"Because she must have resisted the lure of the fragment," Michael reasoned. "That is impressive, but it is too late for this man."

Michael raised his sword to Jackson's chest. Warrick lunged again, and was pulled back harder than before. The angels shoved him down until he was on his knees and the sword was against his throat.

"Please," my lover called, "there has to be another way!"

Michael didn't look at Warrick. He was completely focused on Jackson.

"There isn't."

It happened in the blink of an eye. One moment Jackson was standing in front of Michael, unable to escape the circle of angels. The next moment, the tip of a sword was poking through Jackson's back. Warrick screamed from pain and rage. Michael ignored him, holding Jackson in place with his free hand on his shoulder. The demon slayer's eyes bulged. He looked down at the sword lodged in his torso, like he was trying to understand how it got there. His face mirrored Elle's, and I felt a horrible twist in my stomach.

"You have done your kind a great service," Michael told the man dying on his blade. "I regret we could not have saved you sooner."

Michael stepped back and pulled the sword out of Jackson's body. The big demon slayer collapsed off it, landing on the ground in a heap. His hands went to the enormous gash in his chest. Blood began to seep through his fingers. He blinked, and tilted his head toward Warrick.

His friend struggled and fought the angels, who were having a difficult time holding him down. Eventually they gave up on niceties and punched him in the stomach.

Warrick grunted from the hit and dropped to his knees again. Another hit to his face kept him dazed.

"Sorry, John," Jackson slurred. His skin began to crack.

Warrick lifted his head. His eyes glistened as he watched his best friend decay. In mere seconds, all that was left of Jackson Argyle was a pile of black ash with dots of red. Warrick lost all of his fight, hanging his head to hide his sorrow.

"Two Keys have been destroyed," Michael announced, sliding the bloody sword into the scabbard on his back. "Three, if I am to believe you, Sephiel. Which I am not inclined to do." His eyes shifted to all of us, to Sephiel's shocked expression, to Max's nervous glances, to my steel-eyed rage, to Warrick's obvious grief.

"You shall return with us to draw out Lucifer's spawn. This time you shall not escape, as Raphael is no longer able to take pity on you."

Sephiel stared at his former leader curiously. Then he paled, and his eyes widened with horror.

"You… You killed him?" This was the first time I ever heard Sephiel stutter.

Michael's eyes narrowed furiously. I wondered if it was a shield for his sorrow.

"No, Sephiel. You killed him. When you let the Heaven Gate be destroyed, you killed us all."

Chapter 18

The angels led us through the streets as if they'd lived on them all their lives. I should have been impressed at their navigation, but the entire group had collapsed in some way. Max was as terrified as I'd ever seen him. Sephiel was trapped in a stunned silence. Warrick was lost in mourning.

I couldn't stop thinking about what Jackson said about my sister. That she gave herself up to Lucifer because she couldn't fight what she was anymore. I didn't want to believe it, but death and destruction had followed Dro ever since she was a child. It wasn't the first time she had taken a risk to save my life…

I had to threaten Matt before he let me out of his truck. I gave him the usual spiel– that I would kill him and everyone he loves if he told anyone who I was, who I was looking for, and where he'd dropped me off. I had no intention of acting on any of my threats, but he didn't need to know that.

Dro had taken refuge in a dilapidated motel in Stanton. It was one of those places that you only had to look at once to know the beds would vibrate if you had a quarter to spare.

The woman behind the counter of the front desk looked like a cross between a librarian and a drag queen. She wore thick, square glasses, a blindingly neon pink sweater, chunky gold jewelry, and had painted her eyelids baby blue. She glanced up at me from her gossip magazine, scrunching up her lips and causing her cheap lipstick to crack.

"Looking for a room?" she asked without interest.

"No," I replied. "Looking for a person. A teenage

girl with white hair."

The woman scowled and tossed her hair to the side, showing off its cheap blonde streaks in a motion that she was twenty years too old for. She ignored me and went back to her magazine.

"Ever consider that the people who come here are looking for privacy?" she commented in a bland tone.

I matched it when I answered, "Ever consider I'll smash your face into the desk if you keep ignoring me?"

That got her attention. I gave her a stare that could have frozen a lake, and the magazine began to flap nervously in her shaking hands.

"Take me to her," I demanded. "Now."

The woman didn't need a lot more encouragement. I watched her like I was going to kill her the second she sneezed on me. I don't think I would have, but I was tired, cold, and stuck in the middle of nowhere trying to find my missing sister. My patience was all but gone.

She led me outside to the parking lot of the motel, glancing nervously at all the windows, probably hoping someone would come out and help her.

I rolled my eyes. I didn't even have a knife pulled. If I were going to kill her, I'd have drawn it and pressed it into her back to get her moving. Nothing motivates people like the concept of–

Before I knew what was happening, my senses were overloaded. In the blink of an eye, I felt heat, saw a searing light, smelled smoke, and heard crumbling construction.

I blinked to register it all, and that was when I saw the giant orange blaze rising from the corner of the L-shaped motel.

I knew exactly where Dro was.

I left the motel owner in a shocked state of screaming "Oh my God oh my God oh my God," and I ran for the fire as fast as I could.

None of the other patrons noticed me as I passed them. They launched out of their rooms in various states of undress, shrieking into their cell phones or just shrieking all together. I swung around the banister and darted up the steps, feeling the heat spreading from room to room. Water was building in my eyes and smoke dried out my throat.

"Dro!" I screamed. I didn't think she could hear me past the roar of the flames. Which meant I had to get closer.

It wasn't that I wasn't afraid of fire. I was. Any sane human being who has seen a forest fire on TV thinks, "There is no stopping this," until the fire trucks and water-bombers show up to save the day.

But until then, you're at the mercy of a powerful force set on nothing but destruction. Fire consumes everything, and it doesn't care what stands in its way. It will burn until it decides it wants to be put out.

I kept myself close to the banister, bending away from the flames licking toward me. I could barely see through the tears blurring my eyes, and if I was breathing in oxygen, I couldn't tell.

"Dro!" I shouted again, before I started coughing.

I was standing in front of the open door of her room, staring at a wall of flame. How the hell was I going to get in there? The floor hadn't been totally destroyed, but it wasn't going to last much longer. Every other time I'd seen Dro, she'd been unharmed by the flames she created. But through the racket of the blaze, I heard a noise.

It was faint, but I knew a scream when I heard one.

I covered my mouth with the sleeve of my jacket, and stepped inside the room.

I moved just past the doorway, not trusting the stability of the floor. It was like stepping into an open furnace. Fresh air had been replaced with smoke. The heat slapped my skin and pulled beads of sweat from it. Tears streamed down my cheeks and dried on my face.

I coughed and looked to the left, locking eyes on the bed and the girl in it.

Dro was still screaming, white-hot flames circling her skin and dancing on the edges of her hair. I took a couple more careful steps, wincing whenever the floor groaned underneath me. I got as close to Dro as I dared, too nervous to touch her but unable to back away.

"Dro!" I screamed again. There was no way she could hear me past the fire and her own agonizing screams.

I didn't know what else to do. We couldn't wait for help. God knows how we'd explain her miraculous survival to cops and firemen. And I wouldn't leave her like this, to awake alone in a room full of fire. So I shrugged out of my lucky jacket and tightened it like I was wringing out a towel. I frowned for having to do this, but desperate times, desperate measures.

I whipped the jacket along her stomach.

The reactions were immediate. Hers, and mine.

Dro snapped awake and shot up from the bed, the white flames going out from her body. Me, on the other hand, had to deal with the consequence of sticking my arm over a white-hot flame. I yanked my hand back to my chest, gasping at the razor sharp pain tingling around it. I smelled burning flesh and knew it was horrifically damaged. My new tears of pain mixed with the tears created by the smoke and heat.

I stumbled back, hardly able to see anything anymore. I could barely breathe, and I was getting dizzy from the lack of oxygen. I knew I had to get out of this room, but I couldn't remember where the exit was.

Dro was suddenly in front of me, looking awake and terrified. I smiled stupidly at her, not sure what else to do other than be grateful she was alive.

She hesitated, then grabbed my shirt and led me toward the door. We made it out just as the roof caved in behind us. The change in temperature brought goose bumps to my skin, but I didn't stop following Dro. I cradled my charred hand and practically fell down the steps after my sister. She eventually led us behind the motel, away from prying eyes, even though I knew the motel owner was going to report both of us as soon as the cops arrived.

We lost ourselves in the forest, running until we couldn't move anymore. I leaned back against a tree and slid down it, breathing heavily. I was exhausted, in pain, and I hadn't even gotten into a fight with anybody.

Dro sat next to me, holding her knees to her chest and watching me with tear-filled eyes.

"You found me," she whispered.

I grinned at her. "Course I did. Why wouldn't I?"

She shivered and burst into tears. I reached out with my unburned hand and rubbed her back. She stiffened under my touch, but slowly relaxed. I pulled her closer to me so her head was on my shoulder. We sat there in relative silence, the only sounds coming from the burning motel and my sister's gentle crying...

I stopped thinking about my sister when our Heavenly parade came to a stop outside an abandoned high school. I frowned at it. I went to school until I was fourteen, and was never able to return to it when the demons started chasing us. Dro and I took some homeschooling when we were living with the Blood Thorns, just so we would have some semblance of an education, but it was another regular life-thing that I'd missed.

Not that I would have gotten much from school. I was the average student, coasting by and needing to be forcibly dragged out of bed so I wouldn't be late. Still, it would have been nice to suffer through the mediocrity of school instead of spending the next two years running from demons, living on the streets, and learning how to kill people.

Dro on the other hand, loved school. Of course she would. School was where she made friends, learned new things, got to feel normal. What supernatural child with anxiety issues wouldn't love that?

I sighed. There I went again, trying not to think of my sister, and ultimately thinking about my sister.

The angels led our tragic group inside and locked the door behind us. To my surprise, they didn't immediately tie us to chairs and put swords against our throats. Michael looked at me, as if sensing my confusion.

"You are free to come and go through this building. The hybrid is not with you, so I am not concerned about any resistance."

I had a small fantasy about punching Michael in the mouth and asking, "Are you sure about that?" but I was just too tired and depressed to bother with the attempt. Instead, I walked with the guys down the shadowed halls and cold metal lockers.

After shuffling in silence for the better part of five minutes, I turned in front of the group and looked at them all. No one met my eyes.

"We should get some sleep," I said. "It won't be long until Michael decides to pound answers out of us."

Not one of them moved. My three friends had become three statues. Max was the first one to crack.

"I'm not sure sleep is a good idea for me right now," he whispered.

My chest stung for him. It always amazed me how much Max loved my little sister. Without her, he was like a lost puppy. He was awed by everything she did, happy when she laughed at his lame jokes, and found a purpose in making her feel human. Max wasn't a fighter, but he knew how to protect Dro from herself almost as well as I did.

But almost wasn't enough anymore.

I put my hand on his shoulder. "We'll find her, Max." I said it for myself as much as him.

He nodded automatically, as if he knew I was going to say that. He probably did.

Max walked out from under my hand to the classroom on the left. He closed the door with a silent click. The next person on my radar was Sephiel.

His shoulders were slumped, and there were a couple more streaks of silver at his temples. He looked older and more human every day. I wondered if it was his immortality wearing off, or because being a human in our group was tiring him out.

"It was not supposed to be like this," Sephiel said softly, as though hiding his pain. "I was going to protect her, honor Everiel's last wish. I knew it would be a challenge, that it would test me beyond all measure, but..." He shook his head slowly. "I never imagined how much chaos it would reap."

Sephiel wasn't directly blaming Dro for anything. He had a million chances to turn on us or to just leave all together, but he was fond of Dro. Either because she reminded him of the woman he'd loved for thousands of years, or because he respected her struggle to overcome what she was. He'd stayed, and I wouldn't ask him to leave.

It was selfish, given how much he'd lost and was continuing to lose, but Sephiel was my friend just as much as anyone else's.

"Get some sleep, Sephiel," I told him. "You need it now more than ever."

He looked at me seriously. "I do not trust these angels. I used to, but no longer."

"They aren't going to kill us," I assured him, hoping irony wasn't lurking behind a corner. "They want the same thing we do, and while I think Michael would rather flay himself than work with us, we don't have much of a choice."

Sephiel looked at the ground. I tilted my head to try looking in his eyes. "This is just one more hurdle," I said. "We've been through worse."

Sephiel raised his head, and showed me just how much he believed me.

"If we have, I do not remember it."

I let him turn and walk to a classroom on the right. My pep talks weren't working for anyone. I took a breath to ask Warrick if he was going to shut me down too, only to find he was already walking to another classroom.

"Hey," I said, catching up with him as he gripped the doorknob.

He dropped his hand but didn't look at me. I wrapped my arms around his stomach and pressed my cheek to his back. I felt a sigh leave him, heavy and sad. I didn't waste time telling him how sorry I was.

"I just don't fucking get it," he sighed. "One minute we were ready to kill each other. The next minute he's being erased in front of me."

Warrick's voice was shaky, and I wished I knew what to say to ease his pain.

"He looked like himself before he died," Warrick whispered. "When he looked at me that last time, I wasn't seeing whoever the fragment made him into. He was just Jackson."

Warrick sighed again, and I hugged him tighter.

"Do you want to be alone?" I asked.

"No," he admitted. "But I need to be."

I pulled away from him. Warrick turned around and dropped his head. I cupped his face and kissed him. He didn't hold me. He just closed his eyes and breathed into me.

I stepped back, still holding his face. "I'll be back in a bit. I kinda need some time alone, too."

Warrick slid his hands along my forearms, nodding as he pried my hands from his face. We gave each other weak smiles before he walked into the classroom and closed the door.

I stood alone in the hallway, staring ahead and seeing nothing. I turned away from the door and walked deeper into the school, hoping to leave the air of grief behind me.

All I did was add loneliness to the mix.

I meandered forward, no idea where I was going and not bothering to care. Too much had happened. Being stuck with a fragment. Losing my sister. Watching two slayers die. Seeing the strongest men I knew eaten up by heartache.

I didn't know how much longer I could do this.

I would stop at nothing to save Dro, but I wasn't sure I could save anyone else. Fighting the supernatural was taking its toll. I was tired of constantly looking over my shoulder and watching every shadow. I was tired of running and struggling to survive. I was tired of thinking I would die before my twenty-first birthday.

But stopping Lucifer was the only way to keep him and his demons off our backs. It was the only way any of us could find peace. I could only hope my peace wouldn't end with me lying under six feet of dirt.

Of course, if it did, I wasn't going to be surprised.

Eventually I wound up in the gymnasium. Banners for football and basketball teams hung limply from the rafters. Dirt and dust were smeared along the lined, hardwood floor. The curtains on the stage sagged over the sides of it. Both basketball hoops had been yanked down to sit in piles of broken glass.

I couldn't stand to think anymore, so I drew a knife from inside my jacket and walked to one of the hoops. It was made from plastic, so it would make a good target to practice with.

I flipped my knife end over end, catching it in my fingertips then hurling it at the backboard. The blade crunched into the plastic center right above the mesh hoop.

It felt good to practice, so I threw another one. Then another, then another, on and on until the only weapon I had left was my hatchet.

I took it off my hip and examined the weapon. Not the original that belonged to my father, but Sephiel had gotten a damn good replacement. Thanks to his blessing, I was able to use this weapon with less effort than my previous one. I looked at the Latin phrase engraved on the hilt:

Anima potentis, cor sororis.
Soul of a warrior, heart of a sister.
Where did I go wrong?

I was debating on throwing the hatchet when I felt it behind me. The warm, soothing rush of air so powerful I nearly dropped to my knees. The smell of sulfur was strong, but not as repulsive as usual. It was nearly impossible to resist. I gripped my hatchet so hard that it left an impression in my palm. If I didn't do this now, I was going to lose my mind.

I spun on my heel and launched the hatchet at him.

He raised his slender hand and stopped it a foot away from his face.

I took a deep breath and cursed my anger for making me stupid and impulsive.

I was completely alone and defenseless, and the Devil had come calling.

Chapter 19

Physically, Lucifer was perfect. He was so beautiful he bordered on androgyny, but the muscles of his shoulders and chest made it clear that he was all male. He was seven feet tall with flawless pale skin. He wore a simple black suit under a black overcoat. His tie was as shockingly white as the smooth hair that went to the base of his spine. Lucifer had wings, but I couldn't see them under the suit, though he could have been hiding them with magic, as well.

It didn't matter that I couldn't see them, because I was focused on his eyes. They were glistening and shining black, like someone had replaced his eyes with those of a spider.

I wanted to say that I was scared. Truthfully, I was, but fear wasn't the only thing making my heart beat faster. Being around Lucifer was like being a compulsive drug addict looking at a bag of cocaine in a fire. You knew it was bad for you. You knew touching it would hurt, and the consequences would be worse. But that didn't keep you from staring. It didn't stop the desire.

Lucifer didn't say anything. He stood there, looking past my free-hanging hatchet, and watched me.

I should have screamed. I should have run. I should have done anything to get help against him. I knew I couldn't fight Lucifer. He'd tossed me around like a rag doll when I got in his way, then set me on fire when I slightly annoyed him. Michael might have a chance, but his powers were weakening thanks to me. It would be a small tussle, then a complete bloodbath.

But he was here for a reason. The Devil had a reason for everything. He seemed like the type to plan every miniscule detail, no matter how trivial it seemed.

Having Mateo put the fragment inside of me was no accident.

Not pulverizing me on the spot was no accident, either.

"Why are you here?"

What should have been an intimidating question came out as a quivering whisper. I was glad I found the will to speak at all.

Lucifer didn't answer. He just continued to stare at me. I thought that was all he was going to do, until he looked into my soul.

I squeezed my eyes shut and gasped. It was like two rough, hot hands were reaching into my brain and prying it apart. He could see it all, every memory I shared with my sister.

The day I found her in the forest, alone and wailing in a smoking patch of earth. When she learned how to cook with my mom. The first time she used her powers to heal my wounds. Laughing when I tried to braid her hair. The horrors we'd endured when the demons came for her at Owl Creek. Witnessing the deaths of our parents. Still loving me after I became a killer for the Blood Thorns. Needing her to keep me together. Promising we would leave them. Running after we were betrayed. Losing her and finding her again. Demons hunting us as her powers began to grow. Seeing her rib get torn out. Promising to keep her safe even though I knew I would die. Watching her lose control, and ultimately losing her all over again.

All of my memories surged at once, filling my heart and threatening to break it. I choked out a sob. I nearly begged him for mercy. The pain was crippling, turning my legs into wet noodles. I didn't know what he was looking for, so I couldn't protect myself from him.

Then, after what seemed like an eternity, the hands were pulled from my brain. I heaved and bent at the waist, taking deep breaths to calm myself.

When I looked up again, Lucifer was directly in front of me. I startled and tried to punch him. He caught my wrist easily. Instinct kicked in and I tried to pull away, but he jerked me back. I bumped against his chest. His body heat was smothering, at least twice the heat of a human's. I lifted my head to look at Lucifer, and was painfully aware of how small I was compared to him. He was the Devil. He could crush me, burn me, pull me apart without the slightest effort.

Lucifer gripped my chin and raised my face to his. The floods of dread and yearning fell on my body like drenched clothes. He was too divine. Too terrifying and mighty for me to fight him. I didn't even have a weapon to try.

"You are her protector," he stated. "Your love compels you to defend her, no matter how much she has ruined you."

I don't know how it happened, or why I did it, but suddenly I found the defiance that had been hiding in me.

"She didn't," I breathed out.

"Is that why you are wandering these halls without a purpose? Is that why you are letting your heart break?" He tilted his head ever so slightly, examining me. "Is that why you refuse to let her go?"

I tried to back away, but a sudden ripple of energy shuddered down my spine and through my legs. I couldn't move my feet. They were frozen in place.

"She came to me of her own accord, on the sole promise that I permit you and your friends to live. Given how she has run from me, I was reluctant to adhere to her wish."

Lucifer leaned down like he wanted to kiss me, knowing I couldn't run from him. My heart felt torn— half of it screaming to escape whatever torture Lucifer's kiss would inflict, the other half greedily craving it.

"You think I am being cruel to her. That I would bring her harm. But you are wrong. I have treated her as she deserves to be treated. She is a princess. She belongs. She is happy."

My mind told me it wasn't true. That Dro was working on a ploy, buying time until I could rescue her.

She had to be. It made more sense. She wouldn't give in. Not after everything we'd gone through.

Except…

I can't fight this anymore, Connie.

Those weren't the words of someone who was planning a double-cross. They were honest and sincere. A revelation and an epiphany.

Dro had surrendered.

My heart cracked so sharply I couldn't breathe for a minute. I fought my tears, hoping I looked strong in front of him.

But it didn't matter how I tried to look. He would see right through me.

"I am here to offer you a truce, as I am grateful for what you have done for my child."

I gasped in air, looking at him. Lucifer was *grateful* for me protecting Dro. For unwillingly leading her back to him. If those weren't the words to a trap, I didn't know what was.

"I am indebted to you. Your tenacity has crippled the Heavenly Host. You have valiantly fought for my daughter's life. I am impressed."

Lucifer's hand slid from my chin to my cheek. It pulsed soothing heat and crippling pleasure. It wrapped my body in blankets of comfort, relaxing my tired body and easing my pains. I sighed, aching for more. It wasn't wrong. Couldn't be wrong.

"I shall spare you further pain. You will suffer no more. There will be no need to run, because you shall not know fear. You will know peace, Constance Ramirez. All I ask is that you let her go."

His fingers crept into my brain again, reminding me of everything I wanted. To not be afraid that someone would hurt me, or that I would hurt someone. I wanted to forget about angels and demons and ruthless artifacts. I wanted to be normal. I wanted Sephiel to be relieved of his grief, Max to regain his hope and energy. I wanted Warrick to hold me and tell me how much he loved me, and to have the confidence to give him my whole heart without restraint.

Lucifer could do that for me. All I had to do was stop searching for Dro.

But under all those dreams, I saw the reality of what I really desired. What I needed. A teenage girl to look at me without fear for once. To not see her pulling at her snow-white hair with guilt. To stop icy blue eyes from filling with tears when I came back covered in blood. To fix the mess I had made of our relationship, and stand beside her again.

I wanted to be fearless. I *needed* my sister to be safe.

It took all my strength to breathe and push away the tempting warmth of his promise. The air was sharper in my lungs, almost painful as the heat left it. I held my breath, just in case it was my last one.

"No," I said.

I'd never said a word so quietly before. Never said it with such conviction. No matter how much I ached for that security, for the freedom to live without danger, I wouldn't take the easy road. I wouldn't be seduced into the Devil's trap. Whatever he said, I knew he had something terrible planned for my little sister. You couldn't be the Devil if you didn't have a hidden agenda. Dro's pain and blood would not be on my hands.

I waited to see if Lucifer would kill me. I'd rejected his offer, pushed away his advances. There was nothing in his eyes or on his face to reveal what he was feeling. If he even *could* feel. I concentrated on breathing evenly. I inhaled sharply and squeezed my eyes shut when he forced himself into my head again, drawing out all of my guilt and fear. I dug my nails into my palms, drawing blood. I was trembling, but still didn't give in. I didn't beg for mercy, didn't drop to my knees and cry for release or forgiveness. I didn't think about Dro or Warrick or Max or Sephiel. Lucifer didn't need the ammunition.

"You are brave, Constance Ramirez," crooned the Devil. "Precious few have resisted my comfort. Perhaps you only need more time to break."

I slowly lifted my eyes and looked at Lucifer. He

was already gliding away, moving without a sound, past my free-floating hatchet as if it wasn't even there.

"I'm going to kill you."

The words were out of my mouth before I realized who I was telling them to. Lucifer stopped, and slowly turned back to me. The horrible crush of love and hate flowed over me. I swayed and tried to shake the fog from my mind.

"I do not think so," Lucifer chided. "My daughter would not forgive you for that."

"She's not–" I started to slur.

"She is where she belongs. All the beings I command honor her. In time, her sadness shall fade. As will her memories of you."

I tried to force my body to move, but Lucifer's magic was too strong. He stared at me with empty, abysmal black eyes.

"Do what you will, Constance Ramirez. Hunt the fragments. Search for the girl you believe is your sister. I shall not seek to destroy you."

I blinked, not understanding.

Until he said, "For if you continue down this path, you shall destroy yourself."

And then he was gone, blinking out of sight and leaving me alone in the lifeless school gym. The sudden release from his magic had me pitching forward and listening to my hatchet clatter onto the floor.

It shouldn't have been hard to get up. It was something I'd done a million times before. Just get up, grab my hatchet, and walk away.

But all those times before, I felt whole. I wasn't missing a huge chunk of my life. My foundation was solid.

Now the ground under me had split, and I was falling into darkness.

The pain hit like a bullet to the chest. I put my hand to my chest and tried to breathe through it. Nothing I did seemed to work. I felt as if someone had torn out my heart and filled the hole with piercing wooden splinters. It wasn't long before my cheeks were wet with tears.

I had no idea how long I crouched there, on my hands and knees, crying over everything I had sacrificed, losing the one person I never wanted to lose.

Eventually I ran out of tears. Crying wouldn't bring my sister back. It wouldn't kill Mateo and Drake. It wouldn't stop Lucifer.

The last time I broke down like this, I had Warrick to hold me and anger to draw strength from. Now I was alone and couldn't find the energy to lay blame. Rage had caused me more harm than good. It was time for me to let go and focus on motivation.

Finding Dro was the only thing I needed to do right. I could deal with everything else after as it came along.

I took a deep breath, gathered my weapons, wiped my eyes, and left the gym.

The guys were out of their classrooms when I made my way into the corridor. I followed the sound of their voices until I heard them enter the principal's office.

Two angels were standing on either side of the door, closing it and acting as guards. They saw me approaching and stared at me blankly, but didn't shift to move out of my way.

My patience ran out in microseconds.

"You can move, or you can get punched in the face. Either works for me."

The angels glanced at each other with uncertainty. I almost hoped they would test me. After my encounter with Lucifer and consequential breakdown, I needed to feel strong again. If I had to beat up some angels to do that... Well, I'd be making feathers fly.

"She may enter," came Michael's authoritative voice from beyond the door.

I shared a mutual glare with the angels before they moved aside to let me pass. I yanked open the door a little too aggressively, smacking one of the angels sharply in the arm.

Score one for me.

Angels stood in the reception area, staring at me with untrusting silence. They lined the walls like white leather curtains. I barely gave them a glance.

Weaving into the principal's office, I found Max, Sephiel and Warrick. Sleep didn't seem to have done anything for them. Max was slumped on a couch with his head propped in one hand, depressed and miserable. Warrick was leaning on the wall by the door with his arms folded over his chest. He seemed awake and focused, but the bags under his eyes told a different story. Sephiel stood on the right of the desk, rigid as a soldier. Michael, of course, sat behind the principal's desk with a stony expression.

I walked in like the girl they were about to expel for setting the teacher's lounge on fire.

"Gang's all here," I said, walking straight to the desk and dropping into the chair across from Michael. "Good. Let's talk."

Michael narrowed his eyes, clearly not wanting to be in the same room as me. That was fine. He didn't need to talk. He just needed to listen.

"Who here can find out where Mateo and Drake are going to be next?" I glanced over my shoulder at Max. "Can you?"

He looked at me, frowning as he thought about his answer. He finally shook his head. "It's too murky. Lucifer must be blocking them from wherever he is in the world."

I kept my face blank. "He's in Juárez."

"How do you know?" Warrick asked.

I flicked my eyes at him. "We came here with Dro. I can't see a reason for him to be anywhere else."

Warrick frowned, but it was easier than telling the whole truth right now. Not bothering to return to that recent memory without getting some kind of therapy, I turned back to Michael. The archangel was observing at me with all the interest of a brick wall.

"You can track Lucifer too, right?" I asked. "Maybe not as well as before, but well enough?"

He blinked once. "If you are intending to mock me, I should warn you to stop now."

"Not mocking," I defended. "Asking."

Michael narrowed his eyes yet again. "Yes."

"Good. Because we need to take the fight to Lucifer and his new friends," I bit out.

"You mean the fragments?" Warrick asked.

"If we can get them, sure. But I was thinking we go straight for the two human bastards holding them."

"You think that will make a difference?"

I turned around in the chair so I could face Warrick directly. I don't want to say I was getting annoyed with him, but my temper was on a short leash right now.

"I think Mateo and Drake are playing a major role and know where the remaining fragments are. I think they know where Dro is, and Lucifer by extension."

"Do you believe Andromeda is with Lucifer?"

I twisted in the chair to look at Sephiel. I was glad he asked the question, because I wasn't sure I could stand looking at Max's heartbroken expression. It would only make the gash in my chest feel wider.

I could have lied. Maybe I should have lied. But after everything we'd been through, my group deserved the truth. Michael didn't, but he seemed to be quite comfy in his leather chair. My confidence slipped a little bit, and I slumped in my seat.

"I don't have to believe it. I know it."

Sephiel's heart shot to his eyes, and suddenly I couldn't look at him, either. "How?"

Again, I should have lied. But if I wanted Michael to go through with my idea of luring Lucifer out by targeting Drake and Mateo, then I had to tell the truth. It wasn't something I was used to.

"Same reason I know he's in the city. He came to see me."

The entire room fell silent. Michael's jaw twitched. It was the first semblance of emotion I'd ever really seen from him.

"When?"

"About twenty minutes ago," I confessed.

All my friends gathered their breath to scold me, but I was quicker on the draw.

"He didn't hurt me, I don't know how he found me, and I don't think he wants to kill us."

"That doesn't sound like the Lucifer who tried to kill you a month ago," Warrick said coldly. "What changed his mind?"

I thought back to everything Lucifer had said to me. About walking away and accepting his truce. About Dro being happy with her birth father.

Those were the truths I couldn't seem to tell.

"Does it matter?" I deflected. "The point is he'll think we're going for Dro more than the fragments."

"But if we go after the fragments, we buy more time and draw him into the open," Max said tentatively. "I can't really see what happens, but Constance is right. Each fragment carries a part of Lucifer and the Gate's power. The more we destroy them, the more damage we do to him." Max's expression tightened. "I can see that Carver has one with him."

I glanced back at him. "Your sight is working again?"

Max wobbled his hand. "Still a little spotty, but that part was clear. Carver is our next best shot. I think he'll be with Mateo and Drake. I just can't see where they are."

My gaze shifted back to Michael. I raised an eyebrow. He barely even blinked. I wondered if my gamble of poking at his pride had worked the way I planned. If I'd wasted my breath on a creature that had never loved the company of humans.

Then Michael nodded. It was so small I almost missed it, but there was a conviction in his eyes that hadn't been there before. That was when I knew I'd snared him.

"I shall work with your prophet to discern the locations of all those we seek. Then we shall confront them."

Michael rose out of his chair in one fluid motion. I stayed where I was, watching him carefully. Michael towered over the desk and watched me, thinking God knows what. I never broke eye contact. After a second, he glided out from behind the desk and moved for the door. Sephiel stepped back to give him space. He glanced at me briefly with a look that I swear held some disappointment in it. I didn't know if it was because I'd met Lucifer and not told him, or because Lucifer had been right under his nose and he never knew it.

"Come, Max. Michael is not known for his patience."

Max sighed. "Great. Always wanted to get my brain picked apart by an angel."

I pushed myself out of the chair and turned around its back. "Relax," I said, tapping the hidden tattoo just over my heart, "It's not like you're going to get possessed."

He looked at me like I just told him I wanted to be a ballerina. "Your perception of good and bad is seriously skewed."

I grinned at him. "You'd be amazed how many times people have told me that."

Max rolled his eyes, then suddenly took my hand. I wasn't ready for it, so I didn't have time to pull away. I knew he was searching me for some kind of hope. He wanted to know if Lucifer said something to me suggesting that Dro was all right. I reacted fast, pulling on every ounce of faith I had so he wouldn't know that she might have been happier now than she was with us. I let him feel my confidence in this sudden plan, that I didn't think Lucifer would hurt her, and that I believed we'd get her back.

Only one of those thoughts didn't feel like a lie.

Max took his hand away from mine and gave me a weak smile. I was better at faking it than he was. Sephiel stood by the doorway, watching us silently. Max blew out some air and followed the ex-angel out of the room.

Which left me alone with my annoyed boyfriend.

"Just say it, okay?"

"Say what?" he asked.

"I don't know, whatever's making you look pissed off. I told you that Lucifer showed up and saw me. If he wanted me dead, he would have fried me on the spot. But I'm still here, so everything's fine."

Warrick raised one of his eyebrows. "Everything's fine? That's what you're going with?"

"What do you want me to say?" I shot back. "That I know what the hell I'm doing? That I know it will work? That I'm not fucking terrified of something going wrong?"

My voice had gotten a shake to it that I didn't like. I looked away from Warrick. It wasn't long until he was in front of me, putting his hands on my arms.

"Do you believe we can do this? Stop Drake and Mateo, take the fragments away from Lucifer, make him weak enough to overcome, close the Hell Gate, and get Dro back?"

A sane person would have said no. That we had a better chance at proving Santa Claus was real. It was a much less painful option, too.

But I thought about overcoming impossible obstacles. I thought about stopping one supernatural enemy after the other. I thought about how good it would feel when I stole the dreams from the people who'd given me nightmares.

"Yes," I said.

Warrick read my eyes before giving me an easy smile. He leaned in and gave me a quick kiss. I wanted to make it last longer than it did, but that might make him suspicious.

He pulled back and stroked the hair lying against my face. "Then we better get going."

Warrick kissed the top of my head, took my hand, and led me through the office. I couldn't help but feel he had finally overcome his overprotectiveness for me. Maybe he finally learned that nothing he did or said would keep me out of danger or harm's way.

I hoped that was the case, because I was sure I had

just lied to him.

Chapter 20

No matter how many times I saw a burning building, I was never ready for it.

The smell and sight of the towering smoke pillars always burned my nose and brought tears to my eyes. The heat was always unbearable. The sound of screams was always new.

Michael hadn't said where we were going, or what we'd find when we got there.

With the *movens caeli*'s power enhanced by Michael's teleportation ability, the dozen of us were able to move at once. Max had warned us to be ready for a fight, but when we landed by a green market building called the *Mercado Reforma*, all we saw were the white steeples of the *Cathedral de Ciudad Juárez* erupting with flame. I tore my eyes away from the cathedral and looked at the people screaming on the streets.

There must have been three hundred of them, all crushed together in a mob of flailing limbs. Possessors made of black smoke hovered above their heads, and the smell of blood was thick. It was a full scale riot, with some stragglers being dragged off to the park on the side to be finished off more intimately.

Almost as thick as the blood was the rage. It grew inside me like a cancer, spreading to every cell and making me tighten my grip on my hatchet.

But worse than that was the subtle desire pushing into me. It was hiding under the rage, but it was there, like the heat under a fire.

I gave myself a mental shake and looked at the group. They were fighting the same addiction I was. Not even Michael was able to overcome it, and he wasn't even fully human yet. If anything, he was looking at the madness with more rage than the rest of us.

Wait. He isn't looking at the crowd. He's looking just past them. What could be more...

I was following his line of sight as I thought it, and then I knew.

Standing in front of the burning church, absorbed by the spectacle of bloodshed, was Lucifer's gang.

I spotted Drake and Carver taking whatever stragglers they could and venting on them with their fists. Carver was deadly serious, but I could almost hear Drake's laughter. Behind them, Mateo stood with his fist clenched tightly at his side. He was itching to get into the fight.

I didn't think it could get any worse, until I saw Lucifer.

He was standing with his back to the massacre, as if he had no idea it was happening. He was more interested in the burning cathedral in front of him. At first I thought he was controlling the fire, since he was making sweeping gestures and pointing things out. But he wasn't standing alone.

She raised her hands, and the fire rose with them. She pressed her hands down, and it flattened on command.

When Dro turned her head to see Lucifer, I swore there was a trace of a smile on her lips.

I told myself he had been lying. Deception was what the King of Hell did best. He was trying to trick Dro, and she was playing along to learn his faults. But the smile looked too real for Dro to be faking.

My heart seemed to crumple inward, anger taking its place. I couldn't believe she would fall for this. She had fought too hard for too long. I took my hatchet off my belt. Lucifer would pay for this. I would destroy him, even if I destroyed myself while doing it.

The edges of a white trench coat brushed against my shin. I blinked rapidly to see Michael stalking forward, the *movens caeli* in his hand. Before I could say anything, he immersed himself in the crowd. He was out of sight for a dangerously long time, and then a burst of golden light exploded through the crowd of murder-happy humans. They screamed as the light domed over top of them, and when the light faded, they were gone.

I blinked to clear my eyesight, and found myself staring across the street at my enemies and my sister. Carver, Drake, and Mateo looked furious, Lucifer was as impassive as ever, and Dro seemed caught between indescribable horror and crushing guilt.

Without even blinking or twitching, Lucifer opened a portal. The air parted like sliced skin, blood red fire curling around its edges. Demons tumbled through it, shoving each other aside to get to us.

This had been part of the plan we laid out before we came here. Michael would draw away the distractions, as he was the only one of us who could teleport. While he was gone, we would fight off any demons or Blood Thorns sent our way. The idea was that we could buy enough time for Michael to return and use his powers to strengthen our defense.

Seeing all the demons and possessed Thorns headed our way now, I wasn't so sure we'd have the time we wanted.

I watched them pour out of the torn air, feeling my skin tighten and my heart begin to pound. The monsters rushing through the portal weren't run of the mill demons. There were no brutal Reds, no flesh-hungry ghouls, not even hulking Shredders or howling Wretches.

Bounding out of the red tear were dogs the size of Irish Wolfhounds. But these weren't furry, gentle pets. Not unless you liked your dogs with greasy black skin, curved horns behind sharp ears, razor claws, and serrated teeth. Eyes that were solid black save for a few, stringy red veins stared at us with hunger and hatred. I gripped my hatchet for reassurance. I'd fought hellhounds before, and barely survived. Fighting four of them wasn't going to send the odds into my favor.

But worse were the two shapes morphing behind the hellhounds. The warrior elite of Hell that I didn't stand a chance against. They weren't called Knights for nothing.

Both had the tall, powerful build of a boxer or a professional linebacker. Their bodies were covered in a thick, scaled onyx armor with demonic symbols crudely etched into them. Two wide bat wings stuck out from their backs, and they each held a saw-toothed scythe in their gauntlet-covered hands. Their faces were covered in a helmet pointed like a jouster's, wisps of smoke snaking out from the eye-slits, obscuring the burning red eyes behind the mask.

The angels rushed into the fight before I could tell them not to. Sephiel was even screaming for them to draw back and take out the possessed Blood Thorns first. They forgot they were human now, and it was going to get them all killed.

I wasn't sure what I could do until Michael came back, but I couldn't there and watch them all die. I followed the angels into the fight.

I couldn't save the first one who swung his sword at the Knight he approached. The Knight leaned back, swept his scythe forward, hooking the sword and tearing it from the angel's grip. The scythe flew up on a backswing, and cleaved the angel in two.

Tearing my eyes away from the shower of blood, I turned my head just as a hellhound leaped for my chest. I twisted to the side, seeing the dark blur fly past me. Hellhounds were insanely fast and able to blend into the shadows, literally hunting in darkness. By the time I turned around to find the hellhound, it was already slamming into me.

My back hit the concrete hard, and I barely got my arm under its throat to keep the beast from tearing into my throat. Its weight pressed down on me, the edges of its sharp fur poking into my jacket and the front of my shirt. I crossed my forearms under its neck, turning my head to the side as it snapped at me. Its savage roar was deafening, and the saliva that dripped onto my cheek and throat was burning hot. The smell of wet dog and sulfur gagged me.

Knowing I couldn't hold it off much longer, I pushed my feet into its stomach to force it higher. The hellhound screamed furiously. Still keeping one arm under its neck, my hand darted into my jacket and grabbed a silver knife. I sliced the weapon across the hellhound's throat. It twitched and barked. The skin was thick and hard to break with a single move, but the pressure eased off me. I kept my arm moving, reaching around the hellhound's head until the tip of my knife plunged into its eye.

That got a reaction.

The hellhound yowled and thrashed its head, ripping my knife away from me. Its far paws brushed over my chest as it stumbled away from me, giving me the chance to breathe and get to my feet. I swung the hatchet down for its muzzle, just as it snarled and lunged for me with open jaws. The blade of the hatchet struck the edge of its upper jaw, leaving a shallow cut but still twisting its head to the side.

I stepped back to get distance on the hellhound, when arms coiled around my chest and trapped me.

"Come on now, sweetheart," a Blood Thorn rasped in my ear. I smelled the reek of sulfur coming from his skin. "Give the dog a bone."

I grimaced. "Okay."

I snapped my head back, crushing his nose. He roared and rocked back, too dazed to hang onto me. The hellhound leaped forward just as I twisted to the side. The hellhound crashed into the possessed Blood Thorn. They tumbled and the man screamed, until the scream was replaced by a choking gurgle.

I eased back as the hellhound gorged itself, not ready for the solid punch that landed in my cheek. I stumbled with the hit, unable to get my bearings before someone else grabbed me and picked me up.

I was getting sick of that.

The man behind me hooked my arms while another man rushed in front of me and grabbed my legs. I growled and twisted, jerking one of my feet back until the Thorn in front of me lost hold of my boot. I snapped my foot into his chin, knocking him back and freeing both my legs. I leaned against the man behind me to keep myself elevated, then kicked the man in front of me in the throat. He lurched back and clutched his neck, gasping for air.

The man at my back snarled as we pitched forward, my feet hitting the ground again. He twisted my arms painfully, trying to force another submission hold on me. I stomped on his foot and he howled, loosening his grip. I was able to slip away from his arms, but he thanked me by punching me in the ribs. I hissed and kept twisting until I was in front of him. He swung at my head this time, so I ducked and slammed my hatchet into his leg right above the knee.

He screamed in pain while I reached into my jacket and drew another knife. I silenced him by stabbing the blade into his chin. I ripped it free and looked over my shoulder, seeing the choking Blood Thorn regain his breath to charge me. I tossed the knife with as much strength as I could muster. It was enough, embedding deep into his eye.

Adrenaline was pumping through my veins even as I retrieved my knife. I turned and took a second to see what was happening around me.

I'd been on the edge of the Heaven Gate battle, fighting human enemies while desperately buying Max time to make our escape with the *movens caeli*. It had been a horrible battle to witness, but actually being in this one was worse than I could imagine.

Nearly half of the angels were lying on the ground, blood soaking through the jagged tears of their white coats. Around them were two hellhounds and the gory remains of four Blood Thorns. Black smoke lingered in the air, Possessors in their natural form trying to find a new home. I was terrified they might be able to possess the angels, but they seemed to be deterred when they got too close.

They must have Michael's sigil tattooed on them, too. Thank God.

My gaze shifted from the corpses to the living fighters. The remaining angels were trying to avoid the wickedly fast Knights, kicking away Blood Thorns when they had the chance. I couldn't see Max, but he was probably smart enough to watch the sidelines and shout warnings when we couldn't see a threat behind us. Sephiel was holding off the hellhounds, watching them carefully and lashing out with his short swords when they tried to bite him. The hellhound on his left snapped for his forearm, but Sephiel was just as quick. His left sword hacked down on the monster's neck, causing it to cripple in half. The hellhound on his right charged, but Sephiel swept out his sword and cut open the beast's throat.

Finding Warrick wasn't hard. He was fighting Blood Thorns hand to hand, delivering powerful hits that left his targets stunned if not completely unconscious. Drake had been watching, and was sneaking up behind Warrick with a huge knife. I took in a breath to scream, but Max warned him before I could.

"Drake's behind you!"

That was all Warrick needed to hear. He whirled around and lashed out, catching Drake in the cheek with a powerful back-fist. He grabbed the knife and tried to snap Drake's wrist, but the larger bounty hunter used his free hand to punch Warrick in the head instead.

I was about to run to help him when shadow grew in front of me. Instinct kicked in and I ducked. The air split in half as a scythe barely missed my head. I kept moving, sprinting forward until I thought I had enough distance. I spun on my heel, clutching my hatchet and knife, and saw that I completely misjudged how close the Knight was.

It was three feet from me, coal-red eyes burning into mine as it raised the scythe like an executioner's axe. It descended and I jumped to the side, wincing as the dark blade plunged into the concrete. The Knight dragged the scythe up from the cement, swinging it toward my stomach. I leaped back as far as I could, feeling the air move as the curved blade barely missed me. The demon warrior turned with the blade, lashing out at my head with his fist. I crouched to avoid it, then threw myself back as the scythe crossed up to me.

I watched the blade rise over my head, flip, and descend. I crossed my hatchet and knife to catch the scythe, narrowly avoiding the blade. My strength was nowhere near the Knight's, so the most I could do to save my life was shuffle away and let its black blade screech against my silver ones. I had just pushed away the scythe when the Knight closed in and plunged its fist into my stomach.

I thought it had punched a hole clean through me. I crumpled in half and flew back three feet, tripping on my heels and landing hard on the ground. I grimaced at the pain swelling along my belly, using adrenaline and survival instinct to numb it. I still had my weapons, but they weren't going to do me any good. By the time I was getting back to my feet, the Knight was standing over me. It stood like a black shadow, the red eyes searing into my memory like a branding iron. Its armor clinked as it pulled its arms back, lifting the scythe like a sadistic golfer about to tee off my head.

The blade was just beginning to fall when a blast of gold light exploded behind the Knight. I rolled in the opposite direction of the scythe, scrambling to my feet and backing up. The Knight turned around to see what had attacked it. I peered over its shoulder to see Michael standing in the middle of the battle, his broadsword drawn and his azure eyes glowing with rage.

The second Knight darted for the archangel, swinging its scythe in a powerful arc. Michael didn't move until the very last second, catching the curve of the scythe and sweeping the blade around. It was yanked from the Knight's grip, leaving it defenseless. Michael then cleaved off the Knight's head in a single stroke.

For a second, I thought we could win.

Then Lucifer stepped forward. I could see Carver shifting from foot to foot, as if he couldn't decide whether to join in the fight, or run for his life. Mateo held Dro back while she screamed over and over again.

"No!"

Lucifer didn't listen. He approached Michael and

held out his hand. Hellfire bloomed out of it like a burning flower, funneling toward Michael. The angel spun around, the edge of his white coat twirling with him, and raised his sword.

The blistering hot hellfire engulfed the blade, licking around the sides to try and catch Michael. But the Heavenly Host's Commander held his own against the King of Hell, both supernaturals locked in an intense battle of defense and offence.

I was so damn distracted, that I didn't see the Knight move until its hand clamped around my throat.

It picked me up like I weighed nothing, my feet dangling in the air. I kicked weakly, not even close to touching the Knight. The metal of the gauntlet was blistering the outsides of my neck, getting hotter as its grooves pinched into my skin. I couldn't breathe, pathetically hammering my hatchet down on the Knight's wrist. My silver blade *ping*ed harmlessly off the tough metal armor. I was a mouse trying to bite into a metal cat.

The Knight squeezed my throat again, forcing my bones to grind together. Everything I saw was blurry and dark at the edges. I barely made out the scythe as it was pulled back, ready to sever me at the waist–

Another blast of white light burst through the haze, this time striking against the Knight's back. It didn't make a sound, but it stiffened and dropped me. I landed in a heap, gagging and coughing. Every time I swallowed, the burns on my outer throat throbbed. I was pushing myself up when hands found my arms and lifted me. I snarled and jerked free, ready to fight again.

Dro held her hands up, watching me like she would watch an aggravated cobra. I lowered my hands, and the battle turned into white noise.

"You shouldn't have come here," Dro cried over the commotion. "How did you find me? I was blocking Max."

I narrowed my eyes, glad that Max was too far away to hear his girlfriend. "Does it matter? I found you, and now you can come back."

"No," Dro said.

I absorbed what she said, and blinked when I couldn't believe it. "What the hell do you mean, 'no'?"

Dro's eyes were sad. "I can't go back with you, Con. It's too dangerous." She started shaking her head. "You should have listened to me."

My anger rose, but I pushed it down. Dro wasn't the person I needed to take my frustrations out on. I took a slow, careful step toward her. She tensed, but didn't move back.

"Whatever you're planning, tell me, and I'll help you."

My sister shook her head. "I don't need help."

Some of the anger slipped through the cracks. "You were standing next to Lucifer, burning down a church. Tell me what's right in that picture."

Dro's cheeks took on an embarrassed, annoyed flush. "It isn't what you think."

"Then just tell me what it is." My voice was beginning to rise. A battle was not where I wanted to have a fight with my sister. Especially since I looked out of the corner of my eye and saw that Michael's defense had just broken. His sword could no longer hold back Lucifer's fire.

"You wouldn't understand," Dro said, trying to reign in her own boiling temper.

"Like fuck I wouldn't," I snapped. "How can you say that to me?!"

"*Because you're human!*" she exploded. Her eyes burned like the flame from a welder's torch. "You have no idea what it's like to hold all these powers and thoughts inside of you, always being afraid you'll hurt someone you love, and losing control when you were so sure you had it! I *had* to let it out, Constance! It was tearing me apart not to! Lucifer was the only one who could show me control!"

She took a moment to breathe. I wanted to argue, but I couldn't speak.

"I told Lucifer to look for you. I asked him to give

you a deal that would keep you and the others alive. You should have taken it. You still can. You can't trust me, so you need to let me go."

It was my sister's voice, but they were Lucifer's words. They had to be. Dro knew she was dangerous, but she always wanted to stay with me. It was a promise we had made, that no matter what came across our path, we would overcome it together.

But what if Lucifer didn't tell her to say any of this? What if Dro's finally telling me all the secrets she's kept? What if she really has given up?

I shoved the thought away. I refused to believe it. I couldn't.

"No," I told her flatly. "I'm not going anywhere unless you're coming too."

"Damn it, Constance, I'm trying to save you!" she yelled.

"But you're not!" I shouted back. "You're hurting me!"

I didn't know the words were out of my mouth before it was too late. The stunned expression must have remained on my face, but Dro looked at me with utter despair. If this was the only way I could get Dro to listen to me, then I would do it. Even if I hated myself for it.

"You're hurting me," I repeated.

Seeing the tears form in my sister's eyes cut me deeper than I imagined. My words had caused her pain. But I didn't know what to do. Hurting people was the only thing I knew I would never fail at.

I took one more step, until it felt like just the two of us. I almost forgot about the battle we were losing.

"Andromeda, please," I begged. "This isn't right, and you know it. This isn't what we promised each other."

Tears spilled down Dro's cheeks, but she didn't reach for me. She took a step back.

"Is that what you're banking your hope on? A promise? Like the one where you said nothing bad would ever happen because you, Dad, and Mom would protect me? Or all the times you told me we'd leave Mexico? Or when you said Isabel would never find me?"

Her callousness numbed me for a moment, but it didn't last. Soon the pain crept in, like an icy air that froze everything it touched. It hurt to breathe, my damaged heart cracking again. I didn't want to think it was Dro telling me this. Not my sister, the sweet, innocent, lost girl who was afraid to be alone. Who was kind to those who didn't deserve it. Who loved carefully, but with all her heart. The sister who never wanted me to leave. It couldn't have been her.

But there were no Possessors hovering over her head. No one sticking a knife in her back to make her talk. No sadistic father whispering in her ear.

It was just us.

"You made a million promises to me, Constance. But how many did you really think you could keep? You wanted to save me, but you can't. I wanted you to trust me to save you, but you wouldn't even do that. You held onto me too tight, and now you have to let me go."

Now the tears were building in my eyes. I felt the world crumbling around me, but my feet were glued to the ground.

"I can't," I whispered shakily.

There was no sympathy in her eyes. No regret or guilt. Not even a hint of pity.

"You can," Dro said. "And you will."

She held my eyes a moment longer, then turned on her heel and ran back for the battle. All I could do was stand there and watch a piece of my heart, life, and soul, run away from me. I stood on the sidelines of the battle, unable to find the will to join it. I watched Dro rush to Lucifer's side as Michael fired a blast of heavenfire at the King of Hell. She swept it aside with a stronger flash of her unique hellfire, hurling it directly into another angel and incinerating him instantly. There was no shame on her face.

Michael backed up a step, snapping up his hands and creating a heavenfire so bright it rivaled the sun. I saw Lucifer step in front of Dro protectively, warding off the spell. Michael shouted something I couldn't understand, though I spotted Sephiel grabbing an injured Warrick and helping him limp toward Max. The young prophet was fiddling with the *movens caeli*, as if he'd forgotten how to use it.

My feet moved on their own, survival instinct kicking in over the swelling heartache. As I moved to the much smaller group, I saw Michael move his attention from Lucifer to Carver, who was trying to edge out of range.

He wasn't fast enough.

Michael spun on his heel and hurled his sword at the demon slayer. The blade sank into his chest like butter, nearly cutting him in half. Carver was on his feet for one more second before he began to dissolve into black ash around the blade.

Lucifer's roar sounded through the night like thunder, his strength building over top of Michael's heavenfire wall. White fire smothered the gold, pushing out like daggers that drilled into the archangel's chest. He collapsed onto his back, writhing in pain as a dozen points of flame scorched through him.

I ignored Sephiel's warning, running for Michael. I reached him as he slapped his hands to his chest, using whatever magic he still had to heal himself. I grabbed his arms and was about to pull him back, when a dozen of the white flames shot toward my face. There was no way I could avoid them. I closed my eyes and turned my head away.

Hot air blew in front of me, sweeping out to the left instead of around me. I opened my eyes, seeing the edges of white hellfire push away Lucifer's flaming daggers. When the light and fire cleared, I saw Lucifer staring down at Dro.

She pretended not to see him. She focused solely on me.

"That was the last time, Constance," Dro said. "Don't come back."

I lost all of my senses again. I forgot to breathe. I

forgot what I was holding. I didn't know where I was, or why someone was grabbing onto me. I barely heard the roar of the magic cracking over my head. I stared at my sister until the golden light obscured my vision, and wished I'd seen just a trace of hope in her eyes.

Chapter 21

Maria wasn't in her shop when we crashed into the middle of it. We landed in the front of the shop, all of us stumbling or landing in a heap. I managed to stay on my feet, but I felt weightless. A piece of me was missing, and I couldn't find myself without it. I moved off to the side and looked down at the scrambling humans and the dying archangel.

Warrick and Max were hovering behind Sephiel while the remaining two angels tried to cover the wounds on Michael's chest. The two angels, a brunette woman and an Asian man, pressed their hands to the gory mess spilling from Michael. Whether they were applying pressure or attempting to use their non-existent healing magic, I couldn't tell. It wasn't going to matter soon. Michael was the only one with the power to heal himself, and he wasn't moving.

"Seph, what can we do?" Warrick asked.

Sephiel tossed his head over his shoulder. "Find herbs of grace and archangel root. They should respond with his nature and progress his healing." His face was drawn. "I do not know how much time that will buy before the blood loss completely hinders his consciousness."

Meaning that if Michael didn't wake up soon, he was going to die.

I hurried around the shop with Warrick and Max, who were working together to find the herbs and powders Sephiel had told them to find. Well, it was more like Warrick shouting that nothing was where Max said it was, and Max shouting back that he was looking as hard as he could. Their panic was keeping them from finding what they needed, and none of the angels could think clearly.

Quickly walking to where he was lying, I shouldered in between the angels and touched Michael's neck. His pulse was steady, which meant he was still fighting to live. I slapped him across the face.

Michael's angels gasped in shock, but I didn't look at them, because he groaned. I placed his hands onto his chest. There was no glow coming from them. I glared at the archangel.

"Seriously? This is how you want to go out, Michael? Dying on a floor in an occult shop? You seemed like you wanted to die fighting Lucifer. Guess I was wrong about how tough you were."

I could feel everyone's eyes but Michael's on me. I ignored them all. Still trapped in my grip, Michael's hands began to glow with healing light. I watched as it illuminated the crimson stained white shirt, fresh blood making it stick to the ridges of his muscles. There was a lot of damaged flesh, but I watched intently to see that every hole was closed and all the blackened, blistered skin returned to a healing pink.

Confident that Michael would be able to heal himself, I stepped back. The angels rushed into the place I had been to fuss over their wounded leader.

I wondered how Michael would feel when he was back to his strength. He wasn't the sort of person who wanted to be coddled, any more than he was the type to accept defeat. Lucifer had nearly killed him. Something told me that never would have happened a year ago when the Heaven Gate was still intact.

I slinked back into the shadows, wanting to be alone. I could feel Warrick watching me, but I was moving too quickly for him to follow. I walked through the curtain into the back room, closed the door and locked it behind me. If he didn't get the message before, he would damn sure get it now.

I pressed my back to the door and let my weary body slide down it. I was bruised, sore, exhausted, and heartbroken. It didn't really feel like I was falling on my own. It felt more like someone was pushing me down, dumping weight after weight onto my shoulders until I was trapped under a pile of depression.

Getting my heart broken wasn't new. Feeling overburdened was a daily routine. Hopelessness was as common as despair.

Yet all these familiar emotions were different now. They weren't dull throbs that ached my heart. They were knives that stabbed into my chest whenever I breathed. They were maggots burrowing into my soul to devour me. They were a current that forced me out to sea, shoved me back to shore, then dragged me out again.

Lucifer told me I had lost Dro. I never bought it because I was certain he was just trying to goad me, provoke me into doing something stupid. I was so used to the idea of Lucifer lying to me that I never imagined his telling the truth would hurt me more.

But he wasn't trying to hurt me. Not really. He was warning me, because he knew I wouldn't listen. He knew I would find Dro, and she would hurt me worse than he ever could.

I will destroy you, he'd once promised. Was this what he meant? Had he seen how far apart Dro and I would become? Had he planned this from the beginning, knowing she'd eventually break and go to him, leaving me to suffer in her absence?

Did it matter? After everything Dro had told me, how much she'd been holding back, the distress it was causing her, should I have been surprised that she couldn't hang on anymore?

Yes. I still couldn't process it. Dro wasn't responsible for me. I was the older sister. It was my job to keep us both safe.

But I never did. No matter how dangerous she was, I made it worse every single time. I took the easy route because it was disguised as the tough one. I went to criminals because I wanted human monsters to protect us from demonic ones. I ran when I should have gone straight to demonologists for the answers. I never let Dro get the release she desperately needed, because I refused to believe things were as bad as she claimed. I was so damn certain I could save her from the world. I never imagined I should have been saving her from herself, let alone allow her to save me.

Dro ran from me once. When I found her again, I never asked how it felt for her to be unrestricted by me. Had she felt freer? Had she been happy, if a little guilty? Did she care that I was being selfish in bringing her back to me?

I used to think I knew my little sister like I knew the back of my hand. I began to realize that I never really knew her at all. Pretending to make her human wouldn't change what she was. She had free will, but I had made all the choices for us. She had never been able to make ones that mattered, and I had freaked out whenever she tried. One way or another, I had driven her to Lucifer.

One way or another, I had lost her.

Maybe this was the way it was supposed to be. She had been smiling when she was with Lucifer. He hadn't been hurting her. I would have seen it in her eyes if he were. I still had a chance to run. Michael and his angels wouldn't go, but I could take Warrick and Max and Sephiel with me. We could find a piece of isolation and watch the world fall apart from a distance. A front row seat to the end of the world with my friends didn't seem so bad.

But Dro wouldn't just be missing from the picture. She would be the one burning it.

Deep down, I knew I couldn't stand back and watch the destruction Lucifer would create. I had started this when I hadn't protected Dro from the ritual that summoned Lucifer. I'd made too many mistakes. I was suffering from them now, but I had to make it all right before I died. And now I knew that I would die. When I met with Lucifer, Mateo, Drake, and Dro again, it would be for the last time. Three of them hated me, and one of them had been turned against me. They wouldn't let me walk away again. One of them would kill me.

I didn't really want to die. Missing out on a life

with Warrick and seeing Max and Sephiel find peace were huge sacrifices I didn't want to make. But as much as I tried to admit that I could let Dro stay on her dark path, I knew I would never leave her to that fate. Not when I remembered every time she told me how she wanted to live a normal life. Not when I'd seen how happy and in love she was with Max. Not when I knew she was tired of being hunted and being hated for what she was. Not when I knew her smile was the biggest when she was listening to bad jokes or wandering in forests or helping someone or trying out a new style for her hair.

I'd seen the person Dro really wanted to be. That young woman had surrendered to a demon. She deserved to be free.

That was something I was ready to die for.

Muffled shouts skirted into my grim, resolved thoughts. I caught Sephiel's voice and another woman's, but it didn't sound like Maria. My body protested stiffly as I got to my feet and turned around. I took a deep breath and wiped my cheeks. I hadn't expected them to be as wet as they were.

I hated surprises.

I unlocked the door and walked out of the backroom. To my complete un-surprise, Warrick had been sitting on the floor by the door. He drew himself up quickly, trying to catch my eyes. I shook my head, signaling him that we would talk later. It wasn't going to be a talk we'd enjoy, even though I would be lying through half of it.

"It is pointless, Sephiel!" the female angel cried. I pushed back the curtain and went back into the front of the store. Max was standing by the curtain, his arms wrapped around his middle, his face a sad mix of heartache and worry. I saw it from the corner of my eye, because I wasn't strong enough to look in his face yet.

In front of me, the two angels stood by the door. Michael was still lying on the floor, hands pressed to his chest but breathing deeply from sleep. Sephiel stood next to him, hands open in a pleading gesture.

"We knew this would be a challenge for our kind," he reasoned. "But it is not impossible to defeat Lucifer. Only two fragments remain, both in mortal bodies that have likely fused with their bloodstream. As long as he has one, his power remains insurmountable. If those bodies are destroyed, the Hell Gate can be closed. Lucifer can still be defeated."

"Did you not see the forces Lucifer called with a crook of his finger?" exclaimed the male angel. "Who knows how many more Knights he can bring forth in the next battle! We cannot defeat them as we are, Sephiel. We are human now. We are as breakable as glass."

That stung, mostly since I was crushingly aware of how right he was.

"Humans have done the impossible before," Sephiel insisted. He looked over his shoulder, pointed, and made me wish I had stayed in the backroom. "Constance has been fighting demons since she was a child. She helped keep the demons out of Heaven. She resisted the fragment. She has continually stood up to Lucifer. She thought quickly and saved Michael's life." He stopped pointing at me, but I still felt liable for anything Sephiel said.

"Humans have always been stronger than we gave them credit for. This city has fallen, but we have not. Maybe it is too late to save the souls residing here, but we can cease Lucifer's corruption from spreading." He took a step closer to the two angels. "This is what we were trained for. Defending those who could not defend themselves. Keeping the fiends of Hell locked in their fiery prison. None of that should change now that we are mortal."

Sephiel stood as straight as he could, looking taller and more confident.

"I am staying. Michael shall be staying. What shall you do?"

His speech had been strong. Uplifting. I would have listened to him with rapt attention and followed him through the Gates myself.

But I had been born a human. I hadn't been diminished into a fraction of what I used to be. At least not physically.

The male angel gave Sephiel a sympathetic look. The woman seemed resolved.

"We shall leave," she said. "And we shall live."

When they turned and walked out of the door, no one stopped them. The door slammed closed with a terminal bang. All the height and certainty Sephiel had fell off him. His shoulders slumped, his head dropped to his chest, and he let out a weary sigh. He turned toward us, and this time I was certain I could see new grey streaks in his dark red hair. His steps were heavy and slow as he crossed the room.

"It appears that the term 'Heaven help us,' does not apply to our situation," he said dejectedly.

"You did what you could, Seph," Warrick said from behind me. He was close enough that I could feel traces of his body heat against my back. "This isn't the first time the odds have been against us."

I loved Warrick for his optimism, but we all knew it was a lie. Things had never been worse for us than they were now.

"But she left," Max whispered. We all turned to look at him.

Max had always looked young, but right then he resembled a lost child. It was the same look he'd had when he saw a specter of his father, only to realize that it was a cruel magic trick. He wasn't looking at us, but I could tell he was on the verge of tears.

"She didn't even see me, she…"

Max looked up, the pain in his glistening eyes breaking my heart.

"She's not coming back, is she?"

Hearing the hope in his voice was the worst part. He could see flickers of the future, but he wanted me to lie for him. He wanted to know that Dro would come back, and that we'd find a way to repair everything we'd damaged.

But I couldn't do that to him. Not when I knew the truth as well as he did.

Warrick left my side and put his hands on Max's shoulders.

"We'll find her, Max," he told the boy, repeating words I'd once said with sureness. "Lucifer is confusing her, that's all. We can get through this."

He looked at me as he said the last part, trying to get me to believe him. It didn't work.

"Look, there's nothing more we can do tonight. We need to wait until Michael wakes up before we can make a plan. We should find some food and get some rest. Start over with clear minds."

Max nodded gloomily, drawing back from Warrick's hands. He trudged past the curtains and out of sight.

"Lucifer's hold on Andromeda is strong," Sephiel said once Max was out of hearing range. "It will not be easy to retrieve her from under his spell."

"Nothing's impossible," Warrick insisted. "Just like you told the angels. You aren't wrong, Seph. They just chose to ignore you."

Sephiel set his jaw and nodded grimly. He glanced at me, but I was more interested in the floor.

"Would you like me to take first watch?" Sephiel asked, glancing at us.

"No, I'll do it," Warrick answered. "I'm still pretty wired."

The ex-angel nodded, then slid past me. Once his footsteps turned soft and distant, Warrick put his arms around me and pulled me to his chest. I was too drained to resist, and even under the sour odors of blood, sulfur, and sweat, he smelled safe and comfortable. He smelled like the home I was giving up.

I put my arms around his waist, hugging him tight to me. I wanted to be near him for as long as I could. I was going to lose him soon.

Warrick didn't ask me if I was okay. He didn't try to offer advice or hope or even kiss me. He just stood there, making me feel warm and loved. He started moving his hands through my hair, nearly bringing me to tears.

"I'm sorry about Carver," I got out through a choked voice.

Warrick's motions slowed. He sighed heavily over top of my head.

"Me too," he admitted. "But he made his choice. Nobody could have talked him out of what he thought was right, no matter how big a mistake he was making." He stifled a laugh. "You know, I argued with him more often than not, never really saw things the way he did, but I kind of miss the bastard. Even when he was being a hard-ass, I knew I could always come to him for advice or knowledge or whatever. It's going to be strange, being the last demon slayer in the country."

I had completely forgotten that all of the demonic assaults and possessions were now on Warrick's shoulders. If we succeeded in closing the Hell Gate, he was the one who'd have to clean up the mess. And it was going to be a *huge* mess.

"I'm sorry," I whispered into his chest, closing my eyes.

Warrick's hand rested on the back of my neck. "Don't be. I was kind of hoping to get a new partner."

I opened my eyes and pulled back to look at him. Warrick gazed down at me with hope and a small smile on his lips, truly believing that we'd survive and I would fight off the remaining demons with him.

I was a terrible influence.

"I don't know what to do," I breathed shakily.

Warrick's hands cupped the sides of my face. "Who the hell does? But you'll figure it out. You always do. It's part of the reason I love you so damn much."

He said the right thing, the most perfect thing, and I wanted him to take it back. I didn't want him to love me, because it would hurt him so much more when I was gone.

There was nothing I could say to make him think any different. If I told him not to, he wouldn't listen. If I ran, he would find me. If I told him he meant nothing to me, he wouldn't believe me.

So I didn't say anything. I stood there breathlessly while he leaned down to kiss me. As soon as his lips molded onto mine, I clung to him tighter.

I wasn't just a bad influence and a liar. I was an utterly selfish bitch.

Warrick drew back and pressed his forehead against mine. "Do you want to get some sleep, or stay on watch with me?"

"With you," I whispered back. At least that part wasn't a lie.

Warrick nodded and took my hand, leading me to the middle of store. We stood on either side of the front door, peeking through the curtains to make sure they stayed empty. More than once, I saw Warrick glancing my way and offering me a smile. I did the same, but it didn't reach my heart.

I wasn't sure anything would ever again.

Chapter 22

Sephiel arrived for his watch early, telling Warrick and me to get some sleep. We returned to the storeroom and laid together, me using his chest as a pillow while he used my body as a blanket. He was overly exhausted, and it wasn't long before he fell asleep.

I tried, but couldn't catch more than a couple solid hours. I would nod off, then snap back awake. Eventually I couldn't lie there anymore, no matter how comfortable I was. I eased off Warrick's chest and shrugged out of my jacket, draping it over his chest as a makeshift blanket. As I stood up, he shifted and rolled onto his side, clutching my jacket to his chest before falling back to deep sleep.

So much for promising never to fall in love again. Dro was right about me.

I shook off the painful memory of her and my feelings for Warrick, opening the door and silently closing it behind me. I turned around and jumped near out of my skin when I saw Michael standing in front of me.

I pressed a hand to my chest to slow my racing heartbeat, then glared at the archangel. "You scared the shit out of me," I hissed.

Michael looked at me blankly. "It was not my intent."

It wasn't a full-fledged apology, but it was the most I'd get from him.

Then he surprised me.

"I want to thank you for saving my life," said Michael.

I stared at him, stupefied by what he said. I hadn't expected an apology, let alone him thanking me. Since I was too stunned to speak, Michael took that as an invitation to keep talking.

"I am fully aware that I have been disrespectful and insulting toward you and your followers."

"I think you mean friends," I corrected. "There's a difference, but keep talking."

Michael's upper lip stiffened, but to my utter amazement, he didn't scold me or strike me down. "It appears that my fellow angels have abandoned our cause. I am unfamiliar with the consequences of this."

I shrugged, crossing my arms under my breasts. "Might as well get used to the feeling. It sucks, but it's part of life. Nobody can stay on top forever."

"Not even Lucifer."

My arms tightened around my chest. I wasn't sure he was saying that in hope of me backing him up, or if he was confident in the statement, so I played it smart and didn't answer. Michael stared at me without blinking for what seemed like an eternity. I don't know if he was trying to read my mind or wait for me to speak, but I couldn't think of anything I wanted to say to him. I would have gone into the backroom and slept beside Warrick again if I thought for one second that I would get some rest.

I'll sleep when I'm dead. Won't be much longer now.

Michael took my silence as an opportunity to speak again.

"I feel the need to be forthcoming with you."

I sighed. *Great.*

"Your sister was more of the timid sort before aligning herself with Lucifer."

I slid my hand down to my hatchet as a silent warning. Michael refused to acknowledge it.

"As difficult as this shall be for you to hear, it must be said."

"Then get on with it," I told him impatiently.

Michael took another breath, ready to monologue. "The fragments distort the mind, turning innocent eyes to bloodshed, fuelling sin and ultimately powering the Hell Gate. It is a weapon aimed at humans, but can have a devastating effect in supernaturals." Michael's eyes were so intense it almost hurt to look into them.

"It is my belief that your sister has a fragment inside of her."

It made sense, in its own way. Dro was acting the complete opposite of herself, and Lucifer was the worst catalyst I could imagine. Who knew what he'd done to her in the three days she'd been under his sway? Though at the same time, it seemed more complicated than that.

"Dro's smarter than that. She wouldn't have accepted it. She saw what it did to me."

"And yet, I recognized its power coming from her," Michael insisted. He took a slow step toward me, looking almost sympathetic. "She has become more powerful than I could have perceived. If is has fused with her bloodstream, I fear there is only one way to remove the fragment's influence from her."

My blood turned cold. I gripped my hatchet in a white-knuckle grip, but I was incredibly tempted to draw it and slap Michael across the face with it.

"You have a lot of fucking nerve," I whispered gravely.

"This is not what you wish to hear, but you must understand–"

"No," I interrupted. "This is what *you* need to understand."

For once, Michael didn't try to talk over me.

"Dro is my sister, no matter what she's turned in to. I had a fragment inside of me, and she took it out. I can do the same for her. It will be fucking torture, but I'll do it. So if you get in my way or try to kill her when I'm not around, there is *nothing*, natural or supernatural, that will protect you from me."

I took a step forward this time, looking up into Michael's face even though I had to tilt my head back as far as I could to do it.

"You're human now, Michael. That means anyone can kill you. So don't fucking push me."

If he'd been his old self, he probably would have

obliterated me with a stylish snap of his fingers. But just as he'd given me a cold, hard truth, I gave him one right back. Kill Dro, get killed by me. It was the only simple truth that remained in my life.

"I know what drives these fragments," Michael said. "But I do not understand how they could be removed short of death. Unless yours was a false one."

The idea had never occurred to me. Maybe it should have. Then I remembered the blazing agony, the warped mindset I'd been trapped in, the blood on my hands from the deranged yet innocent people I'd killed. The ash that had dissolved in the vial Maria has shown me.

"It wasn't fake," I told him confidently. "Nothing fake would be that goddamn painful."

Michael opened is mouth to say something else, but turned around as the curtains behind him were drawn apart. Sephiel appeared in the doorway, looking between Michael and me. He seemed amazed that we weren't trying to stab each other. Frankly, so was I.

"It is time for a new watch."

"No," I countered. "It's time to wake everyone up. We're ending this now."

Sephiel hesitated. "Constance, I realize that being without Dro is agonizing to you, but–"

"This isn't about Dro," I cut in. "This isn't about getting revenge or running or waiting for Lucifer's next move. This is about doing what we should have been doing in the first place. Closing the Hell Gate."

I heard Max creaking the floorboards on his way down the stairs. Warrick opened the storeroom door behind me a second later. I looked at Michael, but spoke for all of them.

"You can confirm that Mateo and Drake will have the fragments?"

Michael was practically grinding his teeth when he nodded.

"Then we need to draw them out. If we can lead them out of the city, we can kill them and remove the last two fragments, and close the Hell Gate."

Michael started to protest that we didn't know which of them might have the fragment inside of the, or that Dro might contain one inside of her, but I wasn't going to entertain that idea for myself until I saw her and had more proof.

"If nothing else, we can get them out of the city for a few hours. People might come to their senses and leave. Even if we save one person's life, it will be worth it."

Michael narrowed his eyes defiantly, but I was beyond caring. I'd given him the most important warning I could. He was difficult to read, but I would go with my gut in thinking he would let me handle Dro.

"Lucifer will likely be coming with them," Warrick said. "Dro too."

It hurt to hear him speak her name so grimly. "Focus on destroying the fragments. If we need to escape, we can use the *movens caeli.* Right, Max?"

"Yeah," he confirmed hesitantly. "I guess. But where are we going to go to draw their attention? Mateo and Drake are Lucifer's pet pit-bulls."

"There's one thing we can do that I know will get their attention." I turned to look directly at Max. "Do you trust me?"

He grimaced. "Yeah, but when you say that I wonder if I should."

I grinned for the first time in days. Too bad it was the grin I'd used as an enforcer to terrify my targets. Warrick, Sephiel, and Michael tensed uncomfortably, and Max actually shrank back a little. Good to know I hadn't lost my charm.

"Pack up your stuff, boys. It's time I took you to my place."

***

Mateo hadn't changed anything about the Rocha hacienda since the death of his father. It was still a beautiful, two-story plantation house made of dark brown sandstone. Tall palm trees were behind the perfectly trimmed hedges that lined the cobblestone driveway. The road circled near the front of the house, a huge white marble fountain in the middle of the circle. Dim, gold light shone through the curved arches of the windows. On the left of the main house was a narrow apartment building where the housekeepers, cooks, groundskeepers, and security lived. Where Dro and I used to live.

It was hard not to think about the memories I had attached to this place. Granted, most of them were tainted by Emilio's omnipotence, Mateo's betrayal, or the physical and emotional tortures I'd suffered here, but not every memory was a bad one. Dro and I had been safe from the demons. She'd been loved and accepted by the staff. I learned how to fight and grew stronger. I'd fallen in love. It had been a fucked up life, but it had been a stable one.

I might miss this place one day. But not tonight.

We hid in the trees behind the staff apartment, away from the gates and any guards who might have been walking the grounds. I looked at Max.

"You see anybody inside?" I whispered.

He closed his eyes and sighed. As he concentrated, I looked at the rest of the group. We'd had to raid an auto-repair shop to get dark coveralls for Sephiel and Michael to wear, Max and Warrick had donned darker clothes, and I had raided Maria's closest until I found another plain black shirt to replace the one that had been soaked in blood.

I wondered if I would ever have a time in my life where I could wear a new color and not worry about it getting covered in grime and gore.

Michael was holding one can of gas, and Warrick had the other. Given how many fires were burning in Juárez, you'd think that everyone would be hogging petrol, but that turned out not to be the case. We were lucky, in a brutally ironic way.

Max exhaled and opened his eyes. "You'll get in fine," he said. "The big players aren't inside, but there are guards. You'll have to be careful and sneak around them, because they all have Mateo on speed dial. We light our fire as soon as you get back out here, and then we're gone."

I nodded. When he could see them, Max's visions were usually solid, but that wasn't to say that things couldn't go wrong. We'd play it just as safe as if he hadn't made any confirmation.

"All right," I breathed, rolling my shoulders. "Let's start the barbecue."

I slipped out of the cover of the trees and jogged toward the back of the apartment. Warrick and Sephiel followed me, Sephiel covering the rear while Warrick did his best to keep the sloshing gasoline quiet in its can. I pressed myself to the wall, looking around the corner to make sure the coast was clear. When I didn't see any Blood Thorns coming or going, I sprinted out and ran for the side of the hacienda.

We made it without getting caught. I mentally thanked Max for his gifts, but knew better than to get cocky. I peered around the side of the windowsill and flicked my eyes through the hardwood and sandstone walled room. Two elegantly carved high-backed chairs with wine-colored leather seats were placed on the far ends of the stretching, black wood table. Under the table was a red and black Victorian style carpet. It was the perfect place for cover, among other things.

I stood in front of the window and slipped a knife out of my jacket. I laid the blade flat on the sill, sliding it under the small crack holding it shut. I found the latch and flipped the blade to push it open. My fingers squeezed under the narrow crevice and pushed up. I jumped at the sharp, grinding noise made by the window as it slid up, but no guards came running, so I figured we were still in the clear.

I hooked my leg over the ledge and ducked into the dining room, the familiar smell of roses and spice filling the air. How many meals did I have in here? How many times was I living a lie with the face of a family?

Shutting the memories away, I watched the entranceway while Warrick and Sephiel climbed in.

"Start in here," I whispered, slowly making my way toward the kitchen.

The smell of gas filled the room as they splashed it onto the floor. I stopped at the entranceway and pressed my back to the doorframe. I couldn't see anyone at the front of the house, but I heard voices echoing from the depths of it.

"Hey, you smell that?" one of them said.

"Smell what?"

I looked over my shoulder, seeing Sephiel standing across from me. We nodded to each other.

"Man, it doesn't smell like gas to you?"

They were in perfect range. Before his friend could respond, I swung out from the dining room and jabbed the man closest to the wall in the face. His friend was reaching for a gun when Sephiel appeared and grabbed his wrist. The shocked man tried to swing at the ex-angel, but Sephiel was too quick. He delivered a vicious uppercut to the Blood Thorn's jaw, then crashed his elbow into the top of his head.

While he was doing this, I was moving in on the Blood Thorn I had punched. Now that I had the space, I was able to spin and deliver a roundhouse kick the side of the head. He was unconscious before he hit the floor.

Sephiel and I grabbed them and began dragging them out of sight. Warrick was looking at me for direction, holding the gas can tightly in his fist.

"Do the kitchen next," I told him.

Warrick nodded and darted out of the dining room. Sephiel looked at me as he pulled the second body along the marble floor.

"It does not seem fair to leave them inside when we do this," he panted.

He was right. Yes, these men were Blood Thorns, part of the most ruthless gang in all of Ciudad Juárez, but I didn't recognize them. They had been hired after I'd left, so I didn't know if they'd found themselves in the same hopeless situation I had. Lost and scared, running from something they thought would be more dangerous than what they were running to.

It had been a long time since I felt sympathy for a Blood Thorn.

"Yeah," I agreed, looking around the house. "We'll leave them in the hallway," I said, pointing to the corridor behind the kitchen. "They can get out of the basement that way."

Sephiel nodded and we started dragging the bodies again. A couple minutes later, we left the two men in a heap and hurried back around the corner into the kitchen. The entire room stank of gasoline. I tasted the fumes in the back of my throat and felt them sting my eyes. Warrick finished turning on all the burners on the stove, then grabbed some meat from the fridge and threw it onto the stovetop. He coughed into his sleeve, then turned to look at me. He held out a gas lighter that he'd found in one of the cabinets.

"Care to do the honors?" he asked me.

"Definitely," I replied. "After we get the fuck out of here."

Warrick didn't need to argue with that. The three of us ran back the way we'd come, not caring about subtlety as smoke began to rise from the stove. I stopped at the end of the gas trail, careful not to step in any of it, then took the lighter from Warrick. I hesitated for a moment, hoping that all of the staff was sleeping in the apartment, and that this trick would work. I wondered if Lucifer would find a way to rein Mateo's anger. I doubted it was possible, since Mateo's hatred for me was insatiable, but the King of Hell didn't get his title by being lenient and understanding.

At the same time, I found myself needing this. Burning away a dark part of my life wouldn't wipe the blood from my hands or save my soul. It wasn't right, and doing it for revenge wouldn't make me happier. But it was a part of my life that I wanted to let go. By burning the hacienda to the ground, I could be saving people from a huge mistake. Maybe it wouldn't make a difference. The

Blood Thorns weren't the only gang in Juárez, merely the worst.

But there would be one person out there who might thank me for this. More than that, I could close this chapter of my life forever. The ghost of my old self still lived in these walls. She needed to be set free before we met again on the other side.

I clicked on the lighter, and pressed it to the petrol soaked carpet. The tiny flame ignited the gasoline with a powerful *whump*. I stepped back to avoid the flames, Warrick gripping my shoulders and pulling me toward the window. He saw me through before climbing out to safety. I stepped back, watching the blaze rise from the carpet to the dining table. It ate up the chairs and devoured the curtains. I watched the wall of fire through the box of the window, knowing the fire was following the trail into the kitchen where everything was set to explode.

Warrick grabbed my hand and dragged me out of range. We ran with Sephiel toward the front lawn where Michael and Max were drawing the note in gasoline. I don't remember the last time I'd run that fast. I listened to people shouting from the inside of the hacienda and the staff apartment. We had just reached Max and Michael when half of the hacienda exploded.

Even from the distance, I could feel the heat of the massive blaze. My ears rang as the blasting sound echoed through the night, burning debris flying through the air and landing on the ground. All the lights in the apartment were on now. We had to move fast.

"Is it ready?" I asked.

"Yeah," Max replied, stepping back from the grass and digging the *movens caeli* out of his pocket. "But I don't know how long the effect will last."

I spun the lighter and looked at the gasoline drenched grass. "It'll last long enough for Dro to understand what it means."

The guys stepped back while I bent down and ignited the gas. I lurched away from the blaze, caught by Warrick who held me close while Max opened the golden cap on the heaven-mover. The world erupted into golden light and white noise, but all I could think of was the burning house and the two words I left for my sister.

OWL CREEK.

Chapter 23

Owl Creek RV Park had been abandoned after the massacre nearly seven years ago. After the formal investigation that took months to discern why nearly three hundred people had been suddenly and mysteriously butchered, park officials had wisely closed the park. The investigation became a cold case, since nothing could account for the mangled corpses, missing limbs, and scorched trees. Superstitious believers had claimed that the massacre was caused by everything from werewolves to aliens to the wrath of God.

The only survivors had been Dro and me, and we had been too busy running to come forward and tell the truth. Even if we had gone to the authorities, who would have listened to two orphans claiming it was monsters from another dimension? That was the fast track to a foster home and ultimately separation.

Not that it mattered, did it? You still lost Dro anyway.

Grief stung my heart, but I pushed it down. This was finally going to end tonight. I looked at the grass, and kicked a clump of dirt. Maybe lying underneath it wouldn't be as bad as I thought.

"How long do you think we have?" Warrick asked.

"Not long," Max said. His jaw was set in concentration. "They're just getting the word that something is wrong, but they're still a couple hours away from the hacienda."

"Perhaps it is time to make one final battle call," Michael said. We turned around to look at him. "Every angel wanted to see the end of Lucifer's reign. Perhaps some of them are still willing to fight for it."

Michael held out his hand to take the *movens caeli*

from Max, then looked at Sephiel. The ex-angel who rebelled against Heaven to protect the daughter of Lucifer, was visibly surprised. He looked at us, as if he wasn't sure where he was needed more.

"Go on, Seph," I told him. "Just hurry up."

Sephiel held my eyes and nodded gratefully. There was a small smile on his face, a way of saying he was thankful.

Don't thank me unless we live through this.

Sephiel gripped Michael's arm, then they blinked out into thin air.

"Think they'll be able to find anybody?" Max asked dubiously.

"Guess it doesn't hurt to try." I turned around to face Max. "You're going to stay hidden, right?"

Max frowned. "Look, I know I'm not Hercules or Captain America or whatever, but I can still fight, Constance. You're going to need all the help you can get."

"True, but what I need more is for you to be safe. If something happens to me, but Dro lives–"

"Nothing's going to happen to you."

I forgot whatever I was going to tell him. That was the kind of sentence I would expect from Warrick, not Max. But he looked as determined as I'd ever seen him.

"You're the toughest woman I know. If anybody survives, it's going to be you. Besides, Dro can't live without you." His dark, puppy eyes were sad. "I don't know what she's going through, but she'll come back to herself. When she does, she's going to need you more than she ever needed me."

I didn't want to give him a pitying look, but I couldn't help it.

"Max…"

He waved me off. "It's okay. You both have something that I can't match. I get it, and it doesn't make me upset. Dro needs to be loved, and nobody cares about her as much or the way you do. I love her with my heart and soul, but I can never compare to you. And that's okay, because she'll know that she's always going to be loved by somebody if everyone else is gone."

I'd seen Max as a friend from the moment he stopped being scared of me. Over the last few months, I started seeing more of a brother. We shared the loss of a father figure and cared about the same girl, if in different ways. Max knew what he was and what he wasn't, yet he always stayed, even when he was hopelessly out of his depth. I couldn't have been more grateful to have met him.

I flung out my arms, snared him, and crushed him into a hug. Max sputtered, obviously more shocked than I was. But soon his arms looped around my back and he settled into the embrace.

"Nothing is going to happen to you," I whispered. "I fucking swear it."

I shouldn't have been promising anything, but I couldn't help it. I wanted Max to live. No matter what he said about me, I wasn't going to be alive at the end. I could think of no one better to protect my little sister when my heart finally stopped beating.

Max and I parted and I gave him a phony smile, slapping him on the shoulder. He grinned nervously, then looked over my shoulder.

"Uh, I'm gonna go… wander, or something."

I nodded, watching him walk away. He wasn't gone for more than three seconds before Warrick placed his hand on my shoulder. I turned around to see his worried green eyes.

"He's right, you know," he told me. "I'm not going to let anything happen to you." His expression turned stony and determined. "I want to kill Drake, but if I have to choose between ending him and saving you, I'm going to save you."

My heart went to my throat. I'd never been this deep in love before. It wasn't fair for my soul to ache like this when I knew it wasn't going to last.

I tried to lie, but with the moonlight illuminating his dark hair, the passionate glow in his laser green eyes, and the feel of his warm, strong hand on me, I couldn't find the words.

I reached up to grab his neck and pulled him down to kiss me. It was a little desperate, but I didn't care. This could be the last one. Warrick held me close, kissing me gently and brushing my hair with his fingers to calm me down. It wasn't working.

My body demanded that I breathe, but I was reluctant to let go. I was so close to him that my lips brushed his when I spoke the words he deserved to hear.

"I love you."

Warrick wasn't stupid. He knew I was keeping something from him when I said that. But he must have seen the pleading look in my eyes. I didn't want to talk about it. Not tonight. Maybe not ever. He nodded briefly, then held my face and kissed me again.

It felt like a kiss goodbye, and that was exactly what I needed.

***

Max was right. It wasn't even two hours before Lucifer and his demons came for us.

I was sitting on the dead grass between Warrick and Max, holding my boyfriend's hand, when I smelled the sulfur. I lifted my head and watched the air in front of me rip in half. Fire twisted out of the portal, shadows of monsters and men stepping through.

There were so many of them. Reds, ghouls, Shredders, Wretches, hellhounds, Knights... so many that I lost count. Warrick squeezed my hand, but I wasn't scared. Knowing I was finally confronting the end brought me a peace I hadn't expected. Sure, I wasn't looking forward to the pain coming my way, but at least I would be free of it all one way or another.

The demons didn't charge us. They were twitching with anticipation, hungry for flesh, but waiting for their master's permission.

The fire from the portal belched again, and this time it brought out the beings in control. Drake stepped out first, dressed in a dark hunting jacket and dirty jeans, a smile on his face and malice in his eyes. Both Warrick and Max tensed beside me.

Mateo came out of the portal next. He'd donned a black tactical getup, the same as the one he'd worn when he'd worked with me on the streets. His hair was slicked back and he wore the belt with a rose buckle around his waist. His hand in the black fingerless glove curled around the machete at his hip. His eyes went straight to me, ready to burst into madness.

Stepping out at last, hand in hand, were the King and his daughter. Lucifer looked torturously beautiful, wearing a black frock coat that went all the way to his ankles. He wore dress pants and a black suit jacket but no shirt, revealing the chiseled muscles on his pale skin. The huge claymore sword I'd once seen him carry was resting on his back. He looked like a businessman who part-timed as medieval warrior.

Beside him was my little sister, but she looked nothing like the girl I grew up with and protected for almost seventeen years.

An elegant black dress clung to her body, thin silk hanging around her legs with a slit exposing three quarters of her right leg. The wide leather wrapped around her waist matched the black leather of her ankle boots. The top of the dress was sleeveless black lace cut down the front to show the curves of her breasts. Dro's hair was free of her usual braid, hanging in loose waves down the sides of her torso. Her lips were painted blood red and dark kohl circled her eyes. She looked beautiful, and terrifying.

Dro's eyes met mine, but offered no expression. No joy or fear or hope or even anger. There was nothing. It saddened me to look at her. So I didn't.

"You wish to end your battle where it began," Lucifer's deep, beautiful voice sang to me.

I slowly got to my feet, Warrick and Max rising with me. I started walking forward, feeling Warrick hold onto my hand until he was forced to let go. I steadily crossed the clearing, trying not to see the salivating demon army or the angry eyes of my enemies.

"Yeah," I told Lucifer when I came to a stop. "Something like that."

His obsidian eyes pierced into me as he invaded my mind. I balled my fists and tried to push him out, but he was seeing everything. All of my grief and regrets, the love I had to lose for Warrick, the conviction and understanding that I wasn't going to survive this. I let him see everything.

Except for Michael and Sephiel.

When Lucifer left my brain, I was dizzy. I blinked to clear my head, then stared at Lucifer again.

"You still refused to heed your sister's pleas," he said. "How selfish of you."

"Yeah, I know." I looked at Dro. "She'll understand, though."

Dro's lips formed a narrow line, and her ice blue eyes turned stormy.

Okay, well she wasn't going to understand instantly.

"I do not see the fallen Michael or the disloyal Sephiel," Lucifer went on. "Where have they gone?"

I shrugged. "Disneyland maybe. Mexico's usually beautiful this time of year, but you kind of fucked it up, so they needed to go somewhere else."

Lucifer held out his hand and fired a needle of hellfire at me. I flinched, having nothing to block it and no way to avoid it. The needle stopped inches from my face, so close I thought I was going to breathe it in. I was nervous as hell, but I didn't back down. The needle split in two and circled around my head, dissolving at my back. He was trying to scare me, but I was done with being afraid of him.

"I know Michael too well to assume he has abandoned his attempts at defiance. As you can see, I am prepared for him. But I promised another combat with you."

Oh, joy.

Not to anyone's surprise, Mateo stalked forward. He moved like a bull getting ready to plow into the matador. Warrick must have come up behind me, because Lucifer held up his hand. Wind rushed around me, I whirled my head around and watched him and Max land on the ground ten feet away from me, rolling to catch themselves.

"You will not interfere again."

That was the only thing Lucifer needed to say.

I gave them a despairing look, then turned around to Mateo. He was in the clearing directly in front of me, beyond furious. I wondered what was stopping him from killing me right now, until he started unbuckling his belt.

I gave him a dry look. "Sorry, buddy. I'm not in the mood."

Mateo glared, gripping his machete and holster so tightly I thought his knuckles were going to tear through the leather of his gloves.

"I'm going to have your fucking head by the end of the night," he promised. "But I want you to hurt first. I want you to feel all the pain you caused me."

He tossed the machete and the remainder of his weapons into the grass on his left. He still didn't move his eyes from mine. I sighed, and began taking off my belt and holster.

"How much do you think renovations are gonna cost you?" I asked.

Mateo clenched his fists. "Do you have any idea how long my family had that house? How hard my father fought to maintain it and keep it out of government hands?"

I threw my weapons aside and spread my legs to get balance. "Can't have been too hard when he had everybody in his pocket, could it?"

The second my weapons were out of reach, Mateo lunged for me. His fist shot forward with alarming speed, and I barely leaned away from it in time. I grabbed his wrist and held his arm out, pulling my free hand back to break his arm. Mateo snared my elbow and dragged it down. I kicked for his knee, but he stepped back and drove his far knee into my stomach. Air left my lungs in a huff, but I stayed on my feet and tried to get my arms free. Before I could move, Mateo kicked the back of my leg and buckled me. The arm I'd been holding got free, and soon his hand clamped around my throat.

Mateo kept pushing until I was pinned on the ground, crushed under his weight. He freed his other hand and swung it for me. I tried to block him, but he batted my arm away and hit me before I could get another counter.

Pain exploded as his fist collided with my head, just above the eyebrow. The leather of his gloves scratched over my skin, splitting it open. The world spun as I turned my head straight, feeling Mateo squeeze my neck. He raised his fist again, though this time I caught it before the strike could connect. I wiggled until I knew I had room, then bucked up and pitched Mateo to my right. He fell off me and I was freed. I scrambled to my feet, bringing up my hands when he kicked for my stomach.

He was back on his feet in nanoseconds, punching and kicking furiously. I matched him strike for strike, blocking and dodging, trying to remember the way he fought in our sparring sessions. It was more or less the same style, but a lot more aggressive. He'd hit me during training, claiming that he never wanted to do it but had to make me learn. This wasn't the same, of course. He wasn't going to stop until he'd broken every bone in my body.

Mateo snapped a front kick toward my chest, but I caught it. While he was off balance, I planted my foot in his exposed ribs. He grunted and grimaced as I kicked him again. I dropped his leg and rushed in close, crashing my fist into his jaw. When I tried to punch him again, he grabbed my wrist and yanked it out to the side. Pain shot up my arm as he tried to pull it from its socket. I couldn't get my defense up before he punched me in the chest.

My collarbone reverberated with pain, but I twisted to ease the pressure on my arm and stayed in front of him. I blocked another hit coming for my head, using my free arm to sweep off his hold. Mateo snarled and grabbed a handful of my hair, yanked my head so violently I stumbled.

I let him keep the grip on my hair, focusing on

blocking the punch he aimed at my face. I knocked it aside and shot a jab into his nose. His head rocked back and my hair was released. Furious, I jumped onto him and wrapped my legs around his ribs. I planted one hand on the top of his head and used the other to hit him in the face. It was an awkward position, but I was getting the upper hand.

Until Mateo grabbed my waist, pulled me off him, and hurled me onto the ground.

I rolled on the dead grass, winded from slamming into it. I saw him coming behind me and started to get to my feet. He grabbed one of my ankles and wrenched me back. I flipped around as I was dragged, kicking out with my free foot to catch him in the stomach. My foot skidded against his ribs, but Mateo was on a rampage. He probably wasn't feeling any of the pain I was sending his way.

He tried knocking my legs aside, but I pushed up and slid myself back until I was out of his reach. I shot my knee into his chin, rocking his head back. Mateo shouted, and I thought I saw blood on the insides of his lips. He must have bitten his tongue. I got to my feet and kicked at his head. He batted my leg away and stood up, firing a powerful kick into my abdomen. I stumbled back and barely kept my footing.

When I lifted my head, Mateo was there again. He punched me in the temple, rocking my head to the side, and directly into his second fist. It struck my cheek and wrenched my head again. The world was a blur when his palm slammed into my chest. I staggered for a moment until my feet were swept out from under me. I landed on my back, my head smacking against the hard soil.

I turned to get my bearings, but Mateo was standing over me. He stomped down on my exposed side. I screamed when I felt one of my ribs crack. I rolled onto my back when his foot crashed down again, sending all of the air out of my diaphragm. I coughed as his boot rose again, aiming for my chest. As it descended, I snapped my hands up and caught it. My knuckles dug into my chest, but it was better than him breaking my collarbone.

I pulled his leg forward and swept mine out to trip him. He collapsed onto his back and I tried to get up again. Mateo was faster, his leg swinging up into my chest and knocking me back down. While I was winded, he scissored his foot so his heel dug into the top of my stomach. It was like having the edge of a baseball bat driven into me.

My entire body felt like a bruised mess, and my head was ten sizes too big. I used my elbows to get leverage, but Mateo crawled over to me and drove the tip of his knee into my chest. I cried out from the massive, crushing pain, which only made him press down harder. I swung my fist into his ribs. He jerked once, but didn't get off of me. All I did was shift his knee across my chest.

Mateo punched down, his fist catching me right between the eyes. My head bounced off the dirt, blacking me out for a second. The hits kept coming, filling my vision with darkness. I couldn't see, couldn't move, couldn't fight back.

By the time he was finished, my entire face felt broken. Blood was welling into my head, and I was on the edges of a concussion. My nose was busted, but at least I still had my teeth. Mateo finally got off my chest. My lungs swelled and pushed on the bruises covering my torso. I groaned and rolled onto my stomach, feeling about as strong as a dead fish.

Mateo was walking away. The only reason he would do that was if he was getting his machete. He'd beaten me enough. He was ready to kill me.

I looked up. Some time during the fight, we'd ended up by our weapons. My hatchet was in sight. I crawled for it, forcing myself onto my hands and knees to move faster. My hand had just curled around the neck of the weapon and pulled it free when a foot slammed into my stomach. The motion flipped me through the air until I landed on the grass again.

Mateo knelt down and straddled my chest, gripping my hair with one hand and tugging my head back. The cold metal blade touched my throat, sharp enough to kill me in one swipe. My hands were free, but I didn't dare move. Not yet.

"I would have given you everything, Constance," Mateo said. "I loved you with all my heart." His eyes darkened. "I never thought I would hate you with all my heart, too."

He raised the machete. It gleamed in the moonlight. I heard Warrick screaming. My fingers snaked through the grass.

The blade began to descend, and I moved as fast as I could. I punched Mateo in the stomach. The hit forced his swing to go wide, just barely slicing along my collarbone. With my right hand, I grabbed the hilt of the hatchet and swung it into his unprotected ribs.

Mateo screamed and grabbed my wrist, ditching the machete and trying to tear the hatchet free with both of his hands. I refused to let go. While he was distracted, I grabbed the machete that had fallen next to my head. I swung it up and drove it into his ribs.

Mateo stiffened and gasped in shock as the blade slid home to his heart. He looked down at me, stunned that I had tricked him. My eyes were cold as I twisted the blade. He jerked and coughed, spraying blood onto my neck and face. Mateo's eyes began to glaze over, and it wasn't hard to push him off my chest.

I coughed at the release of pressure, gripping my hatchet and his machete tightly. Mateo lay on his side, staring at me with dying eyes. I rested on my hands and knees, sore and breathing heavily, watching my first love die. After a long, long time, Mateo's eyes rolled into the back of his head. His entire body slumped with a final, sharp breath, then stopped moving all together.

Mateo looked dead to me, but after so many years of running from him, I had to be sure. I crawled closer and cut his throat with my hatchet. Blood squirted out, but he didn't move. His skin began to fill with black veins, tiny cracks zipping over him as his body crumbled in on itself. His remains imploded inside his clothes, and suddenly he was gone.

So was the fragment lodged inside of him.

I moaned painfully, dropping Mateo's machete and clutching my aching stomach. Warrick was still shouting for me, though I didn't raise my head to look at him. I felt sick, but I had to stand up. I used one knee for leverage and slowly rose to my feet. I tilted once, then caught myself and straightened my back. I looked in Warrick's direction, letting him see I was alive.

I must have looked terrible, because his eyes widened with horror and Max turned paper white. Still gripping my stomach and my hatchet, I turned around to face Lucifer. His face was as impassive as always. Beside him, Dro's jaw had dropped. She saw me looking at her, and quickly pressed her lips together.

"That was disappointing," Lucifer said to break the silence. "His anger was palpable. I instilled more strength into him, and yet you survived. I would set you against the bounty hunter," he said, gesturing to Drake, who chuckled at my battered face, "but I have already promised him another's blood."

My own blood went cold. I knew he was talking about Warrick, but if Warrick were killed fighting Drake, the bounty hunter wouldn't stop there. He would see Max, and tear him to pieces.

"But I cannot risk fate smiling upon you," Lucifer said. "I must set you against someone I know you cannot defeat."

He turned his head. Dro looked up at him, her eyes beginning to widen.

"My daughter," Lucifer purred. "Kill her."

Chapter 24

Dro stared at Lucifer as if she couldn't understand what he said. I heard it clear enough, but I still couldn't move. I felt like I would collapse if I budged an inch.

"She— Look at how weak she is," Dro tried. "It won't be much of a fight if I went against her now."

Lucifer's eyes bored into her. Dro flinched.

"I did not tell you to fight her. I told you to kill her."

An unspoken threat hung in the air. If Dro didn't kill me, she would be punished. I knew from experience that being punished by Lucifer could be a fate worse than death.

But the hesitance told me that my sister was still locked under the demon controlling her mind. I looked carefully at Dro's body again, squinting to see if Michael had been right after all. If she didn't have it, Drake did. I would have no problem killing him, though I dreaded how I would deal with my sister if she wasn't being swayed by the supernatural shard.

"But—"

Dro gasped and winced sharply, backing away from whatever invisible pain was being inflicted on her. She slapped a hand to her stomach, right where the leather belt was.

If she has a fragment in her, then that's where it is.

I started walking toward my sister, gripping the hatchet tightly. Not even looking at me, Lucifer flicked his hand in my direction. An invisible momentum slammed into me, knocking me back ten feet. I landed on my ass, not looking forward to more head trauma. But instead of flopping onto the ground again, someone caught me and hauled me to my feet. I swayed, but the hands kept me upright. I breathed deeply, and smelled pine. I would have smiled and thanked Warrick if my face didn't hurt so much.

I turned my attention back to Lucifer and Dro. My sister was clutching her middle, digging her nails into her side to keep from screaming. I started walking forward again, only to have Warrick tug me back. I was ready to shout at him, when I saw Dro relax. She took one more deep breath, then drew herself up and turned in my direction.

I was about twenty feet from her, but I could still see the darkness shimmering in her bright blue eyes. Her smile was malevolent and bloodthirsty.

Michael was right. Dro had a fragment inside of her, not Drake. She wouldn't be looking at me with a smile meant to kill if it weren't. The fragment was dissolving. I had no way to tell if it was dissolved, or if she was holding back. I had to believe she was resisting it. The other option... I couldn't think about it.

She stalked forward like a cat approaching a mouse it had clawed. Max whimpered nervously, and Warrick's hold on me tightened. I didn't move. There had to be a way to get through to her, to let her know that she could be saved if she trusted me.

But I was running out of time, unable to think through the panic taking over my mind. Then Dro froze and frowned. A moment later, the world burst into familiar golden light. We turned around and watched Michael and Sephiel return. And they weren't alone.

A dozen angels strode confidently to our side. Each one of them holding a drawn weapon, wearing a white leather coat, and looking severe. Sephiel scowled unhappily at my injuries, turning his furious blue eyes onto Lucifer. I was still watching the angels emerge from the golden light, not expecting the next man I saw.

"Gabriel?" I choked out.

Michael's second in command smiled a thousand watts at me. The archangel looked like a male model with flawless tanned skin, wavy, sandy blond hair, a youthful face, and glowing hazel eyes.

"You are looking a little worse for wear, Constance Ramirez," he said playfully as he approached me.

I scowled at him, but Gabriel reached out to touch my face. I winced at the initial tingle of his healing magic, but I wasn't about to refuse it. He repaired my nose, my cracked rib, and most of my bruises, though I could tell his magic wasn't nearly as powerful as it should have been. But I was more than grateful to have my worst injuries healed. An extra bruise or two wasn't going to keep me from fighting.

"I thought you were happy to sit on the sidelines until the world ended," I said when he finished healing me.

Gabriel shrugged his broad shoulders. "I was." His luminous eyes held mine. "But family has a way of changing your priorities."

As if those words signaled his entrance, Michael stepped out of the light.

Michael, who still had his motherfucking wings.

Sephiel had had wings before the Heaven Gate was closed, but I never saw them. It was a way of concealing what he was from human eyes, I guess, and they were the reason he'd been able to teleport quickly and invisibly. Dro had been able to see them because she was supernatural. She said they'd been beautiful, but somehow I was willing to bet even his paled in comparison to Michael's.

Two enormous, rounded wings sprouted from his back, beaming with intense white light. It was like he was standing in front of two blinding spotlights. When my eyes reacted to the whiteness, I was able to see the bare edges of feathers on the wings, which shone like crystals. They were so thin they were nearly transparent, veins of gold shimmering through them. Long gold bands traced the edges of the wings, making the entirety of them look like two golden windowpanes under the sun.

I never thought I would see anything that compared to the beauty of the Heaven Gate. I was wrong.

Michael looked right past me, striding forward with

his broadsword in his hand. "This ends tonight, Lucifer. You have left me no choice."

I whipped my head around to find Lucifer. The King of Hell had stripped off his jacket to reveal his own wings. They were as incredible as Michael's, but more terrifying than beautiful. Four bat-like wings tipped with horns protruded from his back, the two larger ones edging along his shoulder blades while the two smaller ones stuck out from his lower ribs. He took the claymore from his back and held it loosely in his left hand. His eyes fixed on Michael, and for the first time, I saw an emotion in them.

Too bad that emotion was complete, utter hatred.

"I never intended to," Lucifer replied.

The King of Hell raised his right hand, snapped his fingers, and let the demons off their leashes.

They charged forward like horses on the racetrack. The angels didn't need Michael's permission to confront them. Dro filled her hands with white-hot hellfire and swept both arcs at the approaching angels. Gabriel suddenly appeared on the frontlines, pushing against Dro's hellfire with his own heavenfire. The white and gold lights slammed into each other, creating a burning explosion that nearly blinded me.

When it faded, Dro was staggering back, scowling and rubbing her eyes. I broke out of Warrick's grip and raced for her. Lucifer was charging for the frontlines, and Michael overtook me. I got in his way before he could do anything to hurt Dro, but it wasn't until I stood in front of her that I realized I might have made a mistake.

Dro's eyes blazed with anger, her beautiful face twisted into a terrible snarl. I couldn't see a trace of the sister I was trying to save, but I knew she was in there. I had to find a way to get her out without really hurting Dro.

Not that it would keep her from hurting me.

Something in Dro must have sparked when she saw me, because she didn't burn me to a crisp. Instead, she fired a punch at my face.

I raised my arm to block her, the force of her strike sending a huge shock through my arm and pushing my block toward my head. She had become incredibly strong thanks to her time with Lucifer. If Gabriel hadn't healed me, Dro would have pounded me into the dirt by now. There were openings I could have taken to turn the table of the fight, but I couldn't bring myself to do it. If anything, I was more cautious about my hand holding the hatchet.

Yet my eyes kept flicking back to her stomach. I had to see if the fragment was in her. If it was, I wasn't going to have a choice. I would have to hurt Dro to save her.

During my distraction, Dro punched up and caught me in the chin. My head rocked back and she kicked me in the chest. For a girl fighting in a dress, she moved with shocking ease.

"Give up, big sister," Dro taunted. Her smile was as cold as her eyes. "We both know you aren't going to hurt me."

Unintentionally, I remembered the first and last time a Possessor had taken control of me. I'd been locked inside my body, struggling and suffering, but never giving up. Dro had known I was in there, and she'd told me to keep fighting. She'd believed I could break free. Being under the influence of a fragment was the same thing. Your soul just didn't know it.

I couldn't let that nightmare come true. I wouldn't let her live with knowing she killed us.

I held my hatchet tightly, meeting Dro's eyes sadly.

"I'm sorry about this, little sister."

Dro scoffed and launched herself at me again. This time I struck first. My fist jabbed into her face, just enough to daze her. Being very careful, I sliced my hatchet along the leather belt at her stomach.

The blade just nicked her skin, but completely ripped open the leather. Beneath it, Dro's flesh was black and corrupted, just as mine had been. She was moving a lot, but I could see the outline of the fragment pressing against her skin.

It was there. *Right there.* If I had been fighting anyone else, I would have already lunged in for the strike.

But I wasn't fighting just anyone. I was fighting my sister.

I hesitated, and it cost me.

Dro roared furiously and pushed a handful of hellfire at me. I dove out of the way, feeling the heat of the white-hot flames rush past me. I caught myself in a roll and kicked back, sweeping her feet from under her. Dro landed on the ground, and I pounced on her before she could get up. She thrashed and screamed and clawed at me, but I took the hits and pressed down on her chest.

Then one of her punches connected with my jaw. It was a hell of a hit, and it knocked me off my sister. I was still recovering from it when Dro pinned me and wrapped one hand around my throat. She splayed her other hand on the ground next to me, white flames creeping along the grass and hovering next to my skull.

I grabbed her wrist with one of my hands. The other held my hatchet. Yet my entire body was frozen.

Oh, God, I can't do it. I can't.

"Dro," I rasped out. "Stop."

"Stop?" she repeated in a dark, mocking voice. "Why should I? You had your chance to run. You didn't listen to me. If you had, it wouldn't have come to this, Constance." Her eyes glowed a shocking blue, the rage in them as alien as the twisted smile on her face.

My sister had truly become a demon.

The heat and flames crept closer, singeing the edges of my hair. I smelled the sharp scent, knew how horrifically close I was to dying, but I couldn't look anywhere but Dro.

"Andromeda," I begged, digging my nails in, trying to reach her one last time. My hatchet was a weight in my hands. "Don't make me…"

"Don't make you what?" she sneered. "Kill me?" She shook her head. "We both know you won't do that, Constance. You should, but you won't. You imagined it differently, didn't you? You really thought you could win."

A tear slipped past my eyelids before I could stop it.

"I didn't want to win," I whispered. "I just wanted to save you."

Dro shook her head, lips twisted between a snarl and a smile.

"That was always your problem, big sister. You always assumed I needed to be saved."

Her grip tightened on my throat. She lifted her burning hand rose from the grass and hovered over my face. I could hardly see her past the heat searing my eyes.

"What I needed was to be let go."

The tears evaporated on my cheeks. In that split second, I knew I couldn't save my sister.

Lucifer had won.

I blinked, the dreaded realization creeping into my stomach.

This was what Lucifer *wanted*. He knew that if Dro killed me, she would be his absolutely. The fragment was meant to skew her perception of me. That was why he'd caused it to flare in her when she hesitated at his first command.

My sister was still in there. I knew she was. Her demon half was trying to strangle and burn me, but it wasn't *Dro*. It wasn't my sister, the girl that I knew was screaming inside, begging me to save her one last time.

At any cost.

My hand tightened around the hatchet, and I looked at the mockery Lucifer had made of my sister. Imaging him behind her eyes made it easier to lift the hatchet, and slash the side of Dro's stomach.

She yelped in surprise and jerked her hands free of my face and throat. I twisted my hips and bucked her onto the scorched ground. I straddled her body, jabbing her once in the face to disorient her and control my weight. I glanced at the cut. It was shallow, far from any major organs.

But I had to make it worse.

Dro thrashed and squirmed beneath me. "Con, you hurt me! How could you cut me?!"

Gritting my teeth, I ignored her betrayed cry and cut

a deeper slice into her stomach. Deep enough that I would be able to reach inside and pluck out the fragment, as she had done for me.

Dro twitched from the pain and started begging.

"No, Connie! This is what Lucifer did to me! Please don't hurt me like he did! Don't, *please!*"

It nearly broke my resolve, seeing the horrible connection to the pain I was putting her through, and the torture Dro had endured when Lucifer tore out her rib to open the Gates.

But I couldn't stop now. As long as the fragment was still in her stomach, she would remain corrupted. She would try to kill me, and there would be no hesitation the second time. I pushed her down again, and reached inside the wound for the fragment. Dro trembled and screamed again, but I felt the small, burning stone between my fingers like a metal splinter. It was whole. Thank God.

I yanked it out of my sister's stomach and hurled it onto the ground. I stared at it as it dissolved in the grass, leaving nothing but a pile of black and red ash. Now that it was dissolved, it wouldn't be able to corrupt me, or anyone else.

Satisfied that the fragment was destroyed, I scrambled back to Dro. She was lying on her back, staring at the black, smoking sky. She looked stunned, catatonic even. I grabbed her wrist and slapped her hand on the cut on her stomach. Dro's hand remained free of healing light. I looked at her face, hoping I hadn't made a soul-crushing mistake.

"Come on, Dro," I pleaded. "I can't heal you by myself!"

There was a sharp, painful scream that caught my attention. I whipped my head around, watching the battle raging. The smell of sulfur and demon blood was thick, but it looked like most of Lucifer's monsters were still alive. The angels fought back with determination, but I could see the exertion in their motions and the blood on their faces.

Sephiel was moving faster than I'd ever seen him

move before, swinging at three Reds that were trying to surround me. The one in front of him swiped its claws at his head, but Sephiel ducked. The demon behind him pounced, but he was already stabbing back with his short swords. The Red shrieked as Sephiel pulled his swords free, and kicked the decaying demon back until it exploded into a cloud of ash. He twirled his swords in his hands, stabbing one into the chest of another Red while swinging and slicing open the throat of the third one.

Max stood at the edge of the battle, silver knives in his hands. Some ghouls ran at him, but he fought back. He kicked one away and stabbed the second one repeatedly until it collapsed. The second ghoul tackled him, but he stabbed at the grey demon's throat until it dissolved.

Warrick stood with the angels, helping them take down a Shredder. The enormous demon batted its hand backward, knocking down two angels. Warrick appeared on its other side, then stabbed his knife into its neck and pulled it across. The demon roared and whirled, stabbing its bone-claws toward him. Warrick slid underneath them, ducking the Shredder's arms until he appeared in front of its chest. His free hand dropped to the ground, and picked up a fallen sword. In the same flowing motion, he drew the sword up and shoved it under the Shredder's chin.

Drake was edging close to Warrick, cutting down every angel he saw as he approached. There was an excited smile on his face that made me sick.

The only creatures I couldn't see were Lucifer and Michael. Before I could look harder for them, a clammy hand snared my wrist. I jumped and whirled around, my eyes finding Dro's. There was no shining madness, no contempt or malice. Her eyes were wide and scared, and behind them I swore I could see a hint of peace.

"You saved me," she whispered.

I squeezed her hand, fighting back tears. "Of course."

"Why?" Her eyes glistened. "I was trying to kill you."

I squeezed her hand. "You could have done it right

when Lucifer told you to, but you didn't. Deep down, you were still the honest, good sister I know."

Dro closed her eyes and rested her head back on the grass. A tear slipped from the corner of her eye.

"You saved me because you saw the good in me," she whispered. "I understand it now," she breathed.

I was about to ask what she was talking about, tell her that we needed to get up and fight, but invisible arms looped around my stomach and pulled me through the air. I screamed involuntarily and the sudden reaction, flying away from my sister until I landed in the middle of the clearing. My side hit the ground and caused me to roll onto my stomach. The same invisible hands clutched my shoulders and yanked me onto my back. I tried to fight against the magic, but the binds were strong, and soon I was lying frozen on the ground, looking up at Lucifer.

His wings were blacker than the sky behind him, as black as the hatred in his eyes. The claymore he held was smeared with blood. Wind and motion moved the edges of his shock-white hair.

"How did you do it?" he asked in an angry whisper.

The binds turned into hooks, and dug into my skin. I squeezed my eyes shut and screamed, unable to block the sudden piercing pain that sank into me.

"I constructed this strategy for centuries, planning what I would do once I produced a child." The hooks plunged deeper and coiled over me, tightening my skin like a constricting wire. "I perfected everything. Creating the fragments and embedding them into humans, making them believe they held enough power to stand beside me, though giving them nothing."

I slowly opened my eyes, heart pounding as Lucifer revealed the details of his plot, too angry to stop himself. He bowed lower, blocking out the world around me until it was just his darkness and me.

"My daughter was to be the Key, the wickedness that would hold the Gates of Hell open. But you stole her from me. You turned her soul from the darkness to the light. You corrupted her."

I would have grinned, but the hooks and coils clenched so tightly I started to see dots in my vision.

"So I chose another. A soul so devious there could be no redeeming it. An image of consummate sin. He did not need prompting as my daughter did."

Drake's laugh seemed louder now. Lucifer knelt down, looking at me as I trembled from pain and fear.

"How did it feel to have a fragment inside of you?" he asked. "Did you feel my influence burning through your veins, or did you feel me when I saved your life?"

Just like that, Lucifer's face shivered. In one smooth transition, it was Maria staring down at me. My heart stuttered.

"All I needed to do was have her touch the fragment," Lucifer said with Maria's voice. "A simple touch to bring her back to me."

I went cold all over. When Dro had taken the fragment out of me, she'd touched it. She'd been mesmerized. Lucifer's magic had invaded her mind, and she didn't know it. That was why she left, why she turned on me, why he was able to put a fragment inside of her and let him control her.

Lucifer's face changed again, back to its awful beauty.

He slowly stood up, standing tall and strong as he towered over me.

"Now you have taken her from me once more. As you have taken something I cherished from me, I shall take the same from you."

An unseen, clawed hand clamped on my head and twisted it sharply to the side. I spotted Michael and Gabriel. The archangels were bloodied and burned, with Gabriel trying to lift Michael to his feet. The Commander's eyes were closed, blood oozing from his gaping wounds. One of his snowy white wings was broken, and his skin was deathly pale.

But Lucifer didn't want me to see them suffer.

Instead, my eyes fixed on Sephiel, leading the angels and fighting for his life. Drake was across the clearing from him, trying intently to murder every angel he could before he got to Warrick.

Then Drake stiffened, like a robot receiving a new command. He shoved aside the angel in front of him and turned on his heel, stalking toward Sephiel with his Bowie knife in hand. I opened my mouth to scream a warning, but an invisible hand covered my mouth. My brain kept screaming, desperately wishing that Sephiel would hear my thoughts. But he couldn't. He was human now.

On the edge of my vision, I saw Max pull himself away from the last ghoul he killed. He winced and suddenly whirled around, eyes going wide when he saw Drake, now just feet away from Sephiel's back.

"*Seph!*" Max shouted.

The auburn-haired angel turned his head at the sound of Max's alarmed voice, seeing the direction of his eyes. Drake raised the knife. I heard Warrick shout in the background just as Sephiel turned.

He swung his swords up to defend himself, but it was too late.

Drake's knife plunged down into the bottom of Sephiel's neck, just above his collarbone. Drake twisted the knife, then tore it free. Sephiel's blood shot out with it. Sephiel dropped one of his swords, planting another hand on the mortal wound. He shook, desperately trying to raise his other sword to fight back and heal himself. But he had no powers. Blood was spilling over his hand.

The hand over my mouth was freed, and I screamed for real.

Drake stared at Sephiel with a cold, evil smile on his face. He let the dying angel swing his sword weakly, laughing as he easily stepping back from the strike. Then he lunged forward again, and stabbed Sephiel in the heart.

My scream turned into a loud aching sob. My eyes blurred and I felt my heart shatter. Drake kicked Sephiel off his knife as though he was nothing. Sephiel landed on the ground, the sword tumbling from his hand. He didn't get back up.

I heard other voices crying– Max, Warrick, Dro– but

I was numb from heartache. Sephiel had given up so much for us, never falling apart or betraying us. He deserved a fresh start. He shouldn't have fallen. I turned my head away, crying in earnest now.

There was a furious war cry and intense heat, both of which came from my sister. I was about to open my eyes to see what she was doing, when the hooks in my body pulled.

I arched my back as much as I could, screaming in agony as Lucifer's magic yanked on my insides. Everything in me– organs, bones, and muscles– were stretched against my skin. I felt as though someone had stuck meat hooks into me, and was ready to suspend me from the ceiling. I screamed until my throat was hoarse, but the pain didn't stop.

"You have a choice, daughter," Lucifer shouted over my cries. "You can remain at my side and save her, or you can defy me and watch her soul be ripped from her body."

To emphasize his point, Lucifer's hooks pulled sharply on my soul. Another hoarse scream escaped my lips as the hooks dragged through me. The pain was blinding, stretching me like an elastic band about to snap. I could almost feel my soul edging against my skin, begging my mind to let it go to escape the pain. Lucifer backed off and I dropped back onto the ground, feeling my eyes close. My mind was heavy, and I knew I was close to passing out. Or worse.

My eyes were sluggish to open, though I still managed to find Dro. She was hesitating, looking from me, to Lucifer, to the battle past us. I lolled my head to the side, hearing angry male shouts.

Warrick and Max had caught up with Drake, and both had jumped him. Drake shoved Max away with an elbow to the stomach, but Warrick got payback by slamming his foot into the bounty hunter's jaw. Drake stumbled, buying Warrick time to drop down and sweep his legs out. He hadn't even fully hit the ground before Max came back and started kicking him in the ribs.

"You taught me so much," Dro said softly. I rolled

my head back to her, but it wasn't me she was talking to. It was Lucifer. "I know how to control it all now. You showed me how much more I can do." Dro stood at her full height, looking confident but sad. She glanced down at me, icy blue eyes knowing and resolved.

"I understand what I have to do. And I hope you will, too."

My heart lurched. She couldn't say yes again. I begged her with my eyes. I couldn't lose her again. Not now. Not when we'd already lost Sephiel. His death couldn't be in vain.

Lucifer's hold on me relaxed. He believed she was coming back to him.

That was when Dro shoved out her hands and blasted him with hellfire.

Lucifer hadn't expected it, so he was engulfed. She held the blaze over him as he screamed with more anger than pain. Once he was consumed, she darted past both of us, running straight for Drake, Warrick, and Max.

As she ran, she passed Gabriel and Michael. The two archangels watched her blur past them, Michael barely hanging onto Gabriel. The dying Commander said something to his second, and Gabriel's eyes widened with shock.

Max was still kicking Drake while Warrick loomed over top of him, holding a knife and looking determined. The fire beside me began to dwindle. Lucifer was dousing the flames, but I was watching my sister.

Warrick raised the knife when Max stepped back. He was ready to get his revenge, for his sister, for Sephiel, for everyone else Drake had helped destroy.

He never saw Dro coming.

Then she was there, pushing Warrick aside, making him miss his strike.

And saving Drake's life.

Nothing happened at first. Then Lucifer screamed.

It took me a moment to realize why he was screaming, and why Drake was rolling around in agony, even though Warrick hadn't touched him with the knife.

Lucifer's howl was one of anguish and frustration. The sound of a man who knew he had lost.

He turned his outrage on me, digging the hooks in as deep as they would go, finding my soul and beginning to rip it from me. I screamed and clutched the grass, feeling the hooks sever my soul's ties to my body.

As this was happening, the air began to change. The power in the air was weakening, crunching down as the Hell Gate closed. Lucifer was losing his power, but he was determined to take my soul before it was gone.

Just as my soul started to break out of my body, Lucifer's hooks disappeared. I dropped onto the ground with a muffled cry, breathing heavily, but suddenly able to move. I felt like I'd been run over by a cement truck, but I turned my head enough to see what had saved me.

Michael and Gabriel appeared, launching the last of their heavenfire at Lucifer. The King of Hell responded by snapping up his hand and throwing hellfire at Gabriel. The archangel wasn't able to move away in time, the ferocious white blast slamming into his chest. His scream was agonizing as he dropped to his knees and batted at the flames.

Lucifer snapped his wings back and launched himself at Michael, his sword extended forward. The powerful angel raised his hands, but was only able to catch Lucifer with them. Michael winced in pain as he collapsed on the ground with Lucifer. I couldn't see where the sword was, but Lucifer was the only one who got up. He whirled around, facing me with murder in his eyes. I pushed myself up as he stalked toward me, grimacing as the air continued to gain weight. Lucifer raised his sword and swung it toward my neck.

That was when the pressure increased, and Lucifer stopped mid-swing. He arched his back and screamed, in more pain than I could imagine. He dropped to his knees, dragging his fingers through the soil and tearing it to pieces. I watched in horror and awe as Lucifer's wings began to lift from his back, the curse of the Hell Gate taking them away. Lucifer struggled to hold onto his wings, but it didn't seem like his curse would let them. They split out of his skin, bones snapping as they broke from his back. Lucifer's blood was darker than any demon's I'd ever seen. His beautiful face was contorted with agony as his wings were torn from him.

But he wasn't the only one screaming. Every living demon, even the one Knight standing, howled in agony. I turned my head in their direction, seeing a portal had opened from the spot where Dro had saved Drake's life. The demons were dragged back toward the portal, as if magnetized to it. They were swallowed up by the portal's fire, disappearing from the clearing.

Another scream cut through my awe, and I turned my head again. Dro was writhing in Max's arms, screaming as the portal tore out her power. Max cradled her close, not sure what to do, but refusing to let go. Warrick was just as lost as he was, looking at me with despair, but not wanting to take his eyes off Drake either.

Lucifer grunted behind me. I twisted to see him. His back was covered in dark, smoking blood. His wings burned to ash on either side of his knees. He looked up at me, obsidian eyes sparking with fury.

I didn't think. I just reacted. I grabbed my hatchet and swung it at Lucifer's head.

He leaned away so my swung went wide. I tumbled onto my hands and knees, giving him the perfect chance to punch me in the stomach. He hit harder than Mateo and Drake combined. Harder than the Knight I fought earlier. He didn't just crack my ribs. He broke them completely.

Done with beating on me, he fisted my hair and yanked my face up to his. I came up swinging, driving my fist into a sloppy uppercut that landed in his jaw. Lucifer's head rolled with the hit, and that was when I swung my hatchet again.

The silver blade landed in his neck with a heavy *thunk*. Lucifer blinked at me, unable to believe that I'd cut him so easily. But he hadn't expected to be weakened from the Hell Gate closing, or for me to have a plan of my own. He thought he could control everything and everyone he set his eyes on. He used to have that power, but he never seemed to understand what simple humans like me would do when we escaped that hold.

We fought back. We overcame the odds. We fucking survived.

Black blood spilled over the hatchet and onto my fingers. A tingling burn went through them, but I barely felt it.

I was just about to rip the hatchet free when a sharp force grabbed hold of Lucifer and pulled him toward the portal. He gripped my wrist and dragged me with him. Frantic, I grabbed at the grass and dug in my heels, but it made no difference. We were moving too fast, and Lucifer wasn't going to let me go. I punched him, clawed at his eyes, even let go of the hatchet.

The portal loomed ahead, drawing closer with each second.

My friends and loved ones saw me as I was pulled through the grass, unable to fight, or escape the fiery door to Hell.

"You are mine," Lucifer whispered, still able to speak despite the blade lodged in his throat. "And I will make every second you endure in Hell agony. You will bleed until you beg for death, and then I shall heal you to repeat your suffering."

My breath hitched. The portal was overhead now. I could feel its heat smothering me. I closed my eyes, rushing through the moments I had with Max and Sephiel. The love I shared with Warrick.

My sister, and how she would be alive when all of this was done–

Lucifer jerked suddenly, his hand suddenly gone from my throat. I dropped heavily onto the grass, opening my eyes and watching the King of Hell gape at the bloody stump of his forearm. Black blood oozed from the ground, right onto the rapidly dissolving shape of a hand.

His head snapped to the side, just as he reached the edge of the portal.

Dro stood over me. One of Sephiel's swords was in

her hands, the blade slick with the Devil's blood.

"She's free of you, demon," Dro cursed. "We both are."

The edges of the portal closed around Lucifer, igniting his face in a blaze of red light. He threw back his head and howled one last time before the portal snapped shut, leaving only his furious echo on the wind.

I lay on the grass, breathing heavily with my broken ribs. Michael and Gabriel were still lying on the ground, barely moving but still alive. I turned around to see the rest of the corpses lying in the blood-soaked clearing. The portal had closed. Piles of demonic ash scattered the dead grass. Angels that had been dying before were now simply dead.

My heart clenched at the thought of Sephiel. My eyes found his body, and I choked on a sob. I kept staring at him with the hope that he would get to his feet.

Sephiel lay on the ground in a motionless heap.

A sword thumped onto the grass. Dro collapsed onto the ground beside me. I tried to reach for her, but even that movement was torture. Broken ribs made pretty much every movement agonizing.

Voices shouted our names, and soon I was scooped up in strong, familiar arms. I winced when Warrick touched my ribs, but it was a small price to pay knowing he was safe and alive. He steadied me so I could look at my sister.

Dro was breathing shallowly in Max's arms, blinking to stay awake. Her eyes stopped fluttering when she looked at me.

"Is he gone?" she whispered shakily. "Is it over?"

I nodded slowly.

Dro slumped with relief. Max kissed her head, holding her tightly to his chest.

"Almost over," Warrick muttered. "I'll be right back."

I gripped his arm. "Help me stand."

"Constance—"

"I'm not going to lie here like a beached whale. I

want to stand."

Warrick frowned and shook his head, muttering something that sounded like, "Stubborn, impossible woman."

Yet he still looped his arm around my back and carefully helped me to my feet. I hissed and swore every time I bent my body, but I was on my feet soon enough. Warrick kept his hand on my shoulder until he was sure I was steadied, then turned and walked to a dark-clothed man on the ground. He picked up his knife along the way.

Warrick put the edge of his boot under Drake's shoulder and flipped him onto his back. Drake's face was a mess of pulped flesh and blood. I couldn't feel sympathy for him as he coughed and spat red saliva.

"How did you know?" Max asked.

"To close the Heaven Gate, we had to destroy something beautiful," I heard Dro mumble. "To close the Hell Gate, we had to save something evil."

It made sense. Lucifer had loved cruel irony.

But he's gone now, and the last piece of his curse is about to meet his fate.

Drake coughed again. "You got some lucky shots in, Johnny-boy," he rasped. He spat out more blood onto the grass. "But you don't got it in you to kill me on my back like this. You're too noble for that."

Warrick stood over him with a knife in his hand.

"I should be," Warrick said evenly. "Dro saved your life to close the Hell Gate. I should honor that." His grip tightened. "But the Gate is closed now, and all I can think about is how you destroyed my sister. You killed a mentor of mine. You kidnapped an innocent girl. You stabbed the woman I love. You murdered my friend."

Warrick knelt down on Drake's chest, ignoring his grimace of pain.

"Somehow, I don't think she's going to stop me now."

When Warrick's knife plunged down into Drake's chest, Dro didn't protest. Nothing magical happened in retribution when Warrick turned the blade slowly. Lucifer didn't return from Hell to incinerate us when Drake Talbot finally died.

After checking to make sure Drake remained dead, Warrick stood up and walked away from his corpse. His eyes were shimmering, but I could see the peace in him. It would be a while before he moved on, but he'd finally be able to sleep and wake in the morning knowing that Drake would never hurt someone close to him again.

He stopped in front of me and curled his arm around my back, bringing me in for a deep kiss. I all but melted into him, not caring how much my ribs hurt as I wrapped my arms around him. Warrick's kiss was no longer desperate, just calming and relieved. I was weak in the knees when he pulled back. He rested his forehead against mine, his fingertips stroking the side of my face tenderly.

The sound of shuffling feet finally broke us apart. I looked over my shoulder as Gabriel approached with Michael.

Both archangels looked horrible. Gabriel had devastating burns on his chest, stretching all the way to his chin. The right side of his handsome face was black with charred flesh. He was sweating from the pain and effort to hold up Michael.

The Commander of the Heavenly Host was slumped over Gabriel's shoulder, breathing rapidly. Sweat glistened on his pale face. His battered wings dragged limply on the ground. One of his hands was pressed to his side. Blood was oozing from between his fingertips. I stared in horror, knowing Lucifer's sword had done that to him when he chose to save my life.

There was a faint shuffling behind me. I watched Dro ease past, Max holding her arm to keep her steady. She stopped in front of the archangels. Her hands stretched out toward Michael, since he was the one closest to death. She touched his wound gently, but no healing glow came from her hands. She held them there longer, pressed a little harder. Nothing happened. She looked up, distraught.

"I– I can't do anything," her voice trembled. "I have

no powers. I... I think I'm human now."

Dro was choked, but Michael did something completely unexpected.

He smiled at her.

"You are, Andromeda. And you are overwhelmingly fortunate. Closing both Gates should have killed you. You were not born human. You were created to be molded, to absorb the powers of Heaven, Hell, and earth." He looked at me. "Perhaps along the way, you absorbed humanity. Likely more than you realize." His eyes turned to Dro again. "It seems that humanity suits with you. The life you have now is a gift. Do not waste it."

"What about you guys?" I asked. "Are you a hundred percent human now?"

Michael shook his head. "Gabriel and I still retain some of our gifts, however."

"Then heal yourselves," Dro pleaded.

Michael shook his head again, looking resigned. "There is another who deserves a gift."

Both Michael and Gabriel looked at the ground behind them. My heart broke again at the sight of Sephiel's body. The utter paleness of his skin, the blood staining his still chest, the closure of his eyes. I kept waiting for him to open his eyes and stand, to reassure us that there was nothing to worry about, and that he was fine.

But he didn't move. He would never move again.

Warrick's hand found mine and gave it a squeeze just as new tears formed in my eyes. It was as much for him as it was for me.

"What are you going to do?" I was afraid to ask, but I needed to know.

"His soul has already left his body," Michael said. "He is behind Saint Peter's Gates. But with the last of my strength, I can put forth a call to the guards watching our half of Heaven. I can tell them to direct the soul of his beloved to him."

My eyes widened. "You mean she's..."

"She was an angel when she died, Constance. Her

soul returned to our afterlife after her passing. I know she did not expect to see Sephiel again, and that she will be elated when she realizes I will allow her to spend the rest of her afterlife with him, on the human side of Heaven." He smirked, as though thinking of a distant memory. "Everiel always had a fondness for humanity. She will be delighted to find Sephiel there."

My heart was torn. On one hand, I knew I would miss Sephiel every day. On the other, I was glad that he would be back with Everiel. He'd be at peace with her. I imagined them sitting together, Sephiel telling her our story as they watched us from the clouds.

Suddenly it wasn't so hard to miss him.

"But that will kill you," Dro said, voice shaking.

"It will," Michael replied sadly. "But humanity does not suit me as well as it did Sephiel and Everiel."

Dro stared at Michael for a long time, desperate to help but knowing there was nothing she could do. Finally, she bowed her head and stepped back.

Michael looked at each of us one last time. Gabriel did the same. They were looks of goodbye, and gratitude. Then they turned away and walked to Sephiel's body. Gabriel slowly and clumsily lowered Michael next to our friend. The Commander gently put his hand on Sephiel's chest. Gabriel did the same. I saw Michael close his eyes, and then all three of them blinked out of existence.

I stared at the spot Sephiel had been, heart in my throat.

Bye, Seph.

Dro stood with her back to us for a long time before she slowly turned to face us. We didn't say anything while she was struggling for words. Her eyes met mine, and that was when she broke.

"I'm sorry," Dro told us. "I'm so sorry. I thought I had control. I hate myself for what I did to you." Tears spilled down her cheeks as she looked at me. "Connie, the things I said... I'm so sorry, big sister."

She couldn't go on. Her eyes squeezed shut and her arms went around her middle. Sobs wracked her body.

"I can't fix it," she cried. "I can't fix it."

I started walking toward Dro. She saw me coming and backed up a step. I moved faster than she did. I stopped in front of her and gently took her elbow. She was tense, but didn't stop me from pulling her forward. I curled my arm around her back and hugged her tight, afraid I would lose her again if I let go. Dro's tears soaked my shoulder as she squeezed me. The hug hurt my ribs, but I didn't care.

"Constance, I–"

"Don't say it," I told her. "There's no need. I'm not angry."

"How? How can you not hate me for what I did? I hurt you, I attacked you, I–"

"I did the same thing to you," I reminded her grimly, guilt pricking my heart with angry fingers. "And believe me, I'm going to kick my ass for that for a while. But it doesn't matter."

Dro pulled back and looked at me, bewildered.

"You heard me. It doesn't matter, Dro. I can't hate you. Yeah, you made mistakes. Yeah, they were terrible ones. But you stopped the demons. You stopped me from getting dragged into Hell." I grinned. "You cut off Lucifer's damn hand." My smile softened. "You've never given up on me. You just got lost. Deep down, we both knew I would find you again."

Dro shivered and burst into fresh tears. I hugged her again.

"I don't know who I am anymore," she whispered.

I pushed her away from me gently to look in her eyes. She had a lot to forgive herself for. There would be ups and downs, nightmares and tears. She wouldn't be the only one enduring them.

"You're who you always were," I said. "You're Dro."

My sister let out a choked laugh, but it was real. That gave me more hope than I could ask for. Dro would move on from her pain and guilt.

As for me, I'd let go, but not of what mattered. I

held on to my sister because she kept me stable. Gave me something to strive for. I did the same for her, and we could both breathe easier.

I had no reason to be vengeful. I could learn to trust. It would be tough, but it was life.

And we had survived worse.

Epilogue

One year later...

"I hate these shoes," I complained again.

Warrick smiled and squeezed my hand. "Relax. You don't have to wear them for much longer."

I frowned at him, but my bitterness didn't last long. Especially when he looked smoking hot in a black suit, white dress shirt, and loose black tie. I was dressed more or less the same, sans the tie, but I felt like Patrick Bateman on his way to the boardroom with an axe.

The analogy would probably fit better if I actually brought my hatchet with me, but it was at home on the nightstand by my side of the bed. I stopped carrying it because I hadn't seen a demon in months, but I still felt naked without it. Sure, I had a throwing knife tucked into my belt and I kept up my strength in sparring practice with Warrick, but I didn't feel right without it yet.

Not that I imagined anyone would attack us in broad daylight in a cemetery. And if they did... Well, I'm sure there was an open plot somewhere for me to hide a body in.

Dro and Max were already at the tombstone. He was dressed in a similar suit to Warrick's, though he didn't fill it as well as my lover did. Dro wore a simple, grey knee length dress, as close to black as she could get it. Black was the one color she refused to wear again. Couldn't really say I blamed her.

Even without her gifts, she sensed me coming. She smiled at me, white roses in one hand and Max's in the other.

"Hey," she said when we made it to the tombstone.

"Hey," I smiled back. "Staying out of trouble?"

Dro's shrug was a sweet, innocent lie. "The movers still haven't brought the couch, but Max saw that it will be here by the end of the week."

"Nice," I said.

After we'd composed ourselves and found the strength to walk, we left Owl Creek behind for good. I never wanted to see that place again. One stolen truck, a trip to a no-questions-asked-hospital, and dozens of miles later, we ended up at our old family house again.

Dro and I sat in the living room and talked for hours. We eventually decided that we needed distance from each other.

I hadn't been that hard to sway for once. It wasn't that I wanted to be away from my sister, but the truth was that we had our own mental and emotional battles to make peace with. We couldn't do that if we smothered each other.

Obviously we didn't move far apart, but we didn't claim ownership of our parent's house. There were too many memories in it.

The few lingering demons that had been too far from the portal to be sucked back into Hell were hunted down by groups of brave– and stupid– vigilantes. The military and the cops had the firepower to track them, but the amount of destruction they had caused wasn't something that could be fixed overnight. The monsters were still hiding in the shadows, and it only took a couple weeks before Warrick and the two demon slayers living in Canada were forced to confess what they were.

Not everybody jumped for joy. A lot of them blamed the slayers for letting this happen, that they should have been protecting one family over another, that they started the war in the first place.

Warrick was happy to ignore all the complaints and do his job, and I was just as happy to join him.

Mexican officials declared Ciudad Juárez a quarantine zone. Nobody was to go in or out unless they had a military escort and express permission from the government. Some of the citizens were able to escape the city, but some chose to stay.

Demons, for all their claws, fangs and savagery, were easy to kill when you knew how. Humans that loved their broken minds, not so much.

It would be at least a decade before anyone was able to enter Juárez again, years before the Blood Thorns relinquished their hold while rival cartels fought to control the city.

I had no intention of going back to help.

So for the first couple of months, we stayed at Warrick's house in San Marcos. It started off as a convenience thing while we looked for jobs and I had a black market forger make fake IDs for me and Dro in return for collecting money from a disloyal customer. It was all too familiar, but I left the customer breathing. It was the last illegal job I ever pulled, deciding that private security would be a good fit for Elisa Diego. I didn't feel like an Elisa or a Diego, but as long as the world bought my lie, I didn't give a shit.

Considering the warrant on me was gone and I had a legitimate job, I was betting the lie would hold. Though I was pretty sure Warrick had pulled some strings with his Marshal pals to get me off the Wanted list.

No one had heard a word about open portals or Lucifer. That was the biggest relief I'd ever had. I hoped the son of a bitch was sulking on his throne, and that the other demons saw his failure on earth and crippled hand as weakness. I hoped that the rebellions and in-fighting would last for eternity, since it would mean that the demons were too selfish and too stupid to try and open the Gates to earth again.

I turned my head and looked at the grave. There was only one plot here, since we couldn't afford to move all our lost loved ones into the same cemetery, but he meant as much to us as the ones we traveled to visit.

Dro knelt down in front of the curved stone, brushing away the dirt that had covered his name over the year. She pulled out the vase hidden in the soil in front of the tombstone. She held the roses in both hands and swallowed her tears.

"We miss you, Sephiel."

Our silence was our agreement.

Dro pulled one of the roses from the bouquet and placed it in the vase. She stared at Sephiel's name for a moment longer, then wiped her eyes and stood up. Max curled his arm around her as she handed the roses to the rest of us.

Max placed his rose in the vase next to Dro's.

"It's not as nice as Heaven, but I hope you still like the plot, buddy."

He patted the top of the tombstone and stepped back. Dro took Max's hand and rested her head on his shoulder.

Warrick went next. He gracefully knelt down and put his rose in the vase. He put his hand on the top of the grave marker and paid a silent tribute to Sephiel. When his minute of silence was finished, he got up and stepped back.

I took his place, my heart filling with heavy grief again. One of my biggest regrets was never fully thanking Sephiel for what he'd done for us. The tombstone wasn't even my idea– it was Dro's. A way to keep him close, she'd said. To let him know we still thought of and missed him as much as our other family members.

I put the rose in the vase, then pressed my fingers against the engraving of his name.

"Thank you," I whispered.

It was the most I could say, and it wasn't just for Sephiel. It was for my mother and father. Raphael and Gabriel. Michael and Rorikel. Manny. Max and Warrick. My sister. All the people gave me the motivation to fight for something I never thought I would have:

A peaceful life.

I stood up and backed away from the tombstone. A small, delicate hand clasped mine. I looked at Dro and smiled when she did.

I couldn't remember the last time I had felt so serene. This might have been the first time. But I had earned this. I deserved it. I would fight to keep it.

But the best part about being free from the curse, was knowing I wouldn't have to.

THE END

Acknowledgments

Well, we've come to the end of a journey. If you'd asked me five years ago if I thought I would ever have an entire book series completed, I probably would have thought you were crazy. But here it is, the last installment of the *Cursed* trilogy. While I'm going to miss the characters and the trouble they got into, I'm also glad to know that they each found their happy ending. I worked hard to bring them the closure they deserved, and I hope that long time and new readers to the series are just as happy with the ending as I am.

This book series wouldn't be here if it weren't for the tremendous love, support, and encouragement from my family and friends. Seeing their proud smiles when I tell them what I've accomplished in a day of writing, or about some exciting news, or a new goal that I had, definitely makes me feel good about myself as a writer, and gives me motivation to write more.

Major thanks to the wonderful artists and teams of Deranged Doctor Design. I didn't know what to expect for the *Damnation's Door* cover, but... Wow. I mean... Wow. Seriously, you guys rock.

Big thanks to Eden Royce, my lovely editor who helped see this series through from beginning to end. She helped me nitpick like crazy, something I'm incredibly grateful for. There's no question that she's helped me improve as an artist.

Thanks to the awesome writers in WritingGIAM Pro (we miss you, Donna) and Weekend Writing Warriors, especially fantasy author and MOD Christina Ochs for reading and reviewing each one of these books. If you're an indie author just starting their career, trust me when I say that you need to find a writing group to be part of. They will do the most amazing things for you just because you ask.

Thank you to all the reviewers who have become lifelong fans of Constance, Dro, Warrick, Max, and Sephiel, especially Ivana and Nell of One Book Two, and Cassandra of The Bookish Crypt. You've offered so many uplifting words, helped with important promotions, and been wonderfully enthusiastic, so I hope that *Damnation's Door* meets your expectations.

Last but not least, thank you to *you* specifically, reader. Whether you're an old or new fan of the *Cursed* series, you've done me a huge honor in simply giving it a chance. That means more than I can ever say, and I will honestly never be able to thank you enough.

So yes, that's it for Constance and Dro and Co. I had an amazing time writing them, and I'm glad they have a chance to relax and enjoy a little quiet for now. I'd say they've earned it.

About The Author

Amy is a Canadian urban fantasy and horror author. Her work revolves around monsters, magic, mythology, and mayhem. She started writing in her early teens, and never stopped. She loves building unique worlds filled with fun characters and intense action. She is the recipient of April Moon Books Editor Award for "author voice, world-building and general bad-assery," and the One Book Two Standout Award in 2015 for her *Cursed* trilogy. She has been featured on various author blogs and publishing websites, and is an active member of the Writing GIAM and Weekend Writing Warrior communities. When she isn't writing, she's reading, watching movies, taking photos, gaming, and struggling with chocoholism and ice cream addiction.

Website: literarybraun.blogspot.ca
Twitter: @amybraunauthor
Facebook: www.facebook.com/amybraunauthor